# THE
# INTERIOR
# COUNTRY

# THE INTERIOR COUNTRY

## Stories of the Modern West

Edited by Alexander Blackburn
with Craig Lesley and Jill Landem

With an Introduction by Alexander Blackburn

*Swallow Press / Ohio University Press*
Athens, Ohio

This project is supported by funding from the Colorado Council on the Arts
and Humanities, a state agency, and the National Endowment for the Arts.
Further funding has been provided by the College of Letters, Arts & Sciences,
University of Colorado at Colorado Springs.

Library of Congress Cataloging-in-Publication Data

The Interior country.

    1. Western stories.    2. American fiction—20th century.
    I. Blackburn, Alexander.    II. Lesley, Craig.    III. Landem, Jill.

| PS 648.W4I58 | 1987 | 813'.0874'08 | 87–1968 |
|---|---|---|---|

ISBN 0–8040–0887–6
ISBN 0–8040–0888–4  (pbk.)

# Acknowledgements

"The Supremacy of the Hunza" from *Rites of Passage* by Joanne Greenberg. Copyright © 1966, 1967, 1968, 1969, 1970, 1971, 1972 by Joanne Greenberg. Reprinted by permission of Henry Holt and Company.

"Winter Count 1973: Geese, They Flew Over in a Storm" from *Winter Count* by Barry Lopez. Copyright © 1981 by Barry Holstun Lopez. Reprinted with the permission of Charles Scribner's Sons.

"The Healthiest Girl in Town" from *The Collected Stories of Jean Stafford*. Copyright © 1951, 1969 by Jean Stafford. Reprinted by permission of Farrar, Straus and Giroux, Inc.

"Black Sun" from *Black Sun* by Edward Abbey. Copyright © 1971 by Edward Abbey. Pp. 133–150, Simon & Schuster edition, reprinted by permission of Don Congdon Associates, Inc.

"Losing Game" from *The Edge of the Desert* by Gladys Swan. Copyright © 1979 by Gladys Swan. Reprinted by permission of University of Illinois Press.

"The Horsebreaker" from *Up Where I Used to Live* by Max Schott. Copyright © 1978 by Max Schott. Reprinted by permission of University of Illinois Press.

"The Indian Well" from *The Watchful Gods & Other Stories* by Walter Van Tilburg Clark. Copyright © 1943, 1971 by Walter Van Tilburg Clark. Reprinted by permission of International Creative Management, Inc.

"So Much Water So Close To Home" from *Fires* by Raymond Carver. Copyright © 1977, 1983 by Raymond Carver. Reprinted by permission of Capra Press, Santa Barbara.

"Lullaby" from *Storyteller* by Leslie Marmon Silko. Copyright © 1981 by Leslie Marmon Silko. Reprinted by permission of Seaver Books, New York.

"The Milagro Beanfield War," pp. 11–19, from *The Milagro Beanfield War* by John Nichols. Copyright © 1974 by John Nichols. Reprinted by permission of Henry Holt and Company, Inc.

"The Woman at Otowi Crossing," pp. 112–119 from *The Woman at Otowi Crossing* by Frank Waters. Copyright © 1966, 1981 by Frank Waters. Reprinted by permission of Swallow Press/Ohio University Press.

"The Death of Sun" reprinted by permission of William Eastlake.

"The Catch" reprinted by permission of Craig Lesley.

"A Winter's Tale" reprinted by permission of Clark Brown.

"My Work in California" reprinted by permission of James B. Hall.

"Field Guide to the Western Birds" from *The City of the Living and Other Stories* by Wallace Stegner. Copyright © 1956 by Wallace Stegner. Reprinted by permission of Wallace Stegner.

"The Van Gogh Field" from *The Van Gogh Field and Other Stories* by William Kittredge. Copyright © 1978 by William Kittredge. Reprinted by permission of William Kittredge.

"The Silence of the Llano" from *The Silence of the Llano* by Rudolfo A. Anaya. Copyright © 1982 by Rudolfo A. Anaya. Reprinted by permission of Rudolfo A. Anaya.

"The Whorehouse Picnic" reprinted by permission of David Kranes.

# Contents

# Introduction

"Beautiful my desire, and the place of my desire," wrote Theodore Roethke in *North American Sequence,* a series of poems depicting the soul's journey spatially into the interior of the continent, temporally into the interior of the past to effect redemption through acceptance, and spiritually into self-transcending depths of interior landscape. It is through place that one exceeds place: one comes to stand outside self with a heightened awareness obtained by relationship with the external world and to the mystery of life itself. The what and the how of Roethke's poetry of place, then, may serve to introduce the serious literature of the various "wests" of the modern American West—truly the heartland, truly the interior country. For the literature of this region is a genuine literature of place, of a real place or series of places inhabited by real people, neither a mythical "country of the mind" (as Archibald MacLeish dismissed it) nor a cultural province existing for the sake of national fantasies or of actual historical exploitation. The interior country is in fact a place of beautiful desire, a symbolic landscape with a power to revitalize the continental soul.

To approach this interior country, we must first remove the shrubbery of capital-W Western literature and film that stands between us and the truth which is beautiful. The shrubbery is not easily cut down: it is stubbornly rooted in morality plays about cowboys and Indians and in stereotyped chivalric romances about hard-riding, fast-shooting heroes who have a kind of messianic ego-identity. Fabulous as the West may have been from the time of the Spanish conquistadors to, roughly, the start of the present century, serious writers want little of this Buffalo Billing. In *Pike's Peak,* an authentic novelistic epic first completed as a trilogy in the 1930's, Frank Waters told the story of New Westerners struggling and failing to attune their psyches to a rightness with the land. In this novel, comparable to Herman Melville's nineteenth-century classic novel *Moby-Dick,* the protagonist's materialistic egotism turns to madness as he seeks the heart of a Great White Mountain. Here, the legendary virtues of western pioneers disintegrate when not balanced with nature's living mystery. Then in *The Ox-Bow Incident,* Walter Van Tilburg Clark's novel published in 1940, the stripping down of frontier fakelore continued in earnest as, behind the façade of retributive justice, the tragic consequences of wrong-minded self-reliance and mob violence lay exposed. And so it has been since then, western writers continuing to feel the need of making a clearing, of turning stereotyped characters and situations on their often nakedly imperialistic heads, without at the same time discarding the real achievements of individualism, the lingering authenticity of innocence, and the possibilities still for realizing the American dream in a land that likes to live in the shape of tomorrow. Whereas some of this effort has been and is the result of a "mock-Western" negative stance, the commitment of anger, like as not, yields a positive force in the attitude of love and respect for a land long-violated yet magnificent and capable of touching us at the core of being. For this reason, the classic capital-W Western hero such as Jack Schaefer's Shane, who is solid and separate and alone in his sense of individuality, cannot be brought down merely by social humiliation—society in the West being still in process of formation, Native American and Hispanic communities aside. The fabulous Western hero has to be humbled in his whole relationship with the universe, that his egoistic will-to-power may be brought into balance with nature and humanity, not asserted too far, not seeking to possess the land or to extract from the world of nature more than nature will allow.

The antiromantic and realistic approach to the interior country has led some western writers of fiction to a conception of personality different from the one found in traditional European and Eastern American literature with its centuries-old emphasis upon the subtle nuances of manners and morals. To be sure, that traditional perspective, often expressed in satirical vein, has not gone dry. Today's Californian and Sun Belt culture calls forth the steady gaze of such powerful moralists as Wallace Stegner in the Pulitzer Prize-winning novel, *Angle of Repose*, and Edward Abbey in the hilariously fulminating novel, *The Monkey-Wrench Gang*. But the traditional perspective may not serve the western writer out in the metaphorical lunar landscape beyond the Sun Belt. So he or she may not be writing traditionally at all, a view championed by such contemporary scholars as Thomas J. Lyon, editor of *Western American Literature*. The reader who approaches all western fiction from the traditional perspective will argue that western writers, overpowered by landscape, neglect the complexity, depth, and realism of characterization one should expect, and create instead of subtle fiction something akin to moral fables. In other words, inferior fiction. And, it is true, western stories often have an ethical and philosophical import that suggests a regional imperative. However, where some of the greatest of western writers are concerned, there is apt to be *more*, not less subtlety of characterization than one finds in manners-and-morals fiction. To view character as weighed in the balance between the sense of the individual self and the sense of its being a part of nature, of the timeless and indivisible whole, demands skill of the highest order.

Whereas European and Eastern and (usually) Southern American fiction has flourished in hierarchic society and tends to rest its case upon individual action in the social sphere, western fiction sometimes goes beyond the social nuances of interpersonal relationships to the nuances of the interior life, where true subtlety lies. It is as if a western writer has to envision something like the whole range of our lives in society, in history, and in nature and to dramatize the effect, like that of ever-widening ripples on a pool, of the microcosmic individual on the macrocosm at every level from the family to social group to the land and, ultimately, to the cosmos itself. Out West, where the individual consciousness is spatially forced to come to terms with a macrocosmic universe oblivious to its presence, the personality may be formed between polarities of reason and intuition, between conscious and unconscious forces. If the polarization prove constructive, a fictionalized character may become attuned to place and discover at-one-ment with it and with humanity; on the other hand, if the polarization prove destructive, a character may destroy the land, its ancient inhabitants, community, and his own humanity. Western fiction at its best is a call for living within the emerging process of creation. A western writer, far from being artistically limited by place, may move through it and from it in a kind of ritual catharsis to therapeutic vision.

What, then, is the West? It comprises the region beyond the 100th meridian, an arid region fragile both socially and ecologically. The West is principally the Rockies—New Mexico, Colorado, Wyoming, Montana, Arizona, Utah, Nevada, Idaho, and the eastern areas of California, Oregon, and Washington—with subregional borders from West Texas to the Dakota Badlands and from Baja California to Puget Sound. This region represents more than half of the continental United States. It is sparsely populated save for patches of wildly growing cities, especially along the Pacific littoral, and aridity limits future population growth. A region half-owned and not infrequently exploited by the federal government, the West has wilderness areas into which urban civilization has been allowed to expand, but the social and economic structure of major cities is likely to remain tentative and shifting.

Wallace Stegner calls the West "an oasis civilization," its history since the arrival of New Westerners one of the importation of humid-land habits into a dry land that will not tolerate them, of the indulgence of personal liberty in a country that experience says can only be successfully tamed and lived in by a high degree of cooperation. In short, the West lives precariously close to a reality which warns of the collapse of its eco-systems and of the consequent physical and psychical impoverishment of its inhabitants. The sheer beauty and mystery of the West is vulnerable indeed.

Yet vulnerability elicits the response of cherishing, as if the West is a child requiring constant care and protection. When this child-like land and the children of it are, unremittingly, raped by the forces of materialism—and metaphors of rape, violence, and mutilation are strongly present in stories of the modern West—then it is easy to understand why western writers often reveal their love through outrage. Here, though, is some explanation of a surprising fact: writers need not be native to the West nor long resident in it to care about it, to derive actual substance from it, and to write about it at depth of import. The same literary phenomenon is less true, if true at all, about other regions. Southern literature, for example, reflects a special historical experience of land and people and of a language shared from the Carolinas to Mississippi; consequently, nonsouthern writers have contributed little to the South's letters. By contrast, Spanish and Native American languages excepted, "western" English has few deeply shared meanings, and its vernacular is in part a fabrication of popular culture, in part an importation from other regions and nations. Freed of linguistic restraint, the newcomer may feel and express solidarity with native writers born with wild rivers, lonely plains, and towering mountains in their blood. This freemasonry among new and native writers may be accounted for, too, by the nature of experience of the interior country: the subtleties not always being traditionally social, they may come readily to the soul's grasp and the heart's concern. A correct compassion, in sum, may be sufficient credentials for a writer to become western and to participate in the West's history.

Now, it may be argued that the West has no history, or rather, as Gerald Haslam puts it, it has been assigned "a permanent, ossified past without a present." Where, indeed, are the connections, and how recover them? The problem is a serious one for western writers, whatever their racial and cultural backgrounds: Anglos of the dominant culture may yet be nostalgic about the "winning of the West" in the past century, whereas Hispanics and Native Americans feel victimized by this conquest, their traditions enervated. Meanwhile, as Eastern assumptions persist that the West is an historical vacuum, nuclear devices will be detonated in the deserts, water and mineral resources will be exploited regardless of human needs, and wilderness will suffer urban encroachment. Because these events have already happened, a restored and properly focused history is a concern for all writers in the modern West. From such restorations as are currently available, a picture emerges not only of relentless plunder but also of the past and continuing genocide against the Indians. In other words, there is a *burden* to western history with profoundly tragic implications, a tragic awareness opening up on two fronts: that of the attempt of New Westerners to comprehend the land psychically, failing which comprehension they subdue it to European and Eastern American patterns; and that of encounter with the Indian, whose enduring presence undermines notions of an heroic Manifest Destiny. As Dee Brown shows in *Bury My Heart at Wounded Knee: An Indian History of the West*, the West was not won but *lost*. This sense of burdensome history continues in Peter Matthiessen's *In the Spirit of Crazy Horse*, an analysis of how a defiant group of Indians has been "neutralized" since the early 1970s by government forces working to clear the way for progress—that is, for multinational energy corporations that will mine the vast mineral resources and pump down water resources from reservation lands as well as from public lands. Once Americans understand the true nature of western history, writers of the modern West will have found their audience.

Western writers often share in and express tragic vision. Tragedy, which is the inevitable result of taking a complete view of the human situation, makes the richness and beauty of life depend on a balance. The basic tenet of this world-view is that all life is maintained by observance of the natural order, that is, perception that what goes on in one sphere affects what goes on in other spheres. Both Greek and Shakespearean literary tragedy reveal that a disorder in the human system is symbolically paralleled by a disorder in the social system and by a disorder in the cosmic system. The core of tragedy's idea of order, by contrast, is the sacredness of the bonds which hold human beings together and establish mutuality between their lives and the natural order. It is at this juncture that western experience and the idea of tragedy are apt to meet. The experience of the New West—a civilization largely made possible through technological achievements such as construction of Hoover Dam in the mid-1930s—is that the power of tragedy's destructive principle has been admitted and constitutes a general threat. Although the industrial, military, agribusiness, and governmental infrastructure has now stretched western development to the breaking point, particularly in terms of resources and of the problems associated with "instant cities" (so named by Peter Wiley and Robert Gottlieb in *Empires in the Sun: The Rise of the New American West)*, the Great Western Boom continues with visions of projects larger than the pyramids, of excavations rivaling the Panama Canal, of trillion-dollar military projects, of

Sun Belt expansions, and of forced relocations of Indians from ancestral
lands. Thus at the very moment of the region's greatest rise to power,
unless there is a dramatic return to the ethics of balance, a hubristic
civilization of the New West may be headed into decadence, catastrophe,
and silence.

Part of the evidence of a tragic vision in western writers lies in their
questioning of the ideology of individualism, which has had a heyday
in the West—the historian Frederick Jackson Turner its most influential
and enthusiastic proponent. The West, Turner wrote in 1920 in *The
Frontier in American History*,

> was another name for opportunity. Here were mines to be
> seized, fertile valleys to be preëmpted, all the natural re-
> sources open to the shrewdest and the boldest. . . The self-
> made man was the Western man's ideal, was the kind of man
> that all men might become. Out of his wilderness experience,
> out of the freedom of his opportunities, he fashioned a for-
> mula for social regeneration—the freedom of the individual
> to seek his own.

Well, that thesis rings a historical freedom bell all right! But its peal is
increasingly hollow now that a metropolitan West is destroying what's
left of the frontier. The national, indeed international myth of a West
of rugged individualism triumphing over a decaying East has proven
itself, in part, a denial of humanity precisely because, in terms of tragic
vision, the ideology of individualism throws the natural order out of
balance, negating tragedy's complete view of the human situation by
vesting authority in the atomic individual regardless of the effects on
the social system and the cosmic system. Of course, the great open
spaces of the West may still enforce an isolation which can make people
independent and resourceful; may call forth a saving, intuitive reluctance
to surrender themselves to the blind ethics of an imperfectly formed,
excessively masculine society; may make it possible to escape from
the moral claustrophobia of ideology, and to open emotional doors to
forces of the natural order that can nurture western civilization without
demanding that it be repudiated altogether.

Journeying to the interior of historical experiences in the full light of
tragic consciousness, Anglo, Hispanic, and Native American writers
may and sometimes do discover that the connections between past and
present are to be found not in a span of centuries but in millennia. At
the Sun Temple at Mesa Verde in southwestern Colorado we can see
the antiquity of the heartland; and in witnessing the unique mystery
plays enacted in Hopi, Pueblo, and Navajo ceremonies we may realize

that this ancient American civilization is a living presence—and more. The symbols of this civilization are pertinent to the future survival of the human species. Historical orientation locates the pulse of the heart-land in pre-Columbian Mexico among Mayan and Aztec cultures, the center being the sacred city of Teotihuacan, at the mythic heart of which lies the Temple of Quetzalcoatl, the "plumed serpent," symbol of the union of heaven and earth, matter and spirit, a self-sacrificing God-Redeemer who taught that the Road of Life is within man himself. An ethic based upon regard for all forms of life, the Road is a psychological affirmation of an evolutionary emergence of mankind to a new stage of increased awareness of our responsibility in the cosmic plan. Astonishing as this deep meaning of western history may seem, it is true to say that Ancient America has power stored up for the redemption of Modern America. Accordingly, some writers of the West, among whom there is the genius of Frank Waters, are able to render the modern world spiritually significant and to fulfill the prime task of mythology, which is to carry the human spirit forward. The West is a region of myth vitalized by the relationship of peoples to the land. For Native Americans especially that relationship is sacred. Other westerners, drawn to similar regard, move spiritually from the damaged terrain of exterior landscape to the interior country where place is important because it is timeless and self-transcending—where, in Roethke's mystical vision, "all finite things reveal infinitude."

The stories collected in this book mirror various facets of the West since the early 1940s and have been selected for their representational quality as well as for intrinsic merit. Writers whose best work belongs to an earlier period have been omitted. Historical novelists have been passed up, as have been sagebrush-and-six-gun romantics, and genteel local colorists. Many fine writers live in the West but don't write about it, some native westerners have decamped without a trace, some marginally western writers seem more southern than western, others more midwestern than western. Although not all of the authors included in this book are native to the West, their stories and novel-excerpts pretty much cover the territory of the interior country both geographically and culturally and touch a variety of literary forms and modes—tragedy, comedy, satire, fable, elegy, gothic, *cuento*, science fiction and "magic realism." As much as possible, work has been included that faithfully represents an author's characteristic voice, style, stance, and thematic concerns.

In arrangement of stories, there has been a glance at racial and cultural contexts and at various occupations. But the reader who expects to find only cowboys, soldiers, outdoorsmen, prospectors, ranchers, carnies, farm workers, gamblers, miners and Indians (or "noble savages" in some expectations) will be partially disappointed. The West has atomic scientists, artists, professors, high-tech entrepreneurs and real-estate developers as well as more familiar types, who in fact are usually depicted here in nonstereotyped guise. There are women in western literature, too, and they are represented as doing quite a lot of things besides interfering with a hero's need to shoot bums at High Noon. Characters in the modern West play a different ballgame, their roles no longer predestined or protected by the old codes of wild justice or portrayed in prose more purple than sage. In William Eastlake's "The Death of Sun," for instance, roles are so reversed that a posse consisting of a white female schoolteacher and Navajo Indians who read Dostoevski sets out on horseback to pursue a rancher who kills eagles from his helicopter. Similarly, in David Kranes's "The Whorehouse Picnic," a newlywed prostitute kisses her husband with the words, "Have to get to work," and he drives her to the brothel. Obviously, there we are light-years away from the cardboard gentility of Bret Harte's nineteenth-century story of gamblers and prostitutes, "The Outcasts of Poker Flat."

The book has been arranged thematically as a kind of symphony in four movements, with the optimistic keynote sounded in Waters's "The Woman at Otowi Crossing" when an apparently ordinary woman undergoes a momentary apperception of timelessness, the experience counterpointed to an ominous power, that of the birth of the Atomic Age. When the book closes, the vision of the effect of nuclear testing has come true, with Kranes's story giving us in surrealistic tones a peek at a nuclear-armed world where the human power to disrupt nature has seemingly become as casual and respectable as a picnic. The four movements—"Nature and Self," "Innocents and Individuals," "Dark Interiors," and "Shapes of Tomorrow"—play variations on this music of place, sometimes majestic, sometimes somber and discordant, sometimes wildly joyous and tender, finally angry but with reconciliations posed or hinted at, as indeed they usually have been throughout. Perhaps this arrangement introduces an element of arbitrariness, because authors with the range of Waters, Stegner, Edward Abbey and Walter Clark, to name but four, might equally well have appeared in an orchestral mode other than that assigned. Be that as it may, "Nature and Self" addresses fundamental spiritual questions, "Innocents and Individuals" serves to remind us that westerners still have a purchase on frontier values not yet dominated by "eastern" despair and alienation, "Dark Interiors" presents moral and historical perspectives, and "Shapes of Tomorrow" airs out resentment at ecological and human depredations and disillusionment with Sun-Belted, Disneylandish, Vegasized cultural vacuity, warning us that those who live for the future without a past may destroy not only traditional values but also the very energy of hope by which westerners are characteristically and congenially driven.

The modern West, then, is the modern world. This beautiful country, though, is not as benighted or as chaotic as a Waste-Land, its special poignancy being that it remains a place of the soul's desire. Western writers confront with urgency and insight and with remembered anguish some of the most tortured racial, moral, and spiritual questions of our time, and some find answers to them. Waters envisions a coming world of consciousness of the timeless essence of both the exterior and the interior country. Stegner calls for an ordering principle that will allow modern culture to stop its drift toward decadence. Other writers assert our needs for less wilfulness and for a return to humanity, to love and passion and community. Still others remind us that, our earthly tenure being brief if not illusory, we should not take the world too seriously, but take it nonetheless, honestly, responsibly, and wholeheartedly. And even when the world seems to have lost all meaning—when, like Abbey's Will Gatlin, we have descended in our quest for meaning to the very pit of the Grand Canyon of our microcosmic selves—there spreads before us the prospect of endurance and the knowledge that we could not imagine doing anything else, any less. In the final analysis, stories of the modern West have the power to lift the gaze of our hearts to a larger sky, as do the very mountains amidst which many of the stories have taken their origin. "Everything is held together with stories," concludes Barry Lopez in one of the stories in this book. "That is all that is holding us together, stories and compasion."

That statement sums up the purpose of this book.

Alexander Blackburn

# THE
# INTERIOR
# COUNTRY

# 1
# Nature
# and
# Self

# FRANK WATERS
## *from* THE WOMAN
## AT OTOWI CROSSING

Born in Colorado Springs, Colorado, in 1902, Frank Waters for most of his life has resided in the Southwest, particularly in Taos, New Mexico. Through fiction and nonfiction, over twenty books in all, he presents a cyclical pattern of life, the possibilities for harmonious relationships to the earth and between people of differing races and cultures, and the truths of intuitive understanding. His best-known novels are *People of the Valley* (1941), *The Man Who Killed the Deer* (1942), *The Woman at Otowi Crossing* (1966), and *Pike's Peak* (1971); his nonfiction includes *The Colorado* (1946), *Masked Gods* (1950), *Book of the Hopi* (1963), *Pumpkin Seed Point* (1969), and *Mountain Dialogues* (1981). Since 1985, Waters has been continuously nominated for the Nobel Prize in literature.

After serving in the 1950s as Information Director of the Los Alamos Scientific Laboratory, Waters wrote *The Woman at Otowi Crossing* in which the secret development of the atomic bomb at Los Alamos is counterpointed to the secret effort of a white woman to understand Indian ways and to unlock her own psychic energy. Neither modern nor "primitive" world suffices for Helen Chalmers: polarization to over-rationalized, scientific, and materialistic culture releases destructive forces; but the intuitive, ceremonial culture poses its own kind of tyranny. The polarities are shown to be transcended in a new creative synthesis, and this self-transcendence is personified in Helen as she grows through stages of unexpected but normal crisis away from modern society and toward a vision of sacred world order consonant with the full radiance of eternity. In one of the most powerful passages in the novel, Helen moves through three-dimensional time of past, present, and future. She unearths a piece of pottery upon which is the thumbprint of a Navawi'i woman, and at the same moment wild geese in a V-formation fly overhead. Centuries of migrating geese are imaginatively transformed into the redemptive god, the plumed serpent Quetzalcoatl, and become symbolic of expanded consciousness, the past of the Navawi'i woman, the future of the trees growing from fallen seeds, and Helen's present time henceforth blessed not only by previous worlds of elements but also by a feather that is arriving to announce a new world.

# *from* THE WOMAN
# AT OTOWI CROSSING

Peeking out the window, Helen saw that a shrill, metallic squeaking came from an ungreased axle on Facundo's old box wagon approaching the narrow suspension bridge. By the time he had arrived at the door, she had hurriedly washed her face in cold well water and regained some measure of composure. Facundo seemed not to notice her wet hair and swollen eyes.

"Maria have that baby," he said casually. "Man-child. Big!"

"That's fine, Facundo, I'll go right over."

"Mebbe don't go," he said softly but positively. "She sleepin' all day. That the way it is." He looked quietly and unhurriedly at the cold, smoking fireplace and around the disordered room, then turned toward the door. "That noisy wheel. I grease him now. Then we go. Good day to get wood in the mountains!" He closed the door behind him.

"Why not?" she thought, dressing quickly in Levis and stout shoes, laying out mittens and a heavy coat. She was making some sandwiches when Facundo came in the kitchen door.

"Them cold sandwiches white peoples eat! No good! Fire and meat. They better in the mountains."

She found some chops, put bread and fruit in a paper sack, filled the coffee bag. Then they started up the canyon. The plodding broomtails in patched harness with ridiculous eye blinders. The springless Studebaker, with an axe bumping around in the empty wagon box. And Facundo and herself sitting on a plank seat covered with a tattered Navajo blanket against splinters.

The old Indian sat comfortably erect, the reins held loosely but without too much slack in his lap. There was a rent in the knee of his trousers, she noticed, and one ripped moccasin was held together with a greased string. Around his coarse graying hair he wore, Santo Domingo style, a brilliant red silk rag. His dark, wrinkled face looked solid as weathered mahogany. He did not talk. Soon she forgot him.

They were plodding steadily uphill now, the horses keeping the traces taut, their breaths spurting out like smoke. The canyon wall to the left

5

was sheer, black basalt. To the right rose a steep slope thickly forested
with spruce and pine. Over them both the mist still hung, silver-gray,
wispy and tenuous as a cobweb. Suddenly she felt its cooling dampness,
and smelled the moist fragrance of sage and pine. Summer had been
so hot and dry, with dust over everything and swarms of grasshoppers,
that Helen now welcomed the mist as a promise of winter snow. It was
so good on her face, so fresh to breathe!

But it was chilling too. Facundo unfolded his shoulder blanket; she
moved closer to him so he could wrap it around both their shoulders.
In this enclosed proximity she became aware of his peculiar, spicy,
Indian smell, so different from the rather sweetish odor of her own
race. It was strong but not disagreeable, and soon she did not notice it.

When the canyon widened out, Facundo turned to follow the faint,
rutted track of wagon wheels. These rough, almost indistinguishable
"wood roads," long used only by those going after firewood, crept
through the whole area. Soon Facundo stopped in a clearing in the
forest. He unhitched, unharnessed and hobbled the horses to graze.
The yellow gramma or bunch grass was short and dry, but Helen knew
it was nutritious; down below in years gone by it had nourished immense
herds of buffalo, and stock could still keep fat on it all year if it were
not overgrazed.

Without a word, Facundo took his axe into the woods with Helen at
his heels. He was not idly gathering dry sticks for a picnic fire now.
He wanted stout logs that would throw up a bulwark of heat against
a long winter's night. Helen watched him select a high pine, dead but
still sound, and measure its length with a sharp eye. Then he set to
work. It was amazing how much strength his thin, aging body still
held, as his axe bit into the trunk. Perhaps it was life-long skill, rather
than strength, for he wasted no strokes. Each bite of his blade deepened
the previous cut; the scarf was smooth as if cut into butter. With a last
stroke he stepped back; the lofty pine crashed neatly into an opening
in the brush where there was room for him to trim off its branches.
And now, without pause, he began to cut the trunk into wagon-lengths.
A strange feeling crept over Helen as she watched him. For how many
generations had a woman followed her man here, watching him gathering their winter's wood?

She wandered deeper into the forest to fill gunny sacks with pine
cones. How dark and cold it was under these great pines whose lofty
tops soughed with the wind! Years of fallen needles had built up underfoot a soft and springy mat upon which lay the cones. Each one, it
seemed to her, was the skeleton tree in miniature; and deep in the heart
of its seed she was sure there must be another microscopic pattern of a

future tree to complete, in a century perhaps, the ceaseless cycle. Occasionally she froze to watch a bird flutter to a nearby branch, fluffing its feathers with a sharp beak, its tiny black eyes shining like glass. How many there were, if she held still: grosbeaks, towhees, juncos, even a bluebird.

Back in the clearing she built a small fire at which she could stand, her coat spread out like a blanket to catch the heat. "These white people's fires," she remembered Facundo complaining once. "They so big, people stand far away and freeze. Little fire under the blanket, Indian way. It warm."

When he came, they cooked their chops, ate bread-and-butter sandwiches and fruit, and sat drinking coffee. The food gave Helen strength; with the hot black coffee she felt life rising within her. Trouble and weather were never so bad when you got out into them. It was always fun to be out here gathering one's own wood. Once she had been taken down a coal mine near Raton. Never thereafter could she abide the thought of burning coal; the very smell of it reminded her of those black, sweating bodies toiling underground like slaves.

Facundo was too busy to talk. The minute he finished lunch, he began sharpening his axe with a rusty file. Helen was content to sit watching the precise movements of his delicate, dark hands. Finally he stood up and smiled.

"Now I cut piñon! Burn good, smell good, too!"

"I'll help!" she offered cheerfully.

His face quieted; he nodded vaguely toward the flat top of the forested mesa behind her.

"Mebbe you climb up there, find something."

"A pueblo ruin, Facundo? Oh, why haven't you told me about it before!"

"Mebbe *pueblito*," he corrected her. "Mebbe some old houses, mebbe all gone." But he could not diminish her quick excitement.

"Yes! What's it called, Facundo?"

"Mebbe no name. Mebbe forgot. Mebbe not tell." As always he shut off her direct questioning. Nor would he point out its location and thus draw off its power. He merely nodded sideways at a rocky point, without looking at it. "Old spring by that rock. Mebbe you find trail close. Then walkin' easy."

She hurried off to the foot of the rocky point. A landslide had covered the spring, but she found where it oozed up through the brush and matted pine needles. The trail was too old to be clearly visible; with difficulty she traced its course up and across the steep slope. Soon she was above the pine tips; the canyon below, filled with mist, looked like a gray and turbulent sea. She kept climbing.

Near the top she could have let out a squeal of delight had she had a spare breath. To the right, a trail led up to the top of the mesa. Straight ahead she saw a wide, sandy passage overhung by the basaltic cap. And here at the fork she saw stuck in the rocks a weathered clump of prayer-sticks—the little feathered plumes, bound with colored yarn to a carved stick, that men had planted here for centuries when their hearts were right.

Without touching them, she hurried ahead on the sandy passage. There she saw it. A small group of cliff houses clustered protectively under the overhanging ledge which had served as its roof. The front wall had fallen, its stones washing down the steep precipice. But the side walls still stood firm and smooth, like two outstretched arms holding between them the crumbling stone partitions of the tiny rooms. Inside, she dropped to her knees and let the ancient, talcum-like dust dribble through her fingers. As she had hoped, it contained a small piece of charcoal. It was then, suddenly, she felt her "radio" tuned in.

Years ago someone had asked her, "Why is it, Helen, that almost anyplace you go you can find sherds—edges, handles, all kinds of pieces of pottery? I go to the same place and hunt hours, and I can't even turn up an arrowhead!"

Helen had laughed a little self-consciously. "Why, I guess it's just my radio, or something like it in me, that seems to turn on. The farther I go in a certain direction, the more excited I get. Pretty soon I'm just so tingly all over I don't know where to turn or anything. Then I just stick out my hand—in a rock crevice, among a heap of stones, oh anyplace!—and whatever it is, it just seems to come right into my hand!"

That's the way it was now. A continually mounting excitement that led her like a radar beam to prod among the tumbled stone partitions, in the debris at the back of the ledge, and finally against the dark back wall. Feverishly now, conscious only of the excitement impelling her, Helen stuck her hand down into the choked mouth of a hollow in the floor.

It leapt to her fingers: a smooth round edge which carefully scooped out became the rim of a large perfectly formed bowl. Helen carried it out to the light with a sob of triumph hovering between laughter and tears. Brushed free of dirt, the bowl glowed reddish-brown in color, with a glazed black symbol of the plumed serpent moving in his sky-path around the rim, its smooth texture unblemished save for a thick blob of clay stuck to the rim. In this Helen now saw the clear imprint of a woman's thumb.

She was still standing on the ledge, tremblingly clutching her discovery, when she heard the faint, familiar honk of wild geese flying south. In a moment she could detect the undulating V sweeping toward her, high in the mist. Always she had believed the flocks followed the course of the river below. Now she knew that some of them used the plateau to mark their high road. That ancient Navawi'i woman, thumb pressing into the wet clay stuck to her cooking pot, must have watched their passage too, as she prepared for winter.

A muffled report from Los Alamos sounded over the ridge. The wild geese swerved, dipped toward her. Helen could see the sharp point of the V, the two trailing lines separating into distinguishable projectiles of lightning speed. Instinctively she braced herself against the airway shock of their hurtling passage.

At that instant it happened again: the strange sensation as of a cataclysmic faulting of her body, a fissioning of her spirit, and with it the instantaneous fusion of everything about her into one undivided, living whole. In unbroken continuity the microscopic life-patterns in the seeds of fallen cones unfolded into great pines. Her fingers closed over the splotch of clay on the bowl in her arms just as the Navawi'i woman released her own, without their separation of centuries. She could feel the enduring mist cooling and moistening a thousand dry summers. The mountain peaks stood firm against time. Eternity flowed in the river below . . . And all this jelling of life and time into a composite *now* took place in that single instant when the wedge of wild geese hurtled past her—hurtled so swiftly that centuries of southward migrations, generations of flocks, were condensed into a single plumed serpent with its flat reptilian head outstretched, feet drawn back up, and a solitary body feather displaced by the wind, which seemed to be hanging immobile above her against the gray palimpsest of the sky.

Nothing, she knew, could ever alter this immemorial and rhythmic order. Not the mysterious explosions on the Hill, nor the ever-increasing mechanism and materialism of successive civilizations. This was the unchanging essence to which the life of mankind was ultimately pitched. With this reassuring conviction, the fierce proudness and humble richness of her life at Otowi Crossing rushed back at her with new significance and challenge. A woman and a cooking pot! They could defy time, bring civilization to heel!

As if a switch had been turned on again, life resumed its movement. The wild geese swept past. The wind soughed through the pines. Her heart took up its beat. But as it had before, the wonder and the mystery and the beauty remained.

When she reached the wagon, Facundo had filled it with wood and lashed the load fast with rope. What could she say? It was all in her shining eyes, in the vibratory aura about her, in the pot in her arms. Facundo stepped back as she held it forth. He was no longer a ragged old man out cutting wood on a cold Saturday. He seemed again a living receptacle into which had been ceremonially instilled the esoteric wisdom of a tribal entity, handed down from a remote past in which mankind had survived only through its direct intuition of the living powers of earth and sky.

"That got the power," he said quietly. "I no touch!"

No. He would neither touch the old bowl nor sit in contact with her all the way home. Helen shivered without a blanket on the plank beside him. She felt too happy, a little too lightheaded, to care. Nor did she mind lighting lamps and fires in the cold, dark adobe while Facundo unloaded his wagon. He showed up quietly with a solemn face at the kitchen door.

"Come in, Facundo! I'll have some supper ready in just a few minutes."

"I go."

"All right. But wait till I fix a little package of nice things for you to take to Maria."

"I wait," he answered patiently.

When the package was tied and stuffed into a brown paper bag, Helen turned around to see him steadily staring at her with a look of grave concern.

"That Luis. No come no more," he said without preamble. "Workin' on that new road. Get rich, he say."

The information struck Helen queerly. Not that Luis had gone to work on the new road being blacktopped between Espanola and the Hill; the high wages were drawing many Indians as well as Spanish men from all the valley. Nor that after all these years of service to her, he had left her without so much as a word. But that Facundo had waited all day to tell her. Why?

"Mebbe that Maria no come too. That baby mebbe make too much work here. Mebbe she go work up there too."

Why hadn't she suspected that long ago? Helen had heard that due to the shortage of help and the makeshift living quarters, almost every woman up on the Hill was working at something on the Project. Maids were at a premium. Every morning busloads of Indian women were transported from San Ildefonso and Santa Clara, and taken home again at night without cost. "A free ride for nothing, and lots of money besides!" Maria had grumbled, watching the crowded busses rumble over the bridge. And now she was going too. Helen had no doubt of it.

"You no got man to chop wood, get water. You no got woman to cook, carry them plates to people. You got nobody mebbe." Facundo's voice was flat and expressionless.

If she had received the dire news this morning, Helen knew she would have been completely stricken; it was a blow even now. Where could she ever get competent, loyal help now, at the modest wages she could afford? But she felt instilled with a new courage.

"No, I haven't," she answered forthrightly. "But I know I'll make it somehow. Just like long ago."

Facundo looked at her a long time, then stated in the same flat voice, "I come. Livin' in that little house mebbe."

"That old adobe out in back? Why, you'll freeze to death!"

"Get new door. Mebbe stove. Me fix!"

"Move here from the pueblo, Facundo? Won't Luis and Maria miss you? And—"

"They goin'. I say."

It was all talk to gain time to catch her breath. For his suggestion had broken upon her immediately with the incontrovertible truth of something long written in invisible ink that she had suddenly learned to read. "All right, Facundo. Tomorrow we'll talk about getting a little stove from Montgomery Ward. I'm going to buy you some new clothes, too. You must be neat and clean to help me with lots of people around. You won't mind, Facundo?" she finished anxiously.

He smiled with a warmth that enveloped her wholly.

"I goin' now."

Alone again, Helen felt reclaimed by a destiny that somehow always overpowered her. She dropped off to sleep without questioning it.

# EDWARD ABBEY
## *from* BLACK SUN

A Pennsylvanian born in 1927, Edward Abbey first saw the West seventeen years later and after World War II studied at the University of New Mexico. By the mid-1960s he settled on a succession of Western homesites, working as a part-time ranger and then as a fire lookout in a number of national parks; at the present time, he lives near Tucson, Arizona. His random seasonal jobs coupled with personal explorations of the Western scene and his observations of the people and places that he saw have provided the materials for most of what Abbey has written in fiction and nonfiction. In *The New West of Edward Abbey*, Ann Ronald declares that he "wings above the landscape in predatory circles and strips naked those who would destroy its beauty." Among many works of nonfiction, *Desert Solitaire* (1968) and *Beyond the Wall* (1984) stand out. Landscapes of the desert and the mind are often lyrically, sometimes satirically presented in novels such as *The Brave Cowboy* (1958), *Black Sun* (1971), and *The Monkey-Wrench Gang* (1975).

Although on the surface the climactic scene of *Black Sun* might be read as sentimental indulgence in romantic self-pity, Abbey's depiction of an allegorical descent into the inferno of the Grand Canyon examines primordial relationships between human beings and between nature and self. Will Gatlin (a name suggestive of aggressive Anglo ego-identity), a middle-aged dropout who prefers life in a fire tower to mere existence as a college professor, finds and then loses an idyllic relationship with a woman half his age. He searches for her deep in a parched and inimical Grand Canyon, but the loss is irrecoverable: Will realizes that his failure to commit himself in love has its source in a failure to reconcile self with nature. The experience of the quest, however, has a purgatorial, not a romantic effect, and points to the need for an ethic of responsibility toward humanity.

# *from* BLACK SUN

I n his pocket, the cool circlet of silver. Cold silver, like the gleam of
moonlight on water. He fingered it, over and over, in his pocket, as
they talked, knowing it would enclose her slender wrist as easily as his
hand enclasped her ankle, as naturally as his hand might lift and cup
her breast.

"He's coming?"

"Next week."

"Did I tell you he wrote me a letter once, about a month ago?"

"*He* told me. You never answered him."

"I'm not a good letter writer."

"Don't I know that. Your letters to me. In our log. One word. *Venez.*
Or *venga.* Or *venite.*"

"Or come."

"Or come. Nothing but commands. Never a tender word of love. I
wonder if you really love me. For all your antics and crazy songs and
wild places and crazy ways to make love . . . you've never really said,
not once, that you love me."

He sang his new song.

> She was the lovely stranger
> who married a forest ranger
> a dog and a duck
> and never was seen again.

"Some proposal. That's your proposal to me?"

"Call it whatever you want."

"Sounds more like a proposition to me, Mr. Gatlin."

"I want you to come with me and stay with me for the rest of my
life. If I live that long."

"Live in a shack in the woods for the rest of my life, eating poached
deer?"

"Yes."

"Raise my children in a treehouse?"

He was silent.

"Do you know that Larry's been calling me every night? *Every night.*

15

And writing to me almost every day. He really needs me, Will. Not like you. He really needs me and really wants me. He always has, or almost always."

He said nothing. The words he was meant to say remained locked in his head. *I love you,* and so forth. *Will you marry me, Miss MacKenzie,* and so on. *I am yours forever, beloved, through all eternity,* and what not. He could not quite get them out.

"He'd do anything for me, Will. He's only a boy but he really loves me."

Really? he thought. He said nothing, although the words which he knew very well she needed to hear were right there, in his brain, resounding through the circuits of his nerves. *I too. Anything. Anything. Die for you. Go back to the schools again. Profess. Die. Live. Work for you, my love, my darling, my heart,* and so forth, in that vein. *Go back to the world again, back to the cities, emerge at last from this miserable pack rat's nest I've made in the forest.* Thusly, in that manner. The words were there, present. He had only to speak them. Presently, perhaps, he could find voice to utter.

"Aren't you going to say anything?"

He felt the bracelet in his jacket pocket, turning it around and around and around.

"Well?" She stared at him across her table. The flowers, the glowing new candles in old wine bottles, the remains of her latest "extravaganza." *Lasagna . . . lasagna!* This girl could do anything, anything. Bake bread. Scale a cliff. Dance on the tip of his finger. Rub his back, wash his hair, touch him with delicate intimacy in the most intimate, delicate places. Conjure the heart out of an oak, charm a rattlesnake into bliss. Did he love her? He loved the scent of her bare feet on the steps of his tower. He loved the edge of her skirt, the hem of her shadow, the sound of her voice within music. The anticipation of her smile. The slightly misaligned little front teeth. The mole on her shoulder, the dimples at the base of her spine, the golden down on the nape of her neck, the words that came out of her mind and mouth. "If only you would say something. Am I supposed to be a mind reader?"

He did not speak. In the air, surrounding, embracing, assuming them, floated a sweet, melancholy music. Sounds of a dying century, infinitely tender and subtle. Lost.

"I want you to need me," she said.

"I want you."

"Then why don't you say so?"

Lost. Lost.

*II*

At the rail, on the bridge of his ship, he races with the sun. Which, rising far behind, passes far above with the speed of a meteor, and blinds him as it descends before his eyes into the enameled clouds of fire, the seas of fascinating brilliance in the west, so vast and open, deep and fathomless.

That yawning abyss which makes us think of sleep.

He turns this way. That way. This way.

Now it is evening; now it is night.

In the cabin at midnight, by the soft light of the lantern, he writes the letters he should have written years before. Burns them. The fire mutters in the stove, the wind pours through the forest outside, moaning in the pine trees, shaking the dry dead yellow leaves of the aspens. The sound of many rivers. The sound of falls. The sound of human voices. Under the old moon deer pass like phantoms through the clearing. Dead limbs of a pine grate against one another, the noise like a groan of pain, and the deer pause for a moment to listen.

*III*

Darling Will,

Darling, I don't think I'll be able to come this evening. What I really mean is I just *can't* come tonight. And the reason is I just have to get away by myself for a few days, try to think things through and figure things out. Larry will be here Sunday and I must decide exactly what I'm going to tell him. And how. You know what I mean.

Sweetheart Will, whatever happens, I love you. I will always love you. You and the forest and mountains are part of my life now and always will be.

Please don't be hurt by my not coming this one time. I am sure you understand how terrible this situation is for me and how important it is that I make absolutely certain I am doing the right thing for once in my life. After this I don't want to hurt anyone ever again.

If only you could help me a little more. But I guess what you want is that I settle this thing myself, on my own, and no doubt that is the best way and the only way to do it.

I love you, darling. I love you, more than you know.

God I hope you find this note. You must. See you soon, I hope. Be patient with me.

*Ya–ha–la–ni, ch'indy begay,*

—S.

*IV*

Early in the morning, before sunrise, he started down the trail into the
canyon. At the head of this trail, near the end of the dirt road, her car
had been seen three days earlier by one of the rangers, before the car
too had disappeared.

Alone, the pack frame on his back, in the pack enough dehydrated
food for ten days, enough water for two days. He would find more
water, he hoped, distill it from the earth if necessary, go clear down to
the river if he had to. Despite the August sun, the heat of the inferno,
water seemed—*for him*—a lesser problem now.

"Look," Wendell had said, "they don't need you. We do."

"I'll be back."

"Who's gonna man the tower?"

"Put somebody else up there."

"I ain't got anybody else."

"Take it yourself."

"You're crazy. You're kidding. We got three fires going right now. You
can't run out on us now, the whole goddamned forest will burn."

"Let it burn."

"Look," Wendell said, "I understand how you feel. But you're going
about it the wrong way. They had a crew up and down that trail twice
since the storm. They've gone through the canyon with helicopters and
planes every day. The boatmen been all the way through on the river
and ain't seen a thing. Besides, the girl isn't even in the canyon."

"You're sure about that, eh?"

"Well, god damn it, Will, her car is gone. She sure as hell didn't take
the car down the canyon."

"Maybe somebody stole the car."

"That don't mean a thing. She could be anywhere in the world now.
Maybe she went home."

"She didn't."

"Maybe she went to the mountains."

"I'm going there next."

"She might be on her way back here right now."

"Maybe."

"Wherever she went, she sure as hell didn't go down in the canyon.
Nobody would go down in there now. Not in August."

"She would. I'll see you."

"When you coming back?"

"In a week. Two weeks."

"They'll be hunting you next."

"Tell them not to. So long, Wendell."

"You are a goddamned idiot. That's what you are. Christ, Will, there's lots easier ways to commit suicide."

"Good-by, Wendell."

The old trail switchbacked down through a slot in the sandstone wall, passing beneath the last frontiers of the forest—scattered jackpines, a stand of Douglas fir in a shady corner of the wall, a clump of young aspens. Down into juniper and piñon pine, an occasional agave, sagebrush, rabbit brush in summer bloom. A thousand feet of descent would bring him into a plant-life zone roughly equivalent to a journey five-hundred miles southward. As he went down, the temperature, even before dawn, went up. In the bottom of the canyon it would be 120 degrees or more.

As he descended, picking his way slowly and carefully across the tumbled rocks and gravel of washouts, Gatlin checked each possible ledge where anyone could have made even a short traverse. He had little hope of finding her tracks, if she had come this way; the storm two days before would have obliterated all such signs, even as it had wrecked portions of the trail. But there was always the fractional chance that she might have sought refuge under some overhang, been trapped by a rockfall, been cut off, injured. A hundred different things could have happened and he intended to explore each separate possibility. In her distracted state of mind she could have gone anywhere, indeed, and of all choices a hike into the canyon at this time of year was the most unreasonable. But if she had gone to the mountains or to the city she was probably well, at least safe; if she had gone down into the canyon she was probably in trouble, if still alive. So Gatlin reasoned, anyway. Her young man, Larry the flyboy, Lawrence J. Turner III, cadet-pilot, USAF, had on the other hand gone off in a frenzy in all directions: flying to her parents in Washington and back; hiring a plane and nearly killing himself winging through the inner gorge at 150 miles an hour; wandering into the forest and almost getting lost himself; until now, exhausted and paralyzed, he simply sat and waited in Sandy's little apartment in the village, dreaming? praying? hoping? for her return. For Gatlin, at their last encounter, he had had no words; he regarded Gatlin as a murderer, or perhaps as something worse.

A mile below the rim, on the first of the lateral benches above the red wall, Gatlin stopped to cache two of the extra water jugs he carried, placing them under a ledge, hiding them with stones, inscribing the location on his memory.

The sun rose out of the desert far beyond and glared through un-clouded sky into the canyon. The heat intensified immediately.

Gatlin hiked westward on the horizontal bench, following no trail—for there was no trail here, only a maze of faint deer paths which meandered in all directions, petering out in rock and brush—until he came to the point where the bench merged with the main canyon wall, a vertical drop-off of hundreds of feet, beyond which only the birds and the lizards could go.

Noon. Around him lay shallow potholes in the solid rock which two days before might have been full of water; now they were empty, sucked dry by the arid winds, the thirsty air. He crawled into the meager shade of a juniper, removed the pack, finished his first quart of water, ate some raisins and jerky. He was not hungry. He unlaced his boots, loosened his clothing, pillowed his head on the pack bag and tried to sleep. He could not sleep.

Nevertheless he forced himself to stay there in the shade till midafter-noon. He then returned by a different, lower route to the trail and the place where he had cached the water. From there he traversed the bench eastward as far as it went, returning through twilight, again by a different route, to the starting point. On each leg of the hike he looked into every possible cranny in the rock big enough to conceal a human body. Found nothing, nothing but the homes of pack rats, the antlers of a buck, the marks of bobcat, coyote, lizards and rattlesnakes in the dust. On the way he drank nearly all of the water he carried. He had to drink it, or give up. Even the relative coolness after sundown was not sufficient to allay his body's greed—and need—for water.

Near the trail, as stars began to appear, he made camp for the night, brushing off a level place for his poncho and blanket, scraping together a few twigs and sticks for a little fire, on which he made tea and a thick soup. He still did not feel actually hungry, but he compelled himself to eat. He was tired, very tired, and thirsty again after eating. He drank the tea and set his canteen close to his bed, knowing that he would wake up during the night craving water.

Letting the fire die, he wrapped himself in the blanket, clasped his hands under his head and stared up at the stars. He thought he would fall asleep at once but he did not.

A bird called to him, off in the dusk.

"Will. Will. Poor-will."

Answered by another in a different direction.

"Poor-will. Poor-will. Poor-will."

Something woke him in the middle of the night. He opened his eyes to see a coyote watching him from ten feet away, standing sideways, head turned, staring at him with a curiosity which seemed almost sympathetic. Yet it was a lean, haggard beast, with the long muzzle of a wolf, and gleaming teeth. Gatlin stared back at the animal, plain enough in the starlight. Satisfied, not intimidated, the coyote after a time left off, turned and trotted away. Gatlin reached for the canteen.

His internal alarm woke him before dawn, when a faint reflected glow in the western sky made it appear that the sun had reversed its course or the earth had begun a counter rotation. All the familiar constellations were down. In this half-light he pulled on his boots, again made tea, and ate for breakfast a dense compound of cereals, nuts, dried fruit and wheat germ, mixed with powdered milk and water.

A corona of light appeared on the east, again in a sky unflawed by a trace of cloud. Gatlin removed one of the water jugs from his cache, refilled his canteens and packed them. He cleaned cup and spoon with his tongue.

The sun was still below the horizon. Gatlin found a sharp stone and dug a hole in the gravelly soil about two feet deep and three feet in diameter. He knocked the fat pads off some prickly pear, pushed them into the hole and cut them up into chunks with the stone. He set the empty water jug, without its lid, in the center of the hole, pushing it down among the broken pads of the cactus. He took a sheet of thin plastic from his pack, stretched it over the hole and fixed it in place with the material he had removed in making the hole, sealing the edges with dirt and sand. He worked slowly and easily, losing no sweat in the cool air of morning. With the transparent sheet firmly in place, he put one round stone in the center of it; the plastic sagged a little beneath the weight, forming an inverted cone with its apex directly over the mouth of the water jug. If he returned this way there would be, he hoped, enough water in the jug, distilled by the sun, to get him up the last mile to the rim.

The other jug, yet full, he packed in his bag, and shouldered pack and frame, buckled the waist strap and started down the trail.

The sun came up.

He reached the top of the Red Wall, a limestone cliff seven hundred feet high which paralleled the course of the canyon for most of its length. Through a fault in this structure, zigzagging down a talus of broken rock, the trail dropped to the world below, a broad gray platform halfway between rim and river, which also followed the windings of the canyon for over a hundred miles. Beyond this platform lay the inner gorge, a defile so deep and narrow that the river which ran through its depths could not be seen from where Gatlin stood.

He descended, feeling the heat rise and the aridity increase with each downward step.

The sun was high when he came to the end of the lowest switchback in the Red Wall and stepped out onto the rolling ground of the bench. Again he paused to cache a water jug, his last full gallon. As he had done the day before, he left the trail to make a traverse to the west, following as closely as he could the base of the limestone cliff. But this time he would go much farther.

He was now in a gray and barren region of saltbrush, blackbrush, cactus and little else. There were no trees, not even the scrubbiest of junipers, nothing but the knee-high brush, the dusty desert, the pale glaring stone which made his squinting eyes burn and ache. Even here, however, were signs of animal life: snakes, lizards, birds, the twisting pathways of wild burros. But no trace of what he was searching for.

What did he really expect to find? A footprint, a message in a log, a scrap of tartan plaid on a thornbush, a faded picture? A broken body draped on rock, a thin cry for help? He knew that the possibility of any of these things was too small to measure, to make sense. His descent into this inferno was itself an act of insanity. Yet he could not have imagined doing anything else, any less. He trudged on under the cliff, under the blaze of the soaring sun.

When the heat became too great, as it finally did, he crept on hands and knees under the overhang of a boulder into a dusty, scat-littered den which might have been the home of coyote or lion. Wearily, shakily, he undid the pack and drew out a canteen and drank deeply, desperately, letting the warm good water course down his throat as if he could never get enough, as if every cell in his body was demanding the liquid of life. When he finally had all that he needed he stretched out in the dust, head on the pack, and closed his eyes. Outside, in the fierce light, a lizard scurried by, dragging its whiplike tail; locusts screamed from the burning brush. Far above, against the blue, a single vulture gyred through space, black wings motionless, and scanned the desert below with magnetic vision—those protruding eyes socketed in the red raw naked flesh of the beaked head.

"Will, wake up!"

She was laughing at him, shaking him gently, her eyes bright with gaiety. The long hair, shining like burnished copper, fragrant as cliff rose, hung across her bare shoulders and trailed in his face. He could smell the perfume of her breasts, taste the sweetness of her arms.

He opened his eyes.

Strands of a cobweb tickled his face. A few inches from his nose a spider, gray as the dust, dangled from the overhanging rock, extruding from its abdomen a hairlike filament of spume. Instinctively, with a shudder of revulsion, Gatlin brushed away both web and spider and rolled out of the den. He looked at the sun. He had slept for nearly two hours and felt the pang of loss, the bewildering pain of something precious, beautiful, irreplaceable swept away forever.

He also felt, at once, the need for water. He drank, emptying one of his two canteens. Then relaced his boots, put on the pack and his hat, and started off again, following an ancient burro path. He staggered a little at first, dazed by sleep, weakened and confused by the heat. But recovered, marched on, feeling his strength and purpose begin to return.

All through the afternoon he trudged toward the sun, into the evening, into the magenta obscurity which followed sundown, until he was forced to halt by the growing darkness. In the sand of a nearby ravine, among boulders and burned-out brittlebush, he dug for water but found none. He opened the other canteen, drank, built a small fire and fixed himself a supper, ate what he could. He licked his cup and spoon dry.

Very tired, stunned by despair, he lay in the blanket and gazed up at the constellations, those glittering chains which enmeshed the sky. The extravagant randomness of their distribution puzzled the will. All space was charged with their inaudible vibrations. (Inaudible, that is, to the unaided ear. Had he not heard often enough, late at night on the shortwave radio, the siren song of Venus? the deep drone of Jupiter? the fanatic signals from beyond Saturn? Or was it merely fancy to imagine that all of those, all of that which seemed so incomprehensibly remote was actually enclosed by his own consciousness? In the madness, the exultation of solar winds? In the heart-chilling bleakness of his own inmost sensations? his outermost thoughts?)

A blue-green meteor slashed down through the tail of Scorpio, melted into nothing.

His life melted into dreams.

Tortured by thirst, he crawled toward the final resource he had prepared days before, the disc of silver gleaming under the fire of the sun. He neared the place, came upon it, eagerly removed the dirt and sand and lifted the transparent sheet. Instead of water he saw a nest of scorpions, a writhing mass which squirmed, piled, crawled upon itself, multiplying as he watched, there in the pit.

He came to the second secret place, exhausted, hopeless; he brushed away the seal and raised a corner of the clear plastic. And what he found here was not water but a giant rose, a rose nested within a rose, a score of roses sparkling with dew, sweeter than love, inviting him down, down, into the nectar of their hearts. As he entered they parted before him, petals like portals opening before him, closing behind, drawing him deeper into another world, down a brown road that wound among strange green vine-covered hills, toward a tall and weathered farmhouse where his mother waited, his father, his brothers. They would all be glad to see him, he thought, at the end of this journey which had taken so much longer than anyone could have imagined; already he could envision the timid, unbelieving, miracle-struck smile that would glow like sunlight on his mother's gothic face. But the road had taken a different turning; instead of a farmhouse was a crescent blaze of shore and sea, a deserted coast where no ships came, where no man lived, where no wings wove invisible patterns through the air. Only the waves advanced and retreated, with gush of foam and slide of surf upon the sleek sands, on a beach beneath a cliff where the skeleton of a home now stood, the barren timbers never sheathed in walls, unroofed, never completed; through the framework of this house, as if looking through an iron grid, he saw the pale sky, the concentric coronets of dawn, the flames and disc of the rising sun.

Waking once again, he was struck nerveless, drawn hollow by the horror of his deprivation. By the senseless sudden blackness of her vanishing.

Lacking appetite, he ate little, drank half of what water he still had left and turned back toward the east, taking a different track across the middle of the vast and open desert below the cliffs, above the inner canyon. Searching for a shred of cloth, the imprint of a girl's foot, a sign of meaning, he found only the maze of paths made by the feral burros among the brush and rocks, and the winding trail of reptiles in the dust.

By noon he was out of water. As before, he rested, or attempted to rest, in the shade of a ledge during the worst hours of the afternoon. Later, after dark, when he came finally to the canyon trail and his water cache he was seriously dehydrated, ill. Anxiously he uncovered the remaining water jug, opened it with trembling, enfeebled fingers and drank. Drank till his belly could hold no more, till the insistent craving of the body was satisfied. He filled his two canteens with the water left in the jug, draining it, and planted it in a hole in the ground as he had done the other, mashing cactus pads around it and stretching a second sheet of transparent plastic over the opening. In the morning he would have to go down to the river. Hungry again, he cooked himself a supper and went to sleep.

All through the next day and the day that followed he hiked along the river, climbing up and down the taluses of debris, trudging over sand dunes, forcing a way through mesquite thickets and tangles of acacia. At midday he stripped and cooled himself in the water; found refuge from the sun and the 120-degree heat in the shade of boulders; made his way around dark crevices in the rock where dun-colored diamondbacks lay coiled, regarding his passage with lidless eyes and black flickering tongues, their rattles whirring like choruses of locusts. The lizards darted out of his way—whiptails, geckos, collared lizards, fat chuckwallas that hissed and blinked and inflated themselves to grotesque proportions, meant as menace. He passed the tunnels of tarantulas; he saw now and then a centipede, a scorpion, a solpugid. He found nothing that could interest him.

On the first of his two nights by the river he made camp near a rapids. The smoke of his fire mixed with spray from the thundering river. Even in the dark he could see the waters crashing over the drop-off, piling up in ten-foot waves against the granite fangs below, hissing past the ledge on shore. The foam of the tumbled water glowed with spectral luminosity in the darkness, under the stars. The white roar filled his dreams all night long.

The second night he slept on a beach. Here the river was quiet, tons of silty water flowing by each second with no more noise than a distant buried dynamo might make—the sound of power, smooth, assured, unfaltering. Above the river on either side stood the black cliffs of polished schist and granite, Precambrian, Archean, more ancient than anything else on the surface of the earth. And here his dreams were haunted by the silence.

Early the next morning he prepared to climb to the desert again, the middle world between the river below and the forested plateau above. He compelled himself to eat a big breakfast; he drank all the water he could hold, mixing it with powdered fruit juice. He filled his canteens and packed them and filled also a pair of plastic bags which he could carry in his hands. He hunted for the foot of the old trail, long out of use, which would lead him up to the bench.

The trail was hard to follow, washed out completely in many places; it took him half the day to reach the desert platform above the inner gorge. On the way, scrambling across taluses of debris, he broke one of the water bladders. The sun blazed through the pure sky; the canyon walls reflected and radiated heat; in the distance, headwalls and pinnacles swayed dreamily behind a film of heat waves. The rock was almost too hot to touch with his bare hand, it burned through the soles of his boots. At noon he sought shelter from the sun but there was none; he kept climbing until he was able to find a little shade under an overhang at the head of a ravine. He stopped and squatted under the rock—there was not room enough to lie down—and waited through the next three hours. Half his water was already gone; he opened one of the canteens.

Waiting there, half asleep on his heels, stupefied by heat and exhaustion, he stared at a buzzard circling in the sky off to the west. One black shape floating in the air, around and around in endless lazy circles. The glare of the sunlight made his eyes ache; he closed them, lowered his head and tried to sleep.

The next time he looked there were three vultures soaring where only one had been before. Instead of rising with the thermal updrafts and drifting on, as they usually did, the birds were gradually descending, in cautious spirals, toward some attraction on the ground.

Gatlin roused himself. He crept out of the shade and willed his body upright. He shouldered the pack frame, put on his hat, climbed out of the ravine and hiked toward the disappearing birds, following the contour of the slope below the red wall. As he made his way among the rocks, skirting prickly pear and thornbush, he saw more black wings appear in the sky. The gathering of the clan. Whatever it was they were coming down for was hidden from him by the successive dips and rises of the terrain. It was impossible for him, in the heat, in his fatigue, to run over the broken ground; but he hastened forward, sliding and stumbling down into one gulch after another, scrambling up the far side and hurrying on. His shirt turned dark with sweat. Tears, of which he was unaware, streamed through the stubble of beard on his face. He groaned, gasped for breath, clawing at the brush and loose stones as he struggled up the final incline and reached the crest.

At first he saw only a mass of black feathers, a cluster of bald red heads. The vultures were so engrossed in their meal they did not immediately notice the man on the skyline above them. He rushed down, they raised their dripping beaks, vomited, scattered, beating the air with long and heavy wings, and skipped nimbly into space.

Halfway down the slope Gatlin stopped. The quarry was only a deer, a small doe battered and partly dismembered by a long fall from the cliff above. He turned aside, stumbling slowly toward the nearest patch of shade, and rested for an hour. He drank a great deal of water, emptying the first canteen. In the sky the vultures soared and reassembled and after a while the boldest of them ventured to begin to descend. They were all feeding by the time Gatlin found the strength to resume his march.

The sun, touching the horizon, burned for a few minutes directly into his face. He paused to rest, turning his back on the glare, and gazed with weary, aching, blood-flecked eyes at the world of the canyon.

He was alone in one of the loneliest places on earth. Above him rose tier after tier of cliffs, the edge of the forest barely apparent on the rim of the uppermost wall; around him the gray desert platform where nothing grew but scrub brush and cactus sloped toward the brink of the inner gorge and the unseen river. From river to forest an ascent of over five thousand feet; from rim to rim ten miles by airline at the most narrow point; from canyon head to canyon mouth two hundred and eighty-five miles by the course of the river. In all this region was nothing human that he could see, no sign of man or of man's work. No sign, no trace, no path, no clue, no person but himself.

Alone. Was he alone?

"Sandy!" he howled. And waited for an answer.

After a moment the cliffs answered. One, then a second, then a third, and more:

> *SANDY*
> > *Sandy*
> > > *sandy . . .*

Echo answered echo, fading out in delicate diminuendo through league on league of empty space, a wave of sound whose farthest ripple died unheard in the twilight air, on the farthest shore of canyon and desert:

> *sandy*
> > *sandy*
> > > *sandy . . .*

# WALTER VAN TILBURG CLARK
## THE INDIAN WELL

Walter Van Tilburg Clark (1909–1971) grew up in Reno, Nevada, where his father was president of the University of Nevada from 1917 to 1937. The West, chiefly Nevada, was his home for most of his life, and his aesthetic reflects this fact, for he wrote of vast space and unaccommodating land wherein characters are often isolated from appropriate contexts for social action. Three novels—*The Ox-Bow Incident* (1940), *The City of Trembling Leaves* (1945), and *The Track of the Cat* (1949)—and a collection of stories, *The Watchful Gods and Other Stories* (1950), reveal Clark's view that nature remains eternal while people come and go.

"The Indian Well" first appeared in *Accent*, No. 3, Spring 1943. A white man comes to an oasis in the American desert, loses his burro to a cougar, and then maintains a winter-long vigil until he finally kills the cougar. Jim Suttler takes it as a personal affront that nature has claimed his burro, and through endurance he is able to change the natural patterns of the Indian-well region for a time. However, when he moves on in the spring, the patterns resume, and it is as though a man had never been there.

# THE INDIAN WELL

I n this dead land, like a vast relief model, the only allegiance was to sun. Even night was not strong enough to resist; earth stretched gratefully under it, but had no hope that day would not return. Such living things as hoarded a little juice at their cores were secret about it, and only the most ephemeral existences, the air at dawn and sunset, the amethyst shadows in the mountains, had any freedom. The Indian Well alone, of lesser creations, was in constant revolt. Sooner or later all minor, breathing rebels came to its stone basin under the spring in the cliff, and from its overflow grew a meadow delta and two columns of willows and aspens holding a tiny front against the valley. The pictograph of a starving, ancient journey, cut in rock above the basin, a sun-warped shack on the south wing of the canyon, and an abandoned mine above it, were the last minute and practically contemporary tokens of man's participation in the cycles of the well's resistance, each of which was an epitome of centuries, and perhaps of the wars of the universe.

The day before Jim Suttler came up in the early spring to take his part in one cycle was a busy day. The sun was merely lucid after four days of broken showers and one rain of an hour with a little cold wind behind it, and under the separate cloud shadows sliding down the mountain and into the valley, the canyon was alive. A rattler emerged partially from a hole in the mound on which the cabin stood, and having gorged in the darkness, rested with his head on a stone. A road-runner, stepping long and always about to sprint, came down the morning side of the mound, and his eye, quick to perceive the difference between the live and the inanimate of the same color, discovered the coffin-shaped head on the stone. At once he broke into a reaching sprint, his neck and tail stretched level, his beak agape with expectation. But his shadow arrived a step before him. The rattler recoiled, his head scarred by the sharp beak but his eye intact. The road-runner said nothing, but peered warily into the hole without stretching his neck, then walked off stiffly, leaning forward again as if about to run. When he had gone twenty feet he turned, balanced for an instant, and charged back, checking abruptly just short of the hole. The snake remained withdrawn. The road-runner paraded briefly before the hole, talking to himself, and then ran angrily up to the spring, where he drank at the overflow, sipping and stretching his neck, lifting his feet one at a time, ready to go into immediate action. The road-runner lived a dangerous and exciting life.

In the upper canyon the cliff swallows, making short harp notes, dipped and shot between the new mud under the aspens and their high community on the forehead of the cliff. Electrical bluebirds appeared to dart the length of the canyon at each low flight, but turned up tilting half way down. Lizards made similar unexpected flights and stops on the rocks, and when they stopped did rapid push-ups, like men exercising on a floor. They were variably pugnacious and timid.

Two of them arrived simultaneously upon a rock below the road-runner. One of them immediately skittered to a rock two feet off, and they faced each other, exercising. A small hawk coming down over the mountain, but shadowless under a cloud, saw the lizards. Having overfled the difficult target, he dropped to the canyon mouth swiftly and banked back into the wind. His trajectory was cleared of swallows but one of them, fluttering hastily up, dropped a pellet of mud between the lizards. The one who had retreated disappeared. The other flattened for an instant, then sprang and charged. The road-runner was on him as he struck the pellet, and galloped down the canyon in great, tense strides on his toes, the lizard lashing the air from his beak. The hawk stooped at the road-runner, thought better of it, and rose against the wind to the head of the canyon, where he turned back and coasted out over the desert, his shadow a little behind him and farther and farther below.

The swallows became the voice of the canyon again, but in moments when they were all silent the lovely smaller sounds emerged, their own feathering, the liquid overflow, the snapping and clicking of insects, a touch of wind in the new aspens. Under these lay still more delicate tones, erasing, in the most silent seconds, the difference between eye and ear, a white cloud shadow passing under the water of the well, a dark cloud shadow on the cliff, the aspen patterns on the stones. Deepest was the permanent background of the rocks, the lost on the canyon floor, and those yet strong, the thinking cliffs. When the swallows began again it was impossible to understand the cliffs, who could afford to wait.

At noon a red and white range cow with one new calf, shining and curled, came slowly up from the desert, stopping often to let the calf rest. At each stop the calf would try vigorously to feed, but the cow would go on. When they reached the well the cow drank slowly for a long time; then she continued to wrinkle the water with her muzzle, drinking a little and blowing, as if she found it hard to leave. The calf worked under her with spasmodic nudgings. When she was done playing with the water, she nosed and licked him out from under her and up to the well. He shied from the surprising coolness and she put him back. When he stayed, she drank again. He put his nose into the water also, and bucked up as if bitten. She continued to pretend, and he returned, got water up his nostrils and took three jumps away. The cow was content and moved off toward the canyon wall, tonguing grass tufts from among the rocks. Against the cliff she rubbed gently and continuously with a mild voluptuous look, occasionally lapping her nose with a serpent tongue. The loose winter shag came off in tufts on the rock. The calf lost her, became panicked and made desperate noises which stopped prematurely, and when he discovered her, complicated her toilet. Finally she led him down to the meadow where, moving slowly, they both fed until he was full and went to sleep in a ball in the sun. At sunset they returned to the well, where the cow drank again and gave him a second lesson. After this they went back into the brush and northward into the dusk. The cow's size and relative immunity to sudden death left an aftermath of peace, rendered gently humorous by the calf.

Also at sunset, there was a resurgence of life among the swallows. The thin golden air at the cliff tops, in which there were now no clouds so that the eastern mountains and the valley were flooded with unbroken light, was full of their cries and quick maneuvers among a dancing myriad of insects. The direct sun gave them, when they perched in rows upon the cliff, a dramatic significance like that of men upon an immensely higher promontory. As dusk rose out of the canyon, while the eastern peaks were still lighted, the swallows gradually became silent creatures with slightly altered flight, until, at twilight, the air was full of velvet, swooping bats.

In the night jack-rabbits multiplied spontaneously out of the brush of the valley, drank in the rivulet, their noses and great ears continuously searching the dark, electrical air, and played in fits and starts on the meadow, the many young hopping like rubber, or made thumping love among the aspens and the willows.

A coyote came down canyon on his belly and lay in the brush with his nose between his paws. He took a young rabbit in a quiet spring and snap, and went into the brush again to eat it. At the slight rending of his meal the meadow cleared of leaping shadows and lay empty in the starlight. The rabbits, however, encouraged by newcomers, returned soon, and the coyote killed again and went off heavily, the jack's great hind legs dragging.

In the dry-wash below the meadow an old coyote, without family, profited by the second panic, which came over him. He ate what his loose teeth could tear, leaving the open remnant in the sand, drank at the basin and, carefully circling the meadow, disappeared into the dry wilderness.

Shortly before dawn, when the stars had lost luster and there was no sound in the canyon but the rivulet and the faint, separate clickings of mice in the gravel, nine antelope in loose file, with three silently flagging fawns, came on trigger toe up the meadow and drank at the well, heads often up, muzzles dripping, broad ears turning. In the meadow they grazed and the fawns nursed. When there was as much gray as darkness in the air, and new wind in the canyon, they departed, the file weaving into the brush, merging into the desert, to nothing, and the swallows resumed the talkative day shift.

Jim Suttler and his burro came up into the meadow a little after noon, very slowly, though there was only a spring-fever warmth. Suttler walked pigeon-toed, like an old climber, but carefully and stiffly, not with the loose walk natural to such a long-legged man. He stopped in the middle of the meadow, took off his old black sombrero, and stared up at the veil of water shining over the edge of the basin.

"We're none too early, Jenny," he said to the burro.

The burro had felt water for miles, but could show no excitement. She stood with her head down and her four legs spread unnaturally, as if to postpone a collapse. Her pack reared higher than Suttler's head, and was hung with casks, pails, canteens, a pick, two shovels, a crowbar and a rifle in a sheath. Suttler had the cautious uncertainty of his trade. His other burro had died two days before in the mountains east of Beatty, and Jenny and he bore its load.

Suttler shifted his old six shooter from his rump to his thigh, and studied the well, the meadow, the cabin and the mouth of the mine as if he might choose not to stay. He was not a cinema prospector. If he looked like one of the probably mistaken conceptions of Christ, with his red beard and red hair to his shoulders, it was because he had been long away from barbers and without spare water for shaving. He was unlike Christ in some other ways also.

"It's kinda run down," he told Jenny, "but we'll take it."

He put his sombrero back on, let his pack fall slowly to the ground, showing the sweat patch in his bleached brown shirt, and began to unload Jenny carefully, like a collector handling rare vases, and put everything into one neat pile.

"Now," he said, "we'll have a drink." His tongue and lips were so swollen that the words were unclear, but he spoke casually, like a club-man sealing a minor deal. One learns to do business slowly with deserts and mountains. He picked up a bucket and started for the well. At the upper edge of the meadow he looked back. Jenny was still standing with her head down and her legs apart. He did not particularly notice her extreme thinness for he had seen it coming on gradually. He was thinner himself, and tall, and so round-shouldered that when he stood his straightest he seemed to be peering ahead with his chin out.

"Come on, you old fool," he said. "It's off you now."

Jenny came, stumbling in the rocks above the meadow, and stopping often as if to decide why this annoyance recurred. When she became interested, Suttler would not let her get to the basin, but for ten minutes gave her water from his cupped hands, a few licks at a time. Then he drove her off and she stood in the shade of the canyon wall watching him. He began on his thirst in the same way, a gulp at a time, resting between gulps. After ten gulps he sat on a rock by the spring and looked at the little meadow and the big desert, and might have been considering the courses of the water through his body, but noticed also the antelope tracks in the mud.

After a time he drank another half dozen gulps, gave Jenny half a pailful, and drove her down to the meadow, where he spread a dirty blanket in the striped sun and shadow under the willows. He sat on the edge of the blanket, rolled a cigarette and smoked it while he watched Jenny. When she began to graze with her rump to the canyon, he flicked his cigarette onto the grass, rolled over with his back to the sun and slept until it became chilly after sunset. Then he woke, ate a can of beans, threw the can into the willows and led Jenny up to the well, where they drank together from the basin for a long time. While she resumed her grazing, he took another blanket and his rifle from the pile, removed his heel-worn boots, stood his rifle against a fork, and, rolling up in both blankets, slept again.

In the night many rabbits played in the meadow in spite of the strong sweat and tobacco smell of Jim Suttler lying under the willows, but the antelope, when they came in the dead dark before dawn, were nervous, drank less, and did not graze but minced quickly back across the meadow and began to run at the head of the dry wash. Jenny slept with her head hanging, and did not hear them come or go.

Suttler woke lazy and still red-eyed, and spent the morning drinking at the well, eating and dozing on his blanket. In the afternoon, slowly, a few things at a time, he carried his pile to the cabin. He had a bachelor's obsession with order, though he did not mind dirt, and puttered until sundown making a brush bed and arranging his gear. Much of this time, however, was spent studying the records, on the cabin walls, of the recent human life of the well. He had to be careful, because among the still legible names and dates, after Frank Davis, 1893, Willard Harbinger, 1893, London, England, John Mason, June 13, 1887, Bucksport,

Maine, Matthew Kenling, from Glasgow, 1891, Penelope and Martin
Reave, God Guide Us, 1885, was written Frank Hayward, 1492, feeling
my age. There were other wits too. John Barr had written, Giv it back
to the injuns, and Kenneth Thatcher, two years later, had written under
that, Pity the noble redskin, while another man, whose second name
was Evans, had written what was already a familiar libel, since it was
not strictly true: Fifty miles from water, a hundred miles from wood, a
million miles from God, three feet from hell. Someone unnamed had
felt differently, saying, God is kind. We may make it now. Shot an
antelope here July 10, 188–, and the last number blurred. Arthur Smith,
1881, had recorded, Here berried my beloved wife Semantha, age 22,
and my soul. God let me keep the child. J.M. said cryptically, Good
luck, John, and Bill said, Ralph, if you come this way, am trying to get
to Los Angeles. B. Westover said he had recovered from his wound
there in 1884, and Galt said, enigmatically and without date, Bart and
Miller burned to death in the Yellow Jacket. I don't care now. There
were poets too, of both parties. What could still be read of Byron Cotter's
verses, written in 1902, said,

> . . . here alone
> Each shining dawn I greet,
> The Lord's wind on my forehead
> And where he set his feet
> One mark of heel remaining
> Each day filled up anew,
> To keep my soul from burning,
> With clear, celestial dew.
> Here in His Grace abiding
> The mortal years and few
> I shall...

but you can't tell what he intended, while J.A. had printed,

> My brother came out in '49
> I came in '51
> At first we thought we liked it fine
> But now, by God, we're done.

Suttler studied these records without smiling, like someone reading a
funny paper, and finally, with a heavy blue pencil, registered, Jim and
Jenny Suttler, damn dried out, March—and paused, but had no way
of discovering the day—1940.

In the evening he sat on the steps watching the swallows in the
golden upper canyon turn bats in the dusk, and thought about the

antelope. He had seen the new tracks also, and it alarmed him a little that the antelope could have passed twice in the dark without waking him.

Before false dawn he was lying in the willows with his carbine at ready. Rabbits ran from the meadow when he came down, and after that there was no movement. He wanted to smoke. When he did see them at the lower edge of the meadow, he was startled, yet made no quick movement, but slowly pivoted to cover them. They made poor targets in that light and backed by the pale desert, appearing and disappearing before his eyes. He couldn't keep any one of them steadily visible, and decided to wait until they made contrast against the meadow. But his presence was strong. One of the antelope advanced onto the green, but then threw its head up, spun, and ran back past the flank of the herd, which swung after him. Suttler rose quickly and raised the rifle, but let it down without firing. He could hear the light rattle of their flight in the wash, but had only a belief that he could see them. He had few cartridges, and the report and ponderous echo under the cliffs would scare them off for weeks.

His energies, however, were awakened by the frustrated hunt. While there was still more light than heat in the canyon, he climbed to the abandoned mine tunnel at the top of the alluvial wing of the cliff. He looked at the broken rock in the dump, kicked up its pack with a boot toe, and went into the tunnel, peering closely at its sides, in places black with old smoke smudges. At the back he struck two matches and looked at the jagged dead end and the fragments on the floor, then returned to the shallow beginning of a side tunnel. At the second match here he knelt quickly, scrutinized a portion of the rock, and when the match went out at once lit another. He lit six matches, and pulled at the rock with his hand. It was firm.

"The poor chump," he said aloud.

He got a loose rock from the tunnel and hammered at the projection with it. It came finally, and he carried it into the sun on the dump.

"Yessir," he said aloud, after a minute.

He knocked his sample into three pieces and examined each minutely.

"Yessir, yessir," he said with malicious glee, and, grinning at the tunnel, "The poor chump."

Then he looked again at the dump, like the mound before a gigantic gopher hole. "Still, that's a lot of digging," he said.

He put sample chips into his shirt pocket, keeping a small, black, heavy one that had fallen neatly from a hole like a borer's, to play with in his hand. After trouble he found the claim pile on the side hill south of the tunnel, its top rocks tumbled into the shale. Under the remaining rocks he found what he wanted, a ragged piece of yellow paper between two boards. The writing was in pencil, and not diplomatic. "I hereby clame this whole damn side hill as far as I can shoot north and south and as far as I can dig in. I am a good shot. Keep off. John Barr, April 11, 1897."

Jim Suttler grinned. "Tough guy, eh?" he said.

He made a small ceremony of burning the paper upon a stone from the cairn. The black tinsel of ash blew off and broke into flakes.

"O.K., John Barr?" he asked.

"O.K., Suttler," he answered himself.

In blue pencil, on soiled paper from his pocket, he slowly printed, "Becus of the lamented desease of the late clament, John Barr, I now clame these diggins for myself and partner Jenny. I can shoot too." And wrote rather than printed, "James T. Suttler, March—" and paused.

"Make it an even month," he said, and wrote, "11, 1940." Underneath he wrote, "Jenny Suttler, her mark," and drew a skull with long ears.

"There," he said, and folded the paper, put it between the two boards, and rebuilt the cairn into a neat pyramid above it.

In high spirit he was driven to cleanliness. With scissors, soap and razor he climbed to the spring. Jenny was there, drinking.

"When you're done," he said, and when she lifted her head, pulled her ears and scratched her.

"Maybe we've got something here, Jenny," he said.

Jenny observed him soberly and returned to the meadow.

"She doesn't believe me," he said, and began to perfect himself. He sheared off his red tresses in long hanks, then cut closer, and went over yet a third time, until there remained a brush, of varying density, of stiff red bristles, through which his scalp shone whitely. He sheared the beard likewise, then knelt to the well for mirror and shaved painfully. He also shaved his neck and about his ears. He arose younger and less impressive, with jaws as pale as his scalp, so that his sunburn was a red domino. He burned tresses and beard ceremoniously upon a sage bush, and announced, "It is spring."

He began to empty the pockets of his shirt and breeches onto a flat stone, yelling, "In the spring a young man's fancy," to a kind of tune, and paused, struck by the facts.

"Oh, yeah?" he said. "Fat chance."

"Fat," he repeated with obscene consideration. "Oh, well," he said, and finished piling upon the rock notebooks, pencil stubs, cartridges, tobacco, knife, stump pipe, matches, chalk, samples, and three wrinkled photographs. One of the photographs he observed at length before weighting it down with a .45 cartridge. It showed a round, blonde girl with a big smile on a stupid face, in a patterned calico house dress, in front of a blossoming rhododendron bush.

He added to this deposit his belt and holster with the big .45.

Then he stripped himself, washed and rinsed his garments in the spring, and spread them upon stones and brush, and carefully arranged four flat stones into a platform beside the trough. Standing there he scooped water over himself, gasping, made it a lather, and at last, face and copper bristles also foaming, gropingly entered the basin, and submerged, flooding the water over in a thin and soapy sheet. His head emerged at once. "My God," he whispered. He remained under, however, till he was soapless, and goose pimpled as a file, when he climbed out cautiously onto the rock platform and performed a dance of small, revolving patterns with a great deal of up and down.

At one point in his dance he observed the pictograph journey upon the cliff, and danced nearer to examine it.

"Ignorant," he pronounced. "Like a little kid," he said.

He was intrigued, however, by more recent records, names smoked and cut upon the lower rock. One of these, in script, like a gigantic handwriting deeply cut, said *Alvarez Blanco de Toledo, Anno Di 1624*. A very neat, upright cross was chiseled beneath it.

Suttler grinned. "Oh, yeah?" he asked, with his head upon one side. "Nuts," he said, looking at it squarely.

But it inspired him, and with his jack-knife he began scraping beneath the possibly Spanish inscription. His knife, however, made scratches, not incisions. He completed a bad Jim and Jenny and quit, saying, "I should kill myself over a phony wop."

Thereafter, for weeks, while the canyon became increasingly like a furnace in the daytime and the rocks stayed warm at night, he drove his tunnel farther into the mountain and piled the dump farther into the gully, making, at one side of the entrance, a heap of ore to be worked, and occasionally adding a peculiarly heavy pebble to the others in his small leather bag with a draw string. He and Jenny thrived upon this fixed and well-watered life. The hollows disappeared from his face and he became less stringy, while Jenny grew round, her battleship-gray pelt even lustrous and its black markings distinct and ornamental. The burro found time from her grazing to come to the cabin door in the evenings and attend solemnly to Suttler playing with his samples and explaining their future.

"Then, old lady," Suttler said, "you will carry only small children, one at a time, for never more than half an hour. You will have a bedroom with French windows and a mattress, and I will paint your feet gold.

"The children," he said, "will probably be red-headed, but maybe blonde. Anyway, they will be beautiful.

"After we've had a holiday, of course," he added. "For one hundred and thirty-three nights," he said dreamily. "Also," he said, "just one hundred and thirty-three quarts. I'm no drunken bum.

"For you, though," he said, "for one hundred and thirty-three nights a quiet hotel with other old ladies. I should drag my own mother in the gutter." He pulled her head down by the ears and kissed her loudly upon the nose. They were very happy together.

Nor did they greatly alter most of the life of the canyon. The antelope did not return, it is true, the rabbits were fewer and less playful because he sometimes snared them for meat, the little, clean mice and desert rats avoided the cabin they had used, and the road-runner did not come in daylight after Suttler, for fun, narrowly missed him with a piece of ore from the tunnel mouth. Suttler's violence was disproportionate perhaps, when he used his .45 to blow apart a creamy rat who did invade the cabin, but the loss was insignificant to the pattern of the well, and more than compensated when he one day caught the rattler extended at the foot of the dump in a drunken stupor from rare young rabbit, and before it could recoil held it aloft by the tail and snapped its head off, leaving the heavy body to turn slowly for a long time among the rocks. The dominant voices went undisturbed, save when he sang badly at his work or said beautiful things to Jenny in a loud voice.

There were, however, two more noticeable changes, one of which, at least, was important to Suttler himself. The first was the execution of the range cow's calf in the late fall, when he began to suggest a bull. Suttler felt a little guilty about this because the calf might have belonged to somebody, because the cow remained near the meadow bawling for two nights, and because the calf had come to meet the gun with more curiosity than challenge. But when he had the flayed carcass hung in the mine tunnel in a wet canvas, the sensation of providence overcame any qualms.

The other change was more serious. It occurred at the beginning of such winter as the well had, when there was sometimes a light rime on the rocks at dawn, and the aspens held only a few yellow leaves. Suttler thought often of leaving. The nights were cold, the fresh meat was eaten, his hopes had diminished as he still found only occasional nuggets, and his dreams of women, if less violent, were more nostalgic. The canyon held him with a feeling he would have called lonesome but at home, yet he probably would have gone except for this second change.

In the higher mountains to the west, where there was already snow, and at dawn a green winter sky, hunger stirred a buried memory in a cougar. He had twice killed antelope at the well, and felt there had been time enough again. He came down from the dwarfed trees and crossed the narrow valley under the stars, sometimes stopping abruptly to stare intently about, like a house-cat in a strange room. After each stop he would at once resume a quick, noiseless trot. From the top of the mountain above the spring he came down very slowly on his belly, but there was nothing at the well. He relaxed, and leaning on the rim of the basin, drank, listening between laps. His nose was clean with fasting, and he knew of the man in the cabin and Jenny in the meadow, but they were strange, not what he remembered about the place. But neither had his past made him fearful. It was only habitual hunting caution which made him go down into the willows carefully, and lie there head up, watching Jenny, but still waiting for antelope, which he had killed before near dawn. The strange smells were confusing and therefore irritating. After an hour he rose and went silently to the cabin, from which the strangest smell came strongly, a carnivorous smell which did not arouse appetite, but made him bristle nervously. The tobacco in it was like pins in his nostrils. He circled the cabin, stopping frequently. At the open door the scent was violent. He stood with his front paws up on the step, moving his head in serpent motions, the end of his heavy tail furling and unfurling constantly. In a dream Suttler turned over without waking, and muttered. The cougar crouched, his eyes intent, his ruff lifting. Then he swung away from the door, growling a little, and after one pause, crept back down to the meadow again and lay in the willows, but where he could watch the cabin also.

When the sky was alarmingly pale and the antelope had not come, he crawled a few feet at a time, behind the willows, to a point nearer Jenny. There he crouched, working his hind legs slowly under him until he was set, and sprang, raced the three or four jumps to the drowsy burro, and struck. The beginning of her mortal scream was severed, but having made an imperfect leap, and from no height, the cat did not at once break her neck, but drove her to earth, where her small hooves churned futilely in the sod, and chewed and worried until she lay still.

Jim Suttler was nearly awakened by the fragment of scream, but heard nothing after it, and sank again.

The cat wrestled Jenny's body into the willows, fed with uncertain relish, drank long at the well, and went slowly over the crest, stopping often to look back. In spite of the light and the beginning talk of the swallows, the old coyote also fed and was gone before Suttler woke.

When Suttler found Jenny, many double columns of regimented ants were already at work, streaming in and out of the interior and mounting like bridge workers upon the ribs. Suttler stood and looked down. He desired to hold the small muzzle in the hollow of his hand, feeling that this familiar gesture would get through to Jenny, but couldn't bring himself to it because of what had happened to that side of her head. He squatted and lifted one hoof on its stiff leg and held that. Ants emerged hurriedly from the fetlock, their lines of communication broken. Two of them made disorganized excursions on the back of his hand. He rose, shook them off, and stood staring again. He didn't say anything because he spoke easily only when cheerful or excited, but a determination was beginning in him. He followed the drag to the spot torn by the small hoofs. Among the willows again, he found the tracks of both the cougar and the coyote, and the cat's tracks again at the well and by the cabin doorstep. He left Jenny in the willows with a canvas over her during the day, and did not eat.

At sunset he sat on the doorstep, cleaning his rifle and oiling it until he could spring the lever almost without sound. He filled the clip, pressed it home, and sat with the gun across his knees until dark, when he put on his sheepskin, stuffed a scarf into the pocket, and went down to Jenny. He removed the canvas from her, rolled it up and held it under his arm.

"I'm sorry, old woman," he said. "Just tonight."

There was a little cold wind in the willows. It rattled the upper branches lightly.

Suttler selected a spot thirty yards down wind, from which he could see Jenny, spread the canvas and lay down upon it, facing toward her. After an hour he was afraid of falling asleep and sat up against a willow clump. He sat there all night. A little after midnight the old coyote came into the dry-wash below him. At the top of the wash he sat down, and when the mingled scents gave him a clear picture of the strategy, let his tongue loll out, looked at the stars for a moment with his mouth silently open, rose and trotted back into the desert.

At the beginning of daylight the younger coyote trotted in from the north, and turned up toward the spring, but saw Jenny. He sat down and looked at her for a long time. Then he moved to the west and sat down again. In the wind was only winter, and the water, and faintly the acrid bat dung in the cliffs. He completed the circle, but not widely enough, walking slowly through the willows, down the edge of the meadow and in again not ten yards in front of the following muzzle of the carbine. Like Jenny, he felt his danger too late. The heavy slug caught him at the base of the skull in the middle of the first jump, so that it was amazingly accelerated for a fraction of a second. The coyote began it alive, and ended it quite dead, but with a tense muscular movement conceived which resulted in a grotesque final leap and twist of the hindquarters alone, leaving them propped high against a willow clump while the head was half buried in the sand, red welling up along the lips of the distended jaws. The cottony underpelt of the tail and rump stirred gleefully in the wind.

When Suttler kicked the body and it did not move, he suddenly dropped his gun, grasped it by the upright hind legs, and hurled it out into the sage-brush. His face appeared slightly insane with fury for that instant. Then he picked up his gun and went back to the cabin, where he ate, and drank half of one of his last three bottles of whiskey.

In the middle of the morning he came down with his pick and shovel, dragged Jenny's much lightened body down into the dry-wash, and dug in the rock and sand for two hours. When she was covered, he erected a small cairn of stone, like the claim post, above her.

"If it takes a year," he said, and licked the salt sweat on his lips.

That day he finished the half bottle and drank all of a second one, and became very drunk, so that he fell asleep during his vigil in the willows, sprawled wide on the dry turf and snoring. He was not disturbed. There was a difference in his smell after that day which prevented even the rabbits from coming into the meadow. He waited five nights in the willows. Then he transferred his watch to a niche in the cliff, across from and just below the spring.

All winter, while the day wind blew long veils of dust across the desert, regularly repeated, like waves or the smoke of line artillery fire, and the rocks shrank under the cold glitter of night, he did not miss a watch. He learned to go to sleep at sundown, wake within a few minutes of midnight, go up to his post, and become at once clear headed and watchful. He talked to himself in the mine and the cabin, but never in the niche. His supplies ran low, and he ate less, but would not risk a startling shot. He rationed his tobacco, and when it was gone worked up to a vomiting sickness every three days for nine days, but did not miss a night in the niche. All winter he did not remove his clothes, bathe, shave, cut his hair or sing. He worked the dead mine only to be busy, and became thin again, with sunken eyes which yet were not the eyes he had come with the spring before. It was April, his food almost gone, when he got his chance.

There was a half moon that night, which made the canyon walls black, and occasionally gleamed on wrinkles of the overflow. The cat came down so quietly that Suttler did not see him until he was beside the basin. The animal was suspicious. He took the wind, and twice started to drink, and didn't, but crouched. On Suttler's face there was a set grin which exposed his teeth.

"Not even a drink, you bastard," he thought.

The cat drank a little though, and dropped again, softly, trying to get the scent from the meadow. Suttler drew slowly upon his soul in the trigger. When it gave, the report was magnified impressively in the canyon. The cougar sprang straight into the air and screamed outrageously. The back of Suttler's neck was cold and his hands trembled, but he shucked the lever and fired again. This shot ricocheted from the basin and whined away thinly. The first, however, had struck near enough. The cat began to scramble rapidly on the loose stone, at first without voice, then screaming repeatedly. It doubled upon itself snarling and chewing in a small furious circle, fell and began to throw itself in short, leaping spasms upon the stones, struck across the rim of the tank and lay half in the water, its head and shoulders raised in one corner and resting against the cliff. Suttler could hear it breathing hoarsely and snarling very faintly. The soprano chorus of swallows gradually became silent.

Suttler had risen to fire again, but lowered the carbine and advanced, stopping at every step to peer intently and listen for the hoarse breathing, which continued. Even when he was within five feet of the tank the cougar did not move, except to gasp so that the water again splashed from the basin. Suttler was calmed by the certainty of accomplishment. He drew the heavy revolver from his holster, aimed carefully at the rattling head, and fired again. The canyon boomed, and the east responded faintly and a little behind, but Suttler did not hear them, for the cat thrashed heavily in the tank, splashing him as with a bucket, and then lay still on its side over the edge, its muzzle and forepaws hanging. The water was settling quietly in the tank, but Suttler stirred it again, shooting five more times with great deliberation into the heavy body, which did not move except at the impact of the slugs.

The rest of the night, even after the moon was gone, he worked fiercely, slitting and tearing with his knife. In the morning, under the swallows, he dragged the marbled carcass, still bleeding a little in places, onto the rocks on the side away from the spring, and dropped it. Dragging the ragged hide by the neck, he went unsteadily down the canyon to the cabin, where he slept like a drunkard, although his whiskey had been gone for two months.

In the afternoon, with dreaming eyes, he bore the pelt to Jenny's grave, took down the stones with his hands, shoveled the earth from her, covered her with the skin, and again with earth and the cairn.

He looked at this monument. "There," he said.

That night, for the first time since her death, he slept through.

In the morning, at the well, he repeated his cleansing ritual of a year before, save that they were rags he stretched to dry, even to the dance upon the rock platform while drying. Squatting naked and clean, shaven and clipped, he looked for a long time at the grinning countenance, now very dirty, of the plump girl in front of the blossoming rhododendrons, and in the resumption of his dance he made singing noises accompanied by the words, "Spring, spring, beautiful spring." He was a starved but revived and volatile spirit.

An hour later he went south, his boot soles held on by canvas strips, and did not once look back.

The disturbed life of the spring resumed. In the second night the rabbits loved in the willows, and at the end of a week the rats played in the cabin again. The old coyote and a vulture cleaned the cougar, and his bones fell apart in the shale. The road-runner came up one day, tentatively, and in front of the tunnel snatched up a horned toad and ran with it around the corner, but no farther. After a month the antelope returned. The well brimmed, and in the gentle sunlight the new aspen leaves made a tiny music of shadows.

# CRAIG LESLEY
# THE CATCH

Craig Lesley was born July 5, 1945, in The Dalles, Oregon, near the Columbia River. He has worked as a rancher in Oregon, a miner in Idaho, and a longshoreman in Alaska. Following completion of a M.F.A. degree in creative writing at the University of Massachusetts, Lesley has made his home in Portland, Oregon. *Winterkill* (1984) won the Pacific Northwest Booksellers Association first prize for fiction and first prize, Best Novel and Best First Novel, from the Western Writers Association. The Columbia River, salmon fishing, and mountains have spiritual and magical significance in this novel which envisions natural cycles beyond the order that man tries to impose.

This is the theme of Lesley's story, "The Catch," first published in *Writers' Forum*, No. 6, 1979. Jake, a riverguide by profession, and his nephew Brent from St. Louis search for a drowned fisherman on the very river where Brent's father had drowned twenty years earlier. When a crayfish-mutilated body is found, Brent is horrified and repudiates any future relationship with Jake, whose devotion to life (and death) on the river has been a kind of atonement for his brother's drowning. Jake's boasting ("You're outdoors and your own boss. I can teach you about this river.") is invalidated by "the black water" where merciless crayfish scuttle. Nature itself is "the catch," the logical snag in man's self-imposed rituals.

# THE CATCH

J ake rowed the driftboat out of the whitewater and held it steady against the eddying current of the dark green pool. Squinting against the midday glare, he searched the shoreline and shallow water among the snags and deadfall. "See anything?" he asked his nephew Brent.

"No, just more submerged logs."

Brent's voice had an edge that made Jake more aware of his own weariness and concern. Two days on the water and no trace of the lost fisherman. He wanted to rest, to tie his boat to one of the aspens that lined the riverbank and take a nap in the shade. But he also wanted to search the water above South Junction by evening. Below South Junction was the Coffeepot, and Jake had refused to take anyone through those rapids after his brother Dave had drowned there twenty years ago. If they didn't find the man today, they'd have to haul the boat out at South Junction, tow it for ten miles of canyon grade, and put back in below the Coffeepot at the next access road to the river. "Half a mile to Deer Island," Jake said. "We can eat lunch and rest. Maybe we'll find him this afternoon."

"Maybe he's not in the water," Brent said. "He could have had a heart attack and be up by the old railroad grade. Or a snake could have bit him."

"We'd see the crows and magpies," Jake said. "Nope, he's in the water."

"Whatever you say." Brent tugged the visor of his fishing cap over his eyes and slouched in the back of the boat.

Jake studied the nose, the jaw, the pouting lower lip. Thirty years ago, Brent's father had those same features. Although Jake couldn't see Brent's shaded eyes, he knew they resembled Dave's too. The boy was smaller, but if he had stayed in Montana, summers spent bucking bales and lifting irrigation pipes would have filled him out.

Brent lifted the visor of his cap when the boat disturbed a pair of Canvasbacks. They churned out of the water and flapped into the air, their raucous quacking breaking the momentary quiet of the river. "Bang," he said, leveling an imaginary shotgun at the birds.

It was almost like having Dave back, Jake thought. Five years without

seeing the boy had been too long, but now that Brent was almost out
of college, perhaps he would come more often and his visits would last
longer. He wished that this trip was only for fishing, but the boy had
wanted to come. Usually, one of the sheriff's men came for a lost fisherman or drowned canoeist, but the sheriff couldn't spare one of his
deputies this week, the opening of hunting season.

They found nothing in the pools and shallows above Deer Island.
When Jake nudged the boat against the shore at the head of the island,
Brent grabbed the line and stepped into the water. His foot sank in
mud and the heel of his trailing hipboot caught the gunwale. For a
moment, he hung suspended—half in the boat, half in the water—his
legs crooked in an awkward V. Throwing the rope into the water, he
used both hands to tug free the bootheel.

"Easy," said Jake as he saw the flush rise in the boy's neck. He handed
him an oar. "Check for snakes."

Brent poked the oar into the grass along the shoreline and waited.
"Nothing," he said.

Jake stepped into the water, grabbed the prow, and together they
dragged the boat onto the rocky beach.

"Look," Brent said.

Jake counted four deer, one a small buck, swimming from the island
to the shore. Heads back, rumps exposed, they swam, their flared
nostrils and wide black eyes visible above the water. As they reached
shore, Jake whistled, and they turned to look. After shaking, they trotted
up the side of the canyon, their glancing hooves starting small ribbons
of rolling pebbles on the talus slopes. At times, the sun glinted from
the buck's antlers. After five minutes, they were about one third of the
distance to the rim.

"Wish I could still move like that," Jake said.

"Seems a shame to disturb them," Brent said.

"After we're gone, they'll be back," Jake said.

Jake reached into the boat and flipped open the seats to get at the
storage compartments. He handed his pack, the grub box, and spinning
poles to Brent. He brought the tarp and cooking utensils. They carried
the gear to a small clearing in the center of the island.

"You want to cook lunch or catch it?" Jake asked.

"Catch."

"Then I'll heat the small skillet. Take a spinner and fish at the head
of the island. Work the slick, just this side of the riffle."

Brent nodded as he looped his bootstraps through his beltloops.

"Don't tie those hipboots inside at the ankle," Jake warned. "You got
to kick them off if you step in a hole."

"I know, I know," Brent said as he left.

Jake spread the tarp and put the grub box and pack on top. He took his hatchet from the side pocket of the pack and split kindling. When he brought the well-sharpened hatchet down, the wood split neatly along the grain. Jake was proud of the hatchet, a present from Dave over twenty years ago. The head had become squared by years of sharpening, and now he had to file the thick metal for hours before he gained a grudging edge. When the original plumb handle broke, he had replaced it with ash after he learned plumb handles were no longer available.

After he had the coffeepot and skillet on the coals, he leaned back and shut his eyes. Even though he had been guiding all fishing season, the rowing wore him out. Years before, he had looked forward to October and the opening of hunting season, but he no longer hunted. Perhaps he had brought too many drowned men out of the river and it spoiled the hunting. He made his living by guiding fishermen, but fishing seemed different somehow. He hadn't figured it out, but he thought about it.

Jake woke up when he heard water sloshing in hipboots. As Brent walked into camp, Jake saw his pants were wet above the boots. "Big one pull you in?"

"I slipped," Brent admitted. He held up four small rainbows. "Lunch."

Jake knew that he should say something. "They'll fry up real good. Just the right size for the pan." When he spit in the skillet, the spit hissed and popped. Jake cut a hunk of butter and watched it turn brown and bubble in the skillet. When Brent handed him the fish, Jake was pleased that his nephew had cleaned them.

"I couldn't hook the big ones," Brent said. "But sometimes they bumped the spinner."

Jake nodded. "This late in the season, they lie deep and eat crayfish. Sometimes they knock against a spinner, but they never really hit it." He rolled the fish in flour and corn meal, then placed them into the bubbling butter.

"If I caught some crayfish, I could use the tails," Brent said.

Jake waited until the fishes' papery skins browned like old parchment, then flipped them, added salt, and squeezed a wedge of lemon over them. He licked some of the tangy lemon from his fingers and put the fish on tin plates. "There's a special way to fish with crayfish. If you want, I'll show you after lunch."

"I'd like that," Brent said.

Jake had fried the fish just right. When he salted the tail and ate it, the thin brittle crackled in his mouth. Inside the papery skin, the pink flesh was very moist and hot. The lemon made the fish taste better.

"They're never as good," Jake said, "as when you eat them on the river."

Brent nodded as he stuffed the last of his fish into his mouth.

After they finished eating, Jake poured steaming cups of coffee from the pot on the coals at the fire's edge. He took a flask of whiskey from the pack and poured a shot and a half into each cup. He handed one to Brent who sipped it carefully and smiled. As he settled back and drank the hot coffee, Jake relaxed; the weariness in his back and shoulders numbed.

"It's times like these," Brent said, "that I know why you never leave this river. You want to trade for St. Louis?"

"I never been to a big city," Jake said. "Sometimes I go to the guide conventions in Missoula."

"Stay away from the big ones," Brent said. "Too crowded. I don't mind the university though. And mom likes the city."

Jake nodded. "I should have gone out there after your father died, but I never got around to it. Then she got married again and never came back here."

"She reads your letters," Brent said. "Three a year. Christmas, her birthday, mine."

"I'm not much of a writer," Jake said.

"That's all I ever do at college," Brent said. "The river is a nice change. Even if this isn't just a fishing trip."

"I'm glad you came," Jake said. "Dave and I used to sit around and talk for hours . . . on this same island. I don't usually have to look for someone this late in the season."

"It's okay," Brent said. "I wanted to come. It's been more than five years. I just hope to catch a big fish to show the guys at school."

"I want to show you this," Jake said. He took out his wallet and carefully removed an old picture from the plastic compartments. The edges were worn and thumbprinted from years of handling. "Me and your dad," he said pointing to the two grinning men in the picture. They stood with their arms around each other's shoulders, fishing poles jutting from their free hands. "And those are the fish," Jake chuckled. In front of the men was an unfinished door set on two sawhorses. The door was covered with large, thick-sided trout. The smallest fish was longer than the ruler on the table. "We caught those lunkers with soft-shelled crayfish. We hiked in the night before and caught two coffee-cans full of crayfish. After we had eaten supper, I saw Dave messing around with his creels, sewing foamrubber pads on the shoulder straps. He said he planned to catch so many fish the straps would cut his shoulder when we walked out of the canyon."

"That's a fish story," Brent said.

"I thought so, but there's proof." Jake tapped the picture. "We caught those fish by two o'clock and it was past dark before we hiked out of the canyon with them. Our creels were full and each one of us carried a potato sack besides."

"Did you catch them here?" Brent asked.

"No," Jake said. He carefully replaced the picture and put the wallet in his pocket. "Below the Coffeepot. This is the last picture of us together."

Jake brought out two crayfish viewers from the storage compartments under the seat. The viewers were made from a pane of glass 15" square and had wooden sides 6" high. Jake showed Brent how to hold the wooden sides and set the glass flat in the water. It was like looking at the riverbottom through a window.

Jake showed him how to carefully turn over the rocks in the quiet pools to avoid muddying the bottom, and how to grab crayfish just behind the claws, and how to replace the rocks so other crayfish could crawl under them. "Just after they moult, they need the protection. But some bastards want to heave the rocks onto the bank. That means no crayfish another year."

If the crayfish they caught had soft, flexible shells, they put them into a coffee-can. If the shells were hard, they returned the crayfish to the river. After forty-five minutes, they had a dozen. "Let's give these a try," Jake said.

They carried the crayfish and their spinning gear to the deep pools at the lower end of the island. Jake rigged the crayfish by cutting a small piece of surgical tubing and running the spinning line through it. With his pliers, he cut a two-inch strip of lead and shoved it into the surgical tubing, wedging the line between the lead and the tubing. "If the lead hangs on the bottom," he said, "you can pull it out of the tubing without losing the crayfish."

Jake tied a loop in the end of the monofilament line. Then he took an ice pick with a flattened, notched end. Placing the loop in the notch, he stuck the pick into the crayfish, just behind the first section of the tail, and shoved the pick through the middle of the crayfish, bringing the loop out just under the head. After withdrawing the pick, he tied a number six treble hook to the line and pulled it back into the soft flesh of the crayfish.

Handing the pole and rigging to Brent, he said, "Cast upstream and let the lead bounce along the bottom. When a fish takes the crayfish, he sort of mouths it to see if it's soft, and if it is, he swallows it. But if he feels the line drag, he lets go, so when it stops, you got to give slack. Back off three turns, count to five, and set the hook."

Brent released the bail and made an awkward swing cast that sent the crayfish and lead splashing into the water about twenty feet offshore.

"You got to cast farther," Jake said, "and more upstream."

Brent lost two more of the soft crayfish before he cast where Jake wanted him to. Jake watched the pole tip; the little bobs showed him the lead was bouncing along the rocky bottom. When the bobbing stopped before the end of the drift, Jake said, "Back it off now."

Brent turned the handle backwards, feeding three coils off the spool and through the guides.

"Now!"

Brent snapped his wrist back, setting the hook. The pole bent nearly double.

"Loosen the drag, damn it!"

The pole jerked again and again while Brent fumbled to release the drag screw. The line screamed out and the reel smoked as the fish coursed downstream with the current.

"Turn that bastard while you still got line!"

Brent snubbed the fish, then began reeling as the trout reversed direction.

When it came out of the roostertail and into the deep pool, Jake warned Brent, "Keep the pole up. Don't let him get snagged on the bottom." The way the fish had run meant it was a lunker, and Jake didn't want it to die on a snag at the riverbottom, the crayfish and hook deep in its gut.

"Why doesn't he jump?"

"Hooked too deep," Jake replied.

When Brent was able to work the fish toward shore, Jake moved quietly below him and waded into the shallow water. His hand and forearm submerged, he held the net close to the riverbottom. Brent backed away from the river, forcing the fish into the shallows. A silver flame spurting out of the dark green pool, the fish paused in the current. Taking care not to foul the line, Jake brought the net up, and, as the fish lunged, man, river, and trout merged into one quick movement.

Jake held the struggling fish high and grinned. "You caught a log!"

"What a fish!"

"A dandy. Four and a half pounds. Maybe five."

Brent caught three smaller fish before they left the island. With each one, he whooped and shouted like a boy at a circus.

Jake didn't want to end it, but he knew they had to get on with the search.

Jake was tired of rowing. His arms and shoulders ached and his chest, back, and rib cage numbed. The sun was almost behind the canyon's rim and long shadows from the trees along the riverbank reached far across the water.

Brent hunched in the back of the boat, his cap turned backward, his hand cupped to shade his eyes. "Maybe we missed him," he said.

"It's getting hard to see," Jake said. "In half an hour, we'll give it up." He knew he had to shoot Whitehorse rapids while the light was still good. Maybe this was one he wasn't going to find. If so, it would be on his mind all winter and early spring.

"There," Brent said hoarsely, "by that deadfall."

Jake strained to see where his nephew pointed. Then he made out the grey-green waders, subtly different in shade from the deep-green shadows of the trees. "Good eyes," he said.

When he rowed closer, Jake saw the current nudging the body back and forth against the deadfall. The man's face was down. Better for Brent, Jake thought. The dead man floated in murky water, but Jake thought it was shallow enough to wade. He measured the depth with an oar, just to make sure.

"It's not over our boots," he told Brent. After snubbing the boat on a snag close to shore, he got the heavy rubber bag from beneath the seat, stepped out of the boat, and carried the bag up the steep cutbank. After unfolding the bag, he unzipped the wide, waterproof zipper. The dull-grey rubber had blocked letters "Jackson County Sheriff's Dept."

"Too bad there's no beach here," he said to Brent as he came down. "We'll have to drag him to shore and heave him up the cutbank."

"Watch your footing," he told Brent as the two of them waded toward the body. "He'll get real heavy next to the shore. No buoyancy. We'll have to rest there a moment."

"Okay," Brent said.

"You take his feet. Grab real good. Just think about the shore." One of the man's arms was crumpled underneath his body. Jake tried to straighten it, but the arm was stiff. When he grabbed under the armpits, the flesh beneath the wet flannel shirt felt soft and slippery from being in the water so long. Jake shivered. You never get used to it, he thought.

"Got a hold?"

Brent didn't say anything. He nodded.

They lugged the sodden body toward the shore. When they reached the bank, Jake felt the weight was too much. "Lift the legs," he said. "Grab below the knees and lift them high." As Brent lifted, fetid water poured out of the waders.

Jake caught his breath. "Heave him up now. One, two, three, go." He grunted as he lifted the heavy body, but lost his grip a moment. The body slipped; the head flopped face up. Jake averted his eyes and pushed hard. The body rolled over, face-down onto the rubber bag.

Brent's throat contracted as he gasped. Standing stiffly, he clenched and unclenched his fists. His mouth moved but no words came out.

"Sit down," Jake said. "Put your head between your knees." Jake scrambled up the cutbank and quickly folded the heavy rubber bag over the body, then zipped it.

Brent sat, his back to Jake. "Jesus!" he said. "What happened to his face?"

"Crayfish," Jake said. "It's usually that way. Better if you don't look." He dragged the bag down the cutbank and waded out to the boat. He swung the end next to shore so they could load the body. After removing the whiskey flask from the pack, he had a long drink. "Want some?"

"No," Brent said. "I feel sick."

"I know," Jake said. "At least we found this one." He took another drink. "I'd like to let you rest some more, but I got to run Whitehorse while it's light. The sheriff can come get us at South Junction."

Brent said nothing.

"Getting dark," Jake said. "You better help me heave this into the boat."

Whitehorse was treacherous in early fall because low water exposed the jagged rocks at the head of the run and the large boulders in the chute. Jake kept to the middle to avoid the jagged rocks closer to shore. Each rapid slammed the boat with a loud "chunk," throwing the nose high and tearing at the bow, trying to spin the boat into the rocks. The seat jarred Jake's spine, his teeth cracked together, and red pain surged through his mind. Fighting the rapids' pull with long, deep oarstrokes, he kept the boat away from the rocks until it was sucked into the chute.

The fastwater hurled the boat downstream like a tobaggan, skimming past the large boulders in the chute. In spite of Jake's efforts to keep the nose downstream, the boat was gripped by a momentary eddy and flung sideways against one of the large boulders. Water poured over the side. When Jake tried to push off with an oar, the blade snapped with a brittle crack. Reaching beneath the ankle-deep water, he grabbed a spare oar from the bottom of the boat and stood, using his full strength to push the waterladen boat off the boulder and into the mainstream.

Brent clutched the gunwales, his knuckles white. His shirtsleeves were wet from the water which had poured over the side. The body bag floated between the men and crowded them both.

They reached the quieter water of the roostertail and Jake said, "There's a bailing can under your seat."

At South Junction, Jake tied the boat to a piling and the two men hauled their gear to a makeshift campground.

"When that oar snapped, I thought we'd bought the farm," Brent said.

"It happens," Jake said. "Can't ever tell when. That was a new oar too."

"So that's Whitehorse," Brent said. "Is that the worst run on the river?"

Jake stood quietly. "Listen below," he said.

"Rapids?"

"The Coffeepot."

"Do you run it?"

"I used to—just to keep my nerve. No more. You never go through there the same twice, no matter where you start. Bad rocks, worse currents. Sometimes, you slide through slick as a whistle; others, you hang on every rock."

"How was it when my father drowned?" Brent asked.

Jake wanted to tell him how it happened. He measured each word to get it right. "The river was too high that spring, but we were in our twenties and thought nothing could stop us. We remembered the fish from the year before and we had a new boat, so we decided to run the Coffeepot instead of hiking in.

"The current swung the boat against a rock, like today. Dave froze. I grabbed one of the oars from him, but I couldn't push us off in time, and a wall of water flipped the boat. Dave went under the rock; I went around. He came up for a second, unconscious, and I grabbed his life-jacket, but the current slammed us against another rock and I couldn't hold him."

Jake stared at his hands, thick with callouses and rough from years on the river. "I tried, but I couldn't hold him. I crawled ashore below the rapids and stayed until dark. Then I walked the old railroad grade to South Junction and called the sheriff. In the morning we found some splinters from the boat and a piece of Dave's shirt. Your mother left for St. Louis a month later. You were two."

"She never talks about it," Brent said.

"I don't much either," Jake said. "I thought about visiting her, but I never made it to St. Louis."

"She wanted to forget it anyway," Brent said.

"I better go call the sheriff," Jake said.

Jake drank a cup of coffee with the farmer after he called the sheriff. When he returned to camp, Brent was cooking six trout in the large skillet. Jake saw his fly-pole was rigged. "Quick work. What did you use?"

"Spent-wing stone. There was an evening hatch on."

The kid's got some savvy, Jake thought. "Smells good. Want to be camp cook? I'm getting too old."

Brent laughed. "You're almost as old as this river. But I don't think so. I'm just filling-in."

"Sheriff said he'll be here in an hour," Jake said. "That ends our part of it. I figure after we get to town and clean up, maybe we should go to the Red Top and have a few drinks. Dave and I used to go there when we got off the river."

Without looking up from the fish he was cooking, Brent said quietly, "Some other time. I'll probably head for St. Louis tomorrow." He put the fish onto the tin plates.

"I was hoping you'd stay a while. Seems like I don't get to see much of you." Jake took a bite of fish. "Say, you cooked this just right."

"Thanks," Brent said. "But I forgot the lemon."

The two men ate in silence. After supper Jake stood and poured a cup of coffee. He was glad they found the body. It would make the winter better and he could look forward to the spring. "You know," he said. "You could work here." He wanted to tell Brent how he felt, but when the words came out, they were about the job. "You're outdoors and your own boss. I can teach you about this river."

Brent poked at the coals with a stick. "It's not for me," he said.

Jake sipped his coffee. Too hot. He knew what Brent was thinking. "Looking for them . . . it's part of the territory. Somebody cares . . . they've got to be found. It's hard to explain, but after Dave drowned . . ."

"Whatever happened," Brent said, "wasn't your fault. You've been here all your life. I don't know why. But I can't."

Jake slowly poured the rest of his coffee on the hissing coals, then stood. His back ached and his chest felt strained from lifting the dead man. He saw headlights flicker on the road winding down the side of the canyon. "That'll be the sheriff. I better check everything in the boat."

Brent said nothing.

Jake dug a flashlight from his pack and followed its beam to the edge of the river. When he stepped into the water, he was surprised it felt so cold. "Must be damn tired," he muttered. "Damn tired and old." As he flashed the beam into the water, he saw a crayfish on the river-bottom dragging a piece of fish entrail. Startled by the light, the crayfish scuttled into the darkness. Jake's foot slipped and he bumped the flashlight against the side of the boat. It went out, then fell into the water. He started to reach for it, but he didn't want to put his hands into the black water. He closed his eyes and groped until he found the light, but it didn't work.

He leaned heavily against the side of the boat. The night wind whipping off the river carried the low, resonant churning of the Coffeepot. Chilled sweat made his flannel shirt cling to his back, and his socks grew clammy inside his hipboots. Clutching the boat in the darkness Jake waited for the sheriff.

# RUDOLFO A. ANAYA
## THE SILENCE OF THE LLANO

Rudolfo Anaya was born October 30, 1937, in Pastura, New Mexico. After studying literature at the University of New Mexico (B.A. 1963, M.A. 1968) and teaching for seven years in the Albuquerque public schools, he joined the faculty of English at his alma mater. *Bless me, Ultima* (1972), his first novel, won the Premio Quinto Sol and other honors and has been followed by three more novels and a story collection, *The Silence of the Llano* (1982). Inspired by the old Spanish and indigenous *cuentos* of the Mexican-American peoples of the Southwest, Anaya evokes in his writing the magic of human experience without sentimentalizing the loneliness and hardship of simple people enduring in a sometimes oppressive environment.

"The Silence of the Llano" internalizes and humanizes that exterior landscape. Having lost his parents in a blizzard, Rafael lives on a isolated ranch in the New Mexico plains and is believed by the villagers of Las Animas to be possessed by the "silence"" or deathly loneliness of the region. He marries, but when his wife dies in childbirth, he rejects his daughter Rita and is indeed claimed by the "eternal silence" of the plains. Then, many years later, Rafael returns to his adobe house to find that Rita has been raped, and for the first time he realizes he must choose between death (his wife's image fused with the archetypal figure of *la muerte*) and life (his wife's image reborn in Rita). When he utters his daughter's name, he brings the power of language to prevail over death.

# THE SILENCE OF THE LLANO

His name was Rafael, and he lived on a ranch in the lonely and desolate llano. He had no close neighbors; the nearest home was many miles away on the dirt road which led to the small village of Las Animas. Rafael went to the village only once a month for provisions, quickly buying what he needed, never stopping to talk with the other rancheros who came to the general store to buy what they needed and to swap stories.

Long ago, the friends his parents had known stopped visiting Rafael. The people whispered that the silence of the llano had taken Rafael's soul, and they respected his right to live alone. They knew the hurt he suffered. The dirt road which led from the village to his ranch was overgrown with mesquite bushes and the sparse grasses of the flat country. The dry plain was a cruel expanse broken only by gullies and mesas spotted with juniper and piñon trees.

The people of this country knew the loneliness of the llano; they realized that sometimes the silence of the endless plain grew so heavy and oppressive it became unbearable. When a man heard voices in the wind of the llano, he knew it was time to ride to the village just to listen to the voices of other men. They knew that after many days of riding alone under the burning sun and listening only to the moaning wind, a man could begin to talk to himself. When a man heard the sound of his voice in the silence, he sensed the danger in his lonely existence. Then he would ride to his ranch, saddle a fresh horse, explain to his wife that he needed something in the village, a plug of tobacco, perhaps a new knife, or a jar of salve for deworming the cattle. It was a pretense, in his heart each man knew he went to break the hold of the silence.

Las Animas was only a mud-cluster of homes, a general store, a small church, a sparse gathering of life in the wide plain. The old men of the village sat on a bench in front of the store, shaded by the portal in summer, warmed by the southern sun in winter. They talked about the weather, the dry spells they had known as rancheros on the llano, the bad winters, the price of cattle and sheep. They sniffed the air and predicted the coming of the summer rains, and they discussed the news

63

of the latest politics at the county seat.

The men who rode in listened attentively, nodding as they listened to the soft, full words of the old men, rocking back and forth on their boots, taking pleasure in the sounds they heard. Sometimes one of them would buy a bottle and they would drink and laugh and slap each other on the back as friends will do. Then, fortified by this simple act, each man returned home to share what he had heard with his family. Each would lie with his wife in the warm bed of night, the wind moaning softly outside, and he would tell the stories he had heard: so and so had died, someone they knew had married and moved away, the current price of wool and yearlings. The news of a world so far away was like a dream. The wife listened and was also fortified for the long days of loneliness. In adjoining rooms the children listened and heard the muffled sounds of the words and laughter of the father and mother. Later they would speak the words they heard as they cared for the ranch animals or helped the mother in the house, and in this way their own world grew and expanded.

Rafael knew well the silence of the llano. He was only fifteen when his father and mother died in a sudden, deadly blizzard which caught them on the road to Las Animas. Days later, when finally Rafael could break the snowdrifts for the horse, he had found them. There at La Angostura, where the road followed the edge of a deep arroyo, the horses had bolted or the wagon had slipped in the snow and ice. The wagon had overturned, pinning his father beneath the massive weight. His mother lay beside him, holding him in her arms. His father had been a strong man, he could have made a shelter, burned the wagon to survive the night, but pinned as he was he had been helpless and his wife could not lift the weight of the huge wagon. She had held him in her arms, covered both of them with her coat and blankets, but that night they had frozen. It took Rafael all day to dig graves in the frozen ground, then he buried them there, high on the slope of La Angostura where the summer rains would not wash away the graves.

That winter was cruel in other ways. Blizzards swept in from the north and piled the snow drifts around the house. Snow and wind drove the cattle against the fences where they huddled together and suffocated as the drifts grew. Rafael worked night and day to try to save his animals, and still he lost half of the herd to the punishing storms. Only the constant work and simple words and phrases he remembered his father and mother speaking kept Rafael alive that winter.

Spring came, the land thawed, the calves were born, and the work of a new season began. But first Rafael rode to the place where he had buried his parents. He placed a cross over their common grave, then he rode to the village of Las Animas and told the priest what had happened. The people gathered and a Mass for the dead was prayed. The women cried and the men slapped Rafael on the back and offered their condolences. All grieved, they had lost good friends, but they knew that was the way of death on the llano, swift and sudden. Now the work of spring was on them. The herds had to be rebuilt after the terrible winter, fences needed mending. As the people returned to their work they forgot about Rafael.

But one woman in the village did not forget. She saw the loneliness in his face, she sensed the pain he felt at the loss of his parents. At first she felt pity when she saw him standing in the church alone, then she felt love. She knew about loneliness, she had lost her parents when she was very young and had lived most of her life in a room at the back of the small adobe church. Her work was to keep the church clean and to take care of the old priest. It was this young woman who reached out and spoke to Rafael, and when he heard her voice he remembered the danger of the silence of the llano. He smiled and spoke to her. Thereafter, on Sundays he began to ride in to visit her. They would sit together during the Mass, and after that they would walk together to the general store where he would buy a small bag of hard sugar candy, and they would sit on the bench in front of the store, eat their candy and talk. The old people of the village as well as those who rode in from distant ranches knew Rafael was courting her, and knew it was good for both of them. The men tipped their hats as they passed by because Rafael was now a man.

Love grew between the young woman and Rafael. One day she said, "You need someone to take care of you. I will go with you." Her voice filled his heart with joy. They talked to the priest, and he married them, and after Mass there was a feast. The women set up tables in front of the church, covering them with their brightest table oil cloths, and they brought food which they served to everyone who had come to the celebration. The men drank whiskey and talked about the good grass growing high on the llano, and about the herds which would grow and multiply. One of the old men of the village brought out his violin, followed by his friend with his accordion. The two men played the old polkas and the varsilonas while the people danced on the hard-packed dirt in front of the church. The fiesta brought the people of the big and lonely llano together.

The violin and accordion music was accompanied by the clapping of hands and the stamping of feet. The dancing was lively and the people were happy. They laughed and congratulated the young couple. They brought gifts, kitchen utensils for the young bride, ranch tools for

Rafael, whiskey for everyone who would drink, real whiskey bought in the general store, not the mula some of the men made in their stills. Even Rafael took a drink, his first drink with the men, and he grew flushed and happy with it. He danced every dance with his young wife and everyone could see that his love was deep and devoted. He laughed with the men when they slapped his back and whispered advice for the wedding night. Then the wind began to rise and it started to rain; the first huge drops mixed with blowing dust. People sought cover, others hitched their wagons and headed home, all calling their goodbyes and buena suerte in the gathering wind. And so Rafael lifted his young bride onto his horse and they waved goodbye to the remaining villagers as they, too, rode away, south, deep into the empty llano, deep into the storm which came rumbling across the sky with thunder and lightning flashes, pushing the cool wind before it.

And that is how the immense silence of the land and the heavy burden of loneliness came to be lifted from Rafael's heart. His young bride had come to share his life and give it meaning and form. Sometimes late at night when the owl called from its perch on the windmill and the coyotes sang in the hills, he would lie awake and feel the presence of her young, thin body next to his. On such nights the stillness of the spring air and her fragrance intoxicated him and made him drunk with happiness; then he would feel compelled to rise and walk out into the night which was bright with the moon and the million stars which swirled overhead in the sky. He breathed the cool air of the llano night, and it was like a liquor which made his head swirl and his heart pound. He was a happy man.

In the morning she arose before him and fixed his coffee and brought it to him, and at first he insisted that it was he who should get up to start the fire in the wood stove because he was used to rising long before the sun and riding in the range while the dawn was alive with its bright colors, but she laughed and told him she would spoil him in the summer and in the winter when it was cold he would be the one to rise and start the fire and bring her coffee in bed. They laughed and talked during those still-dark, early hours of the morning. He told her where he would ride that day and about the work that needed to be done. She, in turn, told him about the curtains she was sewing and the cabinet she was painting and how she would cover each drawer with oil cloth.

He had whitewashed the inside of the small adobe home for her, then plastered the outside walls with mud to keep out the dust which came with the spring winds and the cold which would come with winter. He fixed the roof and patched the leaks, and one night when it rained they didn't have to rise to catch the leaking water in pots and pans. They laughed and were happy. Just as the spring rains made the land green, so his love made her grow, and one morning she quietly whispered in his ear that by Christmas they would have a child.

Her words brought great joy to him. "A child," she had said, and excitement tightened in his throat. That day he didn't work on the range. He had promised her a garden, so he hitched up one of the old horses to his father's plow and he spent all day plowing the soft, sandy earth by the windmill. He spread manure from the corral on the soil and turned it into the earth. He fixed an old pipe leading to the windmill and showed her how to turn it to water the garden. She was pleased. She spent days planting flowers and vegetables. She watered the old, gnarled peach trees near the garden and they burst into a late bloom. She worked the earth with care and by midsummer she was already picking green vegetables to cook with the meat and potatoes. It became a part of his life to stop on the rise above the ranch when he rode in from the range, to pause and watch her working in the garden in the cool of the afternoon. There was something in that image, something which made a mark of permanence on the otherwise empty llano.

Her slender body began to grow heavier. Sometimes he heard her singing, and he knew it was not only to herself she sang or hummed. Sometimes he glanced at her when her gaze was fixed on some distant object, and he realized it was not a distant mesa or cloud she was seeing, but a distant future which was growing in her.

Time flowed past them. He thinned his herds, prepared for the approaching winter, and she gathered the last of the fruits and vegetables. But something was not right. Her excitement of the summer was gone. She began to grow pale and weak. She would rise in the mornings and fix breakfast, then she would have to return to bed and rest. By late December, as the first clouds of winter appeared and the winds from the west blew sharp and cold, she could no longer rise in the mornings. He tried to help, but there was little he could do except sit by her side and keep her silent company while she slept her troubled sleep. A few weeks later a small flow of blood began, as pains and cramps wracked her body. Something was pulling at the child she carried, but it was not the natural rhythm she had expected.

"Go for Doña Rufina," she said, "go for help."

He hitched the wagon and made the long drive into the village, arriving at the break of light to rouse the old partera from her sleep. For many years the old woman had delivered the babies born in the village or in the nearby ranches, and now, as he explained what had happened and the need to hurry, she nodded solemnly. She packed the things she would need, then kneeled at her altar and made the sign of the cross. She prayed to el Santo Niño for help and whispered to the Virgin Mary that she would return when her work was done. Then she turned the small statues to face the wall. Rafael helped her on the wagon, loaded her bags, then used the reins as a whip to drive the horses at a fast trot on their long journey back. They arrived at the ranch as the sun was setting. That night, a child was born, a girl, pulled from the womb by the old woman's practiced hands. The old woman placed her mouth to the baby's and pushed in air. The baby gasped, sucked in air and came alive. Doña Rufina smiled as she cleaned the small, squirming body. The sound was good. The cry filled the night, shattering the silence in the room.

"A daughter," the old woman said. "A hard birth." She cleaned away the sheets, made the bed, washed the young wife who lay so pale and quiet on the bed, and when there was nothing more she could do she rolled a cigarette and sat back to smoke and wait. The baby lay quietly at her mother's side, while the breathing of the young mother grew weaker and weaker and the blood which the old woman was powerless to stop continued to flow. By morning she was dead. She had opened her eyes and looked at the small white bundle which lay at her side. She smiled and tried to speak, but there was no strength left. She sighed and closed her eyes.

"She is dead," Doña Rufina said.

"No, no," Rafael moaned. He held his wife in his arms and shook his head in disbelief. "She cannot die, she cannot die," he whispered over and over. Her body, once so warm and full of joy, was now cold and lifeless, and he cursed the forces he didn't understand but which had drawn her into that eternal silence. He would never again hear her voice, never hear her singing in her garden, never see her waving as he came over the rise from the llano. A long time later he allowed Doña Rufina's hands to draw him away. Slowly he took the shovel she handed him and dug the grave beneath the peach trees by the garden, that place of shade she had loved so much in the summer and which now appeared so deserted in the December cold. He buried her, then quickly saddled his horse and rode into the llano. He was gone for days. When he returned, he was pale and haggard from the great emptiness which filled him. Doña Rufina was there, caring for the child, nursing her as best she could with the little milk she could draw from the milk cow they kept in the corral. Although the baby was thin and sick with colic, she was alive. Rafael looked only once at the child, then he turned his back to her. In his mind the child had taken his wife's life, and he didn't care if the baby lived or died. He didn't care if he lived or died. The joy he had known was gone, her soul had been pulled into the silence he felt around him, and his only wish was to be with her. She was out there somewhere, alone and lost on the cold and desolate plain. If he could only hear her voice he was sure he could find her. That was his only thought as he rode out every day across the plain. He rode and listened for her voice in the wind which moaned across the cold landscape, but there was no sound, only the silence. His tortured body was always cold and shivering from the snow and wind, and when the dim sun sank in the west it was his horse which trembled and turned homeward, not he. He would have been content to ride forever, to ride until the cold numbed his body and he could join her in the silence.

When he returned late in the evenings he would eat alone and in silence. He did not speak to the old woman who sat huddled near the stove, holding the baby on her lap, rocking softly back and forth and singing wisps of old songs. The baby listened, as if she, too, already realized the strangeness of the silent world she had entered. Over them the storms of winter howled and tore at the small home where the three waited for spring in silence. But there was no promise in the spring. When the days grew longer and the earth began to thaw, Rafael threw himself into his work. He separated his herd, branded the new calves, then drove a few yearlings into the village where he sold them for the provisions he needed. But even the silence of the llano carries whispers. People asked about the child and Doña Rufina, and only once did he look at them and say, "My wife is dead." Then he turned away and spoke no more. The people understood his silence and his need to live in it, alone. No more questions were ever asked. He came into the village only when the need for provisions brought him, moving like a ghost, a haunted man, a man the silence of the llano had conquered and claimed. The old people of the village crossed their foreheads and whispered silent prayers when he rode by.

Seven years passed, unheeded in time, unmarked time, change felt only because the seasons changed. Doña Rufina died. During those years she and Rafael had not exchanged a dozen words. She had done what she could for the child, and she had come to love her as her own. Leaving the child behind was the only regret she felt the day she looked out the window and heard the creaking sound in the silence of the day. In the distance, as if in a whirlwind which swirled slowly across the llano, she saw the figure of death riding a creaking cart which moved slowly towards the ranch house. So, she thought, my comadre la muerte comes for me. It is time to leave this earth. She fed the child and put her to bed, then she wrapped herself in a warm quilt and sat by the stove, smoking her last cigarette, quietly rocking back and forth, listening to the creaking of the rocking chair, listening to the moan of the wind which swept across the land. She felt at peace. The chills she had felt the past month left her. She felt light and airy, as if she were entering a pleasant dream. She heard voices, the voices of old friends she had known on the llano, and she saw the faces of the many babies she had delivered during her lifetime. Then she heard a knock on the door. Rafael, who sat at his bed repairing his bridle and oiling the leather, heard her say, "Enter," but he did not look up. He did not hear her last gasp for air. He did not see the dark figure of the old woman who stood at the door, beckoning to Doña Rufina.

When Rafael looked up he saw her head slump forward. He arose and filled a glass with water. He held her head up and touched the water to her lips, but it was no use. He knew she was dead. The wind had forced the door open and it banged against the wall, filling the room with a cold gust, awakening the child who started from her bed. He moved quickly to shut the door, and the room again became dark and silent. One more death, one more burial, and again he returned to his work. Only out there, in the vast space of the llano, could he find something in which he could lose himself.

Only the weather and the seasons marked time for Rafael as he watched over his land and his herd. Summer nights he slept outside, and the galaxies swirling overhead reminded him he was alone. Out there, in that strange darkness, the soul of his wife rested. In the day, when the wind shifted direction, he sometimes thought he heard the whisper of her voice. Other times he thought he saw the outline of her face in the huge clouds which billowed up in the summer. And always he had to drive away the dream and put away the voice or the image, because the memory only increased his sadness. He learned to live alone, completely alone. The seasons changed, the rains came in July and the llano was green, then the summer sun burned it dry, later the cold of winter came with its fury. And all these seasons he survived, moving across the desolate land, hunched over his horse. He was a man who could not allow himself to dream, he rode alone.

2.

And the daughter? What of the daughter? The seasons brought growth to her, and she grew into young womanhood. She learned to watch the man who came and went and did not speak, and so she, too, learned to live in her own world. She learned to prepare the food and to sit aside in silence while he ate, to sweep the floor and keep the small house clean, to keep alive the fire in the iron stove, and to wash the clothes with the scrub-board at the water tank by the windmill.

In the summer her greatest pleasure was the cool place by the windmill where the water flowed.

The year she was sixteen, during springtime she stood and bathed in the cool water which came clean and cold out of the pipe, and as she stood under the water the numbing sensation reminded her of the first time the blood had come. She had not known what it was: it came without warning, without her knowledge. She had felt a fever in the night, and cramps in her stomach, then in the restlessness of sleep she had awakened and felt the warm flow between her legs. She was not frightened, but she did remember that for the first time she became aware of her father snoring in his sleep on the bed at the other side of the room. She arose quietly, without disturbing him, and walked out into the summer night, going to the watertank where she washed herself. The water which washed her blood splashed and ran into the garden.

That same summer she felt her breasts mature, her hips widen, and when she ran to gather her chickens into the coop for the night she felt a difference in her movement. She did not think or dwell on it, a dark part of her intuition told her that this was a natural element which belonged to the greater mystery of birth which she had seen take place on the llano around her. She had seen her hens seek secret nests to hatch their eggs, and she knew the proud, clucking noises the hens made when they appeared with the small yellow chicks trailing. There was life in the eggs. Once when the herd was being moved and they came to the water tank to drink she had seen the great bull mount one of the cows, and she remembered the whirling of dust and the bellowing which filled the air. Later, the cow would seek a nest and there would be a calf. These things she knew.

Now she was a young woman. When she went to the watertank to bathe she sometimes paused and looked at her reflection in the water. Her face was smooth and oval, dark from the summer sun, as beautiful as the mother she had not known. When she slipped off her blouse and saw how full and firm her breasts had grown and how rosy the nipples appeared, she smiled and touched them and felt a pleasure she couldn't explain. There had been no one to ask about the changes which came into her life. Once a woman and her daughters had come. She saw the wagon coming up on the road, but instead of going out to greet them she ran and hid in the house, watching through parted curtains as the woman and her daughters came and knocked at the door. She could hear them calling in strange words, words she did not know. She huddled in the corner and kept very still until the knocking at the door had ceased, then she edged closer to the window and watched as they climbed back on the wagon, laughing and talking in a strange, exciting way. Long after they were gone she could still smell the foreign, sweet odors they had brought to her doorstep.

After that, no one came. She remembered the words of Doña Rufina and often spoke them aloud just to hear the sound they made as they exploded from her lips. "Lumbre," she said in the morning when she put kindling on the banked ashes in the stove, whispering the word so the man who slept would not hear her. "Agua," she said when she drew water from the well. "Viento de diablo," she hissed to let her chickens know a swirling dust storm was on its way, and when they did not respond she reverted to the language she had learned from them and with a clucking sound she drove them where she wanted. "Tote! Tote!" she called and made the clicking sound for danger when she saw the gray figure of the coyote stalking close to the ranch house. The chickens understood and hurried into the safety of the coop. She learned to imitate the call of the wild doves. In the evening when they came to drink at the water tank she called to them and they sang back. The roadrunner which came to chase lizards near the windmill learned to cou for her, and the wild sparrows and other birds also heard her call and grew to know her presence. They fed at her feet like chickens. When the milk cow wandered away from the corral she learned to whistle to bring it back. She invented other sounds, other words, words for the seasons and the weather they brought, words for the birds she loved, words for the juniper and piñon and yucca and wild grass which grew on the llano, words for the light of the sun and dark of the night, words which when uttered broke the silence of the long days she spent alone, never words to be shared with the man who came to eat late in the evenings, who came enveloped in silence, his eyes cast down in a bitterness she did not understand. He ate the meals she served in silence, then he smoked a cigarette, then he slept. Their lives were unencumbered by each other's presence, they did not exist for each other, each had learned to live in his own silent world.

But other presences began to appear on the llano, even at this isolated edge of the plain which lay so far beyond the village of Las Animas. Men came during the season of the yellow moon, and they carried the long sticks which made thunder. In that season when the antelope were rutting they came, and she could hear the sound of thunder they made, even feel the panic of the antelopes which ran across the llano. "Hunters!" her father said, and he spat the word like a curse. He did not want them to enter his world, but still they came, not in the silent, horse-drawn wagons, but in an iron wagon which made noise and smoked.

The sound of these men frightened her, life on the llano grew tense as they drew near. One day, five of the hunters drove up to the ranch house in one of their iron wagons. She moved quickly to lock the door, to hide, for she had seen the antelope they had killed hung over the front of their wagon, a beautiful tan colored buck splattered with blood. It was tied with rope and wire, its dry tongue hanging from its mouth, its large eyes still open. The men pounded on the door and called her father's name. She held her breath and peered through the window. She saw them drink from a bottle they passed to each other. They pounded on the door again and fired their rifles in the air, filling the llano with explosive thunder. The acrid smell of burned powder filled the air. The house seemed to shake as they called words she did not understand. "Rafael!" they called. "A virgin daughter!" They roared with laughter as they climbed in their wagon, and the motor shrieked and roared as they drove away. All day the vibration of the noise and awful presence of the men lay over the house, and at night in nightmares she saw the faces of the men, heard their laughter and the sound of the rifle's penetrating roar as it shattered the silence of the llano. Two of them had been young men, broad-shouldered boys who looked at the buck they had killed and smiled. The faces of these strange men drifted through her dreams and she was at once afraid and attracted by them.

One night in her dreams she saw the face of the man who lived there, the man Doña Ruffina had told her was to be called father, and she could not understand why he should appear in her dream. When she awoke she heard the owl cry a warning from its perch on the windmill. She hurried outside, saw the dark form of the coyote slinking toward the chicken coop. A snarl hissed in her throat as she threw a rock, and instantly the coyote faded into the night. She waited in the dark, troubled by her dream and by the appearance of the coyote, then she slipped quietly back into the house. She did not want to awaken the man, but he was awake. He, too, had heard the coyote, and had heard her slip out, but he said nothing. In the warm summer night each lay awake, encased in their solitary silence, saying nothing, expecting no words, but aware of each other as animals are aware when another is close by, as she had been aware even in her sleep that the coyote was drawing near.

3.

One afternoon Rafael returned home early. He had seen a cloud of dust on the road to his ranch house. It was not the movement of cattle, and it wasn't the dust of the summer dustdevils. The rising dust could only mean there was a car on the road. He cursed under his breath, remembering the signs he had posted on his fence and the chain and lock he had bought in the village to secure his gate. He did not want to be bothered, he would keep everyone away. For a time he continued to repair the fence, using his horse to draw the wire taut, nailing the barbed wire to the cedar posts he had set that morning. The day was warm, he sweated as he worked, but again he paused, something made him restless, uneasy. He wiped his brow and looked towards the ranch house. Perhaps it was only his imagination, he thought, perhaps the whirlwind was only a mirage, a reflection of the strange uneasiness he felt. He looked to the west where two buzzards circled over the coyote he had shot that morning. Soon they would drop to feed. Around him the ants scurried through the dry grass, working their hills as he worked his land. There was the buzz of grasshoppers, the occasional call of prairie dogs, each sound in its turn absorbed into the hum which was the silence of the land. He returned to his work but the image of the cloud of dust returned, the thought of strangers on his land filled him with anger and apprehension. The bad feeling grew until he couldn't work. He packed his tools, swung on his horse and rode homeward.

Later, as he sat on his horse at the top of the rise from where he could view his house, the uneasy feeling grew more intense. Something was wrong, someone had come. Around him a strange dark cloud gathered, shutting off the sun, stirring the wind into frenzy. He urged his horse down the slope and rode up to the front door. All was quiet. The girl usually came out to take his horse to the corral where she unsaddled and fed it, but today there was no sight of her. He turned and looked towards the windmill and the plot of ground where he had buried his wife. The pile of rocks which marked her grave was almost covered by wind-swept sand. The peach trees were almost dead. The girl had watered them from time to time, as she had watered the garden, but no one had helped or taught her and so her efforts were poorly rewarded. Only a few flowers survived in the garden, spots of color in the otherwise dry, tawny landscape.

His horse moved uneasily beneath him; he dismounted slowly. The door of the house was ajar, he pushed it open and entered. The room was dark and cool, the curtains at the window were drawn, the fire for the evening meal was not yet started. Outside the first drops of rain fell on the tin roof as the cloud darkened the land. In the room a fly buzzed. Perhaps the girl is not here, he thought, maybe it is just that I am tired and I have come early to rest. He turned toward the bed and saw her. She sat huddled on the bed, her knees drawn up, her arms wrapped around them. She looked at him, her eyes terrified and wild in the dark. He started to turn away but he heard her make a sound, the soft cry of an injured animal.

"Rafael," she moaned as she reached out for him. "Rafael . . . ."

He felt his knees grow weak. She had never used his name before.

At the same time she flung back the crumpled sheet and pointed to the stain of blood. He shook his head, gasped. Her blouse was torn off, red scratch marks scarred her white shoulders, tears glistened in her eyes as she reached out again and whispered his name. "Rafael. . . Rafael. . . ."

Someone had come in that cloud of dust, perhaps a stray vaquero looking for work, perhaps one of the men from the village who knew she was here alone, a man had come in the whirlwind and forced himself into the house. "Oh God. . . ." he groaned as he stepped back, felt the door behind him, saw her rise from the bed, her arms outstretched, the curves of her breasts rising and falling as she gasped for breath and called his name, "Rafael. . . Rafael. . . ." She held out her arms, and he heard his scream echo in the small adobe room which had suddenly become a prison suffocating him. Still the girl came towards him, her eyes dark and piercing, her dark hair falling over her shoulders and throat. With a great effort he found the strength to turn and flee. Outside, he grabbed the reins of his frightened horse, mounted and dug his spurs into the sides of the poor creature. Whipping it hard he rode away from the ranch and what he had seen.

Once before he had fled, on the day he buried his wife. He had seen her face then, as he now saw the image of the girl, saw her eyes burning into him, saw the torn blouse, the bed, and most frightening of all, heard her call his name, "Rafael. . . Rafael. . . ." It opened and broke the shell of his silence, it was a wound which brought back the ghost of his wife, the beauty of her features which he now saw again and which blurred into the image of the girl. He spurred the horse until it buckled with fatigue and sent him crashing into the earth. The impact brought a searing pain and the peace of darkness.

He didn't know how long he lay unconscious. When he awoke he touched his throbbing forehead and felt the clotted blood. The pain in his head was intense, but he could walk. Without direction he stumbled across the llano only to find that late in the afternoon when he looked around he saw his ranch house. He approached the water tank to wash the clotted blood from his face, then he stumbled into the tool shed by the corral and tried to sleep. Dusk came, the bats and night hawks flew over the quiet llano, night fell and still he could not sleep. Through the chinks of the weathered boards he could see the house and the light which burned at the window. The girl was awake. All night he stared at the light burning at the window, and in his fever he saw her face again, her pleading eyes, the curve of her young breasts, her arms as she reached up and called his name. Why had she called his name? Why? Was it the devil who rode the whirlwind? Was it the devil who had come to break the silence of the llano? He groaned and shivered as the call of the owl sounded in the night. He looked into the darkness and thought he saw the figure of the girl walking to the water tank. She bathed her shoulders in the cold water, bathed her body in the moonlight. Then the owl grew still and the figure in the flowing gown disappeared as the first sign of dawn appeared in the clouds of the east.

He rose and entered the house, tremulously, unsure of what he would find. There was food on the table and hot coffee on the stove. She had prepared his breakfast as she had all those years, and now she sat by the window, withdrawn, her face pale and thin. She looked up at him, but he turned away and sat at the table with his back to her. He tried to eat but the food choked him. He drank the strong coffee, then he rose and hurried outside. He cursed as he reeled towards the corral like a drunken man, then he stopped suddenly and shuddered with a fear he had never known before. He shook his head in disbelief and raised his hand as if to ward away the figure sitting at the huge cedar block at the woodpile. It was the figure of a woman, a woman who called his name and beckoned him. And for the first time in sixteen years he called out his wife's name.

"Rita," he whispered, "Rita. . . ."

Yes, it was she, he thought, sitting there as she used to, laughing and teasing while he chopped firewood. He could see her eyes, her smile, hear her voice. He remembered how he would show off his strength with the axe, and she would compliment him in a teasing way as she gathered the chips of piñon and cedar for kindling. "Rita. . ." he whispered, and moved toward her, but now the figure sitting at the woodblock was the girl, she sat there, calling his name, smiling and coaxing him as a demon of hell would entice the sinner into the center of the whirlwind. "No!" he screamed and grabbed the axe, lifted it, and summoning his remaining strength he brought it down on the dark heart of the swirling vortex. The blow split the block in half and splintered the axe handle. He felt the pain of the vibration numb his arms. The devil is dead, he thought, opened his eyes, saw only the split block and the splintered axe in front of him. He shook his head and backed away, crying to God to exorcize the possession in his tormented soul. And even as he prayed for respite he looked up and saw the window. Behind the parted curtains he saw her face, his wife, the girl, the pale face of the woman who had haunted him.

Without saddling the horse he mounted and spurred it south. He had to leave this place, he would ride south until he could ride no more, until he disappeared into the desert. He would ride into oblivion, and when he was dead the tightness and pain in his chest and the torturous thoughts would be gone, then there would be peace. He would die and give himself to the silence, and in that element he would find rest. But without warning a dark whirlwind rose before him, and in the midst of the storm he saw a woman. She did not smile, she did not call his name, her horse was the dark clouds which towered over him, the cracking of her whip a fire which filled the sky. Her laughter rumbled across the sky and shook the earth, her shadow swirled around him, blocking out the sun, filling the air with choking dust, driving fear into both man and animal until they turned in a wide circle back towards the ranch house. And when he found himself once again on the small rise by his home, the whirlwind lifted and the woman disappeared. The thunder rumbled in the distance, then was gone, the air grew quiet around him. He could hear himself breathe, he could hear the pounding of his heart. Around him the sun was bright and warm.

He didn't know how long he sat there remembering other times when he had paused at that place to look down at his home. He was startled from his reverie by the slamming of a screen door. He looked and saw the girl walk towards the water tank. He watched her as she pulled the pipe clear of the tank, then she removed her dress and began her bath. Her white skin glistened in the sunlight as the spray of water splashed over her body. Her long, black hair fell over her shoulders to her waist, glistening from the water. He could hear her humming. He remembered his wife bathing there, covering herself with soap foam, and he remembered how he would sit and smoke while she bathed, and his life was full of peace and contentment. She would wrap a towel around her body and come running to sit by his side in the sun, and as she dried her hair they would talk. Her words had filled the silence of that summer. Her words were an extension of the love she had brought him.

And now? He touched his legs to the horse's sides and the horse moved, making its way down the slope towards the water tank. She turned, saw him coming, and stepped out of the stream of cascading water to gather a towel around her naked body. She waited quietly. He rode up to her, looked at her, looked for a long time at her face and into her eyes. Then slowly he dismounted and walked to her. She waited in silence. He moved towards her, and with a trembling hand he reached out and touched her wet hair.

"Rita," he said. "Your name is Rita."

She smiled at the sound. She remembered the name from long ago. It was a sound she remembered from Doña Rufina. It was the sound the axe made when it rang against the hard cedar wood, and now he, the man who had lived in silence all those years, he had spoken the name.

It was a good sound which brought joy to her heart. This man had come to speak this sound which she remembered. She saw him turn and point at the peach trees at the edge of the garden.

"Your mother is buried over there," he said. "This was her garden. The spring is the time for the garden. I will turn the earth for you. The seeds will grow."

# II
## Innocents and Individuals

# JOHN NICHOLS
## *from* THE MILAGRO BEANFIELD WAR

John Nichols, born in Berkeley, California in 1940, received his B.A. from Hamilton College in 1963, returning to live in Taos, New Mexico, after the early success of his first novel, *The Sterile Cuckoo* (1969). This book was followed by *The Wizard of Loneliness* (1966), *The Milagro Beanfield War* (1974), *The Magic Journey* (1978), *The Nirvana Blues* (1981), and *The Last Beautiful Days of Autumn* (1982). He also wrote the screenplay for the Costa-Gavras film, "Missing," and has scripted "The Milagro Bean-field War" for a Robert Redford film production.

*The Milagro Beanfield War* is a comic epic with no individual protagonist but, rather, a collective one. This collective personality is composed of a host of "innocent" Mexican-Americans who live, as they have lived for centuries, on a subsistence economy in northern New Mexico. At the heart of their struggle with Anglo land-developers and Anglo law are water rights, so when a member of the community, Joe Mondragón, defies those alien forces by opening a ditch to irrigate his beanfield, the community as a whole responds with characteristic resilience and endures against the odds, much as the minor character Amarante Córdova does in this excerpt from the novel.

# *from* THE MILAGRO BEANFIELD WAR

A marante Córdova had had thirteen children. That is, he and his wife, Elizabeth—known as Betita—had had thirteen children, who either still were or had been Nadia, Jorge, Pólito, María Ana, Berta, Roberto, Billy, Nazario, Gabriel, Ricardo, Sally, Patsy, and Cipriano. Betita, who had never been sick a day in her life, died in 1963, on November 22, on the same day as President Kennedy, but not from a bullet in the head. She had been outside chopping wood during a lovely serene snowstorm when suddenly she set down the ax and began to walk along the Milagro–García spur out onto the mesa. In recalling her death later Amarante would always tell his listeners, "You cannot imagine how beautiful it was that afternoon. The snow falling was as serene as the white feathers of a swan. When the ravens sailed through it they made no sound. You looked up and the big black birds were floating through the snowflakes like faint shadows of our forefathers, the first people who settled in the valley. The tall sagebrush was a lavender-green color because there had been a lot of rain in the autumn, and that was the only color on the otherwise black and white mesa, the pale lavender-green of the sage on which snow had settled. You remember, of course, that Betita's hair was as white as the snow, and she was wearing a black dress and a black woolen shawl that Sally, our daughter who was married to the plumber from Doña Luz, knitted for her on a birthday long ago."

Slowly, taking her time, Betita walked across the mesa to the rim of the gorge. "And there she stood on the edge looking down," Amarante said. "For a long time she was poised there like a wish afraid to be uttered. The walls of the gorge created a faded yellow glow to the flakes falling eight hundred feet down to the icy green river below. Ravens were in the air, circling, their wings whispering no louder than the snow falling. It was very peaceful. I was at the house, I never saw her leave. But when she didn't come in with the wood after a while, I saddled up that lame plow horse we used to have called Buster, and went after her, following her tracks in the snow. Just as I left the road

83

to enter the chamisal an owl dropped out of the darkening sky, landing on a cedar post not ten yards away. An owl is a sure sign from the dead, you know, and it was right then I knew she had disappeared into the gorge. When I arrived at the rim an enormous raven was standing where she had last stood, and when he saw me he spread his wings, which were wider than my outstretched arms, and floated up like a good-bye kiss from my wife into the lazy storm. Next day we opened the church, only the second time that year it was used, not to say prayers for Betita, but to burn candles and shed our tears for the President who had died in Dallas. But I lit my candles for Betita, and nobody noticed. Three months later her body was discovered on the bank of the river two miles below Chamisaville."

The Córdova sons and daughters had scattered, as the saying goes, to the four winds. Or actually, only to the three winds, eastward being anathema to the children of Milagro, whose Mississippi was the Midnight Mountains, that chain running north and south barely a mile or two from all their backyards.

Nadia, a waitress most of her life, first in Doña Luz, then Chamisaville, wound up in the Capital City barrio, dying violently (and recently) at the age of sixty-one in a lover's quarrel. Jorge emigrated to Australia where he tended sheep, same as at home. Pólito, who spent his life wandering around, getting married three or four times and taking care of sheep in Wyoming, Montana, and Utah, had died young of the flu. María Ana wanted to be a dancer, took the train to San Francisco, and after years of strenuous work, heartbreak, and small roles in the city ballet company, she hurt her back and wound up teaching in an Arthur Murray studio. Berta married an Anglo who raised lemons in California, and, curiously, they never had any children. Roberto, Billy, and Nazario became farm workers, mechanics, truck drivers, dishwashers, and short-order cooks in and around Los Angeles; they all raised large families, and although between them they'd had nine sons in Vietnam, only one of Billy's kids, Rosario, had been killed. Gabriel, who miraculously metamorphosed into a run-of-the-mill featherweight boxer in the army, turned pro after his discharge, was known as the Milagro Mauler during his short and undistinguished prime, and died in a plane crash in Venezuela. Ricardo had stayed on as a rancher in Milagro, although he spent half his life in the lettuce, sugar beet, or potato fields of southern Colorado, or else with the big sheep outfits up in Wyoming and Montana. Two of his sons, Elisardo and Juan, had died in Vietnam; another boy was stationed in Germany. Sally married a plumber in Doña Luz and had eleven kids herself, one of whom became a successful pop singer in Mexico City, but never sent any money home, not even after the plumber died when a black widow bit him while he was creeping around somebody's musty crawl space on a job. Patsy, the most beautiful and the sharpest in school, ran West to join a circus, became an Avon lady instead, and died with her husband and all their children except Peter (who was in a Japanese hospital at the time recovering from wounds received in Vietnam) in a head-on car crash in Petaluma. And little Cipriano, the baby of the family, born in 1925, who went farther than everyone else in his education, and, in fact, had just obtained a full scholarship to Harvard when he was drafted, was vivisected by a German machine gun during the first eighteen seconds of the Normandy D-day landings.

All his life Amarante had lived in the shadow of his own death. When he was two days old he caught pneumonia, they gave him up for dead, somehow he recovered. During his childhood he was always sick, he couldn't work like other boys his age. He had rheumatic fever, chicken pox, pneumonia three or four more times, started coughing blood when he was six, was anemic, drowsy all the time, constantly sniffling, weak and miserable, and—everybody thought—dying. At eight he had his tonsils out; at ten, his appendix burst. At twelve he was bitten by a rattlesnake, went into a coma, survived. Then a horse kicked him, breaking all the ribs on his left side. He contracted tuberculosis. He hacked and stumbled around, hollow-eyed, gaunt and sniffling, and folks crossed themselves, murmuring Hail Marys whenever he staggered into view. At twenty, when he was already an alcoholic, scarlet fever almost laid him in the grave; at twenty-three, malaria looked like it would do the job. Then came several years of amoebic dysentery. After that he was constipated for seventeen months. At thirty, a lung collapsed; at thirty-four, shortly after he became the first sheriff of Milagro, that old devil pneumonia returned for another whack at it, slowed his pulse to almost nothing, but like a classical and very pretty but fainthearted boxer, couldn't deliver the knockout punch. During the old man's forties a number of contending diseases dropped by Amarante's body for a shot at the title. The clap came and went, had a return bout, was counted out. The measles appeared, as did the mumps, but they did not even last a full round. For old time's sake pneumonia made a token appearance, beat its head against the brick wall that evidently lined Amarante's lungs, then waved a white flag and retreated. Blood poisoning blew all his lymph nodes up to the size of golf balls, stuck around for a month, and lost the battle.

Amarante limped, coughed, wheezed; his chest ached; he spat blood and gruesome blue-black lungers, drank until his asshole hurt, his flat feet wailed; arthritis took sledgehammers to his knees; his stomach felt like it was bleeding; and all but three of his teeth turned brown and toppled out of his mouth like acorns. In Milagro, waiting for Amarante Córdova to drop dead became like waiting for one of those huge sneezes that just refuses to come. And there was a stretch during Amarante's sixties when people kept running away from him, cutting conversations short and like that, because everybody *knew* he was going to keel over in the very next ten seconds, and nobody likes to be present when somebody drops dead.

In his seventies Amarante's operations began. First they removed a lung. By that time the citizens of Milagro had gotten into the irate, sarcastic, and not a little awed frame of mind which had them saying: "Shit, even if they took out that old bastard's other lung he'd keep on breathing."

A lump in his neck shaped like a miniature cow was removed. After that a piece of his small intestine had to go. There followed, of course, the usual gallbladder, spleen, and kidney operations. People in Milagro chuckled "Here comes the human zipper," whenever Amarante turned a corner into sight. His friends regarded him with a measure of respect and hatred, beseeching him to put in a good word for them with the Angel of Death, or whoever it was with whom he held counsel, even as they capsized over backward into the adobe and caliche darkness of their own graves.

But finally, at seventy-six, there loomed on Amarante's horizon a Waterloo. Doc Gómez in the clinic at Doña Luz sent him to a doctor at the Chamisaville Holy Cross Hospital who did a physical, took X rays, shook his head, and sent the old man to St. Claire's in the capital where a stomach specialist, after doing a number of tests and barium X rays and so forth, came to the conclusion that just about everything below Amarante's neck had to go, and the various family members were notified.

The family had kept in touch in spite of being scattered to the three winds, and those that were still living, including Jorge from Australia, returned to Milagro for a war council, and for a vote on whether or not they could muster the money to go ahead with their father's expensive operation. "If he doesn't have this operation," the Capital City doctor told them, "your father will be dead before six months are out."

Now the various members of the family had heard that tune before, but all the same they took a vote: Nadia, María Ana, Berta, Sally, and Billy voted for the operation; Jorge, Roberto, Nazario, and Ricardo voted against it. And so by a 5–4 margin Amarante went under the knife and had most of his innards removed. He recuperated for several weeks, and then, under Sally's and Ricardo's and Betita's care, went home to Milagro.

But it looked as if this time was really *it*. Slow to get back on his feet, Amarante had jaundice and looked ghastly. He complained he couldn't see anymore, and they discovered he had cataracts in both eyes, so Ricardo and Sally and Betita took him back to St. Claire's and had those removed. Thereafter, he had to wear thick-lensed glasses which made him look more like a poisoned corpse than ever before. His slow, creeping way of progressing forward made snails look like Olympic sprinters. The people of Milagro held their collective breath; and if they had been a different citizenry with a different culture from a different part of the country, they probably would have begun to make book on which day *it* would happen. In fact, the word had spread, so that down in Chamisaville at the Ortega Funeral Home, which handled most of the death from Arroyo Verde to the Colorado border, it became common for Bunny Ortega, Bruce Maés, and Bernardo Medina to wonder, sort of off the cuff during their coffee breaks, when Amarante's body would be coming in. And eventually, although she did not go so far as to have Joe Mondragón or one of the other enterprising kids like him dig a grave out in the camposanto, Sally did drop by Ortega's in order to price coffins and alert the personnel as to what they might expect when the time came.

One gorgeous autumn day when all the mountain aspens looked like a picture postcard from heaven, Amarante had a conversation with Sally. "I guess this old temple of the soul has had it," he began with his usual sly grin. "I think you better write everybody a letter and tell them to come home for Christmas. I want to have all my children gathered around me at Christmastime so I can say good-bye. There won't be no more Navidades for me."

Sally burst into tears, she wasn't quite sure whether of relief or of grief. And, patting her father on the back once she had loudly blown her nose, she said, "All right, Papa. I know everybody who's left will come."

And *that* was a Christmas to remember! The Celebration of 1956. Jorge came from Australia with his wife and their five children. Nadia journeyed up from the capital with her lover. María Ana took off from the Arthur Murray studios in San Francisco, flying in with her husband and four children. Berta and the lemon grower took a train from the San Jose Valley. Roberto, Billy, and Nazario, their wives and fourteen children and some grandchildren, drove in a caravan of disintegrating Oldsmobiles from L.A. And Sally and the remaining two of her brood still in the nest motored up every day from Doña Luz. People stayed at Ricardo's house, at what was left of Amarante's and Betita's adobe, and some commuted from Sally's in Doña Luz.

They had turkeys and pumpkin pie, mince pie and sour cream pie;

they had chili and posole, corn and sopaipillas and enchiladas and empanaditas, tequilla and mescal, Hamms and Coors and Old Crow, and in the center of it all with the screaming hordes revolving happily about him, chest-deep in satin ribbons and rainbow-colored wrapping paper, so drunk that his lips were flapping like pajamas on a clothesline during the April windy season, sat the old patriarch himself, dying but not quite dead, and loving every minute of it. His children hugged him, whispered sweet nothings in his ear, and waited on his every whim and fancy. They pressed their heads tenderly against his bosom, muttering endearing and melodramatic lovey-doveys, even as they also anxiously listened to see if the old ticker really was on its last legs. They took him by the elbow and held him when he wished to walk somewhere, they gazed at him sorrowfully and shed tears of both joy and sadness, they squeezed his feeble hands and reminisced about the old days and about the ones who were dead, about what all the grandchildren were doing, and about who was pregnant and who had run away, who was making a lot of money and who was broke and a disgrace, who was stationed in Korea and who was stationed in Germany. . . and they joined hands, singing Christmas carols in Spanish, they played guitars and an accordion, they wept and cavorted joyously some more, and finally, tearfully, emotionally, tragically, they all kissed his shrunken cheeks and bid him a fond and loving adios, told their mama Betita to be strong, and scattered to the three winds.

Three years later when Jorge in Australia received a letter from Sally in Doña Luz, he replied:

> What do you mean he wants us all to meet again for Christmas so he can say good-bye? What am I made out of, gold and silver? I said good-bye two winters ago, it cost me a fortune! I can't come back right now!

Nevertheless, when Sally a little hysterically wrote that this time was really *it*, he came, though minus the wife and kiddies. So also did all the other children come, a few minus some wives or husbands or children, too. At first the gaiety was a little strained, particularly when Nazario made a passing remark straight off the bat to Berta that he thought the old man looked a hell of a lot better than he had three years ago, and Berta and everyone else within hearing distance couldn't argue with that. But then they realized they were all home again, and Milagro was white and very beautiful, its juniper and piñon branches laden with a fresh snowfall, and the smell of piñon smoke on the air was almost like a drug making them high. The men rolled up their sleeves and passed around the ax, splitting wood, until Nazario sank the ax into his foot, whereupon they all drove laughing and drinking beer down to the Chamisaville Holy Cross Hospital where the doctor on call proclaimed the shoe a total loss but only had to take two stitches between Nazario's toes. Later that same afternoon there was a piñata for the few little kids—some grandchildren, a pocketful of great-grand-children—who had come, and, blindfolded, they pranced in circles swinging a wooden bat until the papier-mâché donkey burst, and every-one cheered and clapped as the youngsters trampled each other scram-bling for the glittering goodies. Then the kids stepped up one after another to give Grandpa sticky candy kisses, and he embraced them all with tears in his eyes. Later the adults kissed Grandpa, giving him gentle abrazos so as not to cave in his eggshell chest. "God bless you," they whispered, and Amarante grinned, flashing his three teeth in woozy good-byes. "This was in place of coming to the funeral," he rasped to them in a quavering voice. "Nobody has to come to the funeral." Betita started to cry.

Out of the old man's earshot and eyesight his sons and daughters embraced each other, crossed themselves, crossed their fingers, and, casting their eyes toward heaven in supplication, murmured, not in a mean or nasty way, but with gentleness and much love for their father:

"Here's hoping..."

When, five years later, Jorge received the next letter from Sally, he wrote back furiously:

NO! I just came for Mama's funeral!

On perfumed pink Safeway stationery she pleaded with him to recon-sider, she begged him to come. For them all she outlined their father's pathetic condition. He'd had a heart attack after Betita's death. He had high blood pressure. His veins were clotted with cholesterol. His kidneys were hardly functioning. He had fallen and broken his hip. A tumor the size of an avocado had been removed from beside his other lung, and it was such a rare tumor they didn't know if it was malignant or benign. They thought, also, that he had diabetes. Then, most recently, a mild attack of pneumonia had laid him out for a couple of weeks. As an afterthought she mentioned that some lymph nodes had been cut from his neck for biopsies because they thought he had leukemia, but it turned out he'd had an infection behind his ears where the stems of his glasses were rubbing too hard.

Jorge wrote back:

What is Papa trying to do to us all? I'm no spring chicken, Sally. I got a heart condition. I'm blind in one eye. I got bursitis

so bad in one shoulder I can't lift my hand above my waist.
And I've *got* diabetes!

He returned, though. He loved his father, he loved Milagro. Since
the last time, Nadia had also died. The other surviving children came,
but none of the grandchildren or great-grandchildren showed up. Times
were a little tough, money hard to come by. And although maybe the
old man was dying, he looked better than ever, better even than some
of them. His cheeks seemed to have fleshed out a little, they were even
a tiny bit rosy. Could it be their imagination, or was he walking less
stooped over now? And his mind seemed sharper than before. When
Jorge drove up the God damn old man was outside chopping wood!

They shared a quiet, subdued celebration. Most of them had arrived
late and would leave early. And after they had all kissed their father
good-bye again, and perhaps squeezed him a little harder than usual
in their abrazos (hoping, maybe, to dislodge irrevocably something vital
inside his body), the sons and daughters went for a walk on the mesa.

"I thought he said he was dying," Jorge complained, leaning heavily
on a cane, popping glycerin tablets from time to time.

"I wrote you all what has happened," Sally sighed. "I told you what
Papa said."

"How old is he now?" asked Berta.

"He was born in 1880, qué no?" Ricardo said.

"That makes him eighty-four," Billy said glumly. "And already I'm
fifty."

"He's going to die," Sally said sadly. "I can feel it in my bones."

And those that didn't look at her with a mixture of hysteria and
disgust solemnly crossed themselves....

For the Christmas of 1970 only Jorge came. He bitched, ranted, and
raved at Sally in a number of three-, four-, and five-page letters, intimat-
ing in no uncertain terms that he couldn't care less if his father *had* lost
all the toes on one foot plus something related to his bladder, he wasn't
flying across any more oceans for any more Christmases to say good-bye
to the immortal son of a bitch.

But he came.

The airplane set down in the capital; he took the Trailways bus up.
Ricardo, who was recovering from stomach surgery but slowly dying
of bone cancer anyway, met him at Rael's store. Sally came up later.
Jorge had one blind askew eye and poor vision in the other, he was
bald, limping noticeably, haggard and frail and crotchety. He felt that
for sure this trip was going to kill him, and did not understand why
he kept making it against his will.

Then, when Jorge saw Amarante, his suspicions were confirmed. His father wasn't growing old: he had reached some kind of nadir ten or twelve years ago and now he was growing backward, aiming toward middle age, maybe youth. To be sure, when Amarante lifted his shirt to display the scars he looked like a banana that had been hacked at by a rampaging machete-wielding maniac, but the light in his twinkling old eyes, magnified by those glasses, seemed like something stolen from the younger generation.

The next day, Christmas Day, in the middle of Christmas dinner, Jorge suffered a heart attack, flipped over in his chair, his mouth full of candied sweet potato, and died.

Bunny Ortega, Bruce Maés, and the new man replacing Bernardo Medina (who had also died), Gilbert Otero, smiled sadly but with much sympathy when Sally and Ricardo accompanied the body to the Ortega Funeral Home in Chamisaville.

"Well, well," Bunny said solicitously. "So the old man finally passed away."

"No-no-no," Sally sobbed. "This is my brother. . . his son! . . ."

"*Ai, Chihuahua!*"

And here it was, two years later more or less, and Joe Mondragón had precipitated a crisis, and Amarante Córdova had never been so excited in his life.

One day, during his Doña Luz daughter's weekly visit, Amarante told her, "Hija, you got to write me a letter to all the family."

Sally burst into tears. "I can't. I won't. No. You can't make me."

"But we have to tell everyone about what José has done. They must see this thing and take part in it before they die. Tell them the shooting is about to start—"

So Sally dutifully advised her surviving siblings about what Joe Mondragón had done; she informed them that the shooting was about to start.

Maybe they read her letters, maybe they only looked at the postmark, but to a man jack they all replied: "Send us your next letter *after* Papa is dead!"

"That's the trouble with this younger generation," Amarante whined petulantly. "They don't give a damn about anything important anymore."

# MAX SCHOTT
# THE HORSEBREAKER

Born in 1935, Max Schott until the age of thirty was a horse trainer as well as story writer, living and ranching in the Klamath Falls, Oregon area and in California's Santa Ynez Valley. He now teaches fiction writing and literature at the University of California, Santa Barbara. A collection of his stories, *Up Where I Used to Live,* was published in 1978 in the Short Fiction Series of the University of Illinois Press. One of his stories, "Murphy's Romance," has been filmed and earned James Garner an Oscar nomination for his portrayal of the titular role.

"The Horsebreaker" first appeared in *Ascent,* No. 2, 1977. Old Clyde has not grown so soft and rich from the real-estate business as to forget how to break a horse. So when the opportunity to break Hornet arrives, he can't resist the temptation. Just as his two-day struggle with Hornet appears triumphant, the horse throws and drags him. Will he be mocked by his wife, brother, the townspeople? As it turns out, they are far more concerned about his banged-up condition than about his heroics. These were foolish enough for a man his age but also admirable: he has lived up to his ideal, an old-fashioned one of "just being himself."

# THE HORSEBREAKER

S ome people just get old, but Clyde got old and rich. And he was pretty old, too, before he took it into his head to get rich. Not only that, if he wanted to brag on himself, but he'd gone to a new town and entered a new business to do it. And there was no reason it had to be chalked up to luck, either, unless he wanted to call just being himself lucky. It was no fluke: when he got too old to do anything else, or to feel much like doing anything else, he just naturally began to make money. It seemed to him now that he always half knew that's how it would be.

Even so, there was too little to it. Selling real estate made and kept him rich, but it wasn't really what he did: he didn't really do anything. He was a has-been—and a has-been is better than a never-was, but not much. The stories he told about himself began to ring false even to his own not unsympathetic ear. They were true, those stories: in case anyone doubted it, his brother could always be called in for a verification. But no one seemed to want to call his brother in, nor was his brother very accommodating.

Clyde had an endless number of true and astounding tales to tell about himself: horses and mules he'd broken and shod, miraculous operations he'd performed on the eyes of cows (cutting cancers off them) after the vets had given up; and there were even people, especially in cold weather, willing to sit in his office and listen. There was a big number of stories, but still some were better than others, and Clyde tended to repeat those.

It wasn't senility. For one thing, he wasn't so old, less than sixty; and as his brother Ben would tell you, he'd always been like that. Only when Clyde called him up one night and announced that he was breaking a horse did Ben begin to wonder about him.

There was not much use arguing with the old fellow, but Ben tried it anyway.

"You say you have a horse you want someone to break?" Ben said. "Talk louder!"

"Try the other ear," Clyde said. (Ben was a little deaf in one ear.)

"What do you want a horse broke for?" Ben said. "You're too lazy to ride one. There's a boy right next door to you who breaks them—at least he has a sign up that says so."

"I know he does," Clyde said. "I don't want one broke—I aim to break one."

"Why mess your nest?" Ben said. "Don't be stunting around—a man of your age. What horse?"

"Little horse belongs to Sterling Green—had his ears stung off."

"Why you know the story on that horse—you're crazier than you act."

"He's never been soft," Clyde said. "Never been properly softened up, that little horse, not till I got ahold of him."

"You'll think soft," Ben said. "I sat in my truck and watched him put two better men than you where it's soft, right in one day."

"I doubt that," Clyde said.

"Doubt it?—doubt what?"

"I doubt two better men. Hey you, don't you remember that pinto mule in Bakersfield? That one who they claimed he—"

"Yes, I have a long memory. I want to talk to you, old son," Ben said.

"How's that skim-milk pig doing?"Clyde said.

"I want to talk horses," Ben said.

"I've got him half soft and soaking tonight. His neck needed pounding. Tomorrow I'll have him in the sack. I'll have him in the sack tomorrow. They don't buck with their head up. You know that. Anybody knows it. What's unknown is how to keep it up. They've got to be soft and you've got to have quick hands. Say, my hands are still fast, you know that? Damn right!"

"You're fast all over," Ben said. "I want to see you in the morning."

"All tied up," Clyde said. "Down to my office at two, be down to my office at two and I'll talk to you then. Squeeze you in. On the instant—whereby all expectorations remaining unramified I'll perpetrate."

"Don't real estate me," Ben said. "You just tell me now that—"

"Hey, let's go to Reno tomorrow night," Clyde said, "what do you say? We'll get this young horsefighter next door to go with us and we'll all get drunk together and puke in each other's hair. He can't do his wife because she's eight months along and out of town. We're sick of this town, all of us. I feel revigorated. How about yourself?"

"I feel as if I shoveled ditch all day on a sour stomach," Ben said. He'd have to try to remember to go to his brother's office the next day at two, and see if he was still alive.

Earlier in the day the young horsefighter next door had lost a fight with a horse, and that was how Clyde got into it.

First of all, weeks ago, he'd seen the boy move in, and he'd gone over and introduced himself. The boy didn't seem big on talking about himself, but that was all right with Clyde. Then from his porch Clyde had off and on watched as the fellow built himself a round corral that could only be a horsebreaking corral. Worked kind of slow but didn't do a half bad job: big juniper posts set *deep* in the ground—judging by the length of time it took him to dig the holes in that easy sandy ground —and then circles of cables in which were inserted a great number of vertical pickets and brushy branches, so that you could hardly even see through it when he was done.

Then he'd hung out a shingle, just a few days ago:

HORSES BROKE, TRAINED AND SHOD
Guaranteed

Clyde figured that the word "guaranteed" gave him away: he wasn't familiar with breaking horses for the public. Most people couldn't stay on top of a sawhorse, and there was no use promising they could.

Then Clyde, sitting by his stove in the morning, had heard a truck gearing down. He went onto the porch and saw Sterling's outfit come by, carrying a lone horse whose head was stuck up as high as possible over the racks, looking out. It was the little horse Sterling called Hornet, who'd been into a bee's nest as a colt and lost the tips of his ears. And Clyde said to himself that wasn't the only story he knew on the horse.

He watched the truck turn into his neighbor's lane and back up to the loading chute. He told his wife to go down to the office and open up; he wouldn't be down. Don't call him unless there was something so live it just couldn't wait. Sterling left, and his wife left, and Clyde wandered around the house. It was midmorning before Wesley finally led the horse out to the wicker corral. None of my business, Clyde thought, but the boy gets to his work kind of late in the day.

Clyde drove over, sneaked up, and peeked through the pickets. It wasn't polite, but what else could he do? The horse was saddled and ready. The horsebreaker was adjusting himself. Clyde counted the times he pulled down his hat and rearranged his chaps. The horse appeared calm, acted gentle to handle, quiet.

Suddenly he wanted to yell through the fence, "Jesus Christ get a short hold on the reins and pull his head around *to* you!" But what did he care? It wasn't him in the corral. The boot went in the stirrup and without so much as an eyeball flicker Hornet jumped ahead and stuck a hind foot in the horsebreaker's belly.

The stirruped boot jammed against the horse's heart; the rest of the horsebreaker's body flew back and his head struck the ground. The horse snorted a little and jumped sideways. The boy was jerked a few inches when the boot came off and hung alone in the stirrup. There it was, stuck, an empty boot, and for the first time the horse seemed really scared. He ran to the fence, hit it, and spun, whistling through his nose and rolling his left eye and all the ears he had toward the boot. With the accuracy of one who had been desperate before, the horse cow-kicked the boot from the stirrup and sent it spinning across the corral. Immediately he subsided and stood where he was.

Clyde looked at the horsebreaker. His hat was off. Stretched out there, he looked still younger. Hardly twenty, and there was a hole in his sock. The horsebreaker had told Clyde his wife would be arriving in a few days, and that she was going to have a baby. Clyde imagined her unable to darn a sock, potbellied and popping with milk, legs like an antelope: delicate! *that* was what he liked. He wondered if they'd been married long enough . . . then he began to wonder if the boy was ever going to get up.

The horsebreaker did sit up then, and began making sure all his parts were operating. Work down from top to bottom, Clyde thought. The best thing for him to do was to sneak away and come back and announce himself. He walked off among the barn and the sheds, turned, and slowly came back.

Clyde yelled. The gate rattled and swung. "Good morning," Clyde said. "Or is it still morning? How are you and Bee-ears getting along?"

"I'm not so sure," the horsebreaker said, blinking. "I haven't been on him yet."

"You haven't, huh? Let me put it to you this way," Clyde said. "How much do you know about this horse?"

The horsebreaker was blinking rapidly, then succeeded in stopping. "Sterling said he was well started."

"He told you the truth then," Clyde said. He laughed, eyes aglitter. "He's been started more than any horse around and by more different men. You don't mind if I sit on the fence and watch?"

"Do whatever you want," the horsebreaker said.

"I like to ask. Some don't want anyone around. To tell the truth, I never did myself. I never liked anyone around." Clyde waited for the horsebreaker to draw him out about his past. "When I was breaking horses," he added. At last he broke silence again himself: "Have you rode many colts?"

"My share of saddlebroncs."

"Rodeos," Clyde said. "Ah now, that's another business altogether now isn't it?"

"Whatever you say."

The horsebreaker caught the horse and led him to the middle of the corral. This time he did try to pull the head around, but the horse's neck was no more pliable than Clyde's stiff old boar's-dick quirt. You never thought of softening him up a little? Clyde said to himself.

He started up the fence. He picked the biggest post. When he grabbed hold of it he felt it was broken off at the bottom, hanging from the cables now instead of supporting them. Could that horse have broken it? Surely Wesley must have backed into it with a pickup. Clyde crawled up the fence and got on top of the post anyway. If they'd gone a little farther out in the hills, he thought, and cut down a little bigger tree, the post would never have broken, would have been stronger in the ground and broader on the top and a little more comfortable sitting.

At least this time the boy was taking a short hold on the reins, and he kept his back near the horse's front end and got a deathhold on the horn before he put his foot in the stirrup. When the horse threw his wingding, the horsebreaker went right on up into the saddle. Clyde was elated. Of course with the horse's head free, the horsebreaker never got seated, nor even a foot in the right stirrup. Down again, soft this time, carefully brushing the shit out of his hat.

Clyde could see that Hornet did only what needed to be done. Like a mule, saving himself. Better and harder things ahead. The boy would never get settled on him the way he was going at it, that was plain. It was a disappointment. He would like to see the horsebreaker get a good seat, just once. He wanted to see if the horse would walk astraddle of his own neck and squeal like a dog, at least for a jump or two, or throw himself on the ground. No, he doubted that last. It was a puzzle, curious, the end predictable but not the action. He himself was shivering; he crossed his arms and wished for his coat.

Up again, the horsebreaker said, "Hornet, he's further along in his education than I am."

"Lookit here, son, maybe it's not mine to say," Clyde said, "but if I was you I believe what I'd do is to—"

The horsebreaker turned on him, cocked his head up to Clyde sitting on the high post like God. "Lookit here yourself. If you were me and I were you, you'd be down here and I'd be up there, but if I was you I'd keep more quiet. I've had all the big-hatted advisers I need."

Clyde was calm. "What would you give a man to start this horse?" he said.

"You'd better watch yourself," the horsebreaker said, and turned away.

Face blanched, Clyde stood, boot-balanced on the highest cable, poised like an eagle. He started to jump, cast his weight forward nimbly as any man, one boot heel jamming between two pickets where they met the cable, the rotted-off post lurching, and he swung forcibly like a hinged board, face first.

"Man overboard," the horsebreaker said.

Clyde dragged himself up, red-faced and spitting sand, and turned to inspect the part of his boot heel that remained in the fence. He dug it out with his knife and put it in his pants pocket. "Two dollars to get it fixed back on," he mumbled.

Yet before the horsebreaker was through smiling Clyde pried him again. "What would you give a man to start this horse for you?"

"Why just what I'd give to see a piss-ant eat a bale of hay. All I have. Which is nothing. At least you couldn't further spoil him."

"What's Sterling paying you?" Clyde said. "No, never mind. You feed him and keep him and let me use your place and I'll start him for you. It won't take long. Five dollars a day and you pay me when Sterling pays you."

"Well I'm not your daddy," the horsebreaker said. "You be the fool and I'll be the audience."

Without unsaddling the horse, the horsebreaker climbed onto Clyde's post. Clyde drove home, lifted *his* saddle from a hook in the barn, opened the old war chest: took out his quirt, a snaffle-bit bridle with soft rope reins, a hobble made of a split and twisted tow sack, a soft cotton rope an inch and a half thick, and a lariat a little mashed by storage. He cut the wires from a bale of hay and twisted them into a slender baling-wire bat.

When he faced the horse, he noticed that even the air in the bottom of the corral was considerably different from that on the post. The horse flicked his foot at a fly and Clyde felt a twitch in his own thigh, like the reflex from a blow. When he bent over to sort his equipment his face got red, and when he stood up it got white—he had that kind of face. Too much pork and chair, he thought. For a moment he felt as if he'd gone by a gully with something dead in it. Then he was all right. He felt good. He disregarded his audience.

With one hand he took hold of the rein up close to the bit and with the other threw the cotton rope over the horse's head and tied a knot in it around the base of the neck. He wondered if the horsebreaker had ever seen anyone tie a bowline with one hand. If he had an eye in his head he'd notice. Clyde flicked the slack of the rope between the hind legs. A foot raised to kick was hooked. The horse didn't throw a fit: apparently this had been done before too, and done well enough so that he was afraid to fight it. Clyde drew the leg up high under the belly, twisted the escape out of the rope, and tied it off. He pulled the saddle and bridle from the fouled horse and went to throw them up on the fence, swinging them neatly off his hip. To his surprise the saddle fell back into his arms. It was too high, he couldn't make it. "Here," said the horsebreaker, and in some embarrassment Clyde handed them up.

Clyde changed his rope. For the horse, then, to jump would be to fall. Hornet wouldn't make the move and Clyde couldn't pull down the braced weight. Facing the horse to the fence, Clyde tied the foot ropes forward to a post and suddenly struck the horse in the face with the heel of the quirt. Hornet in terror jumped backwards, hind legs snatched forward, falling. Clyde was fast: jerked the knot loose from the fence and fell on the falling animal's head. He lay down alongside Hornet, one knee plunged against throat, other knee hooked around muzzle, locked his legs together and twisted the head as hard as he could. He reached up and tightened the leg ropes with his hands.

He was a little surprised the horse didn't thrash his head, even when it was released, or strain against the ropes. This had most likely all been done to him before, yet it must have been a while ago. The horse began to sweat. Clyde noticed it first at the flanks—just a dark turn to the hair. Then all the body oozed at once, or so it seemed. There was water in the crease below the chopped ears; it rolled in and out of the eye sockets and trickled from the nostrils.

With the baling-wire bat Clyde struck the supple part of the neck. The horse curled from the ground, face wet and slick, wet ears pinned flat, mouth striking. Clyde mashed his heel into it, stood on the horse's mouth and continued pounding with a rapid stroke.

Noon, and no one to cook. He fried him some sausage. For business purposes he had a sticker on his car: "Eat beef for health." But pork was really his meat and sausage his cut. "I like the grease off the meat," he was fond of saying. After lunch he hated to leave the shade of his porch. Yet at one sharp he was back in the corral. He rolled the horse over and began pounding the other side of the neck. The horse had turned black and settled the dust around him. Apparently there was no end to the water he could put out. The boy was there on the post. Was he there again or there still? Surely *again*, Clyde thought. Who would sit staring at a tied-down horse for an hour, without even a speck of shade? With veterinary curiosity Clyde reached between the hind legs and stroked the hairless chocolate-colored skin where the testicles had been cut out three or four years ago.

The horse needed hind shoes. Clyde hated the thought. Yet now while he had him down was the time. Rather than build a fire and shape some shoes to fit properly, he drove down to the hardware and bought some pre-shaped and -sized "cowboy" shoes. He asked the horsebreaker to lend him some tools. They included a pair of fine hand-forged nippers that had been worn out once and repinned. He wondered if the boy didn't shoe horses better than he broke them. It was true that his knuckles were scarred and he had a proper curl to his shoulders.

"Don't you tell anyone who shod this horse," Clyde said. "I guessed his size: he only takes an aught shoe and's got a six-year-old mouth. Nice small feet." Clyde unbent his back and glanced down at his own feet, which were also small (the horsebreaker's weren't), proving that he, Clyde, was a rider, not a plodder.

He clinched the shoes on to stay, if not to fit. It seemed his back would never be half straight again—and here he used to shoe sometimes eight or nine head in a day. An idiot's life! Though maybe he hadn't thought so then. . . .

Clyde untied the ropes, hit the horse with the sack hobble; Hornet scrambled up, shook, staggered, planted his feet squarely and stood blinking. With a rope Clyde jacked up a hind leg as before. He hobbled the front legs together and jumped and struggled onto Hornet's back. The horse stood a second, then, even fouled as he was, snorted and erupted, sprang in the air, and fell on his ribs. Clyde was thrown clear on hands and knees, perfectly clear yet arms and legs churning like a pig on ice. He got on his feet and whipped the horse up quickly. When he got on again, Hornet stood. Clyde moved around over the back, petting and massaging for what seemed endless minutes, but the horse never stopped shaking.

Clyde brushed the horse's back and belly with his hand and saddled him. "Let's tie him in your barn," he said. "When he cools off, you can feed him and pack him some water."

"I'll take him," the horsebreaker said. "You're not going to unsaddle him?"

"Uh-uh, I want to see what he does. I don't want to tell you your business, but if you're going to lead him you better get a hold close to his face."

The horsebreaker opened the gate, holding the exhausted horse on twelve inches of slack. Hornet bogged his head and took it. Hind feet crossed the boy's face, hit the brim of his hat.

"I'll get your hat for you," Clyde said. "Rope burn you?"

The horsebreaker flapped his hands and stared fascinated: "Pootah la Maggie, look at him fire."

The horse was mopping the barnyard with his nose on the ground, breath shooting gravel at their knees. Stiff-kneed landings drove the stirrups straight in the air where they clashed repeatedly over the saddle, the stirrup leathers snapping like whips. A fog of dust obscured him and when they saw him again he was running.

"Could you ride your pony if you ever got seated on him?" Clyde said.

"I don't imagine, but that's for me to ask you."

The horse ran down the lane, slid up to the gate, spun and came galloping back. Clyde stood ready in the end of the lane with a loop hidden behind him. He would have liked to turn him a flip, and as the horse shied by he did forefoot him neatly. But the instant the loop enveloped his legs, Hornet planted himself and slid to a stop. They anchored him for the night.

"You're not going to unsaddle him now?" the horsebreaker said.

Clyde said he wasn't. He drove home, wandered out to find his cow, who was waiting for him near the barn, tight-bagged, and he milked her crudely with stiff fingers.

The evening was unpleasant. His wife didn't like what he was up to and said nothing to him except that he must call Ben. No business would be talked tonight. When he'd finished supper and watched television a bit, he did get up and call. But Ben's words and her silences had equally little effect on Clyde.

The next day the horsebreaker limped out of the barn. "I led him to water and tied him back up," he said.

"Uh-huh. How'd he lead this morning?" Clyde said.

"Sudden."

"Huh. You kept ahold of him though, right? You reached and got him and snatched him back. You're waking up. To tell the truth, I saw you from the porch." Clyde untied the horse and led him to the corral. The neck was swollen, a small ridge on each side, but the real soreness would be underneath, in the muscles. Clyde was satisfied. He thought, Bee-ears, you're tender and bendable as a flower. There were mouth corners yet to be done.

He tied the left rein to a ring in the left saddle skirt and had the horse chasing himself, whirling from the pressure and from him—Clyde—who stood there snapping hobbles and kicking dirt. This was done on the other side too, and the skin where the black lips met was peeled down to pink by the bit rings. Clyde tied long ropes to both bit rings, ran the ropes back through the stirrups, and began driving the horse from behind like a plowman.

He jumped the horse into a trot, stayed well back himself, and made the inside circles. Still he had to open his mouth to get enough air, and what he got seemed straight dust.

"Can you open the gate?" he said. Hornet spurted through the opening. Clyde let him run the length of the lines, threw his weight onto one. He had the leverage. The head whipped around, the body flew on, circling the head, unfooted, helpless, ungainly, crashing. It was a while before Clyde could get the horse up. After that he had him turning every which way and stopping, hooves sliding, making short figure elevens in the gravel. He had a good natural stop, Clyde thought. Wasn't it time to quit? He had almost run out of air himself. And if he went too far the horse would be immune to feeling. Soft and watching—and if he was any judge the horse was at that point. Though you never knew if a little less or a little more would do better. Who could say? He looked at his watch: ten-thirty. He'd rest until one, maybe even go without dinner.

At one Clyde brought back a short leather strap with snaps on each end. With this he hobbled the stirrups together, passing the strap across under the horse's belly.

Holding the reins short, and getting the cheek of the bridle tight in his hand, Clyde pulled the horse's head around and made him whirl in a circle. He was at the center, and he kept the horse spinning even after he was in the saddle, until he had the seat he wanted. The horse was grabbing himself, tail clamped, back humped, trying to buck with his head up. Clyde suddenly drove a spur in him, snatched him to the left again, driving the right spur. Pulled him back and forth then and into the fence, loping finally, Clyde's feet driving him on. The horse had a right to scotch, for every time Clyde suspected him of getting wits and balance together he slid a hand down one rein and pulled the horse hard into the fence.

The head busy, the head busy, Clyde thought, soft as butter. The horse lathered white between the legs and specks of blood showed at the mouth corners. They never slowed up. "Swing the gate once more for me, son, if you would," and out they shot.

Clyde let him run halfway across the barnyard, spurs gigging him on, then he set down so hard on one rein that he was afraid the horse would turn another squawdeedo, this time land on him. Hornet did start to fall sideways, stumbling, and Clyde threw the reins to him, let him gather his feet, and then snatched him again, this time the other side, whirled him both directions and off they went right down the center of the highway, Clyde still jerking the horse in circles first one way then the other and gigging him with both spurs, sparks flying off the asphalt, Hornet given no chance to forget he was being used.

The skidding shod and unshod hooves rang on varying pavement. Their tracks would be there in the tarry patches, Clyde thought. Immortal! Or at least until the first hard freeze this fall. For a minute he was afraid the streets would be deserted. Then he straightened his back in the saddle, swelling like an old boar, the bull of the woods, drawing in his belly, increasing by inches. The horse seemed to dwindle.

A motorcycle passed: Hornet rolled an eye, leaped, was pulled easily around, stumbling. Clyde imagined what they'd say tonight in the Frontier Club. . . .

Someone stepped into the street, hailing him. Clyde said, "Is this the horse you think it is? I expect it is. Only horse around's had both ears stung off. . . ." He went on, stopped again: "Uh-huh, I brought him in right off to get used to the boogers. He's never been uptown before, do you imagine? 'Cept just passing through, trying to stare the slats out of a truck. What do you say?"

Ben was standing in front of the office. Faces of children were pressed to the window of one of Clyde's duplexes across the street. He heard the excited hum of voices coming through the walls, though he finally realized this was a television.

Ben bowed and took off his hat, a wild head of hair springing out like the white beard on a goat.

"Yessir!" Clyde said. "Do you want to talk to me?"

"I did but I don't," Ben said. "I changed my mind. You'd best go on before she decides to come out of the office."

"She won't," Clyde said. Yet she might, and he rode on.

Heading out the other side of town he was light-headed. I should have eaten a little, he thought, a piece of bread and honey or some plum jam by itself. He turned across the canal. When the hooves rattled the bridge boards, Hornet snorted and tried halfheartedly to bolt. Clyde pulled him around. "Ante," he said. "If you've got to be a nigger, be a good one." You're in the sack now, he thought.

They jogged on across the juniper flat, skirting town and heading home. He put his reins in one hand now. Something gray appeared at the edge of vision: "Coyote," Clyde said, and lifted his free hand. Hornet jumped sideways and landed stiff-kneed, an ear cocked at Clyde who'd been snapped off center. A hair off, but Hornet took it. Mouth open, Clyde's teeth smashing tongue, Hornet's head gone out of sight and the noise coming up, like a stuck pig or a dog in the mower blades, continuous.

It was this squealing that terrified Clyde. He got his seat back, as good a deep socked-in seat as anyone ever had. Boots jammed to the heels down the hobbled stirrups, spurs jobbed into the cinch and through the cinch to the hide and through the hide, an arch thrown into his back and his weight against the reins trying to control the head, drawing mouth blood too, all he could, though that wouldn't help now.

Clyde grunted. The horse too, whose body couldn't stand its own lock-kneed hitting. Hornet's mouth showering back a bloody salt into Clyde's eyes and he himself spitting air. He refixed the jumping desert each time they landed. Forced himself not to be confused by the sky, to keep refocusing the horse's neck against the ground. His eyes were gauging accurate, but beginning to lag, lagging, falling behind like the bubble on a spinning level. He was being moved, knew he was, crotch drifting, will couldn't stop it. Off center, a hump jerked into his back, the left leg taking too much shock, the right one springing loose, spur popped from the cinch.

He lost the stirrup, felt it go, and only hoped then to lose the left one too. Mane glimpsed against the sky, track all lost of where he was, while he felt it there solid, his foot stirruped, hobbled, spur spurred into the cinch and through it, twisting now like a hook; he the fish now, a whole new set of things to think about, too fast, rising changing sand bushes. Clyde's face passing Hornet's mouth, open, blood on the bit rings, eye glazed visionless. Bucking blind, then quit and ran.

For fifty yards Hornet tried to kick him loose. Clyde dragging. His eye buried in the crook of one arm and the other arm enfolding his head. Even during this he imagined the luck of the foot breaking, getting sluffed out of his boot. The horse hit the badger hole, folded down upon Clyde's leg. He thought this was salvation and spun over onto his back, watched the horse pawing up again, saw himself still hooked, suspended, moving off, face slapped by branches, and discovered his hands lacing around juniper trunk. And him knowing he could pull his leg off if he had to. An explosion in his knee, vision of juniper roots bursting, fibers flayed out like the nerve ends on a lighted chart. The saddle fell on his feet, the horse tangled in bridle reins, stepping on them and brutally stabbing his own mouth. Hornet stopped, tied to his own legs.

Clyde discovered that he was still squeezing his juniper. He let go. Who saw? He turned slowly. She would be there, arms across chest; Ben quizzical, hat off, head at an angle; the boy who wanted to break horses; behind them a great vague crowd of townspeople. No, he saw the buildings of town, that was all, and farther west the ridge of his own canal bank.

He fished up his knife, leaned forward and cut a few strands of cinch away from his spur. If the latigo on the saddle hadn't broken, the strands would have, he thought. He pulled his boot from the stirrup and got up. As far as he could tell, nothing was broken, and neither back nor knee would be impossible until tomorrow. All the rest was skin, the knees and elbows ripped out of his clothes, bruises, teeth. He must have hit his mouth. Where was his hat? There. Way back there. Well, he'd gone a long while with his own teeth, hadn't he? Way longer than Ben.

His inclination was to pull the bridle off Hornet and start walking. But if he left the horse here, this whole story was going to be out an hour after feeding time. And what if he led him in? If he walked alone he could wade the canal anywhere, but the horse wouldn't follow him through the water. He'd have to go to the bridge, which was right by the highway and visible from the horsebreaker's house too. It wouldn't do to be seen leading the horse in, and if he waited till dark, his wife would have the whole town out after him. There was nothing to be done but to mend his latigo and be seen riding in, if he was to be seen at all.

Clyde threw his stirrup hobbles away and hid the spurs in the badger hole. He couldn't control his knee and didn't want to be spurring the horse by accident. This was one ride he wanted to sneak. He hobbled Hornet with a rein, saddled him, and when he went to get on cheeked him tight as the mouth could stand—not much now.

The horse dragged his toes, even over the rattling crossboards of the bridge. But Clyde wasn't taking any chances: he kept his eyes on the horse's head. If he'd dared to look around, he might have seen the listless dragging tracks Hornet was making in the sand, and been less nervous.

Clyde was a couple of days in the house recuperating, and when he did go back to the office he looked pretty bunged up. The horse was loping along like a good one and stuck his foot in a badger hole and took a tumble: that was the story Clyde thought of telling, but he was afraid it wouldn't be believed and changed his mind. Besides the episode as it really was was good enough.

And it was lucky for him that he didn't try to lie. That darned Sterling, the first day Clyde was back at the office, knocked on the door of Clyde's house and asked his wife if it wasn't okay to borrow something out of the tackroom. She told him to go ahead, and under pretense of borrowing something (though he really did borrow something), he looked at Clyde's saddle and found the track of the right spur rowel where it had crossed the seat of the saddle on Clyde's way off—and Sterling told everyone about it.

Ben stopped in at the office a week later, to say the pig he was fattening for Clyde was ready (he also wanted to have a look at him). Once there, he regretted it, and could hardly wait to make his escape.

"You saw yourself," Clyde said to him, "I had him between my two hands. Soft as butter, don't you doubt it."

"I don't doubt it," Ben said wearily. "I saw it myself."

"Only I ought to have kept both hands on the reins at all times. Darned if a man no matter how much he knows and how well he knows it won't always lose his wherewithal at the sight of a coyote or some silly thing."

"Now there's a bit of first-class wisdom for you," Ben said.

Clyde was having some teeth made, but right now he was missing some out of his mouth like an old cow. It didn't make him look younger. And he had a new cane—Ben saw it leaned up against the desk—to help him out with his knee. But for all that, he appeared to be in a lively enough mood.

Ben thought he'd bait him a little. "How long again you say you rode that horse?"

"Two days, so far."

"Two. . . . Pay you, did they?"

"Five a saddle."

"Uh-huh—ten dollars. That pay those dentist bills pretty well, will it?"

"I've just about got that dentist sold a piece of property," Clyde said. "Anyway he's easy money from now on, that horse—you could sit on him backwards."

"Not me," said Ben.

# WILLIAM KITTREDGE
# THE VAN GOGH FIELD

William Kittredge, born in 1932 in Portland, grew up in the Owyhee River country of southeastern Oregon. His first book of stories, *The Van Gogh Field* (1978), won the Fiction International Prize for 1979, and has been followed by a second book of stories, *We Are Not in This Together* (1984). He has taught creative writing at a number of institutions, including Stanford University where he was a Stegner Fellow, and is now on the faculty of the University of Montana. In reading Kittredge, one is reminded of Wallace Stegner's advice to western writers not to close their eyes to the West's cultural and intellectual limitations and not to be carried away by its scenic landscapes, for Kittredge carefully discriminates between pictures and passions and celebrates provincial life without nostalgia or romantic gloss.

"The Van Gogh Field" originally appeared in *The Iowa Review*, No. 3, 1972. The main character, Robert Onnter, while standing at a Chicago art museum before the self-portait of Vincent van Gogh, is reminded of the barley fields of his home in an eastern Oregon valley and of the simple itinerant combine-runner, Clyman Teal, who had been hired annually to mow those fields. Robert has needed to travel, to escape the "stillness" and "desolate small loves" of his valley, to come to terms with the paradoxical "constant motionlessness reflected in the eyes of Clyman Teal and now in the detached and burning eyes of van Gogh." In Chicago, Robert has drifted into a casual affair with a pseudosophisticated married woman in spite of his distaste for "the insincerity of imitations, falsity" and "her insistence on futility." The memory of Clyman's lonely but steady and useful life affect Robert's final inclination to return home where love and death unite in beauty as once they did for van Gogh.

# THE VAN GOGH FIELD

Clyman Teal: swaying and resting his back against the clean-grain hopper, holding the header wheel of the Caterpillar-drawn John Deere 36 combine, a twenty-nine-year-old brazed and wired-together machine moving along its path around the seven-hundred-acre and perfectly rectangular field of barley with seemingly infinite slowness, traveling no more than two miles in an hour, harvest dust rising from the separating fans within the machine and hanging around him as he silently contemplates the acreage being reduced swath by swath, a pale yellow rectangle peeling toward the last narrow and irregular cut and the finished center, his eyes flat and gray, squinted against the sun.

Robert Onnter, standing before the self-portrait of van Gogh, had finally remembered Clyman Teal, his expression beneath that limp sweat-and-grease-stained hat, the long round chin and creased, sun and windburned cheeks and shaded eyes, a lump of tobacco wadded under his thin lower lip, sparse gray week-old whiskers, face of a man getting through not just the pain of his last illness and approaching death, but the glaring sameness of what he saw, at least trying to see through.

Changing position every few moments, as if from some not-yet-discovered perspective he would be able to see into an interior space he felt the picture must have, Robert Onnter faced the self-portrait of van Gogh on temporary display in the marble-floored main lower corridor of the Chicago Art Institute and felt the eyes in the portrait as those of a man looking into whatever Clyman Teal must have seen while watching the harvest fields that occupied the sun-colored impenetrable August days of his life, the sheen brilliant and unresolved as light glaring off buffed aluminum: eye of van Gogh.

In the same place the afternoon before, people dressed for winter occasionally passing, Robert had been distracted by the woman, her gloved hand on his sleeve, while trying to visualize something he could not imagine, what lay beneath and yet over the texture of thick blue paint, how the ridged strokes fixed there changed his memories of slick wheatfield prints under glass in frames on his mother's wall. This morning he had left the woman sleeping in her cluttered brown apartment . . . her fragility only appearance . . . curled like a small aging moth on her side of a too-wide bed in a building that overlooked the northern end of Michigan Boulevard and snow-covered ice of the lake, gone by taxi to his room in the Drake Hotel and showered and shaved and changed clothes, and feeling clean as when outdoors on a long-ago summer morning touched by dew which dampened the leather of his worn-toed childhood boots, caught another taxi and returned to stand again before the picture.

There was a sense in which he had come to Chicago to look the first time at real paintings because of van Gogh. Part of his reaction against the insubstantiality of his life had been founded on those flat wheatfield prints his mother cherished. Robert smoked a cigarette from a crumpled pack, wondered if he should have left a note for the woman, and thought, as when the woman interrupted him the afternoon before, about his mother's life in isolation and her idea of beauty, surely implied by her love of those prints, desolate small loves in the eastern Oregon valley that was his home, the transparently streaked sheen of yellow gold over the ripening barleyfields under summer twilight, views of that and level windblown snow no doubt having something to do with the way he had felt compelled to spend this winter and with what he saw in the eyes of van Gogh, remembered from the simple death of Clyman Teal, and what he thought of his mother's idea, not so much of beauty but of the reasons things were beautiful. The woman's appearance beside him the day before seemed inevitably part of the education he had planned for this winter, escaping stillness. Except for two and a half years at the University of Oregon in liberal arts, studying nothing, a course urged on him by his mother, four years in the air force, a year and a half of marriage to a girl from Vacaville, California, named Dennie Wilson . . . when he lived in Sacramento selling outboard motors . . . he had always lived in the valley. So there was need to travel.

Twenty-seven when he returned to the valley, he worked for his father as he had always known eventually he would, spending his time at chores and drinking in the town of Nyall at the north end of the valley, seeing whichever girl he happened to meet in the taverns. Lately the calm of that existence had fragmented, partly because of his mother's insistence he was wasting his life, more surely because of constant motionlessness, reflected in the eyes of Clyman Teal and now in the detached and burning eyes of van Gogh. Robert had been disconnected from even his parents since the divorce, and now it seemed there had been no one even then. The girl Dennie, addicted to huge dark glasses with shining amber lenses, so briefly his wife, now lived in Bakersfield with another man and a daughter named Felicity who was nearly six years old and ready for school. Robert could recall his wife's face . . . the girl he married . . . could not imagine her with a child, saw with absolute clarity the slender girl from Vacaville, eyes faintly owllike in the evening because her suntan ended at the rim of her glasses. She had grown up while he had not. By missing knowledge of her strength in childbirth he had missed part of what he could have been. His sense of lost contact was constructed at least in part of that.

The previous year, early spring, before winter broke out of the valley, a morning he remembered perfectly, he called Dennie before daylight, a frantic and stupid mistake finally shattering any sort of relationship they might have carried past divorce. Robert had been reading a book pushed on him by his mother, *The Magic Mountain*, written by a German named Mann, which seemed a strange name for a German, his mother saying the book would tell him something about himself and that if he would only begin reading he would see why he must change. The day was a dead Sunday and he was a little hung over and somehow bored with the idea of another slow afternoon in the bars of Nyall, the blotched snow and peeling frame buildings and the same people as always, aimless Sunday drinkers. So he read because there was nothing else to do and then for reasons he did not understand became fascinated and began to struggle seriously with comprehending what the German meant by writing down his story of sickness and escape, seeing why his mother might imagine it applied to him, yet sure it meant something more.

He spent weeks at it, reading and rereading each page and paragraph, savoring the way it was to be German and writing about sickness, staying in his room and working at it each night, waking in the early morning before daylight and thinking about it again. Until at four o'clock the morning of the phone call he turned on his light and began reading about a beautiful epileptic woman and began to feel as if he were himself at the next breath going to descend into a spasm and ended terrified and unable to focus his eyes on the print, or even move, as if the merest responses of his body might cause the heavy and shrouding weight of stillness to settle like a cloud blotting away all connection, and finally he forced himself and called the girl who had been his wife, Dennie, who he sensed might understand, might not have completely deserted him. She told him he was drunk and hung up quickly, and Robert felt himself alone in his cloud and could think of nothing but awakening his mother, begging her to make it go away, ended going for weeks through the motions of days surrounded by terror of something simple as air.

Now the heavy and vivid symbolic color of the self-portrait seemed reality, the expression and agony of a man abruptly giving up, Clyman Teal who had been dying that last summer, a wandering harvest-follow-

ing man who could have been van Gogh, who traveled north with the
seasons along the West Cost in a succession of gray and rust-stained
automobiles, always alone: hard streaked color of the painting ridged
and unlike the wheatfield prints, actual as barley ripe before harvest,
all bound into the stasis Robert was attempting to escape in this city,
while traveling.

The woman's amber-colored hair was long and straight, over her
shoulders, contrasting with the natural paleness of her clear oval face.
She brushed her hair slowly. "I'd just finished washing it," she said,
smiling, "when you called."
So casual she seemed younger, and small and full rather than tiny
and drawn together by approaching age; she sat in a black velvet chair
by a window overlooking the lake, lighted from behind by a gray midwestern sunlight, wearing a deep-and-soft-blue gown which concealed
all but her white shoulders and neck, bare feet curled beneath her.
Worn embroidered slippers lay on the pale, almost white carpet in the
room cluttered with sofas covered by blankets and with tables whose
surfaces reflected intricate porcelain figures. "I like nice things," she'd
said the night before. "Most of these things were my mother's. Is there
anything wrong with that?" Robert told her he imagined not, and she
smiled. "Call me Goldie," she'd said. "Everyone does." He had read
the card inserted in the small brass frame beneath the entry buzzer.
*Mrs. Daniel (Ruth Ann) Brown.* Her husband, she explained, was away
in Europe. "He's no threat," she'd said. "He's gone for the winter."
They'd come here in the evening at her insistence, sat in flickering
near darkness before the artificial fire, and she changed into a dressing
gown and served tiny glasses of a thick pale drink, that tasted like burnt
straw. Finally he kissed her, moving awkwardly across the sofa while
she waited with an icelike smile. "He's away," she said, "to Greece, to
the islands, to walk and think."
In the soft light of afternoon she was completely serene. Robert asked
why her husband had gone. "Because of the clearness," she said. "The
light . . . things have gone badly, with the unrest, and he wanted to
think. . . ." Perhaps, Robert thought, he would follow, to the pale sunlight and dusty white islands and the water of the sea, New York and
then London, Paris, Rome, at last to the islands off Greece, and see the
water moving under the light, flow and continuity that might illuminate
his vision of a desert stream low in a dry summer and water falling
through crevices between boulders, always images of water, the cold
Pacific gray beneath winter clouds, waves breaking in on barren sand
and the heavy movement of the troopship just after leaving San Francisco

for Guam, where he spent a year and a half of his air-force time.

In childhood he had imagined the barleyfields were water. After the last meal of the day, while dishes remained stacked in the sink to be washed later, they would all of them go out into the valley and look at the ripening crop, his mother and father, Robert, and his younger brother and even-younger sister all in the old dark-green Chevrolet pickup. Now his brother had been dead eleven years, killed in an automobile crash his second semester of college, and his sister, married directly out of high school, lived distantly with children in Amarillo, Texas. Then they had all been home, and his father had driven them out over the dusty canal-bank roads until east of the fields, looking toward the last sunlight glaring over the low rim; and those yellowing fields were luminous and transformed into a magic and perfect cloth for them to walk on, and Robert imagined them all hand in hand, walking toward the sun.

His mother had named the largest field on one of those trips, and because of the prints in the house it had seemed she was only silly. But surely she had been right, however inadvertently. The yellowish, rough sheen of bearded, separate, and sunlighted barley heads matched perfectly the reality of van Gogh, glowing paint, his eyes, texture. "The van Gogh field," she said, repeating it as if delighted. "It's so classic." She would often say that. "It's so classic." They stayed until the air began to cool and settle and then went slowly home, Robert and his brother in the back of the pickup, watching the dust rise soft and gray as flour behind them and hang in the air, streaked and filmy as an unlighted aura even after the pickup was parked beneath the cottonwood trees behind the house.

Robert wondered what those evening trips had meant to his father. Nearly sixty, silently beguiled by sentiment, his father wept openly for a month after Robert's brother was killed, sat abruptly upright drinking coffee Robert's mother brought, never going outside until spring irrigation forced him to work, after that revealing emotion only with his hands, gesturing abruptly and reaching to pick up a clod of dry and grainy peat, crumbling it to dust between callused fingers. During planting the man would sometimes walk out over the damp tilled ground and kneel, sink his hands and churn up the undersoil, crouch lower like a trailing animal. "Seeing if it's right," he would say. "If it's ready."

The woman returned with drinks. "I didn't think you'd be back," she said. "I hoped, but. . . ." She smiled, perhaps wishing she were alone, the last night an incident scarcely remembered. "I went back to the painting," Robert said.

"What are you really doing? I don't think I believe what you told me." She continued smiling. He had lied, unable to admit he had borrowed ten thousand dollars from his father, feeling childish over his search for places and cities missed, and told her he was an insurance salesman. "Looking for islands," he said, wondering if she would take him seriously.

She glanced away, stopped smiling. "The wheatfields," she said, "you should see them, the last particularly." Robert didn't answer. "Before he shot himself, I mean," she said, "when you think of what it meant to him . . . the yellow and that field pregnant, those birds . . . his idea of death, and remember it was there he killed himself, in that field, then you see."

"Yellow?"

"Simply love." The afternoon had settled, blue winter light darkening, her face isolated as if detached from her dark gown. "I don't think you can tell from prints," he said, "we had prints and there's nothing in them . . . my mother must have thought he was pretty and bright." Robert could not explain the insincerity of imitations, falsity.

"So?" The woman leaned forward just slightly, perhaps interested and no longer getting politely through an afternoon with a man she'd slept with and would have preferred never seeing again. Her tone was sharper, quick, and she sipped her drink, turned the glass in her hands.

"The way she acted. . . ." Robert stalled.

"Your mother acted improperly." The woman's voice was impatient, dropping the *improperly* as if she had changed her mind while speaking, finishing awkwardly, perhaps not wanting to acknowledge the moral distance implied in her judgment of him and his judgment of his mother.

". . . as if it were an example of something."

"Are you so sure? Perhaps it was all a disguise."

"I don't think she. . . ." Robert hesitated. "A man died and she knew some pictures and so it was beautiful and emblematic of something." His mother had stirred her coffee and smiled with total self-possession. "He finished doing what he loved," she had said. "Until the job was over."

The woman rose from her chair and began walking slowly before the windows, carrying a half-empty glass. "Women see more than you imagine," she said. "Sometimes, perhaps everything."

His mother: Duluth Onnter, what did she see, having come west from Minnesota to marry his father out of college, so taken by color and names? Her parents had moved from Minneapolis to Tucson the year after Robert was born, and although he had visited them as a child, he could not imagine the long-dead people he remembered, a heavy white-haired man and woman, as having lived anywhere not snow covered half the year. His grandfather had been in Duluth the day Robert's mother was born, and because of that had insisted she be named after a cold lakeport city. "Papa always said it was beautiful that morning," his mother told him. "That I was his beauty."

"Maybe the pictures were only warm and nice," Robert said. "Maybe she did see."

"My husband is like that," the woman answered, "imagines he's going to find spirituality in Greece, in some island. I don't. I'm lucky." She continued walking before the windows, gown trailing the carpet, her thin figure silhouetted. "I have what seems necessary and it's not freedom. I'll go Friday and confess having slept with you. That's freedom."

"To a priest?" It seemed totally wrong, sleeping with him and then carrying the news to church, the kind of circularity he had been escaping. "I don't see that at all," he said. "Why do anything in the first place . . . and pretend you didn't?"

"It's not pretending," she said. "It's being forgiven. I go to look as you do, somehow for a moment you helped me see better, look at van Gogh, and even my need to see is a sin, a failure of belief. I sold myself for what you helped me see. If that sounds silly maybe it is, but it wasn't to me then and it's not now. It's my own freedom and I don't need to go anywhere to find it. And it has to be confessed."

Robert wondered if she found him foolish, in Chicago, planning on Europe, if she wished to be rid of him and would regard his going coldly, as his mother had taken the death of Clyman Teal, if for her anything existed but hope. "I must seem stupid," he said.

"No . . . I just don't think there's anything like what you're looking for."

"Like what?"

"I don't know, but it isn't here . . . or Greece or anywhere."

"Perhaps I should stay." There was the easy possibility of a winter in Chicago, walking the street, looking at pictures, going from van Gogh to Gauguin, Seurat, seeing her occasionally, as often as she would permit.

"I wouldn't," she said. "If I were you." Feeling denied some complex understanding she could give if only she would, Robert knew she was right and trying to be kind. "I wouldn't bother you," he said. "Only once in a while, just to talk."

"No," the woman said. "I'll get your coat." Her face was hard and set and he thought how melodramatic she was with her insistence on futility. Standing in the hallway with her door closed behind he saw how much she believed she was right, her belief founded on quick sliding glances at whatever it was van Gogh and Clyman Teal had regarded steadily in their fields of grain.

The next morning he returned to the Art Institute, and she was there, standing quietly in a beige wool suit with a camel's-hair coat thrown over her shoulders, a thin and stylish, nearly pretty woman who was aging. "You came back," he said. She turned as if surprised and then smiled. "Let's be quiet," she said, "the best part is silence, then we can talk."

Beside her, sensing she now wanted some word from him, Robert was drawn to the fierce and despairing painted face, memories of Clyman Teal in the days before he died. Summer had been humid, with storms in June and a week of soft rain in late July, and the crop the best in years, kernels filled without the slightest pinch and heavy by the time harvest started in August. Clyman Teal arrived the day it began, lean and thick shouldered, long arms seeming perpetually broken at the elbows, driving slowly across the field in the latest of his secondhand automobiles, a gray two-door Pontiac. He rubbed his eyes and walked a little into the field with Robert and his father. Dew was just burning off. "Came last night from Arlington," he said. "Finished there yesterday." He'd been working the summer wheat harvest just south of the Columbia River, two hundred and fifty miles north, for twenty years, always coming when it finished to run combine for Robert's father. After this job ended he'd go south to the rice harvest in the Sacramento Valley. Thick heads of barley drooped around them, and Clyman Teal cracked kernels between his teeth and chewed and swallowed, squinting toward the sun. "Going to be fine," he said, "ain't it boy." Leaving the trunk lid open on the Pontiac, heedless of dust sifting over his bedroll and tin-covered suitcase, he dragged out his tools and spent the rest of the morning working quietly and steadily while the rest of them waited, regreasing bearings Robert had greased the afternoon before, tightening chains and belts, running the machine and tightening again, finishing just as the noon meal was hauled to the field in pots with their lids fastened down by rubber bands. They all squatted in the shade to eat, then flipped the scraps from their plates to the sea gulls, and the work began. With the combine motor running, Clyman Teal motioned for Robert to follow him and walked to where Robert's father stood cranking the old D7 Caterpillar, dust goggles already down over his eyes. "When there's time," he shouted, "I want this boy on the machine with me." Then he walked away, climbed the steel ladder to the platform where he stood while tending the header wheel, and waved for Robert's father to begin the first round.

So when there was time between loads, Robert rode the combine, learning to tend the header wheel, what amount of straw to take in so the machine would thrash properly and to set the concaves beneath the thrashing cylinder, adjust the speed of the cylinder according to the heaviness of the crop, regulate the fans that blew the chaff and dust from the heavier grain. "Whole thing works on gravity," the old man said. "Heavy falls and the light floats away."

Sometimes the old man would walk behind the machine in the fogging dust of chaff, his hat beneath the straw dump, catching the straw and chaff, then dumping the hatful of waste on the steel deck and slowly spreading it with thick fingers, kneeling and blowing away the chaff, checking to see if kernels of the heavy grain were being carried over. "You need care," the old man said. "Otherwise you're dumping money."

But most often he just rode with his back braced against the clean-grain hopper. The harvest lasted twenty-seven days, the last swath cut late in the afternoon while Robert was hauling his final truckload on the asphalt road up the west side of the valley to the elevator in Nyall. Returning to the field in time to see the other truck pulling out, a surplus GI six-by-six converted to ranch truck wallowing through the soft peaty soil in low gear, Robert waited at the gate. The other driver stopped. "Claims he's sick," the man said, leaning from the truck window. "Climbed down and curled up and claimed he was sick and said to leave him alone." The combine was parked in the exact center of the field, stopped after the last cut. Tin eyed and balding, the driver lived in the valley just south of Nyall on a sour alkali-infested 160 acres and now seemed impatient to get all this over and back to his quietude. "Your daddy wants you to bring out the pickup," he said.

Robert drove the new red three-quarter-ton International pickup, rough and heavy, out to the combine. Clyman Teal lay curled on the ground in the shade of the machine. Robert and his father loaded the old man into the pickup, and Robert drove slowly homeward over the rutted field while his father supported Clyman Teal with an arm around his shoulders. The old man grunted with pain, eyes closed tightly and arms folded over his belly. Parked at last before the whitewashed bunkhouse, they all sat quiet a moment, nothing in the oppressive empty valley moving but one fly in dust on the slanting windshield. "We'll take him inside," Robert's father said, and Robert was surprised how fragile and light the old man was, small inside his coveralls, like a child, diminished within the folds, his odor like that of a field fire, sharp and acrid. They left him passive and rigid on the bunk atop brown surplus GI blankets. He opened his eyes and grunted something that meant for them to leave him alone, then drew back into himself. The window shelf above the bed was lined with boxes and pills, baking soda and aspirin and home stomach remedies. Robert's mother carried down soup and toast that evening, and the old man lay immobile while Robert's father washed the dust from his face. They tucked him under the blankets and the next morning the meal was untouched. That afternoon Robert's father called a doctor, the only one in Nyall, and after probing at the curled figure the doctor called an ambulance from the larger town fifty miles west. It was evening when the ambulance arrived, a heavy Chrysler staffed by volunteers, red light flickering at the twilight while Robert helped load the old man on a stretcher. Clyman Teal was sealed inside without ever opening his eyes, and Robert never saw him again. During the brief funeral parlor ceremony six days later he didn't go up and look into the coffin, nor did anyone.

Operated on the night he was hauled away, Clyman died. "Eaten up," the doctor said, shaking his head: "Perforations all through his intestines." Robert remembered his mother's reddened hands gripping the tray she carried down the hill, his father's fumbling tenderness while washing the old man's face, the mostly silent actions. Three days after Clyman died the sheriff's office located a brother in Clovis, New Mexico, who said to go ahead and bury him. Six attended the funeral, Robert and his father and mother and the truck driver and his huge smiling wife and a drifter from one of the bars in Nyall. The brother was a grinning old man in a greenish black suit and showed up a week later. He silently loaded Clyman's possessions into the Pontiac and drove away, heading back to New Mexico. He hadn't seen Clyman, he said, in thirty-eight years, hadn't heard from him in all that time. "Just never got around to anything," he said. But the trip was worth his trouble, he said. He'd found hidden in the old man's tin suitcase a bankbook from Bakersfield showing total deposits of eight thousand some odd dollars. He said he thought he'd go home by way of Bakersfield.

The woman took Robert's arm. "I've had enough," she said. "Let's have a cup of coffee." Seated in the noisy cafeteria, she smiled. "I liked that," she said. "Standing there quietly together . . . that's what I first liked about you, that you knew how to be quiet." Robert wondered how often she did this, picked up some stray; what had driven away her husband. "Is that why?" he said, involved in a judgment of her that seemed finally unfair, perhaps because it came so close to being a judgment of himself.

"You could appreciate stillness . . . the moment I love in church is that of prayer, silence before the chant begins." Her hands moved slowly, touching her spoon, turning her cup. "I've changed my mind," she said. "I'd like you to stay the winter.

"You could go with me on Sundays," she said, "and see how the quiet and perfection . . . the loveliness on Easter."

But he couldn't. It was useless, for her perhaps all right, he couldn't know about that, but stillness would mount while they chanted, and not her church or any city in Europe, even clarity of water, would do more for him than going home to those cold wet mornings in early spring while they planted, the motionless afternoons of boredom while the harvest circled to where the combine parked. "Yes," he said, not wanting to hurt her, knowing he might even stay. "I could do that." Wheatfields reared toward the sky under circling birds, evening dust hung still behind his father's pickup, and his brother's childish face was staring ahead toward lights flickering through the poplar trees marking their home, the light yellow color of love, van Gogh dead soon after, nearby.

# JEAN STAFFORD
# THE HEALTHIEST GIRL IN TOWN

Jean Stafford (1915–1979) was born in Covina, California, grew up in Colorado, graduating B.A. and M.A. in 1936 from the University of Colorado at Boulder, and thereafter lived in the East. (She was married for eight years to poet Robert Lowell.) The most western of her novels is *The Mountain Lion* (1947), set partly in a middle-class home in Covina, partly in the rougher, simpler atmosphere of a Colorado cattle ranch, and many of her stories in *Collected Stories* (1969), which won the Pulitzer Prize in 1970, are set in the West and consider the lonely few with strength to resist being trapped in hollow social rituals and in outmoded "eastern" cultural patterns.

"The Healthiest Girl in Town," which appeared in *The New Yorker*, was selected for inclusion in *Best American Short Stories 1952*. The setting for the story in a "high Western town" inhabited in part by tuberculosis patients and their families. (Note: Colorado had various sanatoria in 1924, the most famous of which was Cragmor Sanatorium in Colorado Springs, a city then sometimes called "Little London" for its pretensions to European and Eastern sophistication.) As the narrator's mother is employed by a puritanical family from Massachusetts, the Butlers, she herself, eight years old, is cast into the company of the Butler children, whose cruelty, haughtiness, and witch-hunting tactics make her feel like a pariah in her own territory. The Butler family have "an orthodox aversion to the West" and look down "at the entire population, as if it consisted of nothing but rubes." The narrator has the independence and strength of mind to assert herself, but when she shocks the children into believing she is infected with leprosy, she seems to go too far: the lie will cost her mother her job. So she confesses to the lie and wins the day simply by displaying a healthy individuality against which the girls' genteel maladies have no chance.

# THE HEALTHIEST
# GIRL IN TOWN

In 1924, when I was eight years old, my father died and my mother and I moved from Ohio to a high Western town, which, because of its salubrious sun and its astringent air, was inhabited principally by tuberculars who had come there from the East and South in the hope of cure, or at least of a little prolongation of their static, cautious lives. And those of the town who were not invalids, or the wives, husbands, or children of invalids, were, even so, involved in this general state of things and conversant with its lore. Some of them ran boarding houses for the ambulatory invalids ("the walkers," as we called them) and many were in the employ of the sanitarium which was the *raison d'être* of the community, while others were hired privately as cooks, chauffeurs, or secretaries by people who preferred to rent houses rather than submit to the regulations of an institutional life. My mother was a practical nurse and had come there because there were enough people to need her services and therefore to keep a roof over our heads and shoes on our feet.

My contemporaries took for granted all the sickness and dying that surrounded us—most of them had had a first-hand acquaintance with it—but I did not get used to these people who carried the badge of their doom in their pink cheeks as a blind man carries his white stick in his hand. I continued to be fearful and fascinated each time I met a walker in the streets or on the mountain trails and each time some friend's father, half gone in the lungs, watched me from where he sat in enforced ease on the veranda as other girls and I played pom-pom-pulla-way in his front yard. Once Dotty MacKensie's father, who was soon to die, laughed, when I, showing off, turned a cartwheel, and he cried, "Well done, Jessie!" and was taken thereupon with the last awful cough that finally was to undo and kill him. I did not trust their specious look of health and their look of immoderate cleanliness. At the same time, I was unduly drawn to them in the knowledge that a mystery encased them delicately; their death was an interior integument that seemed to lie just under their sun-tanned skin. They spoke softly and their manners were courteous and kind, as if they must live hushed and on tiptoe, lest the bacilli awaken and muster for the kill. Occasionally, my mother was summoned in the middle of the night to attend someone in his final hemorrhage; at times, these climactic spasms were so violent, she had once told me, that blood splattered the ceiling, a hideous thought and one that wickedly beguiled me. I would lie awake in the cold house long after she had left and would try to imagine such an explosion in myself, until finally I could all but see the girandole of my bright blood mount through the air. Alone in the malevolent midnight darkness, I was possessed with the facts of dying and of death, and I would often turn, heartless and bewitched, to the memory of my father, killed by gangrene, who had lain for weeks in his hospital bed, wasted and hot-eyed and delirious, until, one day as I watched, the poisonous tide deluged him and, as limp as a drowned man, he died. The process had been so snail-paced and then the end of it so fleet that in my surprise I had been unable to cry out and had stood for several minutes, blissful with terror, until my mother came back into the room with a doctor and a nurse. I had longed to discuss with her what I had seen, but her grief—she had loved him deeply—inhibited me, and not until we had come West did I ask her any questions about death, and when I did, I appeared to be asking about her patients, although it was really about my father.

The richer of the tuberculars, especially those who had left their families behind, were billeted in the sanitarium, an aggregate of Swiss chalets that crested the western of our twin hills. If they were not bedridden, they lived much as they might have done at a resort, playing a great deal of bridge, mah-jongg, and cowboy pool, learning to type-write, photographing our declamatory mountain range. Often in the early evening, from the main lodge there came piano music, neither passionate nor complicated, and once, as I was passing by, I heard a flute, sweet and single in the dusk. On walks, the patients slowly ranged the mesas, gathering pasque-flowers in the spring and Mariposa lilies in the summer, and in the winter, when the snow was on the ground, they brought back kinnikinnick, red-berried and bronze-leaved. These pastimes were a meager fare and they were bored, but they were sustained by their stubborn conviction that this way of life was only temporary. Faithfully, winter and summer, spring and fall, they went abroad each day at noon to get the high sun, and because the sanitarium was near my school, I used to see them at the lunch recess, whole phalanxes of them, indulging sometimes in temperate horseplay and always in their interchange of cynical witticisms that banded them to-gether in an esoteric fellowship. In the winter—and our winters were so long and cruel that the sick compared this region to Siberia and their residence there to exile—their eyes and noses alone were visible through their caparisons of sweaters, mufflers, greatcoats, but their sanguine, muted voices came out clearly in the thin air. Like all committed people, whether they are committed to school or to jail, to war or to disease, there was among them a good-natured camaraderie that arose out of a need to vary the tedium of a life circumscribed by rules. I would hear them maligning and imitating the doctors and the nurses, and laying plans to outwit them in matters to do with rest periods and cigarettes, exactly as my schoolmates and I planned to perpetrate mischief in geography class or study hall. I heard them banteringly compare X-rays and temperatures, speak, in a tone half humorous and half apprehensive, of a confederate who had been suspended temporarily (it was hoped) from the fraternity by a sudden onslaught of fever. They were urbane, resigned, and tart. Once, I recall, I met two chattering walkers on a path in the foothills and I heard one of them say, "All the same, it's not the bore a nervous breakdown is. We're not locked in, at any rate," and his companion amiably answered, "Oh, but we are. They've locked us into these ratty mountains. They've 'arrested' us, as they say."

This colony was tragic, but all the same I found it rather grand, for most of the sanitarium patients had the solaces of money and of education (I was sure they all had degrees from Eastern universities) and could hire cars to go driving in the mountains and could buy books in quantity at Miss Marshall's snobbish shop, the Book End, where they could also drink tea in an Old Englishy atmosphere in the backroom. I did not feel sorry for them as I did for the indigent tuberculars, who lived in a settlement of low, mean cottages on the outskirts of the town. Here I saw sputum cups on windowsills and here I heard, from every side, the prolonged and patient coughing, its dull tone unvarying except when a little respite came and its servant sighed or groaned or said, "Oh, God Almighty," as if he were unspeakably tired of this and of everything else in the world. There were different textures and velocities to the coughing, but whether it was dry or brassy or bubbling, there was in it always that undertone of monotony.

It was neither the rich nor the poor that my mother nursed but those in between, who rented solid houses and lived—or tried to live—as they had in Virginia or in Connecticut. Whole families had uprooted themselves for the sake of one member; mothers had come out of devotion to a favorite son. There were isolated individuals as well, men with valets and motorcars and dogs (I thought that the bandy-legged basset belonging to the very rich Mr. Woodham, of Baltimore, was named Lousy Cur, because that was how I always heard Mr. Woodham's man address him), and women who were invariably called grass widows whether they were spinsters or divorcées or had left a loving husband and family behind. Grass widows, walkers, lungers—what a calm argot it was! Many of fhem were not so much ill as bored and restive—lonely and homesick for the friends and relatives and for the landscapes they had left behind. Ma was a valiant, pretty woman and she was engaged more, really, as a companion than as a nurse. She read aloud to her charges or played Russian bank with them or took them for slow walks. Above all, she listened to their jeremiads, half doleful, half ironic, and tried, with kindly derision, to steer them away from their doldrums. It was this attitude of "You're not alone, everyone is in the same boat" that kept them from, as Ma said, "going mental." A few times, solitary gentlemen fell in love with her, and once she accepted a proposal—from a Mr. Millard, a cheerful banker from Providence, but he died a week before they were to be married. I was relieved, for I had not liked to think of living with a stepfather riddled with bugs.

Soon after Mr. Millard died, Ma went to work for a family named Butler, who had come West from Massachusetts, resentfully but in resignation, bringing their lares in crates and barrels, leaving behind only the Reverend Mr. Butler, who, feeling that he could never duplicate his enlightened congregation, remained in Newton to propagate the Low Church faith. Mrs. Butler, a stout, stern woman who had an advanced degree from Radcliffe, had been promised that here her life, threatened twice by hemorrhages, would be extended to its normal span and that the "tendency" demonstrated by all three of her children would perhaps be permanently checked. Besides the mother and the children, there was a grandmother, not tubercular but senile and helplessly arthritic, and it was for her that Ma had been hired. It was the hardest job she had had, because the old woman, in constant pain, was spiteful and peckish, and several times she reduced my intrepid mother to tears. But this was also the best-paid job she had had, and we were better dressed and better fed than we had been since we left Ohio. We ate butter now instead of margarine and there was even money enough for me to take dancing lessons.

Two of the Butler children, Laura and Ada, were in my grade at school. There was a year's difference between them but the elder, Laura, had been retarded by a six-month session in a hospital. They were the same size and they looked almost exactly alike; they dressed alike, in dark-blue serge jumpers and pale-blue flannelette guimpes and low black boots. They were sickly and abnormally small, and their spectacles pinched their Roman noses. All of us pitied them on their first day at school, because they were so frightened that they would not sit in separate seats, and when Miss Farley asked one of them to sing a scale, she laid her head down on her desk and cried. But we did not waste our sympathy on them long, because after their first show of vulnerability we found them to be haughty and acidulous, and they let it be known that they were not accustomed to going to a public school and associating with just anyone. Nancy Hildreth, whose father was a junkman, excited their especial scorn, and though I had always hated Nancy before, I took her side against them and one day helped her write a poison-pen letter full of vituperative fabrication and threats. We promised that if they did not leave town at once, we would burn their house down. In the end, the letter was too dangerous to send, but its composition had given us great pleasure.

After about a month, Laura and Ada, to my bewilderment and discomfort, began to seek me out at recess, acknowledging in their highhanded way that they knew my mother. They did not use the word "servant" in speaking of her but their tone patronized her and their faint smiles put her in her place. Af first, I rebuffed them, for they were too timid to play as I played; they would never pump up in the swings but would only sit on the seats, dangling their feet in their *outré* boots, trying to pretend that they were not afraid but were superior to our lively games. They would not go near the parallel bars or the teeter-totter, and when the rest of us played crack-the-whip, they cowered, aghast, against the storm doors of the grammar school. But when I complained to Ma of how they tagged after me and tried to make me play their boring guessing games, she asked me, for her sake, to be nice to them, since our livelihood depended on their mother, a possessive woman who would ferociously defend her young. It was hardly fair of Ma to say to me, "Just remember, it's Laura and Ada who give you your dancing lessons," but all the same, because she looked so worried and, even more, because I could not bear to think of not going to my lessons, I obeyed her, and the next day grudgingly agreed to play twenty questions while, out of the corner of my eye, I enviously watched the other children organizing a relay race.

Not long after I made this filial compromise, Laura and Ada began asking me to come home with them after school, and though my friends glared at me as we left the playground together, I never dared refuse. Anyhow, the Butlers' house enchanted me.

It smelled of witch hazel. As soon as we entered the cool and formal vestibule, where a gilded convex mirror hung above a polished console table on which there stood a silver tray for calling cards, the old-fashioned and vaguely medicinal fragrance came to meet me, and I envisaged cut-glass bottles filled with it on the marble tops of bureaus in the bedrooms I had never seen. It made me think of one particular autumn afternoon, in the Ohio woods, when my father and I went for a walk in a clean, soft mist and he cut me a witch-hazel wand, with which I touched a young orange salamander orphaned in the road. As palpable and constant as the smell in the house was the hush of an impending death; somewhere, hidden away in such isolation that I could not even guess where she was, whether upstairs or in a room behind the parlor, lay the grandmother, gradually growing feebler, slowly petering out as my mother spooned up medicine for her and rubbed her ancient back with alcohol. There was hardly a sound in that tomb-still house save for the girls' voices and mine, or the footsteps of their older brother, Lawrence, moving about in his chemical laboratory in the basement.

Again, as vivid as the fragrance and the portentous quiet was the sense of oldness in this house, coming partly from the well-kept antique furniture, the precious Oriental rugs, the Hitchcock settles that formed an inglenook beside the hearth, the quaint photographs hung in deep ovals of rich-brown wood (there was a square piano, and a grandfather clock that told the time as if it knelled a death), but coming even more from the Boston accents and the adult vocabularies and the wise, small eyes of my two playmates. I did not think of them as children my own age but rather as dwarfed grownups, and when I walked along between them, towering over their heads, my own stature seemed eccentric, and in my self-consciousness I would stub my toe or list against one of the little girls (who did not fail to call me awkward). Probably they had never been children; if they had, it had only been for a short time and they had long since cast off the customs and the culture of that season of life. They would not stoop to paper dolls, to pig Latin, to riddles, to practical jokes on the telephone, and in their aloofness from all that concerned me and my fellows they made me feel loutish, noisy, and, above all, stupid.

At other houses, visitors were entertained outside in good weather. In the spring and fall, my friends and I roller-skated or stood on our heads and only looked in at the back door to ask for graham crackers or peanut-butter sandwiches; in the winter we coasted down the hills and occasionally made snow ice cream in some tolerant mother's kitchen. If rain or wind quarantined us, we rowdily played jacks with a golf ball or danced to the music of a Victrola. Whatever we did, we were abandoned to our present pleasure.

But at the Butlers' house the only divertissements were Authors and I Spy, and it was only once in a blue moon that we played those. Usually we sat primly, Laura and Ada and I, in the parlor in three wing chairs, and conversed—it is essential to use that stilted word—of books and of our teachers. The Butler girls were dauntlessly opinionated and called the tune to me, who supinely took it up; I would not defend a teacher

I had theretofore admired if they ridiculed her; I listened meekly when they said that *Rebecca of Sunnybrook Farm* was silly. Sometimes they told me of their dreams, every one of which was a nightmare worse than the one before; they dreamed of alligators and gargantuan cats, of snakes, ogres, and quicksand. I would never tell my vague and harmless dreams, feeling that they would arouse the Butlers' disdain, and once, after they had asked me to and I had refused, Ada said, "It's obvious Jessie doesn't have any dreams, Laura. Didn't Father say that people who sleep soundly have inferior intellects?"

Those long words! They angered and they charmed me, and I listened, wide-eyed, trying to remember them to use them myself—"obvious," "intellect," "logical," "literally." On one of my first visits, Ada, picking up a faded daguerreotype of a bearded man, said, "This is my great-grandfather, Mr. Hartford, whom my brother intends to emulate. Great-grandfather Hartford was a celebrated corporation lawyer." My astonishment at her language must have shown in my face, for she laughed rather unkindly, and, in shocking vernacular, she added, "That is, Larry will be a lawyer *if* he doesn't turn into a lunger first." The Butlers, like the patients at the sanitarium, had their intramural jokes.

Laura and Ada told me anecdotes of Lawrence, who went to high school and was at the head of his class and contributed regularly to the *Scholastic* magazine. They adored him and looked on every word of his as oracular. He was a youth of many parts, dedicated equally to the Muses (he was writing an epic on Governor Bradford, from whom the family was obliquely descended) and to the study of chemistry, and often, commingled with the witch hazel, there was a faint odor of hydrogen sulfide wafted up through the hot-air registers from his basement laboratory. "Lawrence is a genius," said Laura once, stating a fact. "Think of a genius having to live *here* all his life! But, of course, he's stoical."

They told me, also, of incidents in the brilliant university career of their mother, who wore her Phi Beta Kappa key as a lavaliere. They spoke of her having studied under Professor Kittredge, as if this were equivalent to having been presented at court. The formidable bluestocking, Mrs. Butler, seldom came into the parlor, for usually she was out shopping or doctoring or was upstairs writing a play based on the life of Carlyle. But when she did make one of her rare appearances, she took no cognizance of me, although it seemed to me that her discerning eyes, small, like her daughters', and monkey-brown, like theirs, discovered my innermost and frivolous thoughts and read them all with disapproval. She would come in only to remind the girls that that night they must write their weekly letters to their father or to remark indignantly that it was difficult to shop when one was nudged and elbowed by barbarians. For Mrs. Butler had an orthodox aversion to the West, and although almost no one was native to our town, she looked down her pointed nose at the entire population, as if it consisted of nothing but rubes.

After we had talked for half an hour, Laura would go out of the room and come back after a while with a tole tray on which stood a china cocoa set and a plate of Huntley & Palmers sweet biscuits, ordered from S. S. Pierce. We would drink in sips and eat in nibbles and continue our solemn discourse. Often, during this unsatisfying meal (the cookies were dry and the cocoa was never sweet enough for me), the talk became medical, and these sophisticated valetudinarians, nine and ten years old, informed me of extraordinary facts relating to the ills that beset the human flesh and especially those rare and serious ones that victimized them. They took such pride in being hostesses to infirmity that I was ashamed of never having suffered from anything graver than pinkeye, and so light a cast of that that Ma had cured it in a day with boric acid. The Butlers, besides being prey to every known respiratory disorder, had other troubles: Laura had brittle bones that could be fractured by the slightest blow, and Ada had a rheumatic heart, a cross she would bear, she said, until the day she died. They had a quinsy, pleurisy, appendicitis; they were anemic, myopic, asthmatic; and they were subject to hives. They started off the morning by eating yeast cakes, and throughout the day popped pellets and capsules into their mouths; at recess, I would see them at the drinking fountain, gorging on pills. Their brother was a little less frail, but he, too, was often ill. The atmosphere of the house was that of a nursing home, and Ma told me that the whole family lived on invalid fare, on custards and broths and arrowroot pudding. The medicine chest, she said, looked like a pharmacy.

I never stayed long at the Butlers' house, for Laura and Ada had to go upstairs to rest. I stayed only until Lawrence came up from the basement, and as I closed the storm door, I saw, through the side lights, the three of them, weak, intellectual, and Lilliputian, carefully climbing the stairs in single file on their way up to their bedrooms, where they would lie motionless until their dinner of soft white food.

I had had friends before Laura and Ada whose lives were far more overcast by tuberculosis than theirs—children born in the same month and the same year as myself who had already spat out blood, children whose mothers had died in the dead of night, whose fathers would never rise from their beds again. But never before had I been made to feel that my health was a disgrace. Now, under the clever tuition of the

Butlers, I began to look upon myself as a pariah and to be ashamed
not only of myself but of my mother, who was crassly impervious to
disease, although she exposed herself to it constantly. I felt left out, not
only in the Butlers' house but in this town of consumptive confederates.
I began to have fantasies in which both Ma and I contracted mortal
illnesses; in my daydreams, Laura and Ada ate crow, admitting that
they had never had anything half so bad and praising my bravery.
Whenever I sneezed, my heart leapt for joy, and each time my mother
told me she was tired or that her head ached, I hoped for her collapse,
anxious for even a vicarious distinction. I stood before the open window
after a hot bath in the hope of getting pneumonia. Whenever I was
alone in the house, I looked at the pictures in a book of Ma's called
*Diagnostics of Internal Medicine* and studied representations of infantile
spinal paralysis, of sporadic cretinism, of unilateral atrophy of the
tongue. Such was my depravity that when I considered the photograph
of a naked, obscenely fat woman who was suffering, so the caption
read, from "adiposis dolorosa," I thought I could endure even that
disfigurement to best the Butlers.

Because my mother valued health above all else (she was not a prig
about it, she was only levelheaded), I knew that these of mine were
vicious thoughts and deeds, but I could not help myself, for while I
hated the sisters deeply and with integrity, I yearned for their approba-
tion. I wanted most desperately to be a part of this ailing citizenry, to
be able casually to say, "I can't come to your house this afternoon. I
have to have an X-ray." If I had known about such things when I was
nine, I might have been able to see the reasons for my misery, but at
nine one has not yet taken in so much as the meaning of the words
"happy" and "unhappy," and I knew only that I was beyond the pale,
bovine in the midst of nymphs. Epidemics of scarlet fever and diphtheria
passed me by. Other children were bitten by rabid dogs and their names
were printed in the paper, but the only dogs I met greeted me affably
and trotted along beside me if the notion took them to. My classmates
broke their collarbones and had their tonsils taken out. But nothing
happened to me that Unguentine or iodine would not cure, and all the
while the Butlers' pallor seemed to me to deepen and their malicious
egotism to grow and spread.

I do not think that Laura and Ada despised me more than they did
anyone else, but I was the only one they could force to come home
with them. "Who wants to be healthy if being healthy means being a
cow?" said Ada one day, looking at me as I reached for a third insipid
cooky. I withdrew my hand and blushed so hotly in my humiliation
that Laura screamed with laughter and cried, "The friendly cow all red

and white, we give her biscuits with all our might."

Oh, I hated them! I ground my anklebones together, I clenched my fists, I set my jaw, but I could not talk back—not here in this elegiac house where my poor ma was probably simultaneously being insulted by the querulous octogenarian. I could do no more than change the subject, and so I did, but my choice was infelicitous, for, without thinking and with a kind of self-defeating desperation which I saw to be calamitous even before the words were finished, I asked Laura and Ada if they did not like the tumbling we were having in gym, and Ada, horrified, appealed to her sister (she rarely spoke directly to me but through Laura, as if she spoke a separate language that must be translated)—"Oh, tell her that we don't *tumble*"—and her sister went on, "While the rest of you tumble, we write essays." Who could scale this Parnassus? On the flatlands of Philistia, I held my tongue, and I endured, for the sake of learning how to execute a *tour jeté* in Miss Jorene Roy's dance salon.

And then, one day, at the height of my tribulation, Ada, quite by accident, provided me with the means to petrify them for an hour with curiosity and awe. It was nearing Christmas, and the parlor was pranked out with holly wreaths in the windows and a tree in the bay window and early greeting cards lined up in military ranks on the mantel. The girls had been uncommonly animated lately, for their father was coming from Boston to spend two weeks with his brood. I would have the privilege, as would everyone else in town, of hearing him deliver a sermon as the guest preacher at St. John's; the girls' implication was that his erudition was so great that not a soul in this benighted place would understand a word he said. That day, in the dark room—a beautiful, obscuring snow was falling and the heavy branches of the cedar trees leaned against the windows—I envied them this tribal holiday, envied them their peopled house, and pitied myself for being a fatherless and only child. I thought I would have given anything at this moment for a brother, even for Lawrence Butler, with his peaked, mean face and the supercilious way he had of greeting me by saying, "How *do* you do?" Ada, as if she had read my melancholy thoughts and wished to twist the knife, said complacently, "What a shame she doesn't have a father, isn't it, Laura? Laura, ask her what her father died of."

My brilliant answer sprang instantly to my lips without rehearsal or embellishment. "Leprosy," I said, and watched the Bostonians freeze in their attitude as if they were playing Statues. I had learned of leprosy some weeks before from the older sister of a friend, who had held me spellbound. The belief that was soon to be current among my friends and me when the movie *Ben Hur* was to enthrall us all was that lepers slowly vanished, through the rotting away of their fingers and toes, and then of their hands and feet, and then of their arms and legs, and that all exterior appointments, as ears and noses, hair and eyes, fell off like decayed vegetables finally falling from the vine. If this had been my first impression of leprosy, I doubt whether I would, even in this emergency, have thus dispatched my father to his grave, but at the time, thanks to the quixotic older sister, who had got her information in some byway trod by no one but herself, I was under the impression that leprosy was a kind of sleeping sickness brought on by the bite of a lion. This intelligence I passed on to Laura and Ada, glib crocodile tears gathering in the corners of my eyes, and never dreamed, as I pursued my monologue, that they had a Biblical acquaintance with leprosy and that what rooted them to the spot was the revelation that I was the daughter of an unclean man.

Before I could finish my story or make the most of its picturesque details, Laura gasped, "He was unclean!"

"Unclean?" I was incensed. "He was *not* unclean! He washed himself exactly like a cat!" I screamed.

"She said he was asleep for thirty months," said Ada. "Ask her how he could wash in his sleep."

"Well, he did, anyway," I said, flummoxed at being caught out. "I don't know how, but he did. He didn't have fleas, if that's what you mean."

"Unclean," repeated Ada, savoring the word. "Tell her to stay where she is until we get out of the room and tell her never to come back to this house again."

"She never will," said Laura. "She'll be sent to the Fiji Islands or someplace. Lepers can't run around loose."

"Oh, Laura, do you think she has it? Do you think we'll get it?" moaned Ada. "Where is Mother? We must tell her *now!*"

"Be careful, Ada," said Laura. "Go out of the room backwards and keep your eye on her, and if she starts to move, scream. We'll be all right as long as she doesn't touch us."

"Poor Grandmother!" wailed Ada. "Did you think of Grandmother being *touched* all this time by that unclean woman?" She backed to the door, her eyes fixed on me, who could not have moved for anything.

"It's awful!" said Laura, following her sidewise, like a crab. "Of all days for Mother to be at the osteopath! Still, Larry will have an idea."

"Yes," said Ada from the doorway. "Probably Lawrence will send for the Black Maria."

My many selves, all bedlamites, clamored in my faint, sick heart. I wished to tell them on the spot that the whole thing had been a lie. I wished to say it had been a joke. "I was only kidding," I would say. But how heartless that would make me! To jest about my dead father, whom I had loved. Still, I must say something, must in some way exonerate myself and my mother and him. But when I opened my mouth to speak, a throttled sound came out, as surprising to my ears as to theirs, and before I had a chance to find my voice, the girls, appalled, had shut the door. I heard them slowly mount the stairs— even in their alarm they were protective of themselves—and I waited, frozen, for the sound of their avenging brother's footsteps up the stairs from the basement that entered into the front hall. When, at last, mobility returned to me, I slipped out of the parlor and made my way down the corridor to the back of the house, fearful of meeting him in the vestibule. I think I had half expected to encounter my mother in these precincts, but the passage I walked along was doorless until I came to the kitchen, a still, enormous room where there was a soft, sporadic hissing from the banked coal fire in the hooded Glenwood range. Against the varnished wainscotting stood ladder-back chairs, demanding perfect posture of their occupants, and on the trestle table there was a fruit bowl full of wholesome prunes. I knew without looking that there would be nothing good to eat in the cupboards—no brown sugar, no mayonnaise, nothing but those corky cookies. Within the pantry was a deer mouse hunched in death in a trap, and the only ray of light coming through the curtained window made an aura around its freckled fur. I bent to look more closely at the pathetic corpse, and as I did so, I heard, from directly overhead, the sound of Laura and Ada Butler giggling. *At what?* It was a high, aquatic giggle that came in antiphonal wavelets, and then one of the girls began to cough. I fled, mystified, and let myself out into the snow that whirlingly embraced me as I ran blindly home. A block from home, I began wildly to call my cat. "Kitty, kitty, kitty, *kitty!*" I shrieked, to drown out the remembered sound of my terrible lies, and Mr. Woodham's valet, passing me with Lousy Cur on a leash, said, "Whoa, there! Hold on! Where's the fire?" Pretending, with great effort, that I was the same person I had been an hour ago, I stopped and forced myself to grin and to stoop down and lightly pat the sad-eyed dog, and when this amenity was done, I continued on the double-quick.

Mine was a desperate dilemma, for I must either stick to my story and force my mother to confirm it, with the inevitable loss of her job and our probable deportation to the Fiji Islands, or grovel before the girls and admit that I had told a lie. I had told many lies before but I had never told one that involved the far future as well as the near. The consequences of telling my mother that, for example, I had been at the public library when in fact I had been prowling on the dump, hunting for colored bottles, were not serious. I might smart under her disapproval and disappointment (I was not forbidden to go to the dump and the needlessness of the lie made her feel, I suppose, that my character, in general, was devious) but I recovered as soon as her reproach was over. But this one, involving everyone—my father, whom I had, it seemed, maligned (although the concept of uncleanness still puzzled me); my mother, whose job and, indeed, whose whole life I had jeopardized; myself, who could never face the world again and must either wear the mark of the beast forever or spend the rest of my days under a banana tree—this lie was calamity. I thought of stowing away on the interurban to the city, there to lose myself forever in the dark alleys under the viaducts or in the Greek Revival comfort stations at the zoo. I thought of setting fire to the Butlers' house, as Nancy Hildreth and I had threatened to do, and burning them all to death. I thought, more immediately, of shaving off my hair by way of expiation.

When I got to the house, I scooped up Bow, the cat, from the rocking chair where she was sleeping, and went to my bedroom. Without taking off my coat, or even my galoshes, I lay down on my bed, my head beneath two pillows, the outraged and struggling cat clutched in my arms. But before I had time to collect my wits to formulate a plan of action (my disappearance in the city had its attractions), the telephone screamed its two hysterical notes, one short, one long, and I catapulted down the stairs to answer it. Bow trotted after me, resumed her place in the rocking chair, and went instantly to sleep.

It was Laura Butler, who, in a muffled voice, as if she did not want to be overheard by someone nearby, said, "Larry has arranged everything. He knows how we can cure you, and no one will ever know. So you come here tomorrow afternoon on the dot of three o'clock."

The next day was Saturday, and at three o'clock on Saturdays I went to Miss Roy's, and so dear to my heart was dancing class that even in this crisis I protested. "Can't I come at four instead?"

"Why should you come at four?" asked Laura imperiously.

"Because I'm the prince in 'The Cameo Girl.'"

"The *what* in the *what?*"

"I mean I go to dancing class at three," I said. "You know? My fancy-dancing class?"

"Dancing will do you very little good, my dear girl, if your legs fall off," Laura said severely.

"If my legs fall off?" I cried. "What has that got to do with it?"

"Larry says that your legs will undoubtedly fall off if you don't come here at three o'clock tomorrow." There was a slight pause; I felt she was conferring with someone, and she said, "By the bye, your mother doesn't have to have the cure, because she was too old to get leprosy, but of course if you don't have the cure, she'll have to go to the Fiji Islands with you. Larry says that's the law."

"Laura?" My voice explored the tiny tunnel of space between our telephones. Shall I tell her now, I thought. "Laura?" I asked again.

"You know it's Laura," she said, so briskly, so contemptuously that on the instant I was stubborn.

"I can't come," I said.

Aside—to Ada or to Lawrence, I presumed—she said, "We may have to take steps after all. Larry says—"

"Wait!" I cried. "Hey, Laura are you still there? Laura, listen, let me come right now!" For I was thinking of the *entrechat* I had almost perfected, and more than anything else in the world I wanted Miss Roy to tell me, in her jazzy way, that it was "a lulu." But I knew that until my mind lay at rest, I could not dance a single step.

I could hear whispers at the other end, and finally Laura said, "Very well, although it will inconvenience us," and then she warned, "If you are late, my mother will come home. I suppose you don't want *her* to know?"

I sighed deeply into the telephone and heard the other receiver being returned to its hook. Immediately the bell rang again, and Laura said, "Come in ten minutes. We have to get things ready."

The stillness of the house unnerved me as I waited those ten minutes, and, perversely, I frightened myself still more by speaking aloud and hearing my voice come hollowly back to me. "What are they going to do to me, Bow? What *things* have they got to get ready?"

It occurred to me to kill myself. I heard the interurban going out and thought again of skipping town. *Cure* me. What did that mean? I picked up Bow and carried her to the window with me and stood there with her face against mine, watching the storm. She was tense, watching Lousy Cur as he trotted home. "Shall I take the cure, Bow?" I said, and she growled deep in her gentle white belly. "Does that mean yes, Bowcat? Or shall I tell them it was a lie?" She growled again, for Lousy Cur was opposite our house, and, as if he sensed her being there, he paused, one foot uplifted, and gazed with interest at our front door. "Which?" I asked her, and in answer she writhed with a howl from my arms, furious at this double invasion of her privacy. She forgot us both and abruptly took a bath.

My hands were so damp that I could hardly peel my mittens off when

I got to the Butlers' front door, and there was a severe pain in my stomach that made me think I had probably got cancer in punishment for my sin (not, as I might have hoped earlier, as a reward for my virtue). Planless still, my parched lips mouthed my alternative opening speeches: "It was a lie" and "I am ready for the cure." The door opened the moment I rang the bell, and Laura and Ada stood waiting for me in the vestibule, ceremonious in odd brown flannel wrappers with peaked hoods attached to the back of the neck. Gnomelike and leering, they ushered me into the parlor, where they had set up a card table and had covered it with a white cloth. On it stood a group of odd-shaped bottles, which, they explained to me, Larry, the chemist, had lent to them. Did they mean to burn me with acids? To sprinkle me with lye? There was also a covered willowware tureen on the table, and an open Bible.

"Ask her if she believes in God," said Ada.

"Yes," I said quickly, although I was by no means sure. "Listen, Laura—" What if I said the joke was on them? What if I said I'd planned this hoodwink for weeks? The worst they could do was get angry. But I knew I could not convince them, and I floundered, stuttering, beginning, stopping dead.

"The prisoner at the dock wishes to speak," said Ada. "Hear ye! Hear ye!"

"Yes?" said Laura, preoccupied. She had lifted the lid of the tureen and to her sister said, "Do you think the insides of one bird will do?"

Ada, looking into the dish, grimaced. "It will simply have to. There's only one to be had. Larry said it would be all right."

"Do you mind asking him again, just to make sure?"

"I wouldn't dream of disturbing him," said Ada. "He's in his laboratory, boiling his spittle. He can make it turn purple and he can make it turn green."

It made me even more uneasy to know that Lawrence was in the house, and again I started to speak. "Laura, listen to me—" But Laura had picked up the Bible now, and she read, " 'Two birds alive and clean, and cedar wood' "—she held up a beaker half full of cedar berries—" 'and scarlet, and hyssop.' " And her sister pointed to two test tubes, which appeared to be filled, one with red ink and the other with blue.

"Laura—"

"One moment. Be quiet, please." She continued to read, " 'And the priest shall command that one of the birds be killed in an earthen vessel over running water.' " She opened the tureen again and poured out water from a cream pitcher while Ada murmured doubtfully, "Of course, it's already dead."

"A very good thing it is that she believes in God, or the cure would never work," said Laura and went on reading. "'As for the living bird, he shall take it, and the cedar wood, and the scarlet, and the hyssop, and shall dip them and the living bird in the blood of the bird that was killed over the running water.'" With this, she put into the bowl the picture of an eagle, which she had probably cut out of a magazine, and she poured in the red ink, the blue ink, and the cedar berries. Then, bearing the vessel in both hands, she came to where I stood and allowed me to look into a dreadful mess of ink and feathers and the entrails of the chicken that they were doubtless going to have that night for dinner. She dipped her fingers into the stew, and though she shuddered and made a face, she persevered, and before my nose she dangled a bit of dripping innards.

This was enough for me. I would not be touched by those slithering, opalescent intestines, and I shrank back and I cried out, "Will you listen to me? I told a lie!"

Laura's look roasted and froze me, sent me to jail, to hell; it drew and quartered me. "A lie!" she exclaimed, as if I had confessed to murder. Ada turned to her sister with a pout and said crossly, "I *told* you it would never work."

Laura continued to look hard at me, but at last her face relaxed and, patronizing, like a minister, speciously kind, like a schoolteacher, she said, "Now, what's all this about a lie?"

"He didn't die of leprosy," I said. I looked at my feet and moved them slightly, so that the toes of my shoes pointed to the hearts of two roses in the carpet.

"Why did you say that he did?"

"Because—"

"It's more important, I should think," said Ada sulkily, "to find out what he *did* die of. It's quite possible that he died of something worse."

"Why did you say that he did?" said Laura ignoring her.

"Because it was a joke."

"A joke? I thought you said you had told a lie. There is a world of difference between the two, Jessie. Well, which was it, a joke or a lie?"

"A joke!" I cried, almost in tears.

"Do you hear that, Laura?" said Ada. "She tells a *joke* about the deceased."

"I mean it was a lie," I said. I was on the verge of a fearful sobbing. "A lie, and I am sorry." The smell of witch hazel was inordinately dense. In the silence, I heard the click of a ball on the Christmas tree. Suddenly, my ignorance of where my mother was in this unhealthy house terrified me, and I loudly said, "How is your grandmother today?"

"Stick to the subject," said Laura.

But Ada was glad to tell me. "Grandmother is not well at all today. She had a bilious attack this morning. So did I."

She smiled smugly at me, and I, magically emboldened by my distaste, moved to the door, and as I went, I said, "*I* am never sick. I have never been sick in my life."

"Lucky you," gloated Ada.

"What did he die of?" persisted Laura.

"He got shot out hunting, if you want to know," I told them. "My father was as tall as this room. The district nurse told Ma that I am the healthiest girl in town. Also I have the best teeth."

Across those small, old faces there flickered a ray of curiosity to know, perhaps, how the other half lived, and for just that split second I pitied them. My mind cleared and I realized that all this torment had been for nothing. If the Butlers had tried to blacken my name for telling a lie, no one would have believed them, for they had no friends, and, by the same token, if they had noised it about that my father had died of leprosy, I could have said *they* were telling lies. Now I was exalted and hungry and clean, and when I had put on my coat and opened the door, I cried exuberantly, "So long, kids, see you in church!"—a flippancy I would not have dared utter in that house two hours before. By way of reply, Ada coughed pitifully, professionally.

Until the grandmother died, in April, and Ma took another job, I went two or three afternoons a week to the Butlers' house, and over our light collation, as Laura and Ada called it, we talked steadily and solely of the girls' grave illnesses. But as I left, I always said, with snide solicitude, "Take care of yourselves." They were unshakable; they had the final word: "We will. We have to, you know." My vanity, however, was now quite equal to theirs. Feeling myself to be immortal and knowing myself to be the healthiest girl in town, I invariably cut an affronting caper on the Butlers' lawn and ran off fast, letting the good mountain air plunge deep into my sterling lungs.

# III
## Dark Interiors

# GLADYS SWAN
## LOSING GAME

Born in New York in 1934, Gladys Swan grew up in southern New Mexico and is a graduate of New Mexico Western University and of Claremont Graduate School. "Losing Game" is from a collection of her stories, *On the Edge of the Desert* (1979). Her first novel, *Carnival of the Gods*, is a 1986 publication in the Random House Vintage Contemporaries Series, and she completed a new collection of stories while serving as Distinguished Writer in Residence at the University of Texas at El Paso in 1984–1985.

In "Losing Game," Jason Hummer searches for his father who had deserted the family in Salida, Colorado, many years before, after losing their home in a poker game. But when Jason sees a carnival worker who could be his father, he decides against making himself known. What Jason seeks is more than a gypsy parent: he seeks to inherit an illuminated Western past stripped of lies and legends. Jason's illegitimate grandfather had boasted of being the son of Wild Bill Hickok; it was this presumably false tale that had misguided Jason's father into acting the maverick, the part of the lonely man without need for human ties. When Jason sees his own probable father, he recognizes their flawed inheritance: the present, like the past, gives a prospect of loneliness until one comes to terms with the desert within and outside one's self. In Swan's story, the dark interior of history has to be faced with truth, not with cards and a six-gun.

# LOSING GAME

Turn the things out of a man's pockets and take their testimony: a soft
brown leather billfold worn to limpness without ever having been
made fat with prosperity, home of a few snapshots, social security card,
driver's license, expired; a gadget combining pocketknife, corkscrew,
and can opener; a book of matches, a pocket comb with teeth broken
out; the stub of a pencil; an old pocket watch with the staff gone, around
the house for years lying broken—his father's and now his, therefore
a piece of inheritance; a letter, the last his father had written, the address
more than five years old; two quarters, three dimes, and four pennies.
His belongings—down to the lint in his pockets. Uneasy from the light-
ness of his jacket, he stood, missing something, as though he weren't
all there. They dumped the stuff on the desk and let it sit in a little
heap while they dug out a few facts—to hold against him, he supposed—
to clinch the evidence of what they'd found on him.

Name? Jason Hummer. He'd have lied if his things hadn't been such
a dead giveaway, his principle being never to tell the truth if it gave
somebody a hold over you. But he wasn't sure the lie would make that
much difference. Another name, another man? Jake Hemphill, suppose.
He saw a school janitor sweeping slow, eyes wedded to wastepaper
and wads of chewing gum. John Harding: solid sort—bust a man in
the crockery for making eyes at his wife; good provider. Junius Holloway:
banker, pillar of the church, a power in the town; storm cloud by day,
pillar of smoke by night. Jay Hay: playboy—white convertible, leopard-
skin seat covers; a creature of speed and spring and back-seat quick-hand.
Nope, for better or worse, he was stuck with himself.

Age? Twenty-eight. Hair, brown; eyes, brown. Distinguishing marks
and characteristics? None. No visible scars, birthmarks, carbuncles, tics,
tattoos, hardly even a mole of any size or interest. True, he was looking
a bit shaggy and unkempt.

Occupation? That was a tough one. He had been either too many
things or too few to add up to something you could write in the space
on a printed form. Not that he hadn't been occupied. Handyman, he
said. He'd done enough of carpentry, wiring, plumbing, to qualify. He
couldn't make out what the deputy wrote down. Bum, maybe; vagabond,

147

derelict, good-for-nothing. Vagrant. At the moment, nothing else could be his occupation.

Fingerprints. Right thumb, right hand. Left thumb, left hand. No two sets alike, it occurred to him—like snowflakes. He stared at the mark of his uniqueness. A man was his fingerprint.

The deputy beckoned him down the corridor to the lockup, held open the door of the cell and then shut him in with a clash of iron reverberating, working down his spine. Bunk, chair, open toilet—the comforts of home. He sat down on the bunk, his nostrils hit by the smell of disinfectant, powerful, yet somehow impure, as though tainted by the corpse of whatever it killed. For just beneath the over-bearing smell another odor leaked in, faint but pervasive, a presence almost that could not be drowned out. The residue of occupancy, an odor of staleness, like dirty socks or dried sweat, but more like something that, deprived of light and air, had taken its last breath and given up the ghost.

Well, here I am, he thought, as if he had reached a destination. And the other, where was he? Probably carted off to a hospital somewhere— the man who had fallen among ruffians. And he saw the fellow again, a vivid presence. He was red—face red, hands red. A figure sitting on the curb of the street, dabbing at his face with a handkerchief— covered with paint, or so it looked. But then, it had flashed through his mind, why would anybody be covered with red paint? Blood, he thought, just as quickly; that's blood. And he was close enough now to see that the face was streaming with blood, and the hands and arms. The handkerchief that the fellow kept dabbing in a slow unhurried way was itself red, a piece of bright rag held up to the flow.

"My God, fella, what happened to you?" he said.

"Some guys jumped me. Beat me up. Six of 'em."

Nothing like a fair fight. "You can't sit here. Where do you live? Want me to call somebody?"

"Better call the cops."

He didn't much want to call the police. As with doctors and lawyers and hospital personnel and public officials in general, he was content to live and let live. But the case seemed pressing. He crossed the street to the pay phone and put in one of his dimes. If he'd had any sense, he'd have quietly disappeared after doing his little duty. But the fellow was beaten up pretty bad. By the time he got back, he had passed out and was lying on the street. So he stayed till the cops came. He told them what he knew, while a few by-standers milled around, soaking up the scene and waiting till the ambulance came with a fine wail of the siren. They would have to start asking him questions. Once they got on the trail, they kept it up till they had him treed: no job, no money, no place to go. So they hauled him in. Did they suspect him of having beaten up the fellow himself? He explained that he'd come to town trying to locate a relative. Looking for somebody to leech onto, he could hear them thinking; yeah, we know all about it. Actually, he had already been to the town from where his father had sent the letter but hadn't found him. They hauled him in.

"Say, man, what'd they grab you for?"

He looked over to the shape leaning against the bars of the cell across the corridor. "For being plain damn dumb."

"Join the club. Never trust a buddy. Remember that—rule of life. Don't even let a guy smoke in here. What a fleabag."

Here he was—among those nameless others who had bequeathed their presence, a part of that brotherhood that had stood on the wrong side of a barred window. The walls bore the marks of their presence. Names and dates, notches to mark off the days, drawings of women with extraordinary breasts and thighs like columns and explicit crotches —goddesses of waiting and boredom. Obscenities, doodles, scribblings, even a bit of verse carefully boxed in. The pencil had smudged a little, blurring some of the words, but he could make them out:

> The five cards in the cradle
> Are the five cards dealt by fate
> You're in a game of poker
> And luck is an inside straight.

Except for a few dirty limericks, he hadn't been much for verse since the fifth grade, when Mrs. Pennuel had made them memorize it and recite it to the class. But it was mostly high-minded and instructive and never stooped to anything so low as a poker game:

> Build thee more stately mansions,
> O my soul, as the swift seasons roll,

he dredged up from somewhere, unable for the life of him to think of the next line—what you did when you found a place you liked, if you ever did, that was clean and livable and not too high in the upkeep. He had not gotten things too well by heart, having lost all interest in scholarship when the teachers quit reading stories out loud and letting the kids draw pictures with crayons. His mother had spent a lot of words and useless grief trying to shame him with the fact that she had always been at the top of her class in school. With slightly more effect, she used to sit with her sewing to keep an eye on him while he struggled through his homework and would thump him on the head with her thimble when she saw his attention lag. Maybe if she had thumped him harder, the thought occurred to him, circumstances would have thumped him less; for he'd maybe have learned whatever it was that was supposed to do him some good. He read on, squinting to make out the words:

> Sometimes a pair is winner,
> Sometimes a flush is not,
> And you'll lose all your singles
> If losing is your lot.

Good grief, he thought—sure for a moment that his father must have stood in that self-same cell. It could have been his voice speaking, except for the rhyme. Whoever it was must have fared just as badly at poker. A descendant of Wild Bill Hickok? Like his father? Was there something at the marrow of things, he wondered, that made a pair of aces and a pair of eights unlucky? Something you'd get shot in the back for holding? . . . At least James Butler Hickok was the sort of man you could feel bad about getting it. Which he'd started doing about the time he was nine years old. Yes indeed. Drama of the Old West, Part I:


### THE TRUE SON OF WILD BILL HICKOCK

or

### Ladies, If you Have a Love-Child, Lie a Little


*Scene: Salida, Colorado, on the banks of the old Arkansas. White frame house with pillars holding up the front porch. A swing on that porch. The noise of that swing as it goes back and forth, not a squeak exactly, but a low-toned rake, a comfortable sort of noise. Himself on the porch swing, listening:*

I tell you, boy, there was no finer man than Wild Bill, handsome and brave. . . .

*The old man, his grandfather, talking—in his eighties now, come down to Salida, Colorado, to fret out his last years—a straight-backed, hawk-nosed old man, impatient of old age.*

When I was grown up some, I went round to all the men I could find who'd known him when he was marshall in Abilene and Hays City. See, looka here, this is his picture.

*The boy looks at the picture, studies it:*

He looks kinda mean with that mustache.

*His grandfather takes the picture, holds it out in front of him, can't hold it steady because his hands shake.*

No, boy, he wasn't mean, nor wild. They called him Wild Bill, only he wasn't mean and ornery, not like the ruffians he was trying to take a little law and order to in them wild cow towns. He never killed a man but in self-defense.

*The boy looks at the picture again to make sure.*

*His grandfather:* Once three men set upon him at the same time and he shot his way out alive. You had to defend yourself in those days. Still do. *(Little sharp laugh.)* And you remember that—the manly art of self-defense. *(Gives the boy a little friendly poke in the chest.)* And remember what you came from. Remember now that when Jack McCall shot him in the back not all his blood ran onto the ground. The blood that is flowing in your veins, just like the blood flowing in mine, is the blood of Wild Bill Hickok. . . .

*The old man holding him by a look, as though he were hypnotizing him. ENTER a thin, long-faced, bony woman.*

Wild Bill Poppycock, you mean. That's the only stuff flowing around here. No blood neither—just hot wind.

*They look up. His mother, having entered upon the scene unnoticed, stands in front of them, arms akimbo.*

*His grandfather:* What do you mean, daughter, coming sneaking up that-a-way? And what do you know about what I'm saying to the boy?

*His mother:* You ain't no more descended from Wild Bill Hickok than I am. I know all about that: Well, I s'pose your ma had to have somebody to lay it on to—ha! Well, she picked one all right. To take the edge off the disgrace.

*The old man stands up, red in the face, the veins in his forehead looking as though they will burst. The boy looks at his mother, then at his grandfather. His stomach hurts the way it did when he ate too much candy and junk at the carnival.*

*His grandfather:* Shame. How dare you say a thing like that to me? And here in front of the boy . . .

*His mother:* And shame on you, filling up his head with lies and tales—all kind of nonsense. Hard enough time I got as it is pounding some sense into him. What's going to happen to him in the world, the kind of stuff you're loading him up with?

*His grandfather (under his breath):* Bitch.

*His mother:* What? Yes, well, I know how it is. You never liked me from the beginning. Thought I wasn't good enough for that precious son of yours. Well, you don't have to like me much longer—that's how it is.

*Words flying back and forth as the lights fade, carrying both his grandfather and mother into the darkness. A single spotlight lingers momentarily on him, held for questioning:*

> *??????? GRANDSON OF A NOTORIOUS LIAR*
> *AND SON OF A BITCH???????*

●     ●     ●     ●

They brought him a tray of food, recalling to him that he hadn't eaten yet that day.

"Don't look too close at them beans," the fellow across the corridor told him. "You might see something move."

"Well, I'm needing a little red meat."

"Haw, well, it'll put hair on your chest."

The beans were hard and sapless like they'd had to be unstuck from the bottom of the pot. There were potatoes and something else swimming around in the gravy. He ate it all, wiped round the plate with a piece of bread, and sat back content, though he knew that the flavors would keep him company the rest of the night. True, he'd eaten worse, but not much worse.

●     ●     ●     ●

But his mother had to be wrong. For if his father didn't bear Wild Bill's blood, he certainly shared his fatality at poker. Not that there was any other resemblance between Wild Bill and his father, a slim, middling sort of man who'd lost most of his hair and gone slack in the gut by the time he was thirty and could only spend the rest of his life getting balder and slacker. The only thing he'd managed to hold onto was a knot of worry above his nose. For the things that belonged to him had a way of deserting him and the rest had a way of going against him. Penniless relatives and stray cats turned up at the door, starving hungry and howling for food; and small-time hoods smelled him out for a little protection money like rats after crumbs. Otherwise he might have done decently enough with the bar he ran there in Salida, Colorado, though his wife never liked to mention what it was that bought the victuals and paid the bills. She'd have been better pleased if he'd run a grocery or even a feed store or traveled around selling some gadget that lightened your chores.

When he thought of his father, he could sometimes hear his voice and remember something of his general shape; but he could but dimly see his face. Nor could he put his impressions together to form a picture of the man. Specifically he remembered the three signs of his father's presence those evenings he was home and it came time for the kids to go to bed. He and his sister would be making a ruckus, chasing each other around the house, teasing and throwing pillows. His father would clear his throat. That was the announcement that they'd better quit horsing around and do what they were told. Nobody would pay any heed. Next his father would rattle his newspaper. They'd keep on. But when he started knocking the ashes out of his pipe, they'd tear upstairs. He didn't know why. He didn't know what his father would have done if they hadn't. Perhaps they knew by instinct that they oughtn't face him with the crisis. For it was his mother that always gave them a hiding. She kept a switch and she knew how to use it.

So what happened afterwards didn't fit in at all; and nobody could say what it was that got into his father the night of the poker game. He wasn't what you'd call a gambling man. Two or three times a month he'd play a game of nickel ante, his one diversion. So there was nothing new in that. It was true that Avery was a stranger in town, and maybe a sharp stranger, though he couldn't picture it. More than likely, Avery simply fell into something. But if he were actually looking for a way to make his fortune, Fate led him to the right place. Even so, that still didn't account for his father. Maybe his father didn't know what was happening to him, found himself in so deep that he couldn't get out. Or maybe he'd thought he could track down the luck that was always giving him the slip. Or maybe he'd picked up the cards as though the next day didn't matter because he didn't want to think about the next day.

Or maybe it was just a kind of fatality. Maybe the moment you were born, somewhere else was born the man who'd do you the dirty—the Jack McCall who'd shoot you down: like the yolk and the white of an egg. No matter how far away he was, something must be that beckoned a man's destroyer. Then the thought came to him, How about if one created him? It was a puzzle.

In any case, he didn't know what had gone on in the back room of the bar. The only part of the drama he knew about came after the game, and perhaps that was the only part that mattered. Drama of the Old West, Part II:

## THE ERRING SON OF WILD BILL HICKOCK
or
When the Chips Are Down, Boys, Never Let a Female
Get the Drop on You

Scene i:

*Darkness. He wakes to find voices rising up, piercing sleep like knives. He is in bed. He lies listening:*

You're crazy. Drunk or plain crazy. Keeping me up till all hours, worried to death you'd got yourself killed or something worse. And now you come telling me you've lost the place. You're drunk or crazy.

*He strains to catch the answering voice, his father's—low but not blurred.*

Yes, lost it.

*His mother:* You mean . . . you mean you'd gamble away our living? You'd risk that? . . .

*His father:* Risked it and lost it.

*His mother:* Fine, oh that's fine, and what are we supposed to do now? Turn us out into the street. And what do you want—me to walk the street now? I'd prob'ly get us a better living than you ever got.

*His father:* Hush up, Ella, you'll wake the kids.

*His mother:* Don't you be telling me when to shut my mouth. I don't care if I wake the dead. You snake in the grass, you crawling, low-bellied, lying, sneaking . . . I could kill you for this. Oh, I could kill you.

*He gets up out of bed and quietly slips downstairs to the doorway of the living room. He blinks in the light.*

*His father:* You never liked the place anyway.

*His mother:* Oh, so that's how it is. She doesn't like it, so the hell with it. So now what are you going to do, you yellow-bellied, slack-gutted flea-brain?

*His father:* I don't know yet.

*His mother turns, rushes to the little cupboard just to the side of the fireplace and takes out the Colt Peacemaker his grandfather swore had belonged to Wild Bill Hickok himself.*

Get out. Get out.

*His father:* Don't wave that thing around—it's loaded.

*He rushes in, throws himself down, and clings to his father's knees.*

*His mother:* What are you doing up? Get yourself out of here. This is nothing to do with you. Go on, get, before I take the switch to you.

*His father:* Put that goddam thing away. But then I s'pose you want my blood too. Don't worry, I'm leaving in the morning.

*His mother:* We can get along without you—all you've ever done around here. Well, all I'm saying is you'd better get your traps and haul your dead ass out of here by noon and not a minute past.

*His mother turns and goes out of the room, throws down a blanket and pillow into the middle of the floor.*

Now get on out. If you want to sleep, you can sleep on the front porch . . . *(then noticing him).* And you get on up to bed.

*He goes back up to bed and lies there in the dark. He can't close his eyes. He lies there holding up the darkness with his eyeballs. Suppose his father could take hold of that Colt and go after the fellow who'd done him in. Then there wouldn't be any more trouble. But there is a question. He slides out of bed, opens the window, and climbs out onto the roof and shinnies down the pillar. His father lies curled up in the porch swing, his head turned toward the back. He squats down beside him.*

Pa, what happened, Pa? Did he cheat you?

*His father turns over, peers at him in the dark.*

Did he cheat you, Pa?

*His father leans over.*

No, boy, he won it fair and square. *(A long pause.)* Sometimes you. . . . There's something . . . and you got to. . . .

*The light goes on inside the house. The sound of steps.*

*His father:* Quick, now, get on back to bed before your ma catches you out here.

## Scene ii

*Carrying his suitcase down the sidewalk of the empty street at half-past noon, his father rides out of town for the last time—on the Greyhound.*

●    ●    ●    ●

It was a night without peace. He'd dropped off to sleep when the door of the cell next to his clashed shut on a pair of drunks they'd hauled in from somewhere. One got sick all over the floor and the other kept yelling for somebody to come and clean it up. Nobody came. The smell was enough to unlatch his innards, and though he tried to escape into sleep, the smell kept pulling him back.

They let him out the next morning after breakfast.

Sunlight took him by surprise, so accustomed had he become to the glare of artificial light, which had its own kind of dimness. But when his eyes were used to the sunlight and he'd filled his lungs with air, he felt good all of a sudden, as though air and sun alone were cause for celebration. Which direction now—north, south, east, west? He had one more place to look before he called it quits and moved on. He was almost afraid to look further, afraid the old man was dead or else lying in an alley somewhere curled up next to an empty bottle of rotgut. The one place he still had to look was the fairgrounds. He'd come upon an old fellow in a grocery store/filling station who seemed to know every- thing that had happened in those parts for the last seventy-five years and who'd told him he thought—yep, name sounds familiar—he knew a Hummer out at the fairgrounds working in the carnival. And if it were his father, what sort of thing would he be doing there?

Jason waited till nearly dark before he set out to answer the question, walking along the highway out to the fairgrounds, where all the cars were headed, a lot of them jammed full of teenagers in a hurry. He found it pleasant walking while the evening dimmed down to the last streaks of sunset fading behind the hills. The air was cool with the lateness of summer, suggesting what would come: the kids starting back to school; the carnival packing up, the rides being taken down in great chunks of metal; the empty grounds left for the wind to pick at scraps of paper.

But there ahead, the sky was all livened up with strings and circles of lights, though it wasn't dark enough yet for them to stand out sharply. As he approached, he thought he smelled hot dogs. Food—and it smelled good. Since he wasn't about to pay for a ticket, he walked around till he found a place where he could slip into the carnival itself, in between the trucks that held the generating equipment.

He came in near where the ferris wheel was in motion to the grind and putt of the motor below. There were people on it, though not many, the empty seats rattling as they swung back and forth. Two girls flew shrieking past, clinging to each other as they went flying up, then down to catch the lights of the town in their laps. It might be, he considered, taking up possibilities, that his father was selling tickets for one of the rides or maybe peddling popcorn or candied apples, though he couldn't feature it.

He threaded his way through a crowd that was beginning to thicken up with ranchers and town folks with all their kids. Little kids yammering and pulling at the big folks to take them on the rides or buy them popcorn, and solemn staring-eyed babies kept up past their bedtime. He had to work his way around a bunch of the older kids laughing and talking, arms knotted, not looking out where they were going. A few of the gray-headed and thickset had plumped themselves down at the bingo game—a row of bottoms along a bench. The caller, with a voice that twanged like catgut, stood in the middle by a table piled up with lamps and waffle irons and sets of glasses and ashtrays on stands and black ceramic panthers, and called out the numbers.

Not at the ferris wheel or the bingo game, nor as a barker for the freak show, where the man with the rubber neck and the amazing man-woman were on display. Nor did he find him with the girlie show, where the girls stood out on the platform with set faces, like plaster casts, not giving anything away for nothing.

He paused a moment by the merry-go-round and breathed in the smell of hot dogs and popcorn and listened to the calliope and watched scenes of Indian maidens and swans, sailboats and islands with palm trees flash by. He'd wandered here and there without seeing anybody that bore the slightest resemblance to his father, but then he couldn't be sure he would recognize him after all these years. And the question occurred to him, What would he do if he did see him? All the time he had been looking, the question had never crossed his mind; only now when there was a real chance of finding him. For now he was convinced that his father would be working one of the booths. His father ought to know something about games of chance.

For the crowd it was a question of whether to throw darts at balloons or balls at weighted dummies, or toss rings around knife handles, or nickels at little squares; whether to pick a number that might come up at the spin of the wheel or place a coin on a horse in a miniature race— so as to win one of the great bright pink or blue pandas on the shelves or a cigarette lighter, pocketknife, or watch that glittered under the lights, but more likely one of the glass ashtrays hidden under the counter. He watched a young fellow throwing balls, three tosses for a quarter, while a girl waited for him to win one of the giant stuffed pandas for her. He had a pile of quarters on the counter and was determined to do it.

When Jason looked their way, the operators caught his eye, shouted to him to try his luck. "You wanna play, mister? You win some of these, eh?" The slang hammered out in a foreign accent made him pause to look at the face: high cheekbones, red hair cruelly dyed. But it was the voice that got him—hard beyond the hardness of things, but keen-edged with the sharper's interest in getting around them. She was turned sharper just like a man. A great screeching racket met his ears before he saw that the next booth was filled with cages of parakeets. "Come on, mister, ya get de boid." The flash of a gold tooth came with the laugh. Jason couldn't imagine his father among the sharpers, a crew that seemed to have come from an alien place, if not a foreign country. Some of them had served time, he knew. Nobody ever gave his right name if he was a carny, and if you were smart, you didn't ask.

Then he saw him, or at least he saw a man that could have started out as his father: an old man, nearly bald, wearing blue jeans and a checkered flannel shirt. The hair he had left was a shaggy fringe of gray above his ears and around his skull, and his belly was such that he had to belt his pants below it, two skinny little legs taking him the rest of the way to the ground. His care was half a dozen Shetland ponies rigged up to a wheel to make them walk in a circle and saddled up for children to ride. He lifted up the children and set them in the saddles and guided their feet into the stirrups and set the little animals to plodding around in a ring. The ride over, he lifted the children down and turned them loose. Then he went around to the ponies in turn, patting each on the head, giving each a bite of the apple he'd taken out of the pocket of the coat lying across the railing. Then he hoisted up a new set of children. But he had no eyes for the children, nor for their folks, who stood smiling and calling and waving to the tots in the ring. He had to get done with them to have his turn with the ponies.

As Jason watched, it came to him quite without premeditation that he would never go up to his father, even if he were positive it was he, and make himself known. For his father was no more linked to the past that included him than was one of the horses: he was a man alone, without wife or child or any other kin. It seemed that he might as well have forsaken humankind altogether and gone to the wilderness to live among mavericks, listening to coyotes and following the track of the wild mustang. But he had affection for the little horses, stroking their heads, giving each a bite of apple, a lump of sugar.

Uncertain for a moment where he ought to head, Jason stepped back into the crowd and drifted on past to the end of the midway. So this is what it all adds up to, he thought, turning to walk down the other side. Losing game or ace in the hole? The manly art of self-defense? He had a mental image of his father taking up the pack of cards and tossing them into the air, as though casting them into the teeth of fate, in that moment of risking everything and losing everything—to win back himself. He stopped for a moment, feeling slightly dizzy, the way he had felt that morning when he came out of jail. He wanted to laugh and he could have wept, and he could not tell an old ache from a new sort of awe, now that he had come and received his father's blessing: "You're all on your lonesome, boy. You're all on your own."

# RAYMOND CARVER
## SO MUCH WATER
## SO CLOSE TO HOME

Raymond Carver was born in 1938 in Clatskanie, Oregon, and graduated from Humboldt State University in Arcata, California, in 1963. In addition to his books of short fiction—notably *Will You Please Be Quiet, Please?* (1978), *Fires: Essays, Poems, Stories 1966-1982* (1983), and *Cathedral* (1983), he has brought out five collections of poetry. In 1985 he received *Poetry* magazine's Levinson Prize. In 1986 he was guest editor of *Best American Short Stories*. A new book of short stories is scheduled for Fall 1987 publication. After teaching at Iowa, Texas, California, and Syracuse universities, Carver returned in 1983 to live in the Pacific Northwest.

"So Much Water So Close to Home," which originally appeared in slightly different form in Carver's *Furious Seasons* (1977), is reprinted from *Fires*. It is the work of a poet with imaginative kinship to classical Greek tragedy as well as to nineteenth-century American literature. Carver's Washington is no more, but probably no less, important to his tale of terror and despair than is Nathaniel Hawthorne's Massachusetts to, for example, "Young Goodman Brown." Both storytellers present characters poised on the edge of the spirit's abyss; both set nature's potential space in contrast to confined consciousness, leaving only implied loopholes for the soul and the rest to savagery. Neither story— Hawthorne's on the early frontier, Carver's on the frontier at its far western expansion—has a community of love and faith for our comfort: Goodman Brown's experience of evil separates him from Faith, his wife, and the onslaught of Claire's suspicions and forebodings separates her from Stuart, her husband, and undermines faith in her yearnings for love and "home." The western frontier is closed. There is no place to go. Dubious is the prospect of human caring, of rational, ritualized behavior that is an alternative to the dark interior of the wilderness. For it is human nature that, in tragic vision, is also part of uncontrollable elements, like an unburied corpse (an image suggestive of Sophocles's *Antigone*). That corpse, for Claire, previsions her own.

# SO MUCH WATER
# SO CLOSE TO HOME

My husband eats with good appetite but he seems tired, edgy. He chews slowly, arms on the table, and stares at something across the room. He looks at me and looks away again. He wipes his mouth on the napkin. He shrugs and goes on eating. Something has come between us though he would like me to believe otherwise.

"What are you staring at me for?" he asks. "What is it?" he says and puts his fork down.

"Was I staring?" I say and shake my head stupidly, stupidly.

The telephone rings. "Don't answer it," he says.

"It might be your mother," I say. "Dean—it might be something about Dean."

"Watch and see," he says.

I pick up the reciever and listen for a minute. He stops eating. I bite my lip and hang up.

"What did I tell you?" he says. He starts to eat again, then throws the napkin onto his plate. "Goddamn it, why can't people mind their own business? Tell me what I did wrong and I'll listen! It's not fair. She was dead, wasn't she? There were other men there besides me. We talked it over and we all decided. We'd only just got there. We'd walked for hours. We couldn't just turn around, we were five miles from the car. It was opening day. What the hell, I don't see anything wrong. No, I don't. And don't look at me that way, do you hear? I won't have you passing judgment on me. Not you."

"You know," I say and shake my head.

"What do I know, Claire? Tell me. Tell me what I know. I don't know anything except one thing: you hadn't better get worked up over this." He gives me what he thinks is a *meaningful* look. "She was dead, dead, dead, do you hear?" he says after a minute. "It's a damn shame, I agree. She was a young girl and it's a shame, and I'm sorry, as sorry as anyone else, but she was dead, Claire, dead. Now let's leave it alone. Please, Claire. Let's leave it alone now."

"That's the point," I say. "She was dead. But don't you see? She needed help."

"I give up," he says and raises his hands. He pushes his chair away from the table, takes his cigarettes and goes out to the patio with a can of beer. He walks back and forth for a minute and then sits in a lawn chair and picks up the paper once more. His name is there on the first page along with the names of his friends, the other men who made the "grisly find."

I close my eyes for a minute and hold onto the drainboard. I must not dwell on this any longer. I must get over it, put it out of sight, out of mind, etc., and "go on." I open my eyes. Despite everything, knowing all that may be in store, I rake my arm across the drainboard and send the dishes and glasses smashing and scattering across the floor.

He doesn't move. I know he has heard, he raises his head as if listening, but he doesn't move otherwise, doesn't turn around to look. I hate him for that, for not moving. He waits a minute, then draws on his cigarette and leans back in the chair. I pity him for listening, detached, and then settling back and drawing on his cigarette. The wind takes the smoke out of his mouth in a thin stream. Why do I notice that? He can never know how much I pity him for that, for sitting still and listening, and letting the smoke stream out of his mouth. . . .

He planned his fishing trip into the mountains last Sunday, a week before the Memorial Day weekend. He and Gordon Johnson, Mel Dorn, Vern Williams. They play poker, bowl, and fish together. They fish together every spring and early summer, the first two or three months of the season, before family vacations, little league baseball, and visiting relatives can intrude. They are decent men, family men, responsible at their jobs. They have sons and daughters who go to school with our son, Dean. On Friday afternoon these four men left for a three day fishing trip to the Naches River. They parked the car in the mountains and hiked several miles to where they wanted to fish. They carried their bedrolls, food and cooking utensils, their playing cards, their whisky. The first evening at the river, even before they could set up camp, Mel Dorn found the girl floating face down in the river, nude, lodged near the shore in some branches. He called the other men and they all came to look at her. They talked about what to do. One of the men—Stuart didn't say which—perhaps it was Vern Williams, he is a heavy-set, easy man who laughs often—one of them thought they should start back to the car at once. The others stirred the sand with their shoes and said they felt inclined to stay. They pleaded fatigue, the late hour, the fact that the girl "wasn't going anywhere." In the end they all decided to stay. They went ahead and set up the camp and built a fire and drank their whisky. They drank a lot of whisky and when the moon came up they talked about the girl. Someone thought they should do something to prevent the body from floating away. Somehow they thought that this might create a problem for them if it floated away during the night. They took flashlights and stumbled down to the river. The wind was up, a cold wind, and waves from the river lapped the sandy bank. One of the men, I don't know who, it might have been Stuart, he could have done it, waded into the water and took the girl by the fingers and pulled her, still face down, closer to shore, into shallow water, and then took a piece of nylon cord and tied it around her wrist and then secured the cord to tree roots, all the while the flashlights of the other men played over the girl's body. Afterwards, they went back to camp and drank more whisky. Then they went to sleep. The next morning, Saturday, they cooked breakfast, drank lots of coffee, more whisky, and then split up to fish, two men upriver, two men down.

That night, after they had cooked their fish and potatoes and had more coffee and whisky, they took their dishes down to the river and rinsed them off a few yards from where the body lay in the water. They drank again and then they took out their cards and played and drank until they couldn't see the cards any longer. Vern Williams went to sleep, but the others told coarse stories and spoke of vulgar or dishonest escapades out of their past, and no one mentioned the girl until Gordon Johnson, who'd forgotten for a minute, commented on the firmness of the trout they'd caught, and the terrible coldness of the river water. They stopped talking then but continued to drink until one of them tripped and fell cursing against the lantern, and then they climbed into their sleeping bags.

The next morning they got up late, drank more whisky, fished a little as they kept drinking whisky. Then, at one o'clock in the afternoon, Sunday, a day earlier than they'd planned, they decided to leave. They took down their tents, rolled their sleeping bags, gathered their pans, pots, fish and fishing gear, and hiked out. They didn't look at the girl again before they left. When they reached the car they drove the highway in silence until they came to a telephone. Stuart made the call to the sheriff's office while the others stood around in the hot sun and listened. He gave the man on the other end of the line all of their names—they had nothing to hide, they weren't ashamed of anything—and agreed to wait at the service station until someone could come for more detailed directions and individual statements.

He came home at eleven o'clock that night. I was asleep but woke when I heard him in the kitchen. I found him leaning against the refrigerator drinking a can of beer. He put his heavy arms around me and rubbed his hands up and down my back, the same hands he'd left with two days before, I thought.

In bed he put his hands on me again and then waited, as if thinking of something else. I turned slightly and then moved my legs. Afterwards, I know he stayed awake for a long time, for he was awake when I fell asleep; and later, when I stirred for a minute, opening my eyes at a slight noise, a rustle of sheets, it was almost daylight outside, birds were singing, and he was on his back smoking and looking at the curtained window. Half-asleep I said his name, but he didn't answer. I fell asleep again.

He was up this morning before I could get out of bed—to see if there was anything about it in the paper, I suppose. The telephone began to ring shortly after eight o'clock.

"Go to hell," I heard him shout into the receiver. The telephone rang again a minute later, and I hurried into the kitchen. "I have nothing else to add to what I've already said to the sheriff. That's right!" He slammed down the receiver.

"What is going on?" I said, alarmed.

"Sit down," he said slowly. His fingers scraped, scraped against his stubble of whiskers. "I have to tell you something. Something happened while we were fishing." We sat across from each other at the table, and then he told me.

I drank coffee and stared at him as he spoke. Then I read the account in the newspaper that he shoved across the table: ". . . unidentified girl eighteen to twenty-four years of age . . . body three to five days in the water . . . rape a possible motive . . . preliminary results show death by strangulation . . . cuts and bruises on her breasts and pelvic area . . . autopsy . . . rape, pending further investigation."

"You've got to understand," he said. "Don't look at me like that. Be careful now, I mean it. Take it easy, Claire."

"Why didn't you tell me last night?" I asked.

"I just . . . didn't. What do you mean?" he said.

"You know what I mean," I said. I looked at his hands, the broad fingers, knuckles covered with hair, moving, lighting a cigarette now, fingers that had moved over me, into me last night.

He shrugged. "What difference does it make, last night, this morning? It was late. You were sleepy, I thought I'd wait until this morning to tell you." He looked out to the patio: a robin flew from the lawn to the picnic table and preened its feathers.

"It isn't true," I said. "You didn't leave her there like that?"

He turned quickly and said, "What'd I do? Listen to me carefully now, once and for all. Nothing happened. I have nothing to be sorry for or feel guilty about. Do you hear me?"

I got up from the table and went to Dean's room. He was awake and in his pajamas, putting together a puzzle. I helped him find his clothes and then went back to the kitchen and put his breakfast on the table. The telephone rang two or three more times and each time Stuart was abrupt while he talked and angry when he hung up. He called Mel Dorn and Gordon Johnson and spoke with them, slowly, seriously, and then he opened a beer and smoked a cigarette while Dean ate, asked him about school, his friends, etc., exactly as if nothing had happened.

Dean wanted to know what he'd done while he was gone, and Stuart took some fish out of the freezer to show him.

"I'm taking him to your mother's for the day," I said.

"Sure," Stuart said and looked at Dean who was holding one of the frozen trout. "If you want to and he wants to, that is. You don't have to, you know. There's nothing wrong."

"I'd like to anyway," I said.

"Can I go swimming there?" Dean asked and wiped his fingers on his pants.

"I believe so," I said. "It's a warm day so take your suit, and I'm sure your grandmother will say it's okay."

Stuart lighted a cigarette and looked at us.

Dean and I drove across town to Stuart's mother's. She lives in an apartment building with a pool and a sauna bath. Her name is Catherine Kane. Her name, Kane, is the same as mine, which seems impossible. Years ago, Stuart has told me, she used to be called Candy by her friends. She is a tall, cold woman with white-blonde hair. She gives me the feeling that she is always judging, judging. I explain briefly in a low voice what has happened (she hasn't yet read the newspaper) and promise to pick Dean up that evening. "He brought his swimming suit," I say. "Stuart and I have to talk about some things," I add vaguely. She looks at me steadily from over her glasses. Then she nods and turns to Dean, saying "How are you, my little man?" She stoops and puts her arms around him. She looks at me again as I open the door to leave. She has a way of looking at me without saying anything.

When I return home Stuart is eating something at the table and drinking beer. . . .

After a time I sweep up the broken dishes and glassware and go outside. Stuart is lying on his back on the grass now, the newspaper and can of beer within reach, staring at the sky. It's breezy but warm out and birds call.

"Stuart, could we go for a drive?" I say. "Anywhere."

He rolls over and looks at me and nods. "We'll pick up some beer," he says. "I hope you're feeling better about this. Try to understand, that's all I ask." He gets to his feet and touches me on the hip as he goes past. "Give me a minute and I'll be ready."

We drive through town without speaking. Before we reach the country he stops at a roadside market for beer. I notice a great stack of papers just inside the door. On the top step a fat woman in a print dress holds out a licorice stick to a little girl. In a few minutes we cross Everson Creek and turn into a picnic area a few feet from the water. The creek flows under the bridge and into a large pond a few hundred yards away. There are a dozen or so men and boys scattered around the banks of the pond under the willows, fishing.

So much water so close to home, why did he have to go miles away to fish?

"Why did you have to go there of all places?" I say.

"The Naches? We always go there. Every year, at least once." We sit on a bench in the sun and he opens two cans of beer and gives one to me. "How the hell was I to know anything like that would happen?" He shakes his head and shrugs, as if it had all happened years ago, or to someone else. "Enjoy the afternoon, Claire. Look at this weather."

"They said they were innocent."

"Who? What are you talking about?"

"The Maddox brothers. They killed a girl named Arlene Hubly near the town where I grew up, and then cut off her head and threw her into the Cle Elum River. She and I went to the same high school. It happened when I was a girl."

"What a hell of a thing to be thinking about," he said. "Come on, get off it. You're going to get me riled in a minute. How about it now? Claire?"

I look at the creek. I float toward the pond, eyes open, face down, staring at the rocks and moss on the creek bottom until I am carried into the lake where I am pushed by the breeze. Nothing will be any different. We will go on and on and on and on. We will go on even now, as if nothing had happened. I look at him across the picnic table with such intensity that his face drains.

"I don't know what's wrong with you," he says. "I don't—"

I slap him before I realize. I raise my hand, wait a fraction of a second, and then slap his cheek hard. This is crazy, I think as I slap him. We need to lock our fingers together. We need to help one another. This is crazy.

He catches my wrist before I can strike again and raises his own hand. I crouch, waiting, and see something come into his eyes and then dart away. He drops his hand. I drift even faster around and around in the pond.

"Come on, get in the car," he says. "I'm taking you home."

"No, no," I say, pulling back from him.

"Come on," he says. "Goddamn it."

"You're not being fair to me," he says later in the car. Fields and trees and farmhouses fly by outside the window. "You're not being fair. To either one of us. Or to Dean, I might add. Think about Dean for a minute. Think about me. Think about someone else besides your goddamn self for a change."

There is nothing I can say to him now. He tries to concentrate on the road, but he keeps looking into the rearview mirror. Out of the corner of his eye, he looks across the seat to where I sit with my knees drawn up under my chin. The sun blazes against my arm and the side of my face. He opens another beer while he drives, drinks from it, then shoves the can between his legs and lets out a breath. He knows. I could laugh in his face. I could weep.

2.

Stuart believes he is letting me sleep this morning. But I was awake long before the alarm sounded, thinking, lying on the far side of the bed, away from his hairy legs and his thick, sleeping fingers. He gets Dean off for school, and then he shaves, dresses, and leaves for work. Twice he looks into the bedroom and clears his throat, but I keep my eyes closed.

In the kitchen I find a note from him signed "Love." I sit in the breakfast nook in the sunlight and drink coffee and make a coffee ring on the note. The telephone has stopped ringing, that's something. No more calls since last night. I look at the paper and turn it this way and that on the table. Then I pull it close and read what it says. The body is still unidentified, unclaimed, apparently unmissed. But for the last twenty-four hours men have been examining it, putting things into it, cutting, weighing, measuring, putting back again, sewing up, looking for the exact cause and moment of death. Looking for evidence of rape. I'm sure they hope for rape. Rape would make it easier to understand. The paper says the body will be taken to Keith & Keith Funeral Home pending arrangements. People are asked to come forward with information, etc.

Two things are certain: 1) people no longer care what happens to other people; and 2) nothing makes any real difference any longer. Look at what has happened. Yet nothing will change for Stuart and me. Really change, I mean. We will grow older, both of us, you can see it in our faces already, in the bathroom mirror, for instance, mornings when we use the bathroom at the same time. And certain things around us will change, become easier or harder, one thing or the other, but nothing will ever really be any different. I believe that. We have made our decisions, our lives have been set in motion, and they will go on and on until they stop. But if that is true, then what? I mean, what if you believe that, but you keep it covered up, until one day something happens that should change something, but then you see nothing is going to change after all. What then? Meanwhile, the people around you continue to talk and act as if you were the same person as yesterday, or last night, or five minutes before, but you are really undergoing a crisis, your heart feels damaged. . . .

The past is unclear. It's as if there is a film over those early years. I can't even be sure that the things I remember happening really happened to me. There was a girl who had a mother and father—the father ran a small cafe where the mother acted as waitress and cashier—who moved as if in a dream through grade school and high school and then, in a year or two, into secretarial school. Later, much later—what happened to the time in between?—she is in another town working as a receptionist for an electronics parts firm and becomes acquainted with one of the engineers who asks her for a date. Eventually, seeing that's his aim, she lets him seduce her. She had an intuition at the time, an insight about the seduction that later, try as she might, she couldn't recall. After a short while they decide to get married, but already the past, her past, is slipping away. The future is something she can't imagine. She smiles, as if she has a secret, when she thinks about the future. Once, during a particularly bad argument, over what she can't now remember, five years or so after they were married, he tells her that someday this affair (his words: "this affair") will end in violence. She remembers this. She files this away somewhere and begins repeating it aloud from time to time. Sometimes she spends the whole morning on her knees in the sandbox behind the garage playing with Dean and one or two of his friends. But every afternoon at four o'clock her head begins to hurt. She holds her forehead and feels dizzy with the pain. Stuart asks her to see a doctor and she does, secretly pleased at the doctor's solicitous attention. She goes away for a while to a place the doctor recommends. Stuart's mother comes out from Ohio in a hurry to care for the child. But she, Claire, spoils everything and returns home in a few weeks. His mother moves out of the house and takes an apartment across town and perches there, as if waiting. One night in bed when they are both near sleep, Claire tells him that she heard some women patients at the clinic discussing fellatio. She thinks this is something he might like to hear. Stuart is pleased at hearing this. He strokes her arm. Things are going to be okay, he says. From now on everything is going to be different and better for them. He has received a promotion and a substantial raise. They've even bought another car, a station wagon, her car. They're going to live in the here and now. He says he feels able to relax for the first time in years. In the dark, he goes on stroking her arm. . . . He continues to bowl and play cards regularly. He goes fishing with three friends of his.

That evening three things happen: Dean says that the children at school told him that his father found a dead body in the river. He wants to know about it.

Stuart explains quickly, leaving out most of the story, saying only that, yes, he and three other men did find a body while they were fishing.

"What kind of body?" Dean asks. "Was it a girl?"

"Yes, it was a girl. A woman. Then we called the sheriff." Stuart looks at me.

"What'd he say?" Dean asks.

"He said he'd take care of it."

"What did it look like? Was it scary?"

"That's enough talk," I say. "Rinse your plate, Dean, and then you're excused."

"But what'd it look like?" he persists. "I want to know."

"You heard me," I say. "Did you hear me, Dean? Dean!" I want to shake him. I want to shake him until he cries.

"Do what your mother says," Stuart tells him quietly. "It was just a body, and that's all there is to it."

I am clearing the table when Stuart comes up behind and touches my arm. His fingers burn. I start, almost losing a plate.

"What's the matter with you?" he says, dropping his hand. "Claire, what is it?"

"You scared me," I say.

"That's what I mean. I should be able to touch you without you jumping out of your skin." He stands in front of me with a little grin, trying to catch my eyes, and then he puts his arm around my waist. With his other hand he takes my free hand and puts it on the front of his pants.

"Please, Stuart." I pull away and he steps back and snaps his fingers.

"Hell with it then," he says. "Be that way if you want. But just remember."

"Remember what?" I say quickly. I look at him and hold my breath.

He shrugs. "Nothing, nothing," he says.

The second thing that happens is that while we are watching television that evening, he is in his leather recliner chair, I on the sofa with a blanket and magazine, the house quiet except for the television, a voice cuts into the program to say that the murdered girl has been identified. Full details will follow on the eleven o'clock news.

We look at each other. In a few minutes he gets up and says he is going to fix a nightcap. Do I want one?

"No," I say.

"I don't mind drinking alone," he says. "I thought I'd ask."

I can see he is obscurely hurt, and I look away, ashamed and yet angry at the same time.

He stays in the kitchen a long while, but comes back with his drink just when the news begins.

First the announcer repeats the story of the four local fishermen finding the body. Then the station shows a high school graduation photograph of the girl, a dark-haired girl with a round face and full, smiling lips. There's a film of the girl's parents entering the funeral home to make the identification. Bewildered, sad, they shuffle slowly up the sidewalk to the front steps to where a man in a dark suit stands waiting, holding the door. Then, it seems as if only seconds have passed, as if they have merely gone inside the door and turned around and come out again, the same couple is shown leaving the building, the woman in tears, covering her face with a handkerchief, the man stopping long enough to say to a reporter, "It's her, it's Susan. I can't say anything right now. I hope they get the person or persons who did it before it happens again. This violence. . . ." He motions feebly at the television camera. Then the man and woman get into an old car and drive away into the late afternoon traffic.

The announcer goes on to say that the girl, Susan Miller, had gotten off work as a cashier in a movie theater in Summit, a town 120 miles north of our town. A green, late model car pulled up in front of the theater and the girl, who according to witnesses looked as if she'd been waiting, went over to the car and got in, leading the authorities to suspect that the driver of the car was a friend, or at least an acquaintance. The authorities would like to talk to the driver of the green car.

Stuart clears his throat then leans back in the chair and sips his drink.

The third thing that happens is that after the news Stuart stretches, yawns, and looks at me. I get up and begin making a bed for myself on the sofa.

"What are you doing?" he says, puzzled.

"I'm not sleepy," I say, avoiding his eyes. "I think I'll stay up a while longer and then read something until I fall asleep."

He stares as I spread a sheet over the sofa. When I start to go for a pillow, he stands at the bedroom door, blocking the way.

"I'm going to ask you once more," he says. "What the hell do you think you're going to accomplish by this?"

"I need to be by myself tonight," I say. "I need to have time to think."

He lets out breath. "I'm thinking you're making a big mistake by doing this. I'm thinking you'd better think again about what you're doing. Claire?"

I can't answer. I don't know what I want to say. I turn and begin to tuck in the edges of the blanket. He stares at me a minute longer and then I see him raise his shoulders. "Suit yourself then. I could give a fuck less what you do," he says. He turns and walks down the hall scratching his neck.

*       *       *

This morning I read in the paper that services for Susan Miller are to be held in the Chapel of the Pines, Summit, at two o'clock the next afternoon. Also, that police have taken statements from three people who saw her get into the green Chevrolet. But they still have no license number for the car. They are getting warmer, though, and the investigation is continuing. I sit for a long while holding the paper, thinking, then I call to make an appointment at the hairdresser's.

I sit under the dryer with a magazine on my lap and let Millie do my nails.

"I'm going to a funeral tomorrow," I say after we have talked a bit about a girl who no longer works there.

Millie looks up at me and then back at my fingers. "I'm sorry to hear that, Mrs. Kane. I'm real sorry."

"It's a young girl's funeral," I say.

"That's the worst kind. My sister died when I was a girl, and I'm still not over it to this day. Who died?" she says after a minute.

"A girl. We weren't all that close, you know, but still."

"Too bad. I'm real sorry. But we'll get you fixed up for it, don't worry. How's that look?"

"That looks . . . fine. Millie, did you ever wish you were somebody else, or else just nobody, nothing, nothing at all?"

She looks at me. "I can't say I ever felt that, no. No, if I was somebody else I'd be afraid I might not like who I was." She holds my fingers and seems to think about something for a minute. "I don't know, I just don't know. . . . Let me have your other hand now, Mrs. Kane."

At eleven o'clock that night I make another bed on the sofa and this time Stuart only looks at me, rolls his tongue behind his lips, and goes down the hall to the bedroom. In the night I wake and listen to the wind slamming the gate against the fence. I don't want to be awake, and I lie for a long while with my eyes closed. Finally I get up and go down the hall with my pillow. The light is burning in our bedroom and Stuart is on his back with his mouth open, breathing heavily. I go into Dean's room and get into bed with him. In his sleep he moves over to give me space. I lie there for a minute and then hold him, my face against his hair.

"What is it, mama?" he says.

"Nothing, honey. Go back to sleep. It's nothing, it's all right."

I get up when I hear Stuart's alarm, put on coffee and prepare breakfast while he shaves.

He appears in the kitchen doorway, towel over his bare shoulder, appraising.

"Here's coffee," I say. "Eggs will be ready in a minute."

He nods.

I wake Dean and the three of us have breakfast. Once or twice Stuart looks at me as if he wants to say something, but each time I ask Dean if he wants more milk, more toast, etc.

"I'll call you today," Stuart says as he opens the door.

"I don't think I'll be home today," I say quickly. "I have a lot of things to do today. In fact, I may be late for dinner."

"All right. Sure." He moves his briefcase from one hand to the other. "Maybe we'll go out for dinner tonight? How would you like that?" He keeps looking at me. He's forgotten about the girl already. "Are you all right?"

I move to straighten his tie, then drop my hand. He wants to kiss me goodbye. I move back a step. "Have a nice day then," he says finally. He turns and goes down the walk to his car.

I dress carefully. I try on a hat that I haven't worn in several years and look at myself in the mirror. Then I remove the hat, apply a light makeup, and write a note for Dean.

> *Honey, Mommy has things to do this afternoon, but will be home later. You are to stay in the house or in the back/yard until one of us comes home.*
>
>                                          *Love*

I look at the word "Love" and then I underline it. As I am writing the note I realize I don't know whether *back yard* is one word or two. I have never considered it before. I think about it and then I draw a line and make two words of it.

I stop for gas and ask directions to Summit. Barry, a forty-year-old mechanic with a moustache, comes out from the restroom and leans

against the front fender while the other man, Lewis, puts the hose into
the tank and begins to slowly wash the windshield.

"Summit," Barry says, looking at me and smoothing a finger down
each side of his moustache. "There's no best way to get to Summit,
Mrs. Kane. It's about a two, two-and-a-half-hour drive each way. Across
the mountains. It's quite a drive for a woman. Summit? What's in Summit,
Mrs. Kane?"

"I have business," I say, vaguely uneasy. Lewis has gone to wait on
another customer.

"Ah. Well, if I wasn't tied up there"—he gestures with his thumb
toward the bay—"I'd offer to drive you to Summit and back again.
Road's not all that good. I mean it's good enough, there's just a lot of
curves and so on."

"I'll be all right. But thank you." He leans against the fender. I can
feel his eyes as I open my purse.

Barry takes the credit card. "Don't drive it at night," he says. "It's
not all that good a road, like I said. And while I'd be willing to bet you
wouldn't have car trouble with this, I know this car, you can never be
sure about blowouts and things like that. Just to be on the safe side I'd
better check these tires." He taps one of the front tires with his shoe.
"We'll run it onto the hoist. Won't take long."

"No, no, it's all right. Really, I can't take any more time. The tires
look fine to me."

"Only takes a minute," he says. "Be on the safe side."

"I said no. No! They look fine to me. I have to go now. Barry. . . ."

"Mrs. Kane?"

"I have to go now."

I sign something. He gives me the receipt, the card, some stamps. I put
everything into my purse. "You take it easy," he says. "Be seeing you."

As I wait to pull into the traffic, I look back and see him watching.
I close my eyes, then open them. He waves.

I turn at the first light, then turn again and drive until I come to the
highway and read the sign: SUMMIT 117 Miles. It is ten-thirty and warm.

The highway skirts the edge of town, then passes through farm
country, through fields of oats and sugar beets and apple orchards,
with here and there a small herd of cattle grazing in open pastures.
Then everything changes, the farms become fewer and fewer, more like
shacks now than houses, and stands of timber replace the orchards. All
at once I'm in the mountains and on the right, far below, I catch glimpses
of the Naches River.

In a little while I see a green pickup truck behind me, and it stays
behind me for miles. I keep slowing at the wrong times, hoping it will

pass, and then increasing my speed, again at the wrong times. I grip the wheel until my fingers hurt. Then on a clear stretch he does pass, but he drives along beside for a minute, a crew-cut man in a blue workshirt in his early thirties, and we look at each other. Then he waves, toots the horn twice and pulls ahead of me.

I slow down and find a place, a dirt road off of the shoulder. I pull over and turn off the ignition. I can hear the river somewhere down below the trees. Ahead of me the dirt road goes into the trees. Then I hear the pickup returning.

I start the engine just as the truck pulls up behind me. I lock the doors and roll up the windows. Perspiration breaks on my face and arms as I put the car in gear, but there is no place to drive.

"You all right?" the man says as he comes up to the car. "Hello. Hello in there." He raps the glass. "You okay?" He leans his arms on the door and brings his face close to the window.

I stare at him and can't find any words.

"After I passed I slowed up some," he says. "But when I didn't see you in the mirror I pulled off and waited a couple of minutes. When you still didn't show I thought I'd better drive back and check. Is everything all right? How come you're locked up in there?"

I shake my head.

"Come on, roll down your window. Hey, are you sure you're okay? You know it's not good for a woman to be batting around the country by herself." He shakes his head and looks at the highway, then back at me. "Now come on, roll down the window, how about it? We can't talk this way."

"Please, I have to go."

"Open the door, all right?" he says, as if he isn't listening. "At least roll the window down. You're going to smother in there." He looks at my breasts and legs. The skirt has pulled up over my knees. His eyes linger on my legs, but I sit still, afraid to move.

"I want to smother," I say. "I am smothering, can't you see?"

"What in the hell?" he says and moves back from the door. He turns and walks back to his truck. Then, in the side mirror, I watch him returning, and I close my eyes.

"You don't want me to follow you toward Summit or anything? I don't mind. I got some extra time this morning," he says.

I shake my head.

He hesitates and then shrugs. "Okay, lady, have it your way then," he says. "Okay."

I wait until he has reached the highway, and then I back out. He shifts gears and pulls away slowly, looking back at me in his rearview mirror. I stop the car on the shoulder and put my head on the wheel.

The casket is closed and covered with floral sprays. The organ begins soon after I take a seat near the back of the chapel. People begin to file in and find chairs, some middle-aged and older people, but most of them in their early twenties or even younger. They are people who look uncomfortable in their suits and ties, sport coats and slacks, their dark dresses and leather gloves. One boy in flared pants and a yellow short-sleeved shirt takes the chair next to mine and begins to bite his lips. A door opens at one side of the chapel and I look up and for a minute the parking lot reminds me of a meadow. But then the sun flashes on car windows. The family enters in a group and moves into a curtained area off to the side. Chairs creak as they settle themselves. In a few minutes a slim, blond man in a dark suit stands and asks us to bow our heads. He speaks a brief prayer for us, the living, and when he finishes he asks us to pray in silence for the soul of Susan Miller, departed. I close my eyes and remember her picture in the newspaper and on television. I see her leaving the theater and getting into the green Chevrolet. Then I imagine her journey down the river, the nude body hitting rocks, caught at by branches, the body floating and turning, her hair streaming in the water. Then the hands and hair catching in the overhanging branches, holding, until four men come along to stare at her. I can see a man who is drunk (Stuart?) take her by the wrist. Does anyone here know about that? What if these people knew that? I look around at the other faces. There is a connection to be made of these things, these events, these faces, if I can find it. My head aches with the effort to find it.

He talks about Susan Miller's gifts: cheerfulness and beauty, grace and enthusiasm. From behind the closed curtain someone clears his throat, someone else sobs. The organ music begins. The service is over.

Along with the others I file slowly past the casket. Then I move out onto the front steps and into the bright, hot afternoon light. A middle-aged woman who limps as she goes down the stairs ahead of me reaches the sidewalk and looks around, her eyes falling on me. "Well, they got him," she says. "If that's any consolation. They arrested him this morning. I heard it on the radio before I came. A guy right here in town. A longhair, you might have guessed." We move a few steps down the hot sidewalk. People are starting cars. I put out my hand and hold on to a parking meter. Sunlight glances off polished hoods and fenders. My head swims. "He's admitted having relations with her that night, but he says he didn't kill her." She snorts. "They'll put him on probation and then turn him loose."

"He might not have acted alone," I say. "They'll have to be sure. He might be covering up for someone, a brother, or some friends."

"I have known that child since she was a little girl," the woman goes on, and her lips tremble. "She used to come over and I'd bake cookies for her and let her eat them in front of the TV." She looks off and begins shaking her head as the tears roll down her cheeks.

3.

Stuart sits at the table with a drink in front of him. His eyes are red and for a minute I think he has been crying. He looks at me and doesn't say anything. For a wild instant I feel something has happened to Dean, and my heart turns.

"Where is he?" I say. "Where is Dean?"

"Outside," he says.

"Stuart, I'm so afraid, so afraid," I say, leaning against the door.

"What are you afraid of, Claire? Tell me, honey, and maybe I can help. I'd like to help, just try me. That's what husbands are for."

"I can't explain," I say. "I'm just afraid. I feel like, I feel like, I feel like. . . ."

He drains his glass and stands up, not taking his eyes from me. "I think I know what you need, honey. Let me play doctor, okay? Just take it easy now." He reaches an arm around my waist and with his other hand begins to unbutton my jacket, then my blouse. "First things, first," he says, trying to joke.

"Not now, please," I say.

"Not now, please," he says, teasing. "Please nothing." Then he steps behind me and locks an arm around my waist. One of his hands slips under my brassiere.

"Stop, stop, stop," I say. I stamp on his toes.

And then I am lifted up and then falling. I sit on the floor looking up at him and my neck hurts and my skirt is over my knees. He leans down and says, "You go to hell then, do you hear, bitch? I hope your cunt drops off before I touch it again." He sobs once and I realize he can't help it, he can't help himself either. I feel a rush of pity for him as he heads for the living room.

He didn't sleep at home last night.

This morning, flowers, red and yellow chrysanthemums. I am drinking coffee when the doorbell rings.

"Mrs. Kane?" the young man says, holding his box of flowers.

I nod and pull the robe tighter at my throat.

"The man who called, he said you'd know." The boy looks at my robe, open at the throat, and touches his cap. He stands with his legs apart, feet firmly planted on the top step. "Have a nice day," he says.

A little later the telephone rings and Stuart says, "Honey, how are you? I'll be home early, I love you. Did you hear me? I love you, I'm sorry, I'll make it up to you. Goodbye, I have to run now."

I put the flowers into a vase in the center of the dining room table and then I move my things into an extra bedroom.

Last night, around midnight, Stuart breaks the lock on my door. He does it just to show me that he can, I suppose, for he doesn't do anything when the door springs open except stand there in his underwear looking surprised and foolish while the anger slips from his face. He shuts the door slowly, and a few minutes later I hear him in the kitchen prying open a tray of ice cubes.

I'm in bed when he calls today to tell me that he's asked his mother to come stay with us for a few days. I wait a minute, thinking about this, and then hang up while he is still talking. But in a little while I dial his number at work. When he finally comes on the line I say, "It doesn't matter, Stuart. Really, I tell you it doesn't matter one way or the other."

"I love you," he says.

He says something else and I listen and nod slowly. I feel sleepy. Then I wake up and say, "For God's sake, Stuart, she was only a child."

# CLARK BROWN
# A WINTER'S TALE

Clark Brown, son of Montanan parents, grew up in San Francisco and took degrees at the University of California at Berkeley (B.A. 1958, M.A. 1959). A novel, *The Disciple* (1968), has been followed by stories, essays, and translations published in various magazines, including "A Winter's Tale" which appeared in *Writers' Forum*, No. 9, 1983, and was reprinted in *Pushcart Prize IX*, 1984. He teaches fiction and creative writing at California State University, Chico.

"A Winter's Tale" is a pseudo-documentary based upon the author's research into the cavalry campaign of 1876 that led to the so-called Sioux wars and to the rush for gold on the Yellowstone. What makes the story a strongly contemporary expression is Brown's depiction of the white man's absurd prejudice and of genocide in the dark side of American history. One Daniel Palmer seems well-disposed toward Indians, but his "scientific" belief in phrenology so obscures his capacity to understand them that he ceases to resist or make protest about a cavalry unit's massacre of innocents. In Palmer we encounter an American version of Joseph Conrad's Kurtz in "Heart of Darkness," though Brown's understated historical irony is not mediated by the Marlowe of Conrad's story; the reader must absorb ironic impact directly, attention at first diverted by such a quaint topic as phrenology.

# A WINTER'S TALE

B y 1876 enthusiasm had begun to wane, yet the whole improbable business, even the sectioned heads (reproduced today on comic T-shirts), retained a respectful hearing on into the twentieth century, and as late as 1911 books appeared such as *Character Building and Reading*, a cheerful popularized treatise complete with jargon and charts.

The foundations of the science were these: since the exercise of any corporeal organ increases its size (Cuvier), and since certain portions of the brain control certain bodily responses and activities, it seemed reasonable to assume that strenuous exercise of, say, the intellectual faculties would increase the frontal lobes. And therefore, since brain size determined skull size, you could conclude merely from looking at a picture of Socrates (for example) that he was a man of profound thought. From such analogies there developed an elaborate system, quaint and ridiculous in our eyes (though no more so, some claim, than psychoanalysis), including the familiar diagrams of a hairless human head mapped and numbered like demarcated illustrations of cuts of beef. Wonderful qualities or "sentiments" were postulated, such as "bibacity"—"the love of liquids and the fondness for bathing, boating, swimming and marine life." Bibacity was thought to reside near the temple, half way between the eye and ear. Its "perversion" was drunkenness and excessive thirst.

One among many of the practitioners of this fanciful discipline (endorsed by Emerson, George Eliot, Herbert Spencer and Gladstone among others, and dignified with a chair at the University of Edinburgh) was Daniel Joseph Palmer, born in 1848 in Brookline, Massachusetts to Ephraim Leonidas Palmer, a manufacturer of stationers' supplies, and to Dorothy Wilcox Palmer, both robust Congregationalists who would convert to Christian Science soon after the publication in 1875 of *Science and Health*.

Matriculating at Harvard, Palmer graduated in 1869, having studied not medicine but theology and being attracted to the Unitarian faith which, now severed from the religion of his parents, would require him as minister to profess no particular doctrine or creed. He did not, however, enter the ministry but undertook a profitable career in his father's business, to which he brought an evangelical zeal.

It seems characteristic of Palmer to combine mercantile and religious fervor. He shied from a career as clergyman, fearing it would remove him from "the world of men," yet that very world—the world, in his case, of inventories, freight rates, price structures and sales volumes—demanded in his eyes some spiritual commitment, something to uplift and redeem what might otherwise remain a sordid grasping and scheming. He wished his life to be pure and worthy, yet he wished it to be active, virile and of this earth. A faith whose adherents dwelt apart held no charm for him. He wished not to renounce the world but to transfigure it.

In college he had read the works of Francis Gall (1758-1828) and John Caspar Spurzheim (1776-1832). He was familiar with the lectures of the Fowlers (Orson and Lorenzo), and he knew that Ferrier and others were even then applying a weak galvanic current to certain exposed portions of living animal brains and noting the muscular reactions. Like other physiognomists Palmer realized that these newly discovered motor centers corresponded to the psychic brain centers located much earlier by Dr. Gall, centers which positively expressed the feeling or emotion naturally arising from the activities of the faculties *in* sections of the brain. Whether this perception decided him or not is unclear, but at some point after graduation—and we do not know precisely when—Palmer journeyed to England where he studied with Dr. Henry Maudsley, F.R.C.P., Professor of Medical Jurisprudence, University College, London.

He—Palmer—was a short, stocky man with curly brown hair, a long square jaw and large, prominent dark eyes which in the few photographs that survive appear unusually lustrous and troubled. The lips are thick, almost pouting, and the face, which Palmer himself analysed or "read" numerous times (consulting, of course, a mirror), combines a suggestion of obscure and solemn sadness with a hint of boyish wonder. His vision was weak, and he usually wore a pince nez, but none shows in the pictures. This absence may explain the naked, surprised expression, the sense of a creature trapped.

From his journals and meditations—highly self-critical and analytical yet lighted by a stubborn optimism—we gather that he represented an unhappy combination of tenacity and shyness. Short but lacking the little man's compensating swagger, he was determined on self-improvement, and by a sheer assertion of will frequently compelled himself to do exactly what his nature most wished him to avoid. Any qualm or reservation which might, under Palmer's stern eye, be taken for cowardice or funk he resolved to extirpate. Thus he entered politics to the extent of campaigning for Rutherford B. Hayes, partly because he approved of the candidate's teetotaling convictions, but mainly as an opportunity to rid himself of a lifelong fear of public speaking. In the same way—or so we may speculate—he journeyed west in the late fall of 1875, intending to make scientific examination of what he persistently called the "savage temperament."

At that time white man and Indian enjoyed a theoretical peace. True, the Civil War had provided opportunities for sporadic rebellion, and there were still in several western territories small bands—mainly young braves—known as "hot-heads." In general, though, most Plains Indians had resigned themselves to treaties purporting to guarantee their territorial rights. Not all Indians understood such agreements, and the tribes' very democracy provided friction. A chief might sign and sincerely promise peace but compelling obedience was not always within his power. To be "chief" was to assume less authority than the white man often realized. Nevertheless, a truce of sorts prevailed. Then in 1873 the discovery of gold on the Yellowstone River altered these precarious arrangements.

That authorities could have stopped the influx of fortune seekers seems doubtful; that they were not interested in trying is certain. Tension rose. As the year in which Daniel Palmer journeyed west came to a close, people on the frontier wondered what the spring would hold. In winter, game and forage being scarce, Indians necessarily split into small scattered groups, but once the snows vanished, the grass got high and the ponies grew strong again, there might be war, and in the light of this dismal possibility a column of cavalry and mounted infantry left Fort Fetterman in the Wyoming Territory in late January ostensibly on reconnaissance. Daniel Palmer, making his own reconnaissance, traveled with it.

As a rule, Indian fighting was a more casual affair than history and cinema have portrayed. The pensions and commendations of "real" war did not apply, pitched battles were rare and since the army was shrinking and promotions were few, an ambitious officer had little chance to make a reputation against the "hostiles." One exception was Major Robert "Fighting Bob" Shannon, who at thirty-six had established himself, first during the Civil War, then in the brilliant if ambiguous confrontation at Deer Creek (near Cheyenne) in 1868. Presently, Major Shannon was north with a contingent of Crow scouts. He would join the column at a place known as Hanging Man's Fork, south of Sulphur Flats.

The soldiers themselves were not crack troops. Life on the frontier posts was dreary and unattractive, and many of those who signed on for the winter were simply "snowbirds," desperate for food and warm clothing and certain to desert in the spring. These and others were often debtors or worse who had fled the East. The army did not inquire scrupulously into anyone's past or worry overmuch about muster roll authenticity. The same tolerance extended to uniforms. Eccentricities of dress and weaponry were ignored, and some men fought in buckskin or outlandish costumes. Officers, too, could be whimsical. Captain Gideon J. Prowt (1821–1892) rode a mule, tied up his beard with bright ribbons and carried a shotgun.

There was, then, a Dickensian bustle and glamor to the whole business, a local "color" which journalists exploited. Then as now relationships between officers and the press were complicated. Rising stars such as George A. Custer (rumored to have Presidential ambitions) and Major Shannon, aware that Indian fighting was good "copy," encouraged publicity. Robert Shannon himself may well have written many of the dispatches printed under various reporters' names.

Certainly material existed for anyone with an eye to the picturesque. Wandering about the fort, you would see the officers in blue and shiny boots, the men in blues and dark forage caps, the muleskinners bearded and greasy in elkskin or buckskin, hung with revolvers and ammunition, butcher knives stuffed in their belts. Then there were scouts and friendly Indians, longhaired and brown, dressed in a motley of buckskin, blankets and cast-off uniforms. And always there was the noise: wagons clattering, bullwhips cracking, animals snorting, whackers swearing, officers snapping orders, boots thumping, rifles and carbines executing the manual with a slap and bang of stocks and barrels and the jingle of sling-belts.

Palmer, alive to this excitement, had arranged to travel as "scientific observer," eating at headquarters mess. His earnestness and his mysterious knowledge both amused and intrigued the officers, some of whom patronized him but made sure he was properly outfitted. His notebooks record the astonishing amount of gear: bedding, canvas, comforter, buffalo robes, beaver robe, mattress (to be rolled and tied to his horse), rubber poncho, a stock saddle instead of the pancake McClellans with their slots and pads and skirts, messkit (should he have to prepare his own rations), cup, canteen, extra clothes, boots, buffalo coat, muskrat cap with earflaps, fifteen pounds of grain (to be packed on the mules), extra horseshoes, wool face mask, fur gloves, mittens, buffalo overshoes and special issue gear for wrists and knees. For his protection he was equipped with a Springfield carbine rather than the infantryman's "Long Tom" (unmanageable on horseback) and a Colt pistol. (Lithographs and films to the contrary, neither Palmer nor anyone else carried bayonets or sabers.)

On January 31st the column rode out—five troops of cavalry, the pack train and the infantry rear guard mounted on mules—moving north through the creek bottoms where the ground was flat, the riding easy, and thick woods kept off the wind. The first day's march was not arduous, but Palmer's journal notes displeasure—mainly, it appears, at himself.

At the fort he had "examined" various Indians, taking measurements and working his observations into a brief, tentative essay. The black eye, he observed, naturally indicated passion, intensity and impulse, but shape was equally significant. A narrow eye could mean secrecy and suspiciousness. The noses were usually aggressive and the straight thicklipped jaws pointed toward firmness and sensuality. The foreheads, he claimed, generally revealed a deficiency in the moral and intellectual sentiments, and the high prominent crowns (recalling Philip the Second of Spain) showed a desire to tyrannize. Then there was the hair. As a rule, Palmer wrote, the darkhaired races possessed more intensity but not necessarily more physical strength.

But all this was dissatisfying. These savages remained disappointingly unsavage. He felt cheated and balked yet relieved—and despised his relief. What exactly he hoped to find through such study is difficult to say, but it is clear in retrospect that he wished in some way to still within himself a kind of silent terror.

For Palmer was afraid—fearfully afraid—and he believed (or so we gather) that only by forcing himself to look unblinkingly upon the face of human darkness and depravity could he conquer his poisonous shame. But the Crow scouts and the copperskinned loafers at the post, though intriguing at first, failed to frighten him. He felt cravenly let off, deprived of his chance for self-mastery.

Whether at heart he *was* more or less a coward than most men is not the point. He *felt* himself a coward. He had sought a test and was privately grateful that none had arrived, and this gratitude, this obscene unconquerable joy at being spared, moved him to paroxysms of self-disgust. *Truly, he wrote, when I consider how my heart palpitates at the mere idea of danger, and when I look about me and remark how calmly other men accept the nearness of combat and the fact of their own mortality, I am filled with icy despair. Are they bluffers? Do they all wear masks? Even fat Captain Fenton—so clearly the lymphatic type with the characteristically active secreting glands, the languid pulse and the retarded vital functions— even he, I say, the least martial of men, seems undismayed by the frightening possibilities. There is nothing for it. I can only conclude that I am a wretch. . . .*

Then, on the third night, after the column had reached Hanging Man's Fork and pitched camp, Major Shannon and his scouts appeared

from the north. With them they brought, as though for display, a captured Sioux brave.

Eight years older than Palmer, Robert Andrew Shannon looks, in
photographs, several years younger. Though there is something youth-
ful, even childlike in Palmer's glum dubious stare, there are in the
pictures of Robert Shannon a blandness, a simplicity and even a lack
of expression that suggest youth. The face is square, Irish and pale,
with thin lips and the long, thin, not particularly prominent nose. In
Palmer's jargon he represented the "motive temperament," characterized
by "a tall, angular form, long, large bones, prominent joints, strong
muscles and ligaments, large, strong, well defined features, and square
or oblong face, hair and skin usually coarse, the movements and gestures
abrupt and striking." The "mental attributes" of this species are, according to Palmer, "constructiveness, firmness, energy, executive power,
stability, constancy and practical insight." *Such types make good builders,*
Palmer wrote, *also construction engineers, surveyors, farmers, stock raisers
and navigators.*

Certainly Shannon was tall, bony, rectilinear and dry. Certainly too
he was laconic and arrogant, and in Palmer's presence affected a bored,
half-lidded stare of contempt. He seems to have despised Palmer from
the start, and Palmer quailed before his lofty gaze.

It appears not to have occurred to Palmer that much about Shannon
might be pose. Such posturing Palmer never understood. He knew of
course of Shannon's military record. West Point '61, Shannon had fought
at the first battle of Bull Run and in McClellan's unsuccessful Peninsular
Campaign. He had led the bloody but indecisive assault on Lee's left
at Antietam, and with Sedgwick had driven Jubal Early from Mayre's
Heights at Chancellorsville—before Early and Lee repulsed Sedgwick
and Hooker. At Gettysburg he had helped turn back Longstreet. Finally,
there was, as always, his stunning victory over the massed Sioux,
Arapaho and Cheyenne at the battle (some said massacre) of Deer Creek.
Thus when Shannon seated himself on a campstool and quietly, matter-
of-factly (so softly officers strained to hear) made his recommendations,
Palmer was stricken.

What would they do? someone asked. What would they *do?* said
Shannon, lifting an eyebrow (his inflection could make you blush at
your own words). Why, he said, they would rest that day, cut all the
grass they could find for the animals and collect all the water they could
carry. Then they would strike out across Sulphur Flats. Probably they
would spend one night if they pushed themselves, two if they did not.
But, someone objected, could it be done? Could it be *done?* Shannon
asked with a laugh. Hadn't Hardass George Custer marched without

water from the Republican River to the Platte—in a single day?

Technically, Shannon was not the commander. The commander was Colonel Hiram Bartholomew Chilldress, diminutive, silverhaired and vague, but no one doubted that the Major had assumed control and direction of the whole enterprise. He might defer—barely—to Chilldress, but there seemed to be in Shannon's bearing and speech and above all his poised silences an expression of will that no one would oppose.

Palmer was shocked and fascinated. In Shannon he saw what he believed he wished to be, and yet there was something blind and stupid and hostile about the Major. He had made himself a force, yes, but a mindless force. Was he any better, Palmer wondered, than the savages themselves? Well, yes, certainly, but still. . . . Then Palmer no doubt stopped worrying about that. Other challenges confronted him.

Why and how Shannon captured the Sioux remain unclear even today. There was talk of the Crow scouts surprising the brave, who may have been sneaking upon them at night. Details are lacking. He was young— possibly seventeen or eighteen—skinny, proud, fierce and bitter, wrapped in a tattered blanket, his hands lashed behind him, a noose about his neck. He had been transported by horseback, but now he was seated among boulders, wrists and ankles bound, the blanket slipping off one bare shoulder while two carbine-bearing troopers stood guard. Palmer requested and was granted permission to make his "examination." How deeply he wished to do anything of the kind we may imagine.

Secretly, he was appalled. His whole being shrank from the task, from the very sight and smell—the mingled odors of dried sweat, damp wool and filthy buckskin. The lank dark hair, the glazed black eyes, the sharp facial bones, the snarling mouth, the blade of a nose—this was what Palmer had traveled two thousand miles to meet, and his spirit seemed to shriek and urge him to bolt. He realized that he was in no danger, that this miserable starving half wild creature—not much more than a boy—so securely bound and watched, could do nothing to him. All the same, Palmer trembled. Swallowing, he approached the man—*as though I were compelled to examine a leopard*, he wrote. *I could not help it. My very nerves seemed to clatter. I was consumed with fear!*

Yet he made his examination, even explaining briefly to those interested how cranial configurations might be mathematically classified (measuring the forehead slope against a perpendicular through the skull) and yielding such categories and "types" as—in ascending order—the Australian Bushman, the Uncultivated, the Improved, the Civilized, the Enlightened, and, at the apex, the Caucasian. Sometimes, he pointed out, with the Caucasian Type, foreheads actually exceeded ninety degrees. It was at this moment, one likes to think, that the captive broke into that unearthly wail which shook Palmer "to the very marrow of my bones."

*. . . I inquired the reason for this eerie keening, and was informed that the subject was singing his death song.* "He thinks you're going to torture him," someone volunteered, "and he's telling you he don't think much of your medicine."

At any rate, Palmer concluded his business, noticing that the Indian, seemingly bent on his own destruction, had refused all food—to the consternation of no one. *I pointed out that the subject would surely starve,* Palmer wrote, *to which I received the gratifying information that that was frequently the result of neglecting to take nourishment. I was not consoled.*

There was in fact a strong capacity for indignation within Palmer, an ability to resent, heatedly, injustice and cruelty. Whether his outrage at this callousness was in some way fanned by his secret fear we cannot say. Possibly in protesting against the prisoner's treatment, Palmer was privately objecting to his own qualms. The truth is, he hated the man (hardly a man at that), hated him because the brave terrified and shamed him, and, as though to compensate or render some balance, Palmer felt compelled to speak out. He received little satisfaction. It was explained, reasonably enough, that the prisoner's hands *had* been untied and a tin dish of hardtack fried in pork grease (the usual staple of enlisted men) had been set before him, along with a cup of water. The "buck" had growled and overturned both offerings. Evidently, Captain Prowt suggested, the man lacked appetite.

"But surely," Palmer protested, "he must be dehydrated?"

It was conceded that such was very likely.

Palmer was distressed. *I do not understand,* he confided to his journal, *this indifference to the death of another human creature, even one so benighted as a savage sunk in barbarism. This heartless unconcern, I say, fills me with black misery.* Such were his sentiments that evening. Soon enough his misery would grow.

The wind shifted in the night. Rushing from the north now, it whistled through the pines. Dawn blew in grey and fiercely cold, the clouds dull pearl and scaly. The men turned out in the clumsy buffalo coats and the muskrat caps, and those with beards and moustaches seemed to bristle from head to foot.

After breakfast the column moved, the prisoner placed somewhere in the middle, bound in his blanket and set upon a mule, a rope around his neck held by the trooper behind.

"Does he have to have *that?*" Palmer objected.

"I'm afraid he does, Dan," Captain Fenton replied.

At the nooning Palmer went back with a tin dish of biscuit and beef. The Sioux sat the mule as though asleep. When Palmer showed the food, he averted his head.

That evening Palmer tried again.

"Eat!" I cried. "Eat! Eat! Eat!" And, rather comically, I think, I took a bite myself to show the way. "Meat!" I said.

Suddenly, to my astonishment, the subject snatched a morsel with his bound hands and popped it into his mouth.

"Mitt!"—he seemed to bark—or something like that.

"Meat!" I said.

"Mittuh!"

Palmer was trembling with excitement and confusion. He has an ability with language, I think, the physiognomist wrote. The faculty, to be sure, is located in the inferior frontal convolution in the lower surface of the anterior lobe. Pressing upon the supraorbital plate, it throws the eye downwards and outwards. A clear enough sign all right, but somehow I missed it!

But in the morning the brave was gone.

At first this disappearance seemed incredible, this vanishing like breath off a mirror. Then it was discovered that several Crow scouts had also deserted. Apparently they had spirited away the prisoner, a Sioux and hence their hereditary enemy. Palmer flew upon Captain Fenton, who avoided his gaze.

There was much to admire about the Crows, Captain Fenton explained: tall, handsome, clean people, lighter than most savages and superb horse thieves. Some, however, were less than exquisite. These loafed about the forts with their squaws and papooses and dogs. When the urge seized them they could be magnificent scouts. Also, the pay attracted them, but they grew restive under discipline. Many were halfbreeds and squaw men. Some were thieves and bounty jumpers, the dregs of the agencies. Half the time they misdirected you or alerted the hostiles. . . .

Yes, Palmer broke in, all that was fine, but what was the point? What were they going to *do* with the prisoner? Captain Fenton looked away again. About that, he said softly, he couldn't say.

Palmer understood—and was horrified. He sought out Shannon, who, as it happened, was walking the picket line with an aide, the two men swollen-looking in the heavy buffalo coats. Shannon kept swinging his gloved fists together, making little pops.

". . . at Chattanooga," he was saying when I arrived, "the horses tried to eat bark, parts of wagons, tried to eat each other's manes and tails." Ignoring me, he paused, knocked his fists together. "Then," he said, "the *men* ate *them."*

*"Major!" I broke in. "About the prisoner—how did the Crows get him?"*

*"No idea," I was told.*

*I persisted. Wasn't the brave someone's responsibility? I asked. Yes, Shannon agreed, and that someone had been fooled. Well then, I inquired, couldn't someone track the party? Couldn't some attempt be made? I pointed out that it still might not be too late.*

*The Major stopped and considered a horse. (All the mounts were covered with blankets and gunnysacks. They stood stamping and shivering and fluttering their nostrils, and their breath puffed out in little clouds.)*

*"Here's what I mean," he said. Then he bent and lifted a hoof. "No way to shoe a horse. Let a horse run barefoot, see how he* wants *to walk. Oh, it looks bully to shoe 'em so all four feet set the same, I know, but it's a bad idea." Then Shannon straightened up.*

*"Major!" I cried—or rather barked, an intemperate burst.*

*"Solferino!" Shannon said, bewildering me. "Before Solferino the French lost ten thousand horses. Think about it!"*

Soon it began to snow. *The sky turned brown,* Palmer wrote, *the wind dropped. The first flakes fell, swirling down like tiny scraps of paper, powdering caps and shoulders, catching in beards and the horses' manes. A profound stillness reigns. I feel a throbbing between my eyes. My skull itself seems to ache, and the frozen air burns my lungs. . . .*

That evening, around the campfire at headquarters mess, he made some sort of official protest. What exactly he said or theatened we do not know, but that he intended to inform various authorities and newspapers seems certain, for a letter directed to the Commissioner of Indian Affairs still exists. Unfinished and unsent, drafted in pencil (his ink had frozen and burst the bottle), it begins: *On January 31st of this year, a column of United States cavalry and mounted infantry operating in response to rumors of hostile Indian movement was joined near Sulphur Flats in the Montana Territory by Major Robert Shannon and a party of Crow scouts. With him Major Shannon brought. . . .* Tersely the document continues, giving details, then asserts: *It is not these matters, distasteful as they are to anyone in whom the faculties of kindness, conscience and friendship are even moderately developed, which move me to write. Rather it is the negligence if not outright collusion. . . .* Here the letter breaks off, and soon afterwards the story with it, for suddenly Palmer's journal, so voluble and indiscreet, the tight spidery prose (the ink portion a faded rust color today on the brittle paper, the pencil almost indecipherable) becomes withdrawn, matter of fact, tightlipped. That inspired, sometimes tedious examination of conscience protracted over two thousand miles, three months and ten ragged notebooks (see the William T. Riggert Rare Book

Collection, University of Montana, Missoula) stops abruptly. We are forced to speculate.

From Palmer's meager details, and from other firsthand accounts, it is possible to make some sort of reconstruction. There was a debate that night, possibly a "scene," the participants shaggy in their coats and caps like so many argumentative bears, their angry faces polished by firelight. We may imagine that Major Shannon sat his campstool and never raised his voice. We may assume that fat, good-natured Captain Fenton tried to make peace, that old goatbearded Captain Prowt was sarcastic and that Colonel Chilldress looked pained. What was said we do not know. Whether Palmer actually mentioned the letter he had begun and his intentions is questionable (though at some point Captain Fenton at least learned of such). What *is* certain is that Palmer, gripped with despair and misery, wandered off, wishing for solitude.

And how much of his suffering, one wonders, was due to some secret relief (which he hated)? Wasn't he glad, after all, the brave was gone? And was it once again himself he wished to assail and punish in his cries for justice?

And, too, one asks, was Major Shannon's hostility, his calculated contempt and pointed rudeness, were *they* in turn provoked by some fear and self-loathing? Did he despise Palmer—his very earnestness and ignorance, his childish persistence—because Palmer represented everything in himself which *Shannon* wished to destroy, every quality that seemed to the Major unmanly and base? Was Palmer the quintessential civilian in Shannon's eyes—a creature unworthy to bear arms? Further too, one asks, was the prisoner's very disappearance *arranged* by Shannon for precisely this result? And did Palmer suspect as much? Did this suspicion inflame him even further and fill him with anguish when he considered that he, in a sense, collaborated with the Major— that is, he wished, secretly, for just that outcome he felt compelled to deplore? Or did he? Did the image and sound of the brave inexplicably struggling to pronounce the white man's language return to haunt him?

Alone among the darkness and trees Palmer knew he must soon return or make a fire. A pale gibbous moon shone, yet it seemed that a few flakes dropped still. The wind had fallen. Palmer found that he was immensely tired. He sat upon a fallen tree, and the dampness and cold seeped into him. He wondered if he could find his way back and recalled that he could, if necessary, fire a shot.

Fumbling out his knife, he dug at a dead tree, scaling bark and pricking out dry slivers. Then he rooted in the snow for seasoned twigs, threw down wet branches for a base and built a little cone of shavings. The feeling was already leaving his feet. His nose and cheekbones ached, "as though I had been beaten about the face."

. . . *The wood began to smoke,* Palmer wrote, in the last entry of any length, the last passionate moment. *I blew and a tiny leaf of flame fluttered up. I placed more twigs, pressing in, as though to embrace the heat, huddling in the pool of light. Outside, the trees rose in columns.*

*I began to doze. Shadows flitted across the firelit trees and over the snow. Then I stiffened. Something seemed to move. I peered through the smoke and the wavering light. A twig snapped in the fire. Branches swayed and brushed together. I heard a plop—snow from a limb. Then my blood froze. Someone was standing among the trees.*

*He glided across the snow, the tracks stringing out behind. Limping, he approached and squatted. I saw the hawknose, the cheekbones like gleaming knuckles, the dark eyes burning with fever and hunger, the lips drawn tight. He stretched out his hands, flexing the long cold fingers. I stared at the buckskin leggings, the dirty bandage, the torn moccasins beaded with quillwork, the heavy blanket smelling of wet wool. He had followed the column. Somehow he had broken free and followed, sneaking in to steal the blanket and scraps of food. He had clung to us!*

*"Get warm!" I said. "You must get warm!" I whispered as though someone might overhear. I smiled. "Mittuh?" I said, though I had no meat. He gave no sign. Then, choosing a twig, he snapped and placed it on the fire, the long dark hands swift and agile now, like the hands of the blind. Quickly he began sorting my twigs, cracking them, setting them in place. The fire swept up.*

*"Mittuh?" I said.*

*He went on with his work. I too seized a twig and broke it. Then he let his hands hang, staring at the flames. Then he looked at me.*

*He had drawn the blanket about him. Suddenly, I wondered what else he might have stolen. I saw the need to make him understand.*

*"If you are armed," I said, "so am I." I mimed pulling a trigger. It did no good. I drew off the mitten, undid the heavy coat and popped the holster flap. I drew the pistol slowly, hefting it, as though to guess the weight. I meant nothing more, only a show. At once he rose, shrinking back, his eyes never leaving me, dark and glittering in the firelight. Then he turned and began to run, the blanket flapping like coattails.*

*"Wait!" I cried. "Wait. You can stay. You must stay!"*

*I hurried after him, trees, rocks and shadows flashing by. I sucked the raw air.*

*He disappeared—then out from the trees, up a bank, down a gully and up again. Then I lost him, among a pile of snow-covered boulders. I wondered: was he waiting for me?*

*My chest was heaving, my heart slamming. I scooped snow and patted my feverish face. I could hear breathing—my own! The feeling was leaving my legs.*

*I feared moving, yielding my back, and yet. . . . A shadow! I screamed. He darted away, but the scream was still in my ears and that burning rush of fear in my bowels.*

*"You!" I cried. "You!" And I saw him. The roar! The flash! "You!" I shouted. I fired again.*

*Emptying the gun it was as though I had burst from some great sea depth. My lungs filled with air. I could breathe. Only . . . the groaning, the noise, the smear of light . . . the shadow crumpling . . . and the joy, the joy, the joy! For a single instant scalding him as my scream scalded me. . . .*

A moment of reflection follows.

*Here it must end. It is the knowledge of that obscene joy I cannot bear. I seem to see the coppery bark of the pines and the bristling needles sprinkled with flakes and the dark half-buried rocks. Near the creek I can see the dingy frozen willows and the softly gleaming ice. Did they hear? I wondered. Would they come, dragging me back to their firelight and noise? I thought of Job: ". . . now shall I sleep in the dust; thou shalt seek me in the morning, but I shall not be."*

But he was! The gunshot alerted the bivouac. Men did seek Palmer out, carried him back, slapping his shoulders and congratulating him, bringing him whiskey and coffee and blankets, rubbing his hands and feet with gunnysacks and ice and painting his extremities—and his nose—with iodine against frostbite. Huddled about the fire in the blankets, his face vivid with color, Palmer struggled feebly to explain, but, pressed for details, proved unhelpful. Did he look at Major Shannon? Did their eyes meet? Did some understanding flow? Did Shannon smile in faint bitter triumph? We do not know.

The column pushed on. By now, however, it had occurred to several officers that the mission itself was foolhardy and unnecessary. Captain Fenton in particular seems to have realized that the Indians were "up" to nothing—and couldn't be if they had tried—and though the Captain could not possibly have foreseen the course of history—the massacre at the Little Big Horn during the nation's centennial celebration, the outrage and resulting suppression of the Indians (ending in the bitter defeat at Wounded Knee), he saw clearly that war was *not* inevitable, that an assault upon some insignificant village could only be the spark to set the plains afire come spring. He—and others—privately consulted with Palmer, who at some point earlier *must* have threatened protest, not only via *The New York Herald* and *The Chicago Times* but also to General Terry in St. Paul, to General Crook in Omaha and to General

Sheridan in Chicago. If there were some sort of objection, the officers insisted, some demand for an accounting—but a demand that for obvious reasons could not come from within the army itself—why if there could be an investigation of the battle of Deer Creek itself—much might be accomplished. Much too might be saved.

We lack Palmer's answer—or rather we find it in the empty pages, the brief notations. He simply records the pleas. If they stirred anything within him he does not mention it. When scouts returned with news of a village, a colloquy followed, more debate, and in the end Shannon prevailed, since no one except Palmer himself possessed a will sufficient to oppose his.

Thirty-five lodges, maybe a hundred fighting braves, Sioux and some Cheyenne camped across a lake in the mouth of a ravine.

"We don't need to do it!" Captain Fenton protested.

"We are at war," Shannon said smoothly, emphasizing each word.

"We're not at war!" Fenton objected.

Shannon made no reply (or so Palmer tells us).

The column left at night. No moon. A stiff wind flung snow in their faces and Shannon pushed everyone hard. They traveled light—a day's rations and ammunition. By midnight they reached the "sentinels"— three big peaks about the same distance apart. The column shoved through a pass and into a valley, rested and drove on, over bluffs and down slopes and into canyons, until the horses were panting and their flanks were streaming and flecked with curls of sweat. Then the troopers dismounted, scooped snow and rubbed their mounts.

Shannon forbade fires, and if a trooper sank into the slush and begged for rest, the officers would haul him up, cursing. Then they were all mounted and riding on, over flat ground until a ridge rose before them, as though from the sea.

Shannon sent a troop east, across the river, to lie in wait for the Indian ponies. Two more slipped around the west ridge, and the last two snuck north, to the ravine. Chilldress, Fenton and Palmer left their horses and climbed the ridge, looking into a wall of darkness, their breath clouding before them. The wind seemed to smother them. It was as though from the lake great wings beat forth waves of icy air, Palmer wrote, one of the few poetic touches he now allowed himself. Sometimes the tinkle of pony bells carried on the wind.

Slowly a pale white light began to flood the valley and the mist drifted into tatters, and they could hear the bells and see the river gleaming and the frozen lake covered with snow and all around, thick white mounds, and near the shore the ragged willows and cottonwoods casting grey shadows. Then, across the river, they saw the mules and ponies—small dark shapes, heads down, rumps to the wind. Then too, looking south, beneath the smoke and haze they saw the lodges scattered in the nooks of the old river bed. Soon afterward the troopers, formed in company front, moved out, spreading across the valley—a long string of mouse-colored horses and blue-clothed men, coats gone, pistols cocked.

. . . *I could see,* Palmer wrote, *the tails switching and the heads lifted, ears back. I could see the glint of metal, the puff of breath—tiny sparkling clouds—and hear the jingle of bits and the squeak of leather. The troopers crossed the lake and mounted the shore, and behind them the prints and crushed snow rolled out. Then in the village someone hooted like a bird, a soldier whooped, the trumpets snarled, the men yelled and spurred, the horses squatted and sprang forward, tails flicking, snow kicking up behind. . . .*

At first it was only a trot, the men shouting and firing—spits of flame and the crackle and the smoke rising and drifting into a blue cloud. The Indians came swarming out, spinning and falling as they were hit, flinging up their arms or stumbling and dropping. Some escaped, most did not. The troopers tore down the lodges and piled them with dry cottonwood and fired everything—blankets and robes and buffalo meat and saddles and halters and powder. The fires smoldered; then the powder went up in great foamy sheets, and the long fir lodgepoles flung into the sky and down again. The snow began to melt; a dark cloud swept across the valley, and on the ridge you could smell the greasy stink of canvas and buffalo and elk hide burning.

They wouldn't leave the ponies and they couldn't handle them. The fires and the smell of white men spooked them, so to save ammunition the troopers bashed their skulls with axes or ripped their throats with knives, and the shrill trumpeting reached the ridge—the breath rushing from the slashed windpipes. Then came the *thoomp* of Captain Prowt's shotgun.

All this Palmer watched and noted, and if at some point his eyes met Major Shannon's we shall never know. In detail but without comment he leaves us his account.

"None of our men was killed," he concludes. "The wounded we dragged on travois."

# BARRY LOPEZ
# WINTER COUNT 1973: GEESE, THEY FLEW OVER IN A STORM

Barry Lopez, who lives in Finn Rock, Oregon, was born in 1945 in Port Chester, New York, and is a 1966 graduate of the University of Notre Dame. Through nonfiction, fiction, and Native American fictional narratives he has earned a widespread reputation as an authoritative writer on the subject of nature and the environment, his style as pared down and elemental as the lives and values he celebrates. *Of Wolves and Men* (1978) won the John Burroughs Medal for distinguished natural history writing and the Pacific Northwest Booksellers Award for excellence in nonfiction. *Winter Count* (1981), a story collection, received the Distinguished Recognition Award from Friends of American Writers.

"Winter Count 1973" presents the reflections of Roger Callahan, an expert on Native American culture, as he prepares to present a paper at a conference being held in a New Orleans hotel. He scorns colleagues who theorize about Indian history and neglect the "poetic view" that would show compassion for the Indians in their sense of land and history. In turn, when he gives his paper, his colleagues pay scant attention, and Roger almost surrenders to a feeling of righteous self-pity. However, he withdraws honorably into a vision of mythic time and of personal histories—the "winter counts" from Dakota, Crow, and Blackfeet experience.

# WINTER COUNT, 1973: GEESE, THEY FLEW OVER IN A STORM

He followed the bellboy off the elevator, through a foyer with forlorn leather couches, noting how low the ceiling was, with its white plaster flowers in bas-relief—and that there were no windows. He followed him down a long corridor dank with an air of fugitives, past dark, impenetrable doors. At the distant end of the next corridor he saw gray thunderheads and the black ironwork of a fire escape. The boy slowed down and reached out to slide a thick key into the lock and he heard the sudden alignment of steel tumblers and their ratchet click. The door swung open and the boy entered, with the suitcase bouncing against the crook at the back of his knee.

He tipped the boy, having no idea what amount was now thought proper. The boy departed, leaving the room sealed off as if in a vacuum. The key with the ornate brass fob lay on a glass table. The man stood by the bed with his hands folded at his lips as though in prayer. Slowly he cleared away the drapes, the curtains and the blinds and stared out at the bare sky. Wind whipped rain in streaks across the glass. He had never been to New Orleans. It was a vague streamer blowing in his memory, like a boyhood acquaintance with Lafcadio Hearn. Natchez Trace. Did Choctaw live here? he wondered. Or Chitamacha? Before them, worshippers of the sun.

He knew the plains better. Best. The high plains north of the Platte River.

He took off his shoes and lay on the bed. He was glad for the feel of the candlewick bedspread. Or was it chenille? He had had this kind of spread on his bed when he was a child. He removed his glasses and pinched the bridge of his nose. In all these years he had delivered so few papers, had come to enjoy much more listening to them, to the stories unfolding in them. It did not matter to him that the arguments were so abstruse they were all but impregnable, that the thought in them would turn to vapor, an arrested breath. He came to hear a story unfold, to regard its shape and effect. He thought one unpacked history, that it came like pemmican in a parfleche and was to be consumed in a hard winter.

The wind sucked at the windows and released them suddenly to rattle in their metal frames. It made him think of home, of the Sand Hills. He lay motionless on the bed and thought of the wind. Crow men racing naked in an April rain, with their hair, five-foot-long black banners, spiraling behind, splashing on the muscled rumps of white horses with brown ears.

> 1847 One man alone defended the Hat in a fight with the Crow

> 1847 White buffalo, Dusk killed it

> 1847 Daughter of Turtle Head, her clothes caught fire and she was burned up

> 1847 Three men who were women came

He got up and went to his bag. He took out three stout willow sticks and bound them as a tripod. From its apex he hung a beaded bag of white elk hide with long fringe. The fringe was wrinkled from having been folded against itself in his suit pocket.

> 1891 Medicine bundles, police tore them open

What did they want from him? A teacher. He taught, he did not write papers. He told the story of people coming up from the Tigris-Euphrates, starting there. Other years he would start in a different place—Olduvai, Afar Valley. Or in Tierra del Fuego with the Onas. He could as easily start in the First World of the Navajo. The point, he told his students, was not this. There was no point. It was a slab of meat. It was a rhythm to dance to. It was a cloak that cut the wind when it blew hard enough to crack your soul.

> 1859 Ravens froze, fell over

> 1804 Heavy spring snow. Even the dogs went snow-blind

He slept. In his rumpled suit. In the flat, reflected storm light his face appeared ironed smooth. The wind fell away from the building and he dreamed.

For a moment he was lost. Starlight Room. Tarpon Room. Oak Room. He was due—he thought suddenly of aging, of illness: *when our children, they had strangulations of the throat,* of the cure for *any* illness as he scanned the long program—in the Creole Room. He was due in the Creole Room. Roger Callahan, Nebraska State College: "Winter Counts

from the Dakota, the Crow and the Blackfeet: Personal Histories." Jesus,
he thought, why had he come? He had been asked. They had asked.
   "Aha, Roger."
   "I'm on time? I got—"
   "You come right this way. I want you in front here. Everyone is
excited, very excited, you know. We're very glad you came. And how
is Margaret?"
   "Yes—. Margaret died. She died two years ago."

   1837 Straight Calf took six horses from the Crow and gave
        them to Blue Cloud Woman's father and took her

   1875 White Hair, he was killed in a river by an Omaha man

   1943 John Badger Heart killed in an automobile crash

He did not hear the man. He sat. The histories began to cover him
over like willows, thick as creek willows, and he reached out to steady
himself in the pool of time.
   He listened patiently to the other papers. Edward Rice Phillips, Pur-
due: "The Okipa Ceremony and Mandan Sexual Habits." The Mandan,
he thought, they were all dead. Who would defend them? Renata Mor-
rison, University of Texas: "The Role of Women in Northern Plains
Religious Ceremonials."

   1818 Sparrow Woman promised the Sun Dance in winter if
        the Cree didn't find us

   1872 Comes Out of the Water, she ran off the Assiniboine
        horses

   1904 Moving Gently, his sister hung herself

He tried to listen, but the words fell away like tumbled leaves. Cottonwoods. Winters so bad they would have to cut down cottonwood trees
for the horses to eat. *So cold we got water from beaver holes only.* And
years when they had to eat the horses. *We killed our ponies and ate them.
No buffalo.*
   Inside the windowless room (he could not remember which floor the
elevator had opened on) everyone was seated in long rows. From the
first row he could not see anyone. He shifted in his seat and his leather
bag fell with a slap against the linoleum floor. How long had he been
carrying papers from one place to another like this? He remembered a
friend's poem about a snowy owl dead behind glass in a museum, no
more to soar, to hunch and spread his wings and tail and fall silent as
moonlight.

1809  Blue feathers found on the ground from unknown birds

1811  Weasel Sits Down came into camp with blue feathers
      tied in his hair

There was distant applause, like dry brush rattling in the wind.

Years before, defense of theory had concerned him. Not now. "I've
thrown away everything that is no good," he told a colleague one summer afternoon on his porch, as though shouting over the roar of a
storm. "I can no longer think of anything worse than proving you are
right." He took what was left and he went on from there.

1851  No meat in camp. A man went to look for buffalo and
      was killed by two Arapaho

1854  The year they dragged the Arapaho's head through camp

". . . and my purpose in aligning these four examples is to clearly
demonstrate an irrefutable, or what I consider an irrefutable, relationship: The Arikara never . . . "

When he was a boy his father had taken him one April morning to
watch whooping cranes on estuaries of the Platte, headed for Alberta.
The morning was crucial in the unfolding of his own life.

1916  My father drives east for hours in silence. We walk out
      into a field covered all over with river fog. The cranes,
      just their legs are visible

His own count would be personal, more personal, as though he were
the only one.

1918  Father, shot dead. Argonne forest

The other years came around him now like soft velvet noses of horses
touching his arms in the dark.

". . . While the Cheyenne, contrary to what Greenwold has had to
say on this point but reinforcing what has been stated previously by
Gregg and Houston, were more inclined. . . ."

He wished for something to hold, something to touch, to strip leaves
barehanded from a chokecherry branch or to hear rain falling on the
surface of a lake. In this windowless room he ached.

1833  Stars blowing around like snow. Some fall to earth

1856  Reaches into the Enemy's Tipi has a dream and can't
      speak

1869  Fire Wagon, it comes

Applause.

He stood up and walked in quiet shoes to the stage. (Once in the middle of class he had stopped to explain his feeling about walking everywhere in silence.) He set his notes on the podium and covered them with his hands. In a clear voice, without apology for his informality or a look at his papers, he unfolded the winter counts of the Sioux warrior Blue Thunder, of the Blackfeet Bad Head, and of the Crow Extends His Paw. He stated that these were personal views of history, sometimes metaphorical, bearing on a larger, tribal history. He spoke of the confusion caused by translators who had tried to force agreement among several winter counts or who mistook mythic time for some other kind of real time. He concluded by urging less contention. "As professional historians, we have too often subordinated one system to another and forgotten all together the individual view, the poetic view, which is as close to the truth as the consensus. Or it can be as distant."

He felt the necklace of hawk talons pressing against his clavicles under the weight of his shirt.

The applause was respectful, thin, distracted. As he stepped away from the podium he realized it was perhaps foolish to have accepted the invitation. He could no longer make a final point. He had long ago lost touch with the definitive, the awful distance of reason. He wanted to go back to the podium. You can only tell the story as it was given to you, he wanted to say. Do not lie. Do not make it up.

He hesitated for a moment at the edge of the stage. He wished he were back in Nebraska with his students, to warn them: it is too dangerous for everyone to have the same story. The same things do not happen to everyone.

He passed through the murmuring crowd, through a steel door, down a hallway, up a flight of stairs, another, and emerged into palms in the lobby.

> 1823   A man, he was called Fifteen Horses, who was heyoka,
> a contrary, sacred clown, ran at the Crow backwards,
> shooting arrows at his own people. The Crow shot him
> in midair like a quail. He couldn't fool them

He felt the edge of self-pity, standing before a plate-glass window as wide as the spread of his arm and as tall as his house. He watched the storm that still raged, which he could not hear, which he had not been able to hear, bend trees to breaking, slash the surface of Lake Pontchartrain and raise air boiling over the gulf beyond. "Everything is held together with stories," he thought. "That is all that is holding us together, stories and compassion."

He turned quickly from the cold glass and went up in the silent elevator and ordered dinner. When it came, he threw back the drapes and curtains and opened the windows. The storm howled through his room and roared through his head. He breathed the wet air deep into his lungs. In the deepest distance, once, he heard the barking-dog sounds of geese, running like horses before a prairie thunderstorm.

# LESLIE MARMON SILKO
# LULLABY

Born in 1948, Leslie Silko was raised in Old Laguna in New Mexico, and is partly Laguna Pueblo Indian. Laguna material forms the basis for nearly all of her work. Because this northwestern part of New Mexico is a uranium-producing area, the people of Laguna are materially well off, but their traditional communal system has been changed, often for the worse. Silko lived through these developments from old to new. After obtaining a B.A. in English at the University of New Mexico in 1969, she began law school but gave it up for writing. Her novel, *Ceremony* (1977), and fiction/poetry/personal narrative *Storyteller* (1981) have placed her in the forefront of Native American authors along with such writers as N. Scott Momaday and James Welch.

"Lullaby" first appeared in *The Chicago Review*, No. 26, 1974, and was featured in *Best American Short Stories 1975*. The story focuses on an old Navajo couple living just north of Laguna Reservation. Ayah, sitting against a tree waiting for Chato to come back from Azzie's Bar after having spent most of the monthly government check, is thinking of the two really important elements in her life: her childhood in the hogan with her mother weaving, and her two small children whom the white doctors have weaned from home until they hardly recognize her. Even though the story is seen through Ayah's eyes and painfully illustrates her loss, it does not condemn the whites but presents a balanced picture. To be sure, we see examples of how Navajos are shabbily treated; but when the doctors come for the children, it is to save them from the tuberculosis which has killed their siblings, and when Ayah signs the papers, it is because Chato has taught her to sign her name but not to understand English. When she realizes what she has done and wants to call in a medicine man, Chato tells her it is too late, and from then on she no longer sleeps at his side, hating him for having introduced her to new ways. Her song for babies (the lullaby of the title) joins death and life, suggesting that time is endless and life perpetual when rooted in familiar soil.

# LULLABY

The sun had gone down but the snow in the wind gave off its own light. It came in thick tufts like new wool—washed before the weaver spins it. Ayah reached out for it like her own babies had, and she smiled when she remembered how she had laughed at them. She was an old woman now, and her life had become memories. She sat down with her back against the wide cottonwood tree, feeling the rough bark on her back bones; she faced east and listened to the wind and snow sing in a high-pitched Yeibechei song. Out of the wind she felt warmer, and she could watch the wide fluffy snow fill in her tracks, steadily, until the direction she had come from was gone. By the light of the snow she could see the dark outline of the big arroyo a few feet away. She was sitting on the edge of Cebolleta Creek, where in the springtime the thin cows would graze on grass already chewed flat to the ground. In the wide deep creek bed where only a trickle of water flowed in the summer, the skinny cows would wander, looking for new grass along winding paths splashed with manure.

Ayah pulled the old Army blanket over her head like a shawl. Jimmie's blanket—the one he had sent to her. That was a long time ago and the green wool was faded, and it was unraveling on the edges. She did not want to think about Jimmie. So she thought about the weaving and the way her mother had done it. On the tall wooden loom set into the sand under a tamarack tree for shade. She could see it clearly. She had been only a little girl when her grandma gave her the wooden combs to pull the twigs and burrs from the raw, freshly washed wool. And while she combed the wool, her grandma sat beside her, spinning a silvery strand of yarn around the smooth cedar spindle. Her mother worked at the loom with yarns dyed bright yellow and red and gold. She watched them dye the yarn in boiling black pots full of beeweed petals, juniper berries, and sage. The blankets her mother made were soft and woven so tight that rain rolled off them like birds' feathers. Ayah remembered sleeping warm on cold windy nights, wrapped in her mother's blankets on the hogan's sandy floor.

The snow drifted now, with the northwest wind hurling it in gusts. It drifted up around her black overshoes—old ones with little metal buckles. She smiled at the snow which was trying to cover her little by

209

little. She could remember when they had no black rubber overshoes; only the high buckskin leggings that they wrapped over their elkhide moccasins. If the snow was dry or frozen, a person could walk all day and not get wet; and in the evenings the beams of the ceiling would hang with lengths of pale buckskin leggings, drying out slowly.

She felt peaceful remembering. She didn't feel cold any more. Jimmie's blanket seemed warmer than it had ever been. And she could remember the morning he was born. She could remember whispering to her mother, who was sleeping on the other side of the hogan, to tell her it was time now. She did not want to wake the others. The second time she called to her, her mother stood up and pulled on her shoes; she knew. They walked to the old stone hogan together, Ayah walking a step behind her mother. She waited alone, learning the rhythms of the pains while her mother went to call the old woman to help them. The morning was already warm even before dawn and Ayah smelled the bee flowers blooming and the young willow growing at the springs. She could remember that so clearly, but his birth merged into the births of the other children and to her it became all the same birth. They named him for the summer morning and in English they called him Jimmie.

It wasn't like Jimmie died. He just never came back, and one day a dark blue sedan with white writing on its doors pulled up in front of the box-car shack where the rancher let the Indians live. A man in a khaki uniform trimmed in gold gave them a yellow piece of paper and told them that Jimmie was dead. He said the Army would try to get the body back and then it would be shipped to them; but it wasn't likely because the helicopter had burned after it crashed. All of this was told to Chato because he could understand English. She stood inside the doorway holding the baby while Chato listened. Chato spoke English like a white man and he spoke Spanish too. He was taller than the white man and he stood straighter too. Chato didn't explain why; he just told the military man they could keep the body if they found it. The white man looked bewildered; he nodded his head and he left. Then Chato looked at her and shook his head, and then he told her, "Jimmie isn't coming home anymore," and when he spoke, he used the words to speak of the dead. She didn't cry then, but she hurt inside with anger. And she mourned him as the years passed, when a horse fell with Chato and broke his leg, and the white rancher told them he wouldn't pay Chato until he could work again. She mourned Jimmie because he would have worked for his father then; he would have saddled the big bay horse and ridden the fence lines each day, with wire cutters and heavy gloves, fixing the breaks in the barbed wire and putting the stray cattle back inside again.

She mourned him after the white doctors came to take Danny and Ella away. She was at the shack alone that day they came. It was back in the days before they hired Navajo women to go with them as interpreters. She recognized one of the doctors. She had seen him at the children's clinic at Cañoncito about a month ago. They were wearing khaki uniforms and they waved papers at her and a black ball-point pen, trying to make her understand their English words. She was frightened by the way they looked at the children, like the lizard watches the fly. Danny was swinging on the tire swing on the elm tree behind the rancher's house, and Ella was toddling around the front door, dragging the broomstick horse Chato made for her. Ayah could see they wanted her to sign the papers, and Chato had taught her to sign her name. It was something she was proud of. She only wanted them to go, and to take their eyes away from her children.

She took the pen from the man without looking at his face and she signed the papers in three different places he pointed to. She stared at the ground by their feet and waited for them to leave. But they stood there and began to point and gesture at the children. Danny stopped swinging. Ayah could see his fear. She moved suddenly and grabbed Ella into her arms; the child squirmed, trying to get back to her toys. Ayah ran with the baby toward Danny; she screamed for him to run and then she grabbed him around his chest and carried him too. She ran south into the foothills of juniper trees and black lava rock. Behind her she heard the doctors running, but they had been taken by surprise, and as the hills became steeper and the cholla cactus were thicker, they stopped. When she reached the top of the hill, she stopped to listen in case they were circling around her. But in a few minutes she heard a car engine start and they drove away. The children had been too surprised to cry while she ran with them. Danny was shaking and Ella's little fingers were gripping Ayah's blouse.

She stayed up in the hills for the rest of the day, sitting on a black lava boulder in the sunshine where she could see for miles all around her. The sky was light blue and cloudless, and it was warm for late April. The sun warmth relaxed her and took the fear and anger away. She lay back on the rock and watched the sky. It seemed to her that she could walk into the sky, stepping through the clouds endlessly. Danny played with little pebbles and stones, pretending they were birds eggs and then little rabbits. Ella sat at her feet and dropped fistfuls of dirt into the breeze, watching the dust and particles of sand intently. Ayah watched a hawk soar high above them, dark wings gliding; hunting or only watching, she did not know. The hawk was patient and he circled all afternoon before he disappeared around the high volcanic peak the Mexicans called Guadalupe.

Late in the afternoon, Ayah looked down at the gray boxcar shack with the paint all peeled from the wood; the stove pipe on the roof was rusted and crooked. The fire she had built that morning in the oil drum stove had burned out. Ella was asleep in her lap now and Danny sat close to her, complaining that he was hungry; he asked when they would go to the house. "We will stay up here until your father comes," she told him, "because those white men were chasing us." The boy remembered then and he nodded at her silently.

If Jimmie had been there he could have read those papers and explained to her what they said. Ayah would have known then, never to sign them. The doctors came back the next day and they brought a BIA policeman with them. They told Chato they had her signature and that was all they needed. Except for the kids. She listened to Chato sullenly; she hated him when he told her it was the old woman who died in the winter, spitting blood; it was her old grandma who had given the children this disease. "They don't spit blood," she said coldly. "The whites lie." She held Ella and Danny close to her, ready to run to the hills again. "I want a medicine man first," she said to Chato, not looking at him. He shook his head. "It's too late now. The policeman is with them. You signed the paper." His voice was gentle.

It was worse than if they had died: to lose the children and to know that somewhere, in a place called Colorado, in a place full of sick and dying strangers, her children were without her. There had been babies that died soon after they were born, and one that died before he could walk. She had carried them herself, up to the boulders and great pieces of the cliff that long ago crashed down from Long Mesa; she laid them in the crevices of sandstone and buried them in fine brown sand with round quartz pebbles that washed down the hills in the rain. She had endured it because they had been with her. But she could not bear this pain. She did not sleep for a long time after they took her children. She stayed on the hill where they had fled the first time, and she slept rolled up in the blanket Jimmie had sent her. She carried the pain in her belly and it was fed by everything she saw: the blue sky of their last day together and the dust and pebbles they played with; the swing in the elm tree and broomstick horse choked life from her. The pain filled her stomach and there was no room for food or for her lungs to fill with air. The air and the food would have been theirs.

She hated Chato, not because he let the policeman and doctors put the screaming children in the government car, but because he had taught her to sign her name. Because it was like the old ones always told her about learning their language or any of their ways: it endangered you. She slept alone on the hill until the middle of November when the first snows came. Then she made a bed for herself where the children had slept. She did not lie down beside Chato again until many years later, when he was sick and shivering and only her body could keep him warm. The illness came after the white rancher told Chato he was too old to work for him anymore, and Chato and his old woman should be out of the shack by the next afternoon because the rancher had hired new people to work there. That had satisfied her. To see how the white man repaid Chato's years of loyalty and work. All of Chato's fine-sounding English talk didn't change things.

It snowed steadily and the luminous light from the snow gradually diminished into the darkness. Somewhere in Cebolleta a dog barked and other village dogs joined with it. Ayah looked in the direction she had come, from the bar where Chato was buying the wine. Sometimes he told her to go on ahead and wait; and then he never came. And when she finally went back looking for him, she would find him passed out at the bottom of the wooden steps to Azzie's Bar. All the wine would be gone and most of the money too, from the pale blue check that came to them once a month in a government envelope. It was then that she would look at his face and his hands, scarred by ropes and the barbed wire of all those years, and she would think, this man is a stranger; for forty years she had smiled at him and cooked his food, but he remained a stranger. She stood up again, with the snow almost to her knees and she walked back to find Chato.

It was hard to walk in the deep snow and she felt the air burn in her lungs. She stopped a short distance from the bar to rest and readjust the blanket. But this time he wasn't waiting for her on the bottom step with his old Stetson hat pulled down and his shoulders hunched up in his long wool overcoat.

She was careful not to slip on the wooden steps. When she pushed the door open, warm air and cigarette smoke hit her face. She looked around slowly and deliberately, in every corner, in every dark place that the old man might find to sleep. The bar owner didn't like Indians in there, especially Navajos, but he let Chato come in because he could talk Spanish like he was one of them. The men at the bar stared at her, and the bartender saw that she left the door open wide. Snowflakes were flying inside like moths and melting into a puddle on the oiled wood floor. He motioned to her to close the door, but she did not see him. She held herself straight and walked across the room slowly, searching the room with every step. The snow in her hair melted and she

could feel it on her forehead. At the far corner of the room, she saw
red flames at the mica window of the old stove door; she looked behind
the stove just to make sure. The bar got quiet except for the Spanish
polka music playing on the jukebox. She stood by the stove and shook
the snow from her blanket and held it near the stove to dry. The wet
wool smell reminded her of new-born goats in early March, brought
inside to warm near the fire. She felt calm.

In past years they would have told her to get out. But her hair was
white now and her face was wrinkled. They looked at her like she was
a spider crawling slowly across the room. They were afraid; she could
feel the fear. She looked at their faces steadily. They reminded her of
the first time the white people brought her children back to her that
winter. Danny had been shy and hid behind the thin white woman
who brought them. And the baby had not known her until Ayah took
her into her arms, and then Ella had nuzzled close to her as she had
when she was nursing. The blonde woman was nervous and kept looking
at a dainty gold watch on her wrist. She sat on the bench near the
small window and watched the dark snow clouds gather around the
mountains; she was worrying about the unpaved road. She was
frightened by what she saw inside too: the strips of venison drying on
a rope across the ceiling and the children jabbering excitedly in a language she did not know. So they stayed for only a few hours. Ayah
watched the government car disappear down the road and she knew
they were already being weaned from these lava hills and from this sky.
The last time they came was in early June, and Ella stared at her the
way the men in the bar were now staring. Ayah did not try to pick her
up; she smiled at her instead and spoke cheerfully to Danny. When he
tried to answer her, he could not seem to remember and he spoke
English words with the Navajo. But he gave her a scrap of paper that
he had found somewhere and carried in his pocket; it was folded in
half, and he shyly looked up at her and said it was a bird. She asked
Chato if they were home for good this time. He spoke to the white
woman and she shook her head. "How much longer?" he asked, and
she said she didn't know; but Chato saw how she stared at the boxcar
shack. Ayah turned away then. She did not say good-bye.

She felt satisfied that the men in the bar feared her. Maybe it was her
face and the way she held her mouth with teeth clenched tight, like
there was nothing anyone could do to her now. She walked north down
the road, searching for the old man. She did this because she had the
blanket, and there would be no place for him except with her and the
blanket in the old adobe barn near the arroyo. They always slept there

when they came to Cebolleta. If the money and the wine were gone, she would be relieved because then they could go home again; back to the old hogan with a dirt roof and rock walls where she herself had been born. And the next day the old man could go back to the few sheep they still had, to follow along behind them, guiding them, into dry sandy arroyos where sparse grass grew. She knew he did not like walking behind old ewes when for so many years he rode big quarter horses and worked with cattle. But she wasn't sorry for him; he should have known all along what would happen.

There had not been enough rain for their garden in five years; and that was when Chato finally hitched a ride into the town and brought back brown boxes of rice and sugar and big tin cans of welfare peaches. After that, at the first of the month they went to Cebolleta to ask the postmaster for the check; and then Chato would go to the bar and cash it. They did this as they planted the garden every May, not because anything would survive the summer dust, but because it was time to do this. The journey passed the days that smelled silent and dry like the caves above the canyon with yellow painted buffaloes on their walls.

He was walking along the pavement when she found him. He did not stop or turn around when he heard her behind him. She walked beside him and she noticed how slowly he moved now. He smelled strong of woodsmoke and urine. Lately he had been forgetting. Sometimes he called her by his sister's name and she had been gone for a long time. Once she had found him wandering on the road to the white man's ranch, and she asked him why he was going that way; he laughed at her and said, "You know they can't run that ranch without me," and he walked on determined, limping on the leg that had been crushed many years before. Now he looked at her curiously, as if for the first time, but he kept shuffling along, moving slowly along the side of the highway. His gray hair had grown long and spread out on the shoulders of the long overcoat. He wore the old felt hat pulled down over his ears. His boots were worn out at the toes and he had stuffed pieces of an old red shirt in the holes. The rags made his feet look like little animals up to their ears in snow. She laughed at his feet; the snow muffled the sound of her laugh. He stopped and looked at her again. The wind had quit blowing and the snow was falling straight down; the southeast sky was beginning to clear and Ayah could see a star.

"Let's rest awhile," she said to him. They walked away from the road and up the slope to the giant boulders that had tumbled down from the red sandrock mesa throughout the centuries of rainstorms and earth tremors. In a place where the boulders shut out the wind, they sat down with their backs against the rock. She offered half of the blanket to him and they sat wrapped together.

The storm passed swiftly. The clouds moved east. They were massive and full, crowding together across the sky. She watched them with the feeling of horses—steely blue-gray horses startled across the sky. The powerful haunches pushed into the distances and the tail hairs streamed white mist behind them. The sky cleared. Ayah saw that there was nothing between her and the stars. The light was crystalline. There was no shimmer, no distortion through earth haze. She breathed the clarity of the night sky; she smelled the purity of the half moon and the stars. He was lying on his side with his knees pulled up near his belly for warmth. His eyes were closed now, and in the light from the stars and the moon, he looked young again.

She could see it descend out of the night sky: an icy stillness from the edge of the thin moon. She recognized the freezing. It came gradually, sinking snowflake by snowflake until the crust was heavy and deep. It had the strength of the stars in Orion, and its journey was endless. Ayah knew that with the wine he would sleep. He would not feel it. She tucked the blanket around him, remembering how it was when Ella had been with her; and she felt the rush so big inside her heart for the babies. And she sang the only song she knew to sing for babies. She could not remember if she had ever sung it to her children, but she knew that her grandmother had sung it and her mother had sung it:

> *The earth is your mother,*
>      *she holds you.*
> *The sky is your father,*
>      *he protects you.*
> *Sleep,*
> *sleep.*
> *Rainbow is your sister,*
>      *she loves you.*
> *The winds are your brothers,*
>      *they sing to you.*
> *Sleep,*
> *sleep.*
> *We are together always*
> *We are together always*
> *There never was a time*
> *when this*
> *was not so.*

# IV

## Shapes
## of
## Tomorrow

# WALLACE STEGNER
# FIELD GUIDE
# TO THE WESTERN BIRDS

After his birth in Lake Mills, Iowa, in 1909, Wallace Stegner lived in such widely separate areas of the West as North Dakota, Washington, Saskatchewan, Montana, and Wyoming before his family finally settled for nine years in Salt Lake City, Utah. He was educated at Utah (B.A. 1930) and at Iowa (Ph.D. 1935) and taught at a number of institutions including Harvard University (1939–1945) before returning West to take a position as Professor of English and Director of the Creative Writing Program at Stanford University, where he remained until his retirement in 1971. The region he imaginatively—and morally—identifies with, in more than twenty books of fiction and nonfiction, is roughly the inter-mountain West; his work often explores the dichotomy between civilization and barbarism, community and anarchy, pioneering and homesteading values rooted in the past and the self-destructiveness of a modernity living in the shape of tomorrow without much comprehension of the past. Stegner's nonfiction books include *Beyond the Hundredth Meridian* (1954), *Wolf Willow* (1962), and two collections of essays indispensable for studies of the West, *The Sound of Mountain Water* (1969) and *One Way to Spell Man: Essays with a Western Bias* (1982). Among his novels are *The Big Rock Candy Mountain* (1943), *All the Little Live Things* (1967), *Angle of Repose* (1971), which earned him the Pulitzer Prize, and *The Spectator Bird* (1976), winner of the 1977 National Book Award.

Stegner's often-praised realism has a surreal and satirical quality that distinguishes his best work as that of the moralist who seeks to find some ordering principle in current change. These distinguishing concerns and characteristics are prominent in the novelette, "Field Guide to the Western Birds," published in 1956 in Stegner's collection, *The City of the Living*. Literary agent Joe Allston has come up the hard way from Iowa to Madison Avenue and retired to California's Bay Peninsula, south of San Francisco, where he views the bird, animal, and human life with a mixture of wryly humorous detachment and cocksure distaste. But when he unmasks a talented charlatan, star of a neighbor's benefit party, as "a cuckoo chick in a robin's nest," he has the humanity to recognize the arrogance in his somewhat voyeuristic research into the complexities of conduct among "western birds" such as aesthetes and beagle-breeders. No longer sure how individuals fit into society, Joe has to resign himself to the limitations of human understanding, though he clings to an unidealized faith in nature's bounty and in the possibilities of cultural achievement.

# FIELD GUIDE
# TO THE WESTERN BIRDS

I must say that I never felt better. I don't feel sixty-six, I have no geron-
tological worries; if I am on the shelf, as we literally are in this place
on the prow of a California hill, retirement is not the hangdog misery
that I half expected it to be. When I stepped out of my office, we sold
our place in Yorktown Heights because even Yorktown Heights might
be too close to Madison Avenue for comfort. The New Haven would
still run trains; a man might still see the old companions: I didn't want
to have to avoid the Algonquin at noon or the Ritz bar after five. If
there is anything limper than an ex-literary agent it is an ex-literary
agent hanging around where his old business still goes on. We told
people that we were leaving because I wanted to get clear away and
get perspective for my memoirs. Ha! That was to scare some of them,
a little. *What I Have Done for Ten Percent*. I know some literary figures
who wish I had stayed in New York where they could watch me.

But here I sit on this terrace in a golden afternoon, finishing off an
early, indolent highball, my shanks in saddle-stitched slacks and my
feet in brown suede; a Pebble Beach pasha, a Los Gatos geikwar. What
I have done for ten percent was never like this.

Down the terrace a gray bird alights—some kind of towhee, I think,
but I can't find him in the bird book. Whatever he is, he is a champion
for pugnacity. Maybe he is living up to some dim notion of how to be
a proper husband and father, maybe he just hates himself, for about
ten times a day I see him alight on the terrace and challenge his reflection
in the plate glass. He springs at himself like a fighting cock, beats his
wings, pecks, falls back, springs again, slides and thumps against the
glass, falls down, flies up, falls down, until he wears himself out and
squats on the bricks panting and glaring at his hated image. For about
ten days now he has been struggling with himself like Jacob with his
angel, Hercules with his Hydra, Christian with his conscience, old retired
Joe Allston with his memoirs.

I drop a hand and grope up the drained highball glass, tip the ice
cubes into my palm, and scoot them down the terrace. "Beat it, you

fool." The towhee, or whatever he is, springs into the air and flies away. End of problem.

Down the hill that plunges steeply from the terrace, somewhere down among the toyon and oak, a tom quail is hammering his ca-*whack*-a, ca-*whack*-a, ca-*whack*-a. From the horse pasture of our neighbor Shields, on the other side of the house, a meadowlark whistles sharp and pure. The meadowlarks are new to me. They do not grow in Yorktown Heights, and the quail there, I am told, say Bob White instead of ca-*whack*-a.

This terrace is a good place just to lie and listen. Lots of bird business, every minute of the day. All around the house I can hear the clatter of house finches that have nested in the vines, the drainspouts, the rafters of the carport. The liveoaks level with my eyes flick with little colored movements: I see a redheaded woodpecker working spirally around a trunk, a nuthatch walking upside down along a limb, a pair of warblers hanging like limes among the leaves.

It is a thing to be confessed that in spite of living in Yorktown Heights among the birdwatchers for twenty-four years I never got into my gaiters and slung on my binoculars and put a peanut butter sandwich and an apple in my pocket and set off lightheartedly through the woods. I have seen them come straggling by on a Sunday afternoon, looking like a cross between the end of a YWCA picnic and Hare and Hounds at Rugby, but it was always a little too tweedy and muscular to stir me, and until we came here I couldn't have told a Wilson Thrush from a turkey. The memoirs are what made a birdwatcher out of Joseph Allston; I have labored at identification as much as reminiscence through the mornings when Ruth has thought I've been gleaning the busy years.

When we built this house I very craftily built a separate study down the hill a hundred feet or so, the theory being that I did not want to be disturbed by telephone calls. Actually I did not want to be disturbed by Ruth, who sometimes begins to feel that she is the Whip of Conscience, and who worries that if I do not keep busy I will start to deteriorate. I had a little of that feeling myself: I was going to get all the benefits of privacy and quiet, and I even put a blank wall on the study on the view side. But I made the whole north wall of glass, for light, and that was where I got caught. The wall of glass looks into a deep green shade coiling with the python limbs of a liveoak, and the oak is always full of birds.

Worse than that for my concentration, there are two casement windows on the south that open onto a pasture and a stripe of sky. Even with my back to them, I can see them reflected dimly in the plate glass in front of me, and the pasture and the sky are also full of birds. I wrote a little thumbnail description of this effect, thinking it might go into the memoirs somewhere. It is something I learned how to do while managing the affairs of writers: "Faintly, hypnotically, like an hallucination, the reflected sky super-imposed on the umbrageous cave of the tree is traced by the linear geometry of hawks, the vortical returnings of buzzards. On the three fenceposts that show between sky and pasture, bluejays plunge to a halt to challenge the world, and across the stripe of sky lines of Brewer's blackbirds are pinned to the loops of telephone wire like a ragged black wash." I have seen (and sold) a lot worse.

I am beginning to understand the temptation to be literary and indulge the senses. It is a full-time job just watching and listening here. I watch the light change across the ridges to the west, and the ridges are the fresh gold of wild oats just turned, the oaks are round and green with oval shadows, the hollows have a tinge of blue. The last crest of the Coast Range is furry with sunstruck spikes of pine and redwood. Off to the east I can hear the roar, hardly more than a hum from here, as San Francisco pours its commuter trains down the valley, jams El Camino from Potrero to San Jose with the honk and stink of cars, rushes its daytime prisoners in murderous columns down the Bayshore. Not for me, not any more. Hardly any of that afternoon row penetrates up here. This is for the retired, for the no-longer-commuting, for contemplative ex-literary agents, for the birds.

Ruth comes out of the french doors of the bedroom and hands me the pernicious silver necklace that my client Murthi once sent her in gratitude from Hyderabad. The bird who made it was the same kind of jeweler that Murthi is a writer: why in *hell* should anyone hand-make a little set screw for a fastener, and then thread the screw backwards?

I comment aloud on the idiocy of the Hyderabad silversmith while I strain up on one elbow and try to fasten the thing around her neck, but Ruth does not pay attention. I believe she thinks complaints are a self-indulgence. Sometimes she irritates me close to uxoricide. I do not see how people can stay healthy unless they express their feelings. If I had that idiot Murthi here now I would tell him exactly what I think of his smug Oxonian paragraphs and his superior sniffing about American materialism. If I hadn't sold his foolish book for him he would never have sent his token of gratitude, and all the comfortable assumptions of my sixty-six years would be intact. I drop the screw on the bricks: *invariably* I try to screw it the wrong way. Cultural opposites; never the twain shall meet. Political understanding more impossible than Murthi thinks it is, because the Indians insist on making and doing and thinking everything backwards.

"No fog," Ruth says, stooping. At Bryn Mawr they taught her that a lady modulates her speaking voice, and as a result she never says anything except conspiratorially. A writer who wrote with so little regard for his audience wouldn't sell a line. On occasion she has started talking to me while her head was deep inside some cupboard or closet so that nothing came out but this inaudible thrilling murmur, and I have been so exasperated that I have deliberately walked out of the room. Five minutes later I have come back and found her still talking, still with her head among the coats and suits and dresses. *"What?"* I am inclined to say then. The intent is to make her feel chagrined and ridiculous to have been murmuring away to herself. It never does. A Bryn Mawr lady is as unruffled as her voice.

*"What?"* I say now, though this time I have heard her well enough. It just seems to me that out on the terrace, in the open air, she might speak above a whisper.

"No fog," she says in exactly the same tone. "Sue was afraid the fog would come in and chase everybody indoors."

I get the necklace screwed together at last and sink back exhausted. I am too used up even to protest when she rubs her hand around on my bald spot—a thing that usually drives me wild.

"Are you ready?" she says.

"That depends. Is this thing black tie or hula shirt?"

"Oh, informal."

"Slacks and jacket all right?"

"Sure."

"Then I'm ready."

For a minute she stands vaguely stirring her finger around in my fringe. It is very quiet; the peace seeps in upon the terrace from every side. "I suppose it isn't moral," I say.

"What isn't?"

"This."

"The house? What?"

"All of it."

I rear up on my elbow, not because I am sore about anything but because I really have an extraordinary sense of well-being, and when I feel anything that strongly I like a reaction, not a polite murmur. But then I see that she is staring at me and that her face, fixed for the party, is gently and softly astonished. It is as definite a reaction as they taught her, poor dear. I reach out and tweak her nose.

"I ought to invest in a hair shirt," I say. "What have I done to deserve so well-preserved and imperturbable a helpmeet?"

"Maybe it's something you did for ten percent," she whispers, and that tickles me. I was the poor one when we were married. Her father's money kept us going for the first five or six years.

She laughs and rubs her cheek against mine, and her cheek is soft and smells of powder. For the merest instant it feels *old*—too soft, limp and used and without tension and resilience, and I think what it means to be all through. But Ruth is looking across at the violet valleys and the sunstruck ridges, and she says in her whispery voice, "Isn't it beautiful? Isn't it really perfectly beautiful!"

So it is; that ought to be enough. If it weren't I would not be an incipient birdwatcher; I would be defensively killing myself writing those memoirs, trying to stay alive just by stirring around. But I don't need to stay alive by stirring around. I am a bee at the heart of a sleepy flower; the things I used to do for a living and the people I did them among are as remote as things and people I knew in prep school.

"I am oppressed with birdsong," I say. "I am confounded by peace. I don't want to move. Do we have to go over to Bill Casement's and drink highballs and listen to Sue's refugee genius punish the piano?"

"Of course. You were an agent. You know everybody in New York. You own or control Town Hall. You're supposed to help start this boy on his career."

I grunt, and she goes inside. The sun, very low, begins to reach in under the oak and blind me with bright flashes. Down at the foot of our hill two tall eucalyptuses rise high above the oak and toyon, and the limber oval leaves of their tips, not too far below me, flick and glitter like tinsel fish. From the undergrowth the quail cackles again. A swallow cuts across the terrace and swerves after an insect and is gone.

It is when I am trying to see where the swallow darted to that I notice the little hawk hovering above the tips of the eucalyptus trees. It holds itself in one spot like a helicopter pulling somebody out of the surf. The sparrow hawk or kestrel, according to the bird book, is the only small hawk, maybe the only one of any kind, that can do that.

From its hover, the kestrel stoops like a falling stone straight into the tip of the eucalyptus and then shoots up again from among the glitter of the leaves. It disappears into the sun, but just when I think it has gone it appears in another dive. Another miss: I can tell from its angry *kreeeeee!* as it swerves up. All the other birds are quiet; for a second the evening is like something under a belljar. I watch the kestrel stop and hover, and down it comes a third time, and up it goes screeching. As I stand up to see what it can be striking at, it apparently sees me; it is gone with a swift bowed wingbeat into the sun.

And now what? Out of the eucalyptus, seconds after the kestrel has gone, comes a little buzzing thing about the size of a bumblebee. A hummingbird, too far to see what kind. It sits in the air above the tree just as the kestrel did; it looks as if it couldn't hold all the indignation it feels: I think of a thimble-sized Colonel Blimp with a red face and asthmatic wheezings and exclamations. Then it too is gone as if shot out of a slingshot.

I am tickled by its tiny wrath and by the sense it has shown in staying down among the leaves where the hawk couldn't hit it. But I have hardly watched the little buzzing dot disappear before I am rubbing my eyes like a man seeing ghosts, for out of this same eucalyptus top, in a kind of Keystone Kop routine where fifty people pour out of one old Model T, lumbers up a great owl. He looks as clumsy as a buffalo after the speed and delicacy of the hawk and the hummingbird, and like a lumpish halfwit hurrying home before the neighborhood gang can catch and torment him, he flaps off heavily into the woods.

This is too much for Joseph Allston, oppressed with birdsong. I am cackling to myself like a maniac when Ruth comes out onto the terrace with her coat on. "Ruthie," I tell her, "you just missed seeing Oliver Owl black-balled from the Treetop Country Club."

"What?"

"Just as Big Round Red Mr. Sun was setting over the California hills."

"Have you gone balmy, poor lamb?" Ruth whispers, "or have you been nibbling highballs?"

"Madame, I am passionately at peace."

"Well, contain your faunish humor tonight," Ruth says. "Sue really wants to do something for this boy. Don't you go spoiling anything with your capers."

Ruth believes that I go out of my way to stir up the animals. Once our terrier Grumpy—now dead, but more dog for his pounds than ever lived—started through the fence in Yorktown Heights with a stick in his mouth. He didn't allow for the stick and the pickets, and he was coming fast—he never came any other way. The stick caught solidly on both sides and pretty near took his head off. That, Ruth told me in her confidential whisper, was the way I had approached every situation in my whole life. In her inaudible way, she is capable of a good deal of hyperbole. I have no desire to foul up Sue's artistic philanthropies. I can't do her boy any good, but I'll sip a drink and listen, and that's more help than he will get from any of the twelve people who will be there when he finally plays in Town Hall.

II

In California, as elsewhere, alcohol dulls the auricular nerves and leads people to raise their voices. The noise of cocktail parties is the same whether you are honoring the Sitwells in a suite at the Savoy Plaza, or whether you are showing off a refugee pianist on a Los Gatos patio. It sounds very familiar as we park among the Cadillacs and Jaguars and one incredible sleek red Ferrari and the routine Plymouth suburbans and Hillman Minxes of the neighbors. The sound is the same, only the setting is different. But that difference is considerable.

Dazed visitors from the lower, envious fringes of exurbia—and those include the Allstons, or did at first—are likely to come into the Casement cabaña and walk through it as if they have had a solid thump on the head. This cabaña has a complete barbecue kitchen with electrically operated grills thirty feet long. It has a bar nearly that size, a big television screen and a hi-fi layout, a lounge that is sage and gray and tangerine or lobster, I am not decorator enough to tell. It is chaste and hypnotically comfortable and faintly oppressive with money, like an ad for one of the places where you will find *Newsweek* or see men of distinction.

The whole glass side of the cabaña slides back and the cabaña becomes continuous with a patio that spreads to the edge of the pool, which is the color of one of the glass jars that used to sit in the windows of drugstores in Marshalltown, Iowa, when I was a boy. Across the pool, strung for a long distance along the retaining wall that holds the artificial flat top onto this hill, are the playing fields of Eton. I think I have never toured them all, but I have seen a croquet ground; a putting green; a tennis court and a half-sized paddle-tennis court; a ping-pong table; a shuffle-board court of smooth concrete; and out beyond, a football field, full-sized and fully grassed, that was built especially for young Jim Casement and his friends and so far as I have observed is never used. Beyond the retaining wall the hill falls away steeply, so that you look out across it and across the ventilators of the stables below the wall, and into the dusk where lights are beginning to bloom in beds and borders down the enormous garden of the Santa Clara Valley.

A neighborhood couple of modest means—and there are some—contemplate gratefully their admission to these splendors. A standing invitation amounts to a guest card at an exclusive club, and the Casements are generous with invitations. At some stage of their first tour through the layout any neighbor couple is sure to be found standing with their heads together, their eyes gauging and weighing and estimating, and you can hear the IBM machinery working in their heads. Hundred thousand? More than that, a lot more. Hundred and fifty? God knows what's in the house itself, in which the Casements do not entertain but only live. Couldn't touch the whole thing for under two hundred thousand, probably. A pool that size wouldn't have come at less than ten thousand; the cabaña alone would have cost more than our whole house . . .

I have been around this neighborhood for more than six months, and in six months the Casements can make you feel like a lifelong friend. And I have not been exactly unfamiliar in my lifetime with conspicuous consumption and the swindle sheet. But I still feel like whistling every time I push open the gate in the fence that is a design by Mondrian in egg crates and plastic screen, and look in upon the pool and the cabaña and the patio. The taste has been purchased, but it is taste. The Casement Club just misses being extravagantly beautiful; all it needs is something broken or incomplete, the way a Persian rug weaver will leave a flaw in his pattern to show that Allah alone is perfect and there is no God but God. This is all muted colors, plain lines, calculated simplicities. As I hold open the gate for Ruth, with the noise of the party already loud in the air, I feel as if I were going aboard a brand new and competitively designed cruise ship, or entering the latest Las Vegas motel.

We have not more than poked our heads in, and seen that the crowd is pretty thick already, before Sue spots us and starts over. She has a high-colored face and a smile that asks to be smiled back at, a very warm good-natured face. You think, the minute you lay eyes on her, What a nice woman. And across clusters of guests I see Bill Casement, just as good-natured, waving an arm, and with the same motion savagely beckoning a white-coated Japanese to intercept us with a tray. It is one of Bill's beliefs that guests at a Casement party spring into the splendid patio with bent elbows and glasses in their hands. He does not like awkward preliminaries; he perpetuates a fiction that nobody is ahead of anybody else.

"Ah," Sue says, "it's wonderful of you to come!" The funny thing is, you can't look at that wide and delighted smile and think otherwise. You are doing her an enormous favor just to *be*; to be at her party is to put her forever in your debt.

I scuff my ankles. "It is nothing," I say. "Where are the people who wanted to meet me?"

Sue giggles, perfectly delighted. "Lined up all around the pool. Including the next-most-important guest. You haven't met Arnold, have you?"

"I don't think he has met me," I say with dignity.

She has us by the elbows, starting us in. I twist and catch up two glasses off the tray that has appeared beside me, and I exchange a face of fellowship with the Japanese. Then the stage set swallows us. Mr. and Mrs. Allston, Ruth and Joe, the Allstons, neighbors, we are repeated every minute or two to polite attentive people, and we get people thrown at us in turn. Names mean less than nothing, they break like bubbles on the surface of the party's sound. We are two more walk-ons

with glasses in our hands; our voices go up and are lost in the clatter
that reminds my bird-conscious ears of a hundred blackbirds in a tree.
   Groups open and let us in and hold us a minute and pass us on. My
recording apparatus makes note of Mr. Thing, a white-haired and astonishingly benevolent-looking music critic from San Francisco; and Mr.
and Mrs. How-d'ye-do, whose family has supported music in the city
since Adah Menken was singing "Sweet Betsy from Pike" to packed
houses at the Mechanics' Hall. We shake the damp glass-chilled hand of
Mr. Monsieur, whom we have seen on platforms as the accompanist of a
celebrated Negro soprano, and Ruth has her hand kissed by a gentleman
whom I distinguish as Mr. Budapest, a gentleman who makes harps,
or harpsichords, and who wears a brown velvet jacket and sandals.
   Glimpses of Distinguished Guests, *filets* of conversation *au vin, ver-
schiedene Kalter Aufschnitt* of the neighborhood:
   Sam Shields, he of the robust cement mixer and the acres of home-
made walks and patios and barbecue pits and incinerators, close neighbor to the Joseph Allstons; homebuilder who erected by hand his own
house, daring heaven and isostasy, on the lip of the San Andreas fault.
With a Navy captain and a Pan-Am pilot, both of the neighborhood
(the pilot owns the Ferrari) he passes slowly, skinny-smiling, blue-
bearded, with warts, ugly as Lincoln, saying: *I do not kid you. A zebra.
I rise up from fixing that flat tire and I am face to face with a zebra. I am
lucky it wasn't a leopard. Hearst stocked that whole damn duchy with African
animals, including giraffes. It wouldn't surprise me if pygmies hunt warthogs
through those hills with blowguns* . . . And as he passes, the raised glass,
the *salud:* Ah there, Joe!
   Four Unknowns, two male and two females, obviously not related
by marriage because too animated, but all decorous, one lady with
cashmere sweater draped shawl-like over her shoulders, the other winking of diamonds as she lifts her glass; the gentlemen deferential, gray,
brushed, double-breasted, bent heads listening: *Bumper to bumper, all
the way across, and some idiot out of gas on the bridge* . . .
   Mrs. Williamson, beagle-breeder extraordinary, Knight of the AKC,
leather-faced, hoarse-voiced (*Howdy, Neighbor!*) last seen on a Sunday
morning across the canyon from the Allstons' house, striding corduroy-
skirted under the oaks, blowing her thin whistle, crying in the barroom
voice to a pack of wag-tailed long-coupled hounds, *Pfweeeet! Here Esther!
come Esther!* Here we go a-beagling. Wrists like a horsewoman, maybe
from holding thirty couple of questing hounds on leash. Now, from
quite a distance, rounding the words on the mouth, with a white smile,
brown face, tweed shoulders, healthy-horsy-country woman, confidential across forty feet of lawn: *How are the memoirs?*

More Unknowns, not of the local race. City or Upper Peninsula, maybe Berkeley, two ladies and a gentleman, dazzled a little by the Casement Club, watchful. Relax and pass, friends. It is no movie set, it was made for hospitality. The animals who come to drink at this jungle ford are not what they seem. No leopards they, nor even zebras. Yon beagle-breeding Amazon is a wheelhorse of the League of Women Voters, those two by the dressing-room doors at the end of the pool spend much of their time and all of their surplus income promoting Civil Liberties and World Government. Half the people here do not work for a living, for one reason or other, but they cannot be called idlers. They all do something, sometimes even good. And you do not need, as on Martha's Vineyard, to distinguish between East Chop and West Chop. Here we live in a mulligan world, though it is made of prime sirloin . . . *Ah, how do you do? Yes, isn't it? Lovely* . . .

Bill Casement, with his golfer's hide, one eye on the gate for new arrivals—shake of the head, *Quite a struggle, boy*, stoops abstractedly to listen to a short woman with a floury face. Somebody comes in. *Excuse me, please*. Short woman looks around for another anchorage— turn away, quick.

And what of the arts? Ah there, again, in a group: Mr. Thing, Mr. Budapest, Mr. and Mrs. How-d'ye-do, surnamed Ackerman, a tight enclave of the cognoscenti, on their fringes an eager young woman, not pretty, perhaps a piano teacher somewhere; this her big moment, probably, thrilled to be asked here, voice shaking and a little too loud as she wedges something into the conversation, *But Honegger isn't really—do you think? He seems to me* . . . And to me, thou poor child. You have not gone to heaven, you do not have to prove angelhood, you are still in the presence of mortals. Listen and you shall hear.

And what of the Great Man? He is coming closer. There is a kind of progress here, though constantly interrupted, like walking the dog around Beekman Place and up to 51st and back down First Avenue. Magnetic fields, iron filings, kaleidoscopic bits of colored glass that snap into pattern and break again.

On around the diving board, onto the lawn, softer and quieter and with a nap like a marvelous thick rug. Something underfoot—whoop! what the hell? Croquet wicket. Half a good drink gone—on Ruth's dress? No. To the rescue another Japanese, out of the lawn like a mush-room. Thank you, thank you. Big tooth-gleaming grin, impossible to tell what they think. Contempt? Boozing Americans? But what then of all the good nature, the hospitality, the generosity? What o that, my toothy alert impeccable friend? Would you prefer us to be French aristo-crats out of Henry James? Absurd. Probably has no such thoughts at all, good waiter, well trained.

"Ah," Sue says, "there he is!"

It is in her face like a sentence or a theorem: Here is this terrific musician, the best young pianist in the world. And here is this ex-literary agent, knows everybody in New York, owns Town Hall, lunches with S. Hurok twice a week. And here I have brought them together, carbide and water, and what will happen? Something will—there will be an explosion, litmus paper will change color, gases will boil and fume, fire will appear, a gleaming little nugget of gold or radium will form in the crucible.

Mr. Kaminski, Mr. and Mrs. Allston. Arnold, Joe and Ruth.

Now hold your breath.

### III

My first impression, in the flick of an eye, is *What in hell can Sue be thinking of?* My second, all but simultaneous with the first, is *Bill Casement had better look out.*

Taking inventory during the minute or two of introductions and Ruth's far inland murmur and Sue's explanations of who we all are, I can't pick out any obvious reason why Kaminski should instantly bring my hackles up. His appearance is plus-minus. His skin is bad, not pitted by smallpox or chickenpox but roughened and lumpy, the way a face may be left by a bad childhood staphylococcus infection. His head is big for his body, which is both short and slight, and his crew-cut hair, with that skin, makes him look like a second in a curtain-raiser at some third-rate boxing arena: his name somehow ought to be Moishe, pronounced Mushy. But he has an elegant air too, and he has dressed for the occasion in a white dinner jacket. His eyes are large and brown and slightly bulging; some women would probably call them "fine." They compensate for his mouth, a little purse-slit like the mouth of a Florida rock fish.

The proper caption for the picture in its entirety is "Glandular Genius." I suppose if you are sentimental about artistic sensibility, or fascinated by the neurotic personality, you might look at a face like Kaminski's with attention, respect, perhaps sympathy and shared anguish. He has all the stigamata of the type, and it is a type some people respond to. But if you are old Joe Allston, who has had to deal in his time with a good many petulant G.G.'s, you look upon this face with suspicion if not distaste.

It makes, of course, no difference to me what he is. Nevertheless, Bill Casement had better look out. This pianist is pretty expressionless, but such expression as he permits himself is so far a little shadowy sneer, a kind of controlled disdain. Bill might note not only that expression, but the air of almost contemptuous ownership with which Kaminski wears Sue's hand on his white sleeve. And it does not seem to me that even Sue can look as delighted and proud as she looks now out of simple good nature. It is true that she is as grateful for a friendly telephone call as if it had cost you fifty dollars to make it, and true that if you notice her and speak to her and joke with her a little she is constitutionally unable to look upon you as less than wonderful. It is a kind of idiotic and appealing humility in her: she is as happy for a smile as Sweet Alice, Ben Bolt. But right now she looks at Kaminski in a way that can only be called radiant; no woman of fifty should look at any young man that way, even if he *can* play the piano. If she knew how she looks, she would disguise her expression. The whole tableau embarrasses me, because I like Sue and automatically dislike the cool smirk on Kaminski's face, and I am sorry for Sue's sake that no chemical wonder is going to take place at our meeting. As for Kaminski, he is not stupid. Within three seconds he is giving me back my dislike as fast as I send it.

Sue stands outside the closed circuit of our hostility like a careless person gossiping over an electric fence.

"People who have so much to give as you two ought to know each other. Though what the rest of us do to deserve you both is more than I know. It's so *good* of you to be here! And shall I tell you something, Joe? Do you mind being *used*? Isn't that an awful question! But you see, Arnold, Joe was a literary agent for years and years in New York—the best, weren't you, Joe? For who? Hemingway? John Marquand? Oh, James Hilton and James M. Cain and all sorts of people. And we know he couldn't be what he was without having a lot of influence in the other arts too. So we're going to use you, unscrupulously. Or *I* am. Because it's so difficult to make a career as a concert pianist. It's as if there were a conspiracy . . ."

She is holding a glass, but does not seem to have drunk from it. Her hand is on Kaminski's arm, and her face shines with such goodness that I am ready to grind my teeth.

It is Ruth's belief that I take instant and senseless dislikes to people and that when I do I go out of my way to pick quarrels. Nothing, in fact, could be more unjust. Right now I am aching to harpoon this Kaminski and take the smirk off his face, or at least make him say something dishonestly modest, but what do I say? I say, "I'm afraid you're wrong about my having any influence where it would count. But we're looking forward to hearing you play." I could not have bespoke him more fair. He drops his arrogant head a little to acknowledge that I live.

"It's a wonder you haven't heard him clear over on your hill," Sue says. "All he does all day and night is sit down in the cottage and practice and practice and practice—terribly difficult things. He doesn't even remember meals half the time; I have to send them down on a tray." She gives his arm a slap—you naughty boy. "And he's got such power," she cries. "Look at his hands!"

She turns over his hand, which is the hand of a man half again as big as he is, a big thick meaty paw like a butcher's. The little contemptuous shadow of his expression turns toward her. "If I make too much noise?" he says. These are the first actual words we have heard him say.

I am not a Glandular Genius. I am not even an Artist, and hence I am not Sensitive. But I can recognize a challenge when I hear one, especially when there is an edge of insult in it. Poor Sue takes his remark, apparently, as some sort of apology.

"Too much noise nothing! If the neighbors hear you, that's their good luck. And when you break down and play Chopin—which is never often enough—then they're double lucky. You know what we did the other night, Ruth —Joe? We heard Arnold playing Chopin down below, to relax after all the terribly difficult things, and we all just pulled up chairs on the patio and had marvelous concert for over an hour. Even Jimmy, and if you can make *him* listen! Really *nobody* plays Chopin the way Arnold does."

Arnold's expression says that he concurs in this opinion, though generally opinions from this source are uninformed.

He stands there aloofly, not contaminating his art by brushing too close to Conspicuous Consumption. I am reminded irritably of my ex-client Murthi, who would have been astonished by nothing in this whole evening: he would have recognized it as the American Way from old Bob Montgomery movies. He would have recognized Kaminski too: the Artist (imported, of course—the technological jungle could only borrow, not create) captive to the purse and whim of the Nizam-rich, the self-indulgent plutocracy. Murthi would have welcomed in Kaminski a fellow devotee of the Spirit.

Nothing gives me a quicker pain than that sort of arrogance, whether it is Asian, European, or homegrown. I suppose I am guilty of impatience. Our neighbor Mrs. Shields, who does a good deal of promoting of International Understanding among foreign and native students at Stanford, ropes us in now and then for receptions and such. Generally we stand around making polite international noises at one another, but sometimes we really get a good conversation going. It seems to me that invariably, when I get into the middle of a bunch of thoroughly sensible Indians and Siamese and West Germans and Italians and Japanese and Guamanians, and we begin to get very interested in what the other one thinks, there is sure to come up someone in the crowd with a seed in his teeth about American materialism. This sets my spirituality on edge, and we're off.

It will not do for me to be too close to Kaminski tonight. He has hardly said a word, but I can see the Spirit sticking out all over him.

The Japanese passes with a tray. "Arnold?" Sue says. He makes a gesture of rejection with his meaty hand. He is above a drink. But I am pleased to see that when Ruth engages him in one of her conspiratorial conversations he is as vulnerable as other mortals. He listens with his head bent and a pucker between his eyes, not hearing one damned word, but forced to listen.

Well out of it, I stand back and watch, and remember nights when my ten percent involvement in artists didn't permit me to stand back— such a night as the Book-of-the-Month party when the Time-Life boy got high and insulted his publisher's wife, and punches flew, and in the melee someone—I swear it was a *Herald Tribune* reviewer—bit a chunk out of the lady's arm. She got blood poisoning and nearly died. A critic's bite is as deadly as a camel's, apparently. None of that for me, ever again. Let Art pursue its unquiet way, be content to be a birdwatcher of Los Gatos.

I hear Sue say lightly, "You're so dressed *up*, Arnold. You're the dressiest person at your party."

And wouldn't that be true, too: wouldn't Caliban, in this crowd where nothing is conventional except the thinking, just have to be correct as a haberdasher's clerk? Oh, a beauty. I bury my nose in a third highball, feeling ready and alert and full of conversational sass, but not wanting to get involved with Kaminski, and have no one else handy. Sue and her pianist are listening intently to Ruth's whisper. Teetering on my toes, I catch fragments of talk from people passing by, and think of Sam Shields and his zebra, and of Murthi again, and of how zebras roaming the California hills would not surprise Murthi at all. He would have seen them in some movie. Spiritually empty Americans are always importing zebras or leopards or crocodiles for pets. Part of the acquisitive and sensational itch. Roman decadence.

The whole subject irritates me. How in hell do zebras get into an intelligent conversation?

Some god, somewhere, says Let there be light, and a radiance like moonlight dawns over the patio and the clusters of guests. A blue underwater beam awakes in the pool; the water smokes like a hot spring.

Sue's eyes are on the velvet-coated man, who is describing something with gestures to the music-patronizing Ackermans. One of the neighbors, in a loud plaid tweed, stands aside watching the musicians as he would watch little animals digging a hole. I have a feeling that I have failed Sue; Kaminski and I have already practically dropped one another's acquaintance. Her eyes wander around to me. She looks slightly puzzled, a little tired. She rounds her eyes to indicate how pleasantly difficult all this is, and bursts into laughter.

"Everybody here?" I ask.

"Almost, I think. At least the ice seems to be getting broken. Honestly, I don't know half the people here myself. Isn't that a giveaway? This is the first stock I ever bought in musical society."

"Very pretty party," I say. It is. From across the pool it is strikingly staged: lights and shade, compositions of heads and shoulders, moving faces, glints of glass and bright cloth. For a moment it has the swirl and flash of a Degas ballet, and I say so to Sue. I hear Bill Casement's big laugh; white coats dart around; the Mondrian gate opens to spill four late arrivals into the patio.

"Excuse me," Sue says. "I must go greet somebody. But I particularly wanted Arnold to meet the Ackermans, so I'm going to steal him now. Arnold, will you come . . ."

He stands with his fish mouth flattened; he breathes through his nose; he does not trouble to keep his voice down. He says, "For God's sake, how long is this going to go on?"

Sue's eyes jump to his; her lips waver in an imbecilic smile. Her glance swerves secretly to me, then to Ruth, and back to Kaminski. "Well, you know how people are," she says. "They don't warm up without a . . ."

"Good God!" says Kaminski, in a sudden, improbable rage, gobbling as if his throat were full of phlegm. "I am supposed to play for pigs who swill drinks and drinks and drinks until they are falling-down drunk and then will stuff themselves and sleep in their chairs? These are not people to listen to music. I can't play for such people. They are the wrong people. It is the wrong kind of party, nothing but drinks."

Ruth is already trying to pull me away, and I am pretending to go with her while at the same time holding back for dear life; I wouldn't for a fat fee miss hearing what this monster will say next. Sue swings him lightly around, steers him away from us, and I hear her: "Oh, please, Arnold! There's no harm done. We talked about it, remember? We thought, break the ice a little first. Never mind. I'm sorry if it's wrong. We can serve any time now, they'll be ready to listen as soon as . . ."

I am dragged out of earshot, and wind up beside Ruth, over against the dressing rooms under a cascade of clematis. Ruth looks like someone who has just put salt in her coffee by mistake. With her white hair and black eyebrows, she has a lot of lady-comedian expressions, but she doesn't seem to know which one to use this time. Our backs against the dressing-room wall, we sneak a cautious look back where we have just casually drifted from. Sue's Roman-striped cotton and Kaminski's white coat are still posed there at the far edge of the illumination. Then he jerks his arm free and walks off.

Ruth and I look at each other and make a glum mouth. There goes the attempt of a good-natured indiscreet well-meaning culture-craving woman to mother an artistic lush. Horrible social bust, tiptoes, hush-hush among her friends. Painful but inevitable. She looks forlorn at the edge of the artificial moonlight of her patio. A performance is going on, but not the one she planned. The audience is there, but it will have no recital to attend, and will not see the real show, which is already over.

Now don't be stupid and go after him, I say to Sue in my mind, but I have hardly had the thought before she does just that. What an utter fool.

That is the moment when the white coats line up in front of the cabaña, and one steps out ahead of the others. He raises his hands with the dramatics of an assistant tympani player whose moment comes only once, and knocks a golden note from a dinner gong.

An arm falls across my shoulders, another sweeps Ruth in. "Come on," says Bill Casement's gun-club golf-course dressing-room voice. "Haven't had a word with you all night. By God, it's a pleasure to see a familiar face. How's it going? O.K.? Good, let's get us some food."

IV

Assembly line along a reach of stainless steel; the noisy, dutiful, expectant shuffling of feet, the lift of faces sniffing, turning to comment or laugh, craning to look ahead. *Mnnnnnnnnn!* Trenchers as big as cafeteria trays, each hand-turned from a different exotic wood. Behind the counter white coats, alert eyes, ready tongs, spoons, spatulas. A state fair exhibit of salads—red lettuce crinkly-edged, endive, romaine, tomatoes like flowers, hearts of artichokes *marineé*, little green scallions, *caveat emptor*. Aspic rings all in a row. A marvelous molded crab with pimento eyes afloat in a tidepool of mayonnaise. Some of that . . . that . . . that.

*Refugees from Manhattan. Load these folks up, they haven't had a square meal since 1929.*

A landslide, an avalanche: slabs of breast from barbecued turkeys, gobs of oyster dressing, candied yams dripping like honeycomb. A man with a knife as long as a sword and as limber as a razorblade whips off paper-thin slices from a ham, leafs them onto trenchers. Another releases by some sleight of hand one after another of a slowly revolving line of spits from a Rube Goldberg grill. Shishkebab. Tray already dangerous, but still pickles, olives, celery frizzled in crushed ice, a smörgasbord of smoked salmon, smoked eel, smoked herring, cheeses. Ovens in the opulent barbecue yield corn fingers, garlic bread.

No more, not another inch of room—but as we turn away we eye three dessert carts burdened with ice cream confections shaped like apples, pears, pineapples, all fuming in dry ice. Also pastries, petits fours, napoleons, éclairs. Also batteries of coffee flasks streaming bright bubbles. Also two great bowls in which cherries and fat black berries and chunks of pineapple founder in wine-colored juice. Among the smokes of broiling, freshness of scallions, stink of camembert, roquefort, liederkranz, opulence of garlic butter, vinegar-bite of dressings, sniff that bouquet of cointreau and kirsch in which the fruits are soaked. Lucullus, Trimalchio, *adsum.*

But hardly Trimalchio. Instead, this Bill Casement, tall and brown, a maker and a spender loaded with money from lumber mills in the redwood country; no sybarite, but only a man with an urgent will to be hospitable and an indulgent attitude toward his wife's whims. He herds us to a table, looks around. "Where the hell's Sue?" A man behind the counter flashes him some signal. "Excuse me, back in a second. Any of these musical characters tries to sit down here, say it's saved, uh?" Down-mouthed, with his head ducked, he tiptoes away laughing to show that this party is none of his doing, he only works here.

The lawn where Sue and Kaminski have been standing until just a few minutes ago stretches empty and faultless in the dusk. No hostess, no guest of honor. "Quite an evening," I say.

Ruth smiles in a way she has. "Still oppressed with birdsong?"

"Why don't you save that tongue to slice ham with?" I reply crossly. "I'm oppressed all right. Aren't you?"

"If she weren't so nice it would be almost funny."

"But she *is* so nice."

"Yes," she says. "Poor Sue."

As I circle my nose above the heaped and delectable trencher, the thought of Kaminski's bald scorn of food and drink boils over in my insides. Is he opposed to nourishment? "A pituitary monster," I say, "straight out of Dostoevsky."

"Your distaste was a little obvious."

"I can't help it. He curdled my adrenal glands."

"You make everything so endocrine," she says. "He wasn't that bad. In fact, he had a point. It *is* a little alcoholic for a musicale."

"It's the only kind of party they know how to give."

"But it still isn't quite the best way to show off a pianist."

"All right," I say. "Suppose you're right. Is it his proper place to act as if he'd been captured and dragged here? He's the beneficiary, after all."

"I expect he has to humiliate her," Ruth says.

Sometimes she can surprise me. I remark that without an M.D. she is not entitled to practice psychiatry. So maybe he does have to humiliate her. That is exactly one of the seven thousand two hundred and fourteen things in him that irritate the hell out of me.

"But it'll be ghastly," says Ruth in her whisper, "if she can't manage to get him to play."

I address myself to the trencher. "This is getting cold. Do we have to wait for Bill?" When I fill my mouth with turkey and garlic bread, my dyspeptic stomach purrs and lies down. But Ruth's remark of a minute before continues to go around in me like an augur, and I burst out again: "Humiliate her, uh? How to achieve power. How to recover from a depressing sense of obligation. How to stand out in every gathering though a son of a bitch. Did it ever strike you how much attention a difficult cross-grained bastard gets, just by being difficult?"

"It strikes me all the time," Ruth murmurs. "Hasn't it ever struck you before?"

"You suppose she's infatuated with him?"

"No."

"Then why would she put up with being humiliated?"

Her face with its black brows and white hair is as clever as a raccoon's. But as I watch it for an answer I see it flatten out into the pleasant look of social intercourse, and here is Bill, his hand whacking me lightly on the back. "Haven't been waiting for me, have you? Fall to, fall to! We're supposed to be cleared away by nine-thirty. I got my orders."

Our talk is of barbecuing. Do we know there are eighteen different electric motors in that grill? Cook anything on it. The boys got it down to a science now. Some mixups at first, though. Right after we got it, tried a suckling pig, really a shambles. Everybody standing around watching Jerry and me get this thing on the spit, and somebody bound to say how much he looks like a little pink scrubbed baby. Does, too. Round he goes, round and round over the coals with an apple in his mouth and his dimples showing, and as his skin begins to shrink and get crisp, damn if his eyes don't open. By God! First a little slit, then wide open. Every time he comes round he gives us a sad look with these baby blue eyes, and the grease fries out of him and sizzles in the fire like tears. If you'd squeezed him he'd've said mama. He really clears the premises, believe me. Two or three women are really *sick* . . .

Big Bill Casement, happy with food and bourbon, looks upon us in friendship and laughs his big laugh. "Pigs and all, barbecuing is more in my line than this music business. About the most musical I ever get is listening to Cottonseed Clark on the radio, and Sue rides me off the ranch every time she catches me." He rears back and looks around, his forehead wrinkles clear into his bristly widow's peak. "Where d'you suppose she went to, anyway?"

Ruth gives him one of her patent murmurs. It might as well be the Lord's Prayer for all he hears of it, but it comforts him anyway. Sue and Kaminski are nowhere to be seen—having a long confab somewhere. Thinking of what is probably being said at that meeting, I blurt out, "What about the performer? Who is he? Where'd Sue find him?"

"Well," Bill says, "he's a Pole. Polish Jew," he adds apologetically, as if the word were forbidden. "Grew up in Egypt, went back to Poland before the war, just in time to get grabbed by the Polish army and then by the Nazis. His mother went into an incinerator, I guess. He never knew for sure. I get all this from Sue."

His animation is gone. I am damned if he doesn't peek sideways and bat his eyes in a sheepish way around the patio pretending to be very disinterested and casual. He seems set to start back to attention at any slightest word with "What? Who? Me?"

"Very bright guy," he says with about the heartiness of a postscript sending love to the family. "Speaks half a dozen languages—German, Polish, French, Italian, Arabic, God knows what. Sue found him down here in this artist's colony, What's-its-name. He was having a hell of a time. The rest of the artists were about ready to lynch him—they didn't get along with him at all for some reason. Sue's been on the board of this place, that's how she was down there. She can see he's this terrific prospect, and not much luck so far except a little concert here and there, schools and so on. So she offers him the use of the cottage, and he's been here three weeks."

I watch his hand rubbing on the creased brown skin of cheek and jaw. The hand is manicured. I can imagine him kidding the manicurist in his favorite barbershop. He is a man the barbers all know and snap out their cloths for. He brings a big grin to the shoeshine boy. The manicurist, working on his big clean paw, has wistful furtive dreams.

"You met him yet?" Bill asks.

"We talked for a little while."

"Very talented," Bill says. "I *guess*. Make a piano talk. You'd know better than I would—artists are more in your line. I'm just a big damn lumberjack out of the tall timber."

In that, at least, he speaks with authority and conviction. Right now he would be a lot more at home up to his neck in a leaky barrel in some duck marsh than where he is.

Now I see Sue coming down along the fence from the projecting wing of the main house. She is alone. She stops at a table, and in the artificial moonlight I can see her rosy hostess's smile. "Here comes your lady now," I say.

Bill looks. "About time. I was beginning to . . . Say, I wonder if that means I should be . . . Where's Kaminski? Seen *him*?"

"Over across the pool," Ruth whispers, and sure enough there he is, walking pensively among the croquet wickets with his hands behind his white back. The Artist gathering his powers. I cock my ear to the sounds of the party, but all is decorous. All's well, then.

"Maybe I better push the chow line along, I guess," Bill says. He raises an arm and a white coat springs from beside the cabaña wall. In a minute we are confronted by a pastry cart full of all those éclairs and petits fours and napoleons and creampuffs. An arm reaches down and whisks my plate away, slides another in. Right behind the pastry cart comes another with a bowl of kirsch-and-cointreau-flooded fruit and a tray of fruity ice cream molds. Forty thousand calories stare me in the face: my esophagus produces a small protesting conscientious *pwwk!* From the pastry man with his poised tongs and poised smile Ruth cringes away as if he were Satan with a fountain pen.

"Pick something," I tell her. "Golden apples of the sun, silver apples of the moon. You have a duty."

"Ha, yeah, don't let that bother you," Bill says, like a man who gets a nudge without letting it distract him from what he is looking at. Sue has stopped at a nearby table to talk to the Ackermans and the white-haired critic and the harpsichord man. The little music teacher, type-cast for the homely sister of a Jane Austen novel, has managed to squeeze into the musical company. It is all out of some bird book, how the species cling together, and the juncoes and the linnets and the seed-eaters hop around in one place, and the robins raid the toyon berries en masse, and the jaybirds yak away together in the almond trees. The party has split into its elements, neighbors and unknown visitors and the little cluster of musicians. And now Sue, bending across them, beckons Kaminski, and he comes around the diving board, the hatchings of some cuckoo egg whose natural and unchangeable use it is to thrust his bottomless gullet up from the nest and gobble everything a foolish foster mother brings.

The rather dour accompanist moves to make place for him. Sue will not sit down: she stands there animated, all smiles. And Kaminski has changed his front. His politeness is as noticeable as perfume. He talks. He shows his teeth in smiles. The little music teacher leans forward, intent to hear.

With a tremendous flourish the waiter serves Ruth a bowl of fruit. "You do that like Alfredo serving noodles," I say, but Ruth, who knows what I mean, does not say anything, and the waiter, who may or may not, smiles politely, and Bill, who hasn't the slightest idea, comes back beaming into the conversation as if glad of any innocent conversational remark. With a bite of éclair in my mouth I wag my head at him, how delicious. I force down a few spoonfuls of ambrosial fruit. I succeed in forestalling ice cream. The carts go away. Jerry comes around with a coffee flask. I dig out a couple of cigars.

I am facing the musical table, but I have lost my interest in how they all act. Full of highballs, food, smoke, coffee, my insides coil around heavily like an overfed boa constrictor. The only reason I don't slide down in my chair and get really comfortable is that Kaminski is sitting where he can see *me*, and I will not give him the satisfaction of seeing me contented and well nourished. For his performance I shall make it a point to be as wide-awake as a lie-detector, and though I shall listen with an open mind, I shall not be his most forgiving critic.

But there is a clash between comfort and will, and a little balloony pressure in my midsection. Damn Kaminski. Damn his Asiatic spirituality and his coddled Art and his ghetto defensiveness and his refugee arrogance. My esophagus comes again with a richly flavored *brwwp!* Just an echo, hoo hoo.

"Say," says Bill, "how would a brandy go? Or calvados? I got some damn good calvados. You never had any till you taste this."

The impetuous arm goes up, but Sue, who must have had her sharp eye on him, is there before the waiter. "Bill, do me a favor?"

"Surest thing you know. What?"

"Have Jerry close the bar. Don't serve any more now till afterward."

"I was just going to get Joe a snifter of calvados to go with his cigar."

"Please," she said. "Joe won't mind postponing it."

I have not been asked, but I do not mind.

"O.K.," Bill says. "You know what you're doing, I guess. Did you get anything to eat? I kept looking around for you."

"I'll get something later. As soon as people seem to be through, Jerry can start arranging the chairs. I went over it with him this afternoon."

"Check," says Bill. A smile, puzzled, protective, and fond, follows her back to the musician's table. "Bothers her," Bill says. "She's got her heart set on something great. Old Arnold had better be good."

We are silent, stuffed. I commune with my cigar, looking sleepily around this movie set where the standard of everything is excess. Somewhere down deep in my surfeited interior I conduct a little private argument with my client and conscience, Murthi. He is bitter. He thinks it is immoral to fill your stomach. In India, he tells me, the only well-fed people are money-changers and landlords, grinders of the faces of the poor. But these people, I try to tell him, grind no poor. They are not money-changers or landlords. They are the rich, or semi-rich, of a rich country, not the rich of a poor one. Their duty to society is not by any means ignored; they do not salve their own consciences with a temple stuck with pieces of colored glass. They give to causes they respect, and many of them give a great deal. And they don't put on a feast like this because they want to show off, or even because they are themselves gluttonous. They do it because they think their guests will enjoy it; they do it to introduce a struggling young artist. And anyway, why should good eating be immoral?

You pay nothing for it, Murthi says. It is too easy. It does not come after hard times and starvation, but after plenty. It is nothing but self-indulgence. It smothers the spiritual life. In the midst of plenty, that is the time to fast.

I am too full to argue with him. I feel as if I might lift into the air and float away, and the whole unreal patio with me, bearing its umbrella of artificial moonlight and its tables and people and glass-fronted cabaña, its piano and its Artist, high above the crass valley. It is like a New Yorker cartoon, and me with my turned-up Muslim slippers and baggy pants, one of the Peninsula pashas on a magic carpet of the latest model, complete with indirect lighting, swimming pool, Muzak, and all modern conveniences.

All? Nothing forgotten? My feet insist on my notice. I stoop on the sly and feel the cement. Sure enough, the magic carpet has radiant heating too.

V

Kaminski is booted and spurred and ready to ride. The audience is braced between the cabaña and the pool. The moonlight is turned off. The air is cool and damp, but the pavement underfoot radiates its faint expensive warmth. Inside, one light above the piano shines on Kaminski's white jacket as he sits fiddling with the knobs, adjusting the bench. The shadow of the piano's open wing falls across his head. The Degas has become a Rembrandt.

On a lounge sofa between Sue and Ruth, old Joe Allston, very much overfed, is borne up like a fly on meringue. Bill has creaked away somewhere. A partition has slid across the barbecue, and from behind it, during pauses in the hum of talk, comes the sound of a busy electric dishwasher.

"Are people too comfortable, do you think?" Sue asks. "Would it have been better to put out undertaker's chairs?"

I assure her that she has the gratitude of every overburdened pelvis in the house. "There is no such thing as *too* comfortable," I say, "any more than there is such a thing as a large drink of whiskey."

Her hands pick at things on her dress and are held still. Her laugh fades away in a giggle.

I say, "What's he going to play?" and quite loudly she bursts out, "I don't know! He wouldn't tell me!" One or two shadowy heads turn. Kaminski stares out into the dusk from his bench, and the shadow wipes all the features off his face.

We are sitting well back, close to the edge of the pool. "How did you manage to get him to play after all?" Ruth murmurs.

It is as improbable to see the sneering curl of Sue's lip as it would be to see an ugly scowl on her face. "I *crawled!*" she says.

The cushions sigh as Ruth eases back into them. But I am sitting where I can watch Sue's face, and I am not so easily satisfied. "Why?" I ask.

"Because he's a great artist."

"Oh." After a moment I let myself back among the cushions with Ruth. "I hope he is," I say, and at least for the moment I mean it.

The eyeless mask of Kaminski's face turns again. Even when he speaks he does not seem to have lips. "For my first number I play three Chopin Nocturnes. I play these as suitable to the occasion, and especially for Mrs. Casement."

Beside me I can feel Sue shrink. I have a feeling, though it is too dark to see, that she has flushed red. While the murmur rising from the audience says How nice, handsome gesture, what a nice compliment, she looks at her hands.

At the piano, Kaminski kneads his knuckles, staring at the empty music rack. When he has held his pose of communing with his *Giest* long enough for the silence to spread to the far edges of the audience, but not long enough so that any barbarian starts talking again, he drops into the music with a little skip and a trill. It is well timed and well executed. Without knowing it, probably, Sue takes hold of my hand. She is like a high school girl who shuts her eyes while the hero plunges from the two-yard line. Did he make it? Oh, did he go over?

The cabaña acts like a shell; the slightest pianissimo comes out feathery but clear, and Kaminski's meaty hands are very deft. Behind us the faint gurgle and suck of the pool's filter system is a watery night-sound under the Chopin.

God spare me from ever being called a critic or even a judge of music— even a listener. Like most people, I think I can tell a dub from a competent hand, and it is plain at once that Kaminski is competent. The shades of competence are another thing. They are where the Soul comes in, and I look with suspicion on those who wear their souls outside. I am not capable in any case of judging Kaminski's soul. Maybe it is such a soul as swoons into the world only once in a hundred years. Maybe, again, it is such a G.G. soul as I have seen on Madison Avenue and elsewhere in my time.

But I think I can smell a rat, even in music, if it is dead enough, and as Kaminski finishes one nocturne and chills into abashed silence those who have mistakenly started to applaud too soon, and pounds into the second with big chords, I think I begin to smell a rat here. Do I imagine it, or *is* he burlesquing these nocturnes? Is he contemptuous of them because they are sentimental, because they are nineteenth century, because they don't strain his keyboard technique enough, or because he knows Sue adores them? And is he clever enough and dirty enough to dedicate them to her as an insult?

It is hard to say. By the third one it is even harder, because he has played them all with great precision even while he gives them a lot of bravura. I wish I could ask Ruth what she thinks, because her ear for music and her nose for rats are both better than mine. But there is no chance, and so I am still nursing the private impression that Kaminski is hoaxing the philistines when I am called on to join in the applause, which is loud, long, and sincere. If the philistines have been hoaxed, they are not aware of the fact. Beside me, Sue wears her hands out; she is radiant. "Oh, didn't he play them *beautifully*? They loved it, didn't they? I told you, *nobody* can play Chopin the way Arnold can."

In the second row of lounge chairs the musical crowd, satisfactorily applauding, bend heads each to other. Mr. Ackerman's big droopy face lifts solemnly against the light. Kaminski, after his bow, has seated himself again and waits while the clapping splatters away and the talk dies down again and a plane, winking its red and white wing lights, drones on down and blinks out among the stars over Black Mountain. Finally he says, "I play next the Bach Chaconne, transcribed for piano by Busoni."

"What is it?" Sue says. "Should I know it?"

Over Sue's head Ruth gives me one of her raccoon looks. I am delighted; I rouse myself. This time my lie detector is going to be a little more searching, because I have heard a dozen great pianists play the Chaconne, and I own every recording ever made, probably. Every time I catch a competent amateur at a piano I beg it out of him. In my opinion, which I have already disparaged, it is only the greatest piece of music ever written, a great big massive controlled piece of mind. If Kaminski can play the Chaconne and play it well, I will forgive him and his bad manners and his tantrums and the Polish soul he put into Chopin. It takes more than Polish soul to play the Chaconne. It takes everything a good man has, and a lot of good men don't have enough.

Maybe Kaminski does have enough. He states those big sober themes, as they say in music-appreciation circles, with, as they also say, authority. The great chords begin to pile up. Imagine anyone writing that thing in the first place for the violin. As usual, it begins to destroy me. Kaminski is great, he's tremendous, he is tearing into this and bringing it out by the double handful. A success, a triumph. Listen to it roll and pour, and not one trace, not a whisker, of Polish soul. This is the language you might use in justifying your life to God.

As when, in the San Francisco Cow Palace, loudspeakers announce the draft horse competition, and sixteen great Percherons trot with high action and ponderous foot into the arena, brass-harnessed, plume-bridled, swelling with power, drawing the rumbling brewery wagon lightly, Regal Pale: ton-heavy but light-footed they come, the thud of their hoofs in the tanbark like the marching of platoons, and above them the driver spider-braced, intent, transmits through the fan of lines his slightest command: lightly he guides them, powerfully and surely they bring their proud necks, their plumed heads, their round and dappled haunches, the blue and gold wagon Regal Pale—sixteen prides guided by one will, sixteen great strengths respondent and united: so the great chords of Bach roll forth from under the hands of Arnold Kaminski.

And as, half trained or self-willed, the near leader may break, turn counter to his driver's command, and in an instant all that proud unanimity is a snarl of tangled traces and fouled lines and broken step and cross purposes and desperate remedies, so at a crucial instant fails the cunning of Kaminski. A butch, a fat, naked, staring discord.

To do him credit, he retrieves it instantly, it is past and perhaps not even noticed by many. But he has lost me, and when I have recovered from the momentary disappointment I am cynically amused. The boy took on something too big for him. A little later he almost gets me back, in that brief lyrical passage that is like a spring in a country of cliffs, but he never does quite recover the command he started with, and I know now how to take him.

When he finishes there is impressed silence, followed by loud admiration. This has been, after all—Allston *dicens*—the most magnificent piece of music ever written, and it ought to be applauded. But it has licked Kaminski in a spot or two, and he can't help knowing it and knowing that the musicians present know it. As he stands up to take a bow, his face, thrust up into the light, acquires features, a mask of slashes and slots and knobs, greenish and shadowed. He looks like a rather bruised corpse, and he bows as if greeting his worst enemy. In the quiet as the applause finally dies out I hear the gurgle of the pool's drain and catch a thin aseptic whiff of chlorine, a counter-whiff of cigar smoke and perfume.

Says Sue in my ear, tensely, "What did I tell you?"

"For my last number," Kaminski's thick voice is saying, "I play the Piano Pieces of Arnold Schoenberg, Opus 19."

I have had Schoenberg and his followers explained to me, even urged upon me, several times, generally by arty people who catch me with my flank exposed at a cocktail party. They tell me that these noises are supposed, among other things, to produce *tension*. Tension is a great word among the tone-row musicians. God bless them, they are good at it. It astonishes me anew, as Kaminski begins, that sounds like these can come out of a piano. They can only be recovered from through bed rest and steam baths, maybe shock therapy.

For no amount of argument can convince me that this music does not hurt the ears. And though I am prepared to admit that by long listening a man might accustom himself to it, I do not think this proves much. Human beings can adjust to anything, practically; it is a resilient race. We can put up with the rule of kings, presidents, priests, dictators, generals, communes, and committees; we learn to tolerate diets of raw fish, octopus, snails, unborn ducklings, clay, the bleeding hearts of enemies, our own dung; we learn to listen without screaming to the sounds of samisens, Korean harps, veenas, steam whistles, gongs, and Calypso singers; we adjust bravely to whole-tone, half-tone, or quarter-tone scales, to long skirts and short skirts, crew cuts and perukes, muttonchops and dundrearies and Van Dykes and naked chins, castles and paper houses and *barastis* and bomb shelters. The survival of the race depends upon its infinite adaptability. We can get used to anything in time, and even perhaps develop a perverted taste for it. But *why?* The day has not come when I choose to try adapting to Schoenberg. Schoenberg hurts my ears.

He hurts some other ears, too. The audience that has swooned at the Chopin and been respectful before the Bach is systematically cut to ribbons by the saw edges of the Piano Pieces. I begin to wonder all over again if Kaminski may have planned this program with perverse cunning: throw the philistines the Chopin, giving it all the *Schmalz* it will stand; then stun them with the Bach (only the Bach was too much for him); then trample them contemptuously underfoot with the Schoenberg, trusting that their ignorance will be impressed by this wrenched and tortured din even while they writhe under it. A good joke. But then what is he after? It is his own career that is at stake, he is the one who stands to benefit if the musicians' corner is impressed. Does he mean to say the hell with it on these terms, or am I reading into a not-quite-good-enough pianist a lot of ambiguities that don't exist in him?

It slowly dawns on me, while I grit my teeth to keep from howling like a dog, that Kaminski *means* this Schoenberg. He gives it the full treatment; he visibly wrestles with the Ineffable. Impossible to tell whether he hits the right notes or the wrong ones—probably Schoenberg himself couldn't tell. Wrong ones better, maybe—more tension. But Kaminski is concentrating as if the music ties him into bundles of raw nerves. For perhaps a second there is a blessed relief, a little thread of something almost a melody, and then the catfight again. Language of expressionism, tension and space, yes. Put yourself in the thumbscrew and any sort of release is blessed. Suite for nutmeg grater, cactus, and strings. A garland of loose ends.

He is putting himself into it devotionally; he *is* Schoenberg. I recall a picture of the composer on some record envelope—intense staring eyes, bald crown, temples with a cameo of raised veins, cheeks bitten in, mouth grim and bitter, unbearable pain. Arnold Schoenberg, Destroyer and Preserver. Mouthful of fire and can neither swallow nor spit.

In the cone of light under which Kaminski tortures himself and us, I see a bright quick drop fall from the end of his nose. Sweat or hay fever? Soul or allergy? Whatever it is, no one can say he isn't trying.

The piano stops with a noise like a hiccup or a death rattle. Three or four people laugh. Kaminski sits still. The audience waits, not to be caught offside. This might be merely space, there might be some more tension coming. But Kaminski is definitely through. Applause begins, with the overenthusiastic sound of duty in it, and it dies quickly except in the musical row, where the accompanist is clapping persistently.

Sue is clapping her hands in intense slow strokes under her chin. "Isn't that something?" she says. "That's one thing he's been working on a lot. I just don't see how anybody plays it at all—all those minor ninths and major sevenths, and no key signature at all."

"Or *why* anybody plays it," I am compelled to say. But when her hands start another flurry I join in. Kaminski sits, spiritually exhausted, bending his head. Encore, encore. For Sue's sake, try. My arms begin to grow tired, and still he sits there. A full minute after my impertinent question, her hands still going, Sue says, "I admit *I* don't understand that kind of music, but because I'm ignorant is no reason to throw it away."

So I am rebuked. She is a noble and innocent woman, and will stoop to beg Kaminski and leave a door open for Schoenberg, all for the disinterested love of art. Well, God bless her. It's almost over, and she can probably feel that it was a success. Maybe she can even think of it as a triumph. Later, when nothing has come of all her effort and expense, she can console herself with a belief that there is a conspiracy among established musicians to pound the fingers of drowning genius off the gunwale.

"Well, anyway, *he's* terrific," I say like a forktongued liar. "Marvelous." Rewarded by all the gratitude she puts into her smile, I sit back for the encore that is finally forthcoming. And what does Kaminski play? Some number of Charles Ives, almost as mad as the Schoenberg.

Probably there might have been enough politeness among us to urge a second encore, but Kaminski cuts us off by leaving the piano. Matches flare, smoke drifts upward, the moonlight dawns again, Bill Casement appears from somewhere, and a discreet white coat crosses from the barbecue end of the cabaña and opens the folding panels of the bar.

### VI

It seems that quite a number of times during the evening I am condemned to have Sue at me with tense questions. She is as bad as a Princeton boy with a manuscript: *Have I got it? Is it any good? Can I be a writer?* "What do you think?" Sue says now. "Am I wrong?"

"He's a good pianist."

Her impatience is close to magnificent. For a second she is Tallulah. "Good! Good heavens, I know that. But does he have a chance? Has he got so *much* talent they can't deny him? They say only about one young pianist in a hundred . . ."

"You can't make your chances," I say. "That's mostly luck."

"I'll be his luck," she says.

The crowd is rising and drifting inside. Trapped on the lounge, I lean back and notice that over our heads, marbled by the lights, white mist has begun to boil on some unfelt wind. The air is chilly and wet; the fog has come in. Ruth stands up, shivering her shoulders to cover the significant look she is giving me. I stand up with her. So does Sue, but Sue doesn't let me go.

"If you're his luck, then he has a chance," I say, and am rewarded by one of her smiles, so confident and proud that I am stricken with remorse, and add, "But it's an awful skinny little chance. Any young pianist would probably be better off if he made up his mind straight off to be a local musician instead of trying for a concert career."

"But the concert career is what he *wants*. It's what he's been preparing for all his life."

"Sure. That's what they all want. Then they eat their hearts out because they miss, and when you look at it, what is it they've missed? A chance to ride a dreary circuit and play for the local Master Minds and Artists series and perform in the Art Barn of every jerk town in America. It might be better if they stayed home and organized chamber groups and taught the young and appeared once a year as a soloist with the local little symphony."

"Joe, dear," Sue says, "can you imagine Arnold teaching grubby little unwilling kids to play little Mozart sonatas for PTA meetings?"

She could not have found a quicker way to adjust my thermostat upward. It is true that I can't imagine Kaminski doing any such thing as teaching the young, but that is a commentary on Kaminski, not on the young. Besides, I am the defender, self-appointed, of the good American middle class small-town and suburban way of life, and I get almighty sick of Americans who enjoy all its benefits but can't find a good word to say for it. An American may be defined as a man who won't take his own side in an argument. "Is Arnold *above* Mozart?" I ask. "For that matter, is he above the PTA?"

She stares at me to see if I'm serious. "Now you're being cute," she says, and blinks her eyes like a fond idiot and rushes inside to join the group around Kaminski. I note that Kaminski now has a highball in his hand. The Artist is only mortal, after all. If we wait, we may even see him condescend to a sandwich.

"Shall we get out of this?" I ask Ruth.

"Not yet."

"Why not?"

"Manners," she says. "You wouldn't understand, lamb. But let's go inside. It's cold out here."

It is, even with the radiant-heated magic carpet. The patio is deserted already. The air above boils with white. Between the abandoned chairs and empty lawn the transparent green-blue pool fumes with underwater light as if it opened down into hell. Once inside and looking out, I have a feeling of being marooned in a space ship. Any minute now frogmen will land their saucers on the patio or rise in diving helmets and snorkels from the pool.

Inside there are no frogmen, only Kaminski, talking with his hands, putting his glass on a tray and accepting another. The white head of the critic is humorously and skeptically bent, listening. The dour accompanist, the velvet-coated Mr. Budapest, the solid Ackermans, Sue, three or four unknowns, the little piano teacher, make a close and voluble group. Kaminski pauses amid laughter; evidently these others don't find him as hard to take as I do. As if he feels my thoughts, he looks across his hearers at Ruth and me, and Ruth raises her hands beside her head and makes pretty applauding motions. Manners. I am compelled to do the same, not so prettily.

Sam Shields goes past us, winks sadly, leaving. His wife is crippled and does not go out, so that he is always among the first to leave a party. This time he has five or six others for company, filing past Bill and being handshook at the door. To us now comes Annie Williamson, robust dame, and inquires in her fight-announcer's voice why we don't join the Hunt. They have fourteen members now, and enough permissions so that they can put hurdles on fences and get a run of almost fourteen miles. Of course we're not too old. Come on . . . Herman Dyer will still take a three-bar gate, and he's five years older than God. Or maybe we'd like the job of riding ahead dragging a scent or a dead rabbit. Make me Master of the Hunt, any office I want. Only come.

"Annie," I tell her sadly, "I am an old, infirm, pathetic figure. I have retired to these hills only to complete my memoirs, and riding a horse might cut them untimely short. Even art, such as tonight, can hardly make me leave my own humble hearth any more."

"What's the matter?" she says. "Didn't you like it? I thought it was swell. The last one was kind of yowly, but he played it fine."

"Sure I liked it," I say. "I thought it was real artistic."

"You're a philistine," Annie says. "An old cynical philistine. I'd hate to read your memoirs."

"You couldn't finish them," I say. "There isn't a horse or a beagle in them anywhere."

"A terribly limited old man," she says, and squeezes Ruth's arm and goes off shaking her head and chuckling. She circles the Kaminski crowd, interrupts something he is saying. I see her mouth going: Thank you, enjoyed it very much, blah blah. She first, and now a dozen others, neighbors and unknowns . . . so much . . . envy Sue the chance to hear you every day . . . luck to you . . . great treat. Some more effusive than others, but all respectful. Kaminski can sneer at his overfed alcoholic audience, but it has listened dutifully, and has applauded louder than it sometimes felt like doing, and has stilled its laughter in embarrassment when it didn't understand. If he had played nothing but Chopin they would have enjoyed him more, but he would have to be even more arrogant and superior and cross-grained than he is to alienate their good will and sour their wonderful good nature. Luck to you. . . . And mean it. Would buy tickets, if necessary.

"Madame," I say to my noiseless wife, "art is troublesome and life is long. Can't we go home?"

For answer she steers me by the arm into the musical circle. Except for four people talking over something confidential in a corner, and the white coats moving around hopefully with unclaimed highballs on their trays, the musical circle now includes the whole company. Kaminski, we find, is still doing most of the talking. His subject is—guess what? The Artist. Specifically, the Artist in America.

I claim one of the spare highballs in self-defense. I know the substance of this lecture in advance, much of it from Murthi. And if Kaminski quotes Baudelaire about the great gaslighted Barbarity that killed Poe, I will disembowel him.

The lecture does not pursue its expected course more than a few minutes, and it is done with more grace and humor than I would have thought Kaminski had in him. A couple of highballs have humanized his soul. Mainly he talks, and without too obvious self-pity, about the difficulties of a musical career: twenty years or so of nothing but practice, practice, practice; the teachers in Boston and New York and Rome; the tyranny of the piano (I can't be away from a piano a single day without losing ground. On the train, and even in an automobile, I carry around a practice keyboard to run exercises on). It is (with a rueful mouth) a rough profession to get established in. He wonders sometimes why one doesn't instead take the Civil Service examinations. (Laughter.) But it is understandable, Kaminski says, why the trapdoor should be closed over the heads of young musicians. Established performers and recording companies and agencies clinging to what they know is profitable, are naturally either jealous of competition or afraid to risk anything on new music or new men. (That charming little Ives that I used for an encore, for instance, has practically never been played, though it was composed almost fifty years ago.)

The case of Kaminski is (with a shrug) nothing unique. The critic and the Ackermans know how it goes. And of course, there is the problem of finding audiences. Whom shall one play for? Good audiences so few and so small, in spite of all the talk about the educational effect of radio and recordings. People who really know and love good music available only in the large cities or—with a flick of his dark eyes at Sue—in a few places such as this. Oh, he is full of charm. The little music teacher bridles. But generally, Kaminski says, there is only the sham audience with sham values, and the whole concert stage which is the only certain way of reaching the audiences one can respect is dominated by two or three agencies interested only in dollars.

"Shyme, shyme," says old Joe Allston from the edge of the circle, and draws a started half-smile from his neighbors and a second's ironic stare from Kaminski.

"What, a defender of agents in the crowd?" the critic says, turning his white head.

"Literary only," I say. "And ex, not current. But a bona fide paid-up member of the Agents' Protective Association, the only bulwark between the Artist and the poor farm."

"Are agents so *necessary*?" Sue says. "Isn't it possible to break in somehow without putting yourself in the clutches of one of them?"

"Clutches!" I say. "Consider my feelings."

Ruth gives me an absolutely expressionless, pleasant look in which I read some future unpleasantness, but what the hell, shall a man keep quiet while his lifework is trampled on?

"Would you admit," says Kaminski with his tight dog-fish smile, "that an agent without an artist is a vine without an oak?"

The little music teacher brings her hands together. Her eyes are snapping and her little pointed chin, pebbled like the Pope's Nose of a plucked turkey, quivers. Oh, if she were defending the cause of music and art against such commercial attacks, she would . . . She is listening, comprehending, participating, right in the midst of things. Kaminski turns to her and actually winks. As a tray passes behind him he reaches back and takes a third highball. Joe Allston collars one too. The benevolent critic pokes his finger at old Joe and says encouragingly, "How about it, Agents' Protective Association? Can you stand alone?"

"I don't like the figure," I say. "I don't feel like a vine without an oak. I feel like a Seeing Eye dog without a blind man."

This brings on a shower of protests and laughter, and Sue says, "Joe, if you're going to stick up for agents you'll have to tell us how to beat the game. How could an agent help Arnold, say, get a hearing and get started?"

"Any good agency will get him an audition, any time."

"Yes, along with a thousand others."

"No, by himself."

"And having had it, what does he get out of it?" murmurs Mr. Ackerman. He has winesap cheeks and white, white hair, but his expression is not benevolent like the critic's, mainly because his whole face has come loose, and sags—big loose lips, big drooping nose, a forehead that hangs in folds over his eyebrows. He reminds me of a worried little science-fiction writer I used to know who developed what his doctor called "lack of muscle tone," so that his nose wouldn't even hold up his glasses. It was as if he had been half disintegrated by one of his ray guns. Mr. Ackerman's voice sags like his face; he looks at me with reddish eyes above hound-dog lower lids.

They all obviously enjoy yapping at me. Here is the Enemy, the Commercial Evil Genius that destroys Art. This kind of thing exhilarates me, I'm afraid.

"That's not the agent's fault," I say. "It's a simple matter of supply and demand. A hundred good pianists come to New York every year all pumped full of hope. They are courteously greeted and auditioned by the agents, who take on anyone they can. Agents arrange concerts, including Town Hall and Carnegie Hall concerts, for some of them, and they paper the hall and invite and inveigle the critics and clip the reviews, and if the miracle happens and some young man gets noticed in some special way, they book him on a circuit. But if ninety-nine of those young pianists slink out of New York with a few pallid clippings and no rave notices and no bookings, that isn't the agents' fault."

"Then whose fault is it?" cries Sue. "There are millions of people who would be thrilled to hear someone like Arnold play. Why can't they? There seems to be a stone wall between."

"Overproduction," murmurs old Devil's-Advocate Allston, sips his insolent bourbon.

Mr. Ackerman's face lifts with a visible effort its sagging folds; the critic looks ironical and skeptical; Kaminski watches me over his glass with big shining liquid eyes. His pitted skin is no longer pale, but has acquired a dark, purplish flush. He seems to nurse some secret amusing knowledge. The music teacher at his elbow twists her mouth, very incensed and impatient at old commercial Allston. Her mouth opens for impetuous words, closes again. Her pebbled chin quivers.

"Overproduction, sure," I say again. "If it happened in the automobile industry you'd blame it on the management, or the government, or on classical capitalist economics, or creeping socialism. But it's in music, and so you want to blame it on the poor agent. An agent is only a dealer. He isn't to blame if the factory makes too many cars. All he can do is sell the ones he can."

"I'm afraid Mr. Allston is pulling our leg," the critic says. "Art isn't quite a matter of production lines. Genius can't be predicted and machined like a Chevrolet, do you think, Mr. Casement?"

He catches Bill by surprise. Evidently he is one of those who like to direct and control conversations, pulling in the hangers-on. But his question is no kindness to Bill, who strangles and waves an arm. "Don't ask me! I don't know a thing about it." Even after the spotlight has left him, he stands pulling his lower lip, looking around over his hand, and chuckling meaninglessly when he catches anyone's eye.

"So you don't think a New York concert does any good," Sue says—pushing, pushing. After all, she held this clambake to bring us all together and now she has what she wanted—patrons and critics and agents in a cluster—and she is going to find out everything. "If they don't do any good, why bother?"

"Why indeed," I say, and then I see that I have carried it too far, for Sue's face puckers unhappily, and she insists, "But Joe . . ."

The critic observes, "They may not do much good, but nothing can be done *without* one."

"So for the exceptional ones they *do* do some good."

"For the occasional exception they may do everything," the critic says. "Someone like William Kapell, who was killed in a plane crash just a few miles from here. But Kapell was a *very* notable exception."

I cannot read Kaminski—it is being made increasingly clear to me that one of my causes of irritation at him is precisely that I don't know what goes on inside him—but I can read Sue Casement without bifocals, and the look she throws at Kaminski says two things: One is that here, just five feet from her, is another Notable Exception as notable as Kapell. The other is that since Kapell has been killed on the brink of a brilliant career, he has obviously left a vacancy.

"A lot of young pianists can't afford it, I expect," she says—hopefully, I think.

The critic spreads his hands. "Town Hall about fifteen hundred, Carnegie two thousand. Still, a lot of them find it somewhere. It's a lot of money to put on the turn of a card."

Determination and resolve, or muscular contractions that I interpret in these terms, harden in Sue's rosy face. "Is it hard to arrange?"

I can't resist. "Any good agent will take care of it for you," I say. She throws me a smile: you old devil, you.

"But no one can count on one single thing's coming from it," the critic says, and he looks kindly upon both Sue and her protégé. I respect this benevolent old creature in spite of his profession. He is trying to warn them.

Not being one of these socially clairvoyant people, I would not feel extraordinarily at home in a Virginia Woolf novel. But I get a glimpse, for the most fragmentary moment, of an extreme complexity pressing in upon us. There is of course Ruth emanating silent disapproval of her husband's big argumentative mouth, and there is Sue, radiant and resolute, smiling promises at Kaminski. There is Kaminski with his deer

eyes wide and innocent, his mouth indifferently half smiling—a pure
enigma to me, unidentifiable. And there are the critic, ruminating kindly
and perhaps with friendly sorrow his own private doubts, and Ackerman
incognito behind the heavy folds of his face, and Mrs. Ackerman who
looks as if she would like nothing better than to get off her aching feet
and start home, and the music teacher bristling with excitement and
stimulation, saying to Kaminski, "But *imagine* getting up on the stage
at Carnegie Hall with Virgil Thompson and Olin Downes and everybody
there . . ." Also there is Bill Casement with his long creased face that
looks as overworked as Gary Cooper trying to register an emotion. What
emotion? Maybe he is kissing two thousand dollars goodbye and wondering if he is glad to see it go. Maybe he is proud of his wife, who
has the initiative and the culture to do all this of this evening. Maybe
he is contemplating the people in his cabaña and thinking what funny
things can happen to a man's home.

So only one thing is clear. Sue will stake Kaminski to a New York
concert. I don't know why that depresses me. It has been clear all along
that that is exactly what she has wanted to do. My depression may
come from Kaminski's indifference. I would like to see the stinker get
his chance and goof it good.

An improbable opening appears low down in the droops and folds
of Mr. Ackerman's face, and he yawns. "Darling," his wife says at once,
"we have a long drive back to the city."

In a moment the circle has begun to melt and disintegrate. Sue is
accosted with gratitude from three sides. The accompanist and the velvet-
coated Mr. Budapest stay with Kaminski to say earnest friendly things:
I want you to come up and meet . . . He will be interested that you
have appeared with . . . of course they will have heard of you . . . I
should think something of Hovhaness' . . . yes . . . excellent. Why not?

Since the discussion took his career out of his hands, Kaminski has
said nothing. He bows, he smiles, but his face has gone remote; the
half-sneer of repose has come back into it. He is a Hyperborean, beyond
everybody. All this nonsense about careers bores him. Why do the
heathen rage furiously together? Beyond question, he is one of the
greatest bargains I have ever seen bought.

Also, as he turns and shakes hands with Mr. Budapest and recalls
himself for the tiresomeness of goodnights, I observe that perhaps what
I took for snootiness is paralysis. He does not believe in alcohol, which
is drunk only by pigs, but I have seen him take four highballs in twenty
minutes, and Bill Casement's bartenders have been taught not to spare
the Old Granddad.

## VII

While the other ladies are absent getting their coats, Kaminski holds collapse off at arm's length and plays games of solemn jocularity with the homely little music teacher. He leans carefully and whispers in her ear something that makes her flush and laugh and shake her head, protesting. "Eh?" he cries. "Isn't it so?" With his feet crossed he leans close, rocking his ankles. Out of the corner of the music teacher's eye goes an astonishingly cool flickering look, alert to see if anyone is watching her here, tête-a-tête with the maestro. All she sees is old Joe Allston, the commercial fellow. Her neck stiffens, her eyes are abruptly glazed, her face is carefree and without guile as she turns indifferently back. Old Allston is about as popular as limburger on the newlyweds' exhaust manifold. He hates us Youth. The Anti-Christ.

"You can joke," she says to Kaminski, "but I'm serious, really I am. We know we aren't very wonderful, but we aren't so bad, either, so there. We've got a very original name: The Chamber Society. And if you don't watch out, I *will* sign you up to play with us sometime. So don't say anything you don't mean!"

"I never say anything I don't mean," Kaminski grins. "I'd love to play with you. All ladies, are you?"

"All except the cello. He's a math teacher at the high school."

"Repulsive," Kaminski murmurs. The teacher giggles, swings sideways, sees me still there, nails me to the wall with a venomous look. Snoop! Why don't I move? But I am much too interested to move.

"Three ladies and one gentleman," Kaminski says, smiling broadly and leaning over her so far he overbalances and staggers. "A Mormon. Are the other ladies all like you?"

Because I know that none of this will sound credible when I report it to Ruth, I strain for every word of this adolescent drooling. I see the music teacher, a little hesitant, vibrate a look at Kaminski's face and then, just a little desperately, toward the group of men by the door. Kaminski is greatly amused by something. "I tell you what you should do," he says. "You reorganize yourself into the Bed-chamber Society. Let the Mormon have the other two, and you and I will play together. Any time."

He has enunciated this unkind crudity very plainly, so plainly that at fifteen feet I cannot possibly have misheard. The little teacher does not look up from her abstract or panicky study of certain chair legs. Her incomplete little face goes slowly scarlet, her pebbled chin is stiff. That little cold venomous glance whips up to me and is taken back again. If I were not there, she would probably run for her life. As it is, she is tempted into pretending that nothing has been said. She is like Harold Lloyd in one of those old comedies, making vivacious and desperate chatter to a girl, while behind the draperies or under the tablecloth his accidentally snagged pants unravel or his seams burst or his buttons one by one give up the ghost. Sooner or later the draperies will be thrown open by the butler, or someone's belt buckle will catch the tablecloth and drag it to the floor, and there will be Harold in his hairy shanks, his Paris garters. Oh Lord. I am not quite able to take myself away from there.

Kaminski leans over her, catches himself by putting a hand on her shoulder, says something else close to her red hot ear. That does it. She squirms sideways, shakes him off, and darts past the ladies just returning from the cloakroom. Kaminski, not so egg-eyed as I expect to see him, looks at me with a smile almost too wide for his mouth, and winks. He could not be more pleased if he had just pulled the legs off a live squirrel. But the music teacher, darting past me, has given me quite another sort of look. There is a dead-white spot in the center of each cheek, and her eyes burn into mine with pure hatred. That is what I get for being an innocent bystander and witnessing her humiliation.

For a few seconds Kaminski stands ironically smiling into thin air; he wears a tasting expression. Then he motions to one of the Japanese at the bar, and the Japanese scoops ice cubes into a glass.

It is time for us to get away from there. The elegant cabaña smells and looks like Ciro's at nine o'clock of a Sunday morning. Outside, the pool lights are off, but the air swirls and swims, dizzy with moonlighted fog. The sliding doors are part way open for departing guests. Sue comes and catches Kaminski by the arm, holding his sleeve with both hands in a too friendly, too sisterly pose. They stand in the doorway with the mist blowing beyond them.

"Now please do come and see me," Ackerman says. "One never knows. I would like to introduce you. Perhaps some evening, a little group at my home."

"Good luck," says the critic. "I shall hope before long to write pleasant comments after your name."

"Ah, *vunderful*," says Mr. Budapest, "you vere *vunderful!* I have so enjoyed it. And if you should write to Signor Vitelli, my greetings. It has been many years."

"Not at all, not at all," says Bill Casement. "Happy to have you."

"It was so good of you all to come," Sue says. "You don't know how . . . or rather, you do, all of you do. You've been generous to come and help. I'm sure it will work out for him somehow, he has such great talent. And when you're as ignorant as I am . . . I hope when you're down this way you won't hesitate . . . Goodbye, goodbye, goodbye."

The women pull June fur coats around them, their figures blur in the mist and are invisible beyond the Mondrian gate. But now comes the music teacher with a bone in her teeth, poor thing, grimly polite, breathless. She looks neither to left nor right past Sue's face: Goodnight. A pleasant time. You have a very beautiful place. Thank you. And gone.

Her haste is startling to Sue, who likes to linger warmly on farewells, standing with arms hugged around herself in lighted doorways. Kaminski toasts the departing tweed with a silent glass. The figure hurries through the gate, one shoulder thrust ahead, the coat thrown cape-wise over her shoulders. Almost she scuttles. From beyond the gate she casts back one terrible glance, and is swallowed in the fog.

"Why, I wonder what's the matter with her?" Sue says. "Didn't she act odd?"

Bill motions us in and slides the glass door shut. With his back against the door Kaminski studies the ice cubes which remain from his fifth highball. All of a sudden he is as gloomy as a raincloud. "I'm the matter with her," he says. "I insulted her."

"You *what*?"

"Insulted her. I made indecent propositions."

"Oh, Arnold!" Sue says with a laugh. "Come on!"

"It's true," Arnold says. "Ask the agent, there. I whispered four-letter words in her ear."

She stares at him steadily. "And if you did," she says, "in heaven's name *why* did you?"

"Akh!" Kaminski says. "Such a dried-up little old maid as that, so full of ignorance and enthusiasm. How could I avoid insulting her? She is the sort of person who invites indecent exposure." There is a moment of quiet in which we hear the sound of a car pulling out of the drive. "How could I help insulting her?" Kaminski shouts. "If I didn't insult people like that I couldn't keep my self-respect." Nobody replied to this. "That is why nobody likes me," he says, and looks around for a white coat but the white coats are all gone. Automatically Sue takes his empty glass from him.

Ruth says, quite loudly for her, "Sue, we must go. It was a lovely party. And Mr. Kaminski, I thought you played beautifully."

His flat stare challenges her. "I was terrible," he says. "Ackerman and those others will tell you. They are saying right now in their car how bad it was. The way I played, they will think I am fit for high school assemblies or Miss Spinster's chamber society. I am all finished around here. Nothing will come of any of this. I have muffed it again."

"Finished?" Sue cries. "Arnold, you've just begun."

"Finished," he says. "All done."

"Oh, what if you did insult Miss What's-her-name," Sue says. "You can go and apologize tomorrow. It's your playing that's important, and you played so beautifully . . ."

Bill Casement, by the door jamb, rubs one cheek, pulling his mouth down and then up again. He gives me a significant look; I half expect him to twirl a finger beside his head. "Well, goodnight," I say. "I'm tired, and I imagine you all are."

Bill slides the door open a couple of feet, but Sue pays no attention to me. She is staring angrily at Kaminski. "How can you *talk* that way? You did beautifully—ask anybody who heard you. This is only the first step, and you got by it just—just wonderfully! I told you I'd back you, and I will."

I have never observed anyone chewing his tongue, but that is what Kaminski is doing now, munching away, and his purple cheeks working. His face has begun to degenerate above the black and white formality of jacket and pleated shirt and rigid black tie. "You're incurably kind," he says thickly—whether in irony or not I can't tell. He spits out his tongue and says more plainly, "You like me, I know that. You're the only one. Nobody else. Nobody ever did. This is the way it was in Hollywood too. Did you know I was in Hollywood for a while? I had a job playing for the soundtrack of a Charles Boyer movie. So what did I do? I quarreled with the director and he got somebody else."

With a resolute move, Ruth and I get out the door. Pinpricks of fog are in our faces. From inside, Sue says efficiently, "Arnold, you've had one too many. It was a great success, really it was."

"Every time, I fail," wails Kaminski. His Mephisto airs have been melted and dissolved away; he is just a sloppy drunk with a crying jag on. His eyes beg pity and his mouth is slack and his hands paw at Sue. She holds him off by one thick wrist. "Every time," he says, and his eyes are on her now with a sudden drunken alertness. "Every time. You know why? I *want* to fail. I work like a dog for twenty years so I'll have the supreme pleasure of failing. Never knew anybody like that, did you? I'm very cunning. I plan it in advance. I fool myself right up to the last minute, and then the time comes and I know how cunningly I've been planning it all the time. I've been a failure all my life."

I am inclined to agree with him, but I am old and tired and fed up. I would also bet that he is well on his way to being an alcoholic, this anti-food-and-drink Artist. He has the proper self-pity. If you don't feel sorry for yourself in something like this you can't justify the bottle that cures and damns you. This Kaminski is one of those who drink for the hangover; he sins for the sweet torture of self-blame and confession.

A crying jag is as good a way of holding the stage as playing the piano or bad manners.

Now he is angry again. "Why should a man have to scramble and crawl for a chance to play the soundtrack in a Boyer picture? That is how the artist is appreciated in this country. He plays offstage while a ham actor fakes for the camera. Why should I put up with that? If I'm an artist, I'm an artist. I would rather play the organ in some neon cocktail bar than do this behind-the-scenes faking."

"Of course," Sue says. "And tomorrow we can talk about how you're going to go ahead and be the artist you want to be. You can have the career you want, if you're willing to work hard—oh, so hard! But you have to have *faith* in yourself, Arnold! You have to have confidence that nothing on earth can stop you, and then it can't."

"Faith," says Kaminski. "Confidence!" He weaves on his feet, and his head rolls, and for a second I hope he has passed out so we can tote him off to bed. But he gets himself straightened up and under control again, showing a degree of co-ordination that makes me wonder all anew whether he is really as drunk as he seems or if he is putting on some fantastic act.

And then I find him looking out the open door with his mouth set in a mean little line. "You don't like me," he says. "You disliked me the minute you met me, and you've been watching me all night. You want to know why?"

"Not particularly," I say. "You'd better go to bed, and in the morning we can all be friends again."

"You're no friend of mine," says Kaminski, and Sue exclaims, "Arnold!" but Kaminski wags his head and repeats, "No frien' of mine, and I'll tell you why. You saw I was a fake. Looked right through me, didn' you? Smart man, can't be fooled just because somebody can play the piano. When did you decide I wasn't a Pole, eh? Tell me tha'."

I lift my shoulders. But it is true, now that I have had my attention called to it, that the slight unplaceable accent that was present earlier this evening is gone. Now, even drunk and chewing his tongue, he talks a good deal like . . .

"Well, what is the accent?" I ask. "South Boston?"

"See, wha' I tell you?" he cries, and swings on Sue so that she has to turn with him and brace herself to hold him up. Her face puckers with effort, or possibly disgust, and now for the first time she is looking at Bill as a wife looks toward her husband when she needs to be got out of trouble. "See?" Kaminski shouts. "Wasn't fooled. You all were, but he wasn'. Regnize Blue Hill Avenue in a minute."

Again he drags himself up straight, holding his meaty hand close below his nose and studying it. "I'm a Pole from Egypt," he says. "Suffered a lot, been through Hell, made me diff'cult and queer. Eh?" He swings his eye around us, this preposterous scene-stealer; he holds us with his glittering eye. "Le' me tell you. Never been near Egypt, don't even know where Poland is on the map. My mother was not made into soap; she runs a copper and brass shop down by the North Station. So you wonner why people detes' me. Know why? I'm a fake, isn't an hones' thing about me. You jus' le'me go to Hell my own way, I'm good at it. I can lie my way in, and if I want I can lie my way out again. And what do you think of that?"

Bill Casement is the most good-natured of men, soft with his wife and overgenerous with his friends and more tolerant of all sorts of difference, even Kaminski's sort, than you would expect. But I watch him now, while Kaminski is falling all over Sue, and Sue is making half-disgusted efforts to prop him up, and I realize that Bill did not make his money scuffing his feet and pulling his cheek in embarrassment at soirées. Underneath the good-natured husband is a man of force, and in about one more minute he is due to light on Kaminski like the hammer of God.

Even while I think of it, Bill reaches over and yanks him up and holds him by one arm. "All right," he says. "Now you've spilled it all. Let's go to bed."

"You too," Kaminski says. "You all hate me. You'll all wash your hands of me now. Well, why not? That Carnegie Hall promise, that won't hold when you know what kin' of person I am, eh? You'll all turn into enemies now."

"Is that what you *want*, Arnold?" Sue says bitterly. She looks ready to burst into tears.

"Tol' you I wanted to fail," he says—and even now, so help me, even out of his sodden and doughy wreckage, there looks that bright, mean, calculating little gleam of intelligence.

Bill says, "The only enemy you've got around here is your own mouth."

"My God!" Kaminski cries loudly. Either the fog has condensed on his face or he is sweating. I remember the bright drop from his nose while he struggled with the Piano Pieces. "My God," he says again, almost wearily. He hangs, surprisingly frail, from Bill's clutch; it is easy to forget, looking at his too-big head and his meaty hands, that he is really scrawny. "I'll tell you something else," he says. "You don't know right now whether what I've tol' you is true or if it isn'. Not even the smart one there. You don't know but what I've been telling you all this for some crazy reason of my own. Why would I? Does it make sense?"

He drops his voice and peers around, grinning. "Maybe he's crazy. *C'est dérangé.*"

"Come on," Bill says. He lifts Kaminski and starts him along, but Kaminski kicks loose and staggers and almost falls among the chairs in the foggy patio, and now what has been impossible becomes outrageous, becomes a vulgar burlesque—and I use the word vulgar deliberately, knowing who it is that speaks.

"Don't you worry about me!" Kaminski shouts, and kicks a chair over. "Don't you worry about a starving kike pianist from Blue Hill Avenue. Maybe I grew up in Egypt and maybe I didn't, but I can still play the piano. I can play the God damn keys off a piano."

He comes back closer, facing Sue with a chairback in his hands, bracing himself on it. "Don't worry," he says. "I can see you worrying, but don't worry. I'll be out of your damned gardener's cottage in the morning, and thank you very much for nothing. Will that satisfy you?" With a jerk he throws the chair aside and it falls and clatters.

Bill Casement takes one step in Kaminski's direction, and the outrageous turns instantly into slapstick. The pianist squeaks like a mouse, turns and runs for his life. Behind a remoter chair he stops to show his teeth, but when Bill starts for him again he turns once more and runs. For a moment he hangs in mid-air, his legs going like a cat's held over water, and then he is in the pool. The splash comes up ghostly into the moonlight and the fog, and falls back again.

Maybe he can't swim. Maybe in his squeaking terror of what he has stirred up he has forgotten that the pool is there. Maybe he is so far gone that he doesn't even know he has fallen in. And maybe, on the other hand, he literally intends to drown himself.

If he does, he successfully fails in that too. By the time Bill has run to flip on the underwater lights the white coat is down under, and Kaminski is not struggling at all. While the women scream, Bill jumps into the water, and here he comes wading toward the shallow end dragging Kaminski under his arm. He hauls him up the corner steps and dangles him, shaking the water out of him, and Kaminski's arms drag on the tile and his feet hang limp.

"Oh, my God," Sue whispers, "is he dead?"

Bill looks disgusted. After all, Kaminski couldn't have been in the pool more than a minute altogether. As Bill lowers him onto the warm pavement and straightens him out with his face turned sideways on his arm, Kaminski shudders and coughs. His hands make tense, meaty grabs at the concrete. The majordomo, Jerry, pops out of the kitchen end of the cabaña in his undershirt, takes one look, and pops back in again. In a moment he comes running with a blanket.

Kaminski is not seriously in need of a blanket. For the first time that evening, he is not seriously in need of an audience, either. We stay only long enough to see that Bill and Jerry have everything under control, and then we get away. Sue walks us to the gate, but it is impossible to say anything to her. She looks at us once so hurt and humiliated and ashamed that I feel like going back and strangling Kaminski for keeps where he lies gagging on the patio floor, and then we are alone in the surrealist fog-swept spaces of the parking area. In the car we sit for a minute or two letting the motor warm, while the windshield wipers make half-circles of clarity on the glass.

"I wonder what . . ." Ruth begins, but I put my hand over her mouth.

"Please. I am an old tired philistine who has had all he can stand. Don't even speculate on what's biting him, or why he acts the way he does. I've already given him more attention than I can justify."

As soon as I take my hand away, Ruth says softly, "The horrible part is, he played awfully well."

We are moving now out the fog-shrouded drive between curving rows of young pines. "What?" I say. "Did you think so?"

"Oh yes. Didn't you?"

"He hit a big blooper in the chaconne."

"That could happen to anybody, especially somebody young and nervous. But the interpretation—didn't you hear how he put himself into first the one and then the other, and how the whole quality changed, and how really authoritative he was in all of them? Some pianists can only play Mozart, or Beethoven, or Brahms. He can play anybody, and play him well. That's what Mr. Arpad said, too."

"Who's Mr. Arpad?"

"The one that accompanies singers."

"He thought he was good?"

"He told me he had come down expecting only another pianist, but he thought Kaminski had a real chance."

Tall eucalyptus trees are suddenly ghostly upreaching, the lights shine on their naked white trunks, the rails of a fence. I ease round a turn in second gear. "Well, all right," I say in intense irritation. "All right, he was good. But then why in the hell would he . . ."

And there we are back on it. Why would he? What made him? Was he lying at first, lying later, or lying all the time? And what is more important to me just then, where in God's name does he belong? What can the Sue Casements do for the Arnold Kaminskis, and where do the Bills come in, and what function, if any, is served by the contented, beagle-running, rabbit-chasing, patio-building, barbecuing exurbanites on their hundred hills? How shall a nest of robins deal with a cuckoo chick? And how should a cuckoo chick, which has no natural home except the one he usurps, behave himself in a robin's nest? And what if the cuckoo is sensitive, or Spiritual, or insecure? Christ.

Lights come at us, at first dim and then furry and enormous, the car behind them vaguely half seen, glimpsed and gone, and then the seethe of white again. I never saw the fog thicker; the whole cloudy blanket of the Pacific has poured over the Coast Range and blotted us out. I creep at ten miles an hour, peering for the proper turnoff on these unmarked country lanes.

The bridge planks rumble under us as I grope into our own lane. Half a mile more. Up there, the house will be staring blindly into cotton-wool; my study below the terrace will be swallowed in fog; the oak tree where I do my birdwatching will have no limbs, no shade, no birds. Leaning to see beyond the switching wiper blades, I start up the last steep pitch, past the glaring-white gate, and on, tilting steeply, with the brown bank just off one fender and the gully's treetops fingering the fog like seaweed on the left. All blind, all difficult and blind. I taste the stale bourbon in my mouth and know myself for a frivolous old man.

In the morning, probably, the unidentifiable bird, towhee or whatever he is, will come around for another bout against the plate glass, hyp-notized by the insane hostility of his double. I tell myself that if he wakes me again at dawn tomorrow with his flapping and pecking I will borrow a shotgun and scatter his feathers over my whole six acres.

Of course I will not, I know what I will do. I will watch the fool thing as long as I can stand it, and ruminate on the insanities of men and birds, and try to convince myself that as a local idiocy, an individual aberration, this behavior is not significant. And then when I cannot put up with the sight of this towhee any longer I will retire to my study and sit looking out the window into the quiet shade of the oak, where nuthatches are brownly and pertly content with the bugs in their home bark. But even down there I may sometimes hear the banging and thrashing of this dismal towhee trying to fight his way past himself into the living room of the main house.

We coast into the garage, come to a cushioned stop, look at each other.

"Tired?" Ruth whispers.

Her pert coon face glimmers in the dim light of the dash. Her eyes seem to be searching mine with a kind of anxiety. I notice that tired lines are showing around her mouth and eyes, and I am filled with gratitude for the forty years during which she has stood between me and myself.

"I don't know," I say, and kiss her and lean back. "I don't know whether I'm tired, or sad, or confused. Or maybe just irritated that they don't give you enough time in a single life to figure anything out."

# JAMES B. HALL
## MY WORK IN CALIFORNIA

A native of Ohio born in 1918, James B. Hall since 1954 has been a
writer-in-residence at a number of Western universities; from 1968 until
his retirement in 1983 he was founding provost of the arts college at
University of California, Santa Cruz. His works include poetry, a novel,
*Racers to the Sun* (1960), and collections of stories: *Us He Devours* (1964)
and *The Short Hall* (1981). He is coeditor of the anthology *The Realm of
Fiction* (1965–77).

"My Work in California" was first published in *The Missouri Review*,
I, 1978, and reprinted in *Pushcart Prize IV*, 1981. An imaginatively complex, surrealistic satire set in the not-so-distant future, the story envisions
California as a grimly artificial world of fantasy that has become the
model for all cultures and that is smoothly orchestrated by a hollow
man, the narrator. As he shows various foreign visitors the high-tech
exhibitions in urban and mountain areas, his "faith" in modern Hell
becomes for the reader increasingly appalling, yet his thoughts remain
"for tomorrow"—the next erotic encounter.

# MY WORK IN CALIFORNIA

*I. The Younger Factory*

Of the one hundred passengers arriving from Seattle (Boeing) my job was only with thirty-four industrialists from Asia. Of this group a dozen were unexpectedly tall; a few wore dark, prescription glasses; only one man had two briefcases as carry-on. Not one delegate looked back at the aircraft or took a picture of the Oakland charter terminal.

My welcome sign at the baggage claim area read in Japanese and Hindi: Industry Tour Delegates Here. They manufactured something or were of engineering backgrounds; therefore they were urbane and kept my placard in view but did not cluster about. Most of them spoke Oriental languages, but to me they used English: "Our weather is identical of here weather." "We have eaten considerately while at flying," and so on.

At the luggage carousel one man from Korea claimed only a backpack and a pair of blue skis. By way of explanation their chief delegate, a Mr. Hognisko, said our gentleman from Korea join this California Inspection at last minute: all very good.

Beyond the terminal entrance our bus was parked, its engine running. For this I was relieved. In my work a great many things can go wrong.

Finally, our bus headed south towards San Leandro and the plant which was not far beyond Fremont.

By courtesy, Mr. Hognisko had boarded first and had claimed a seat immediately behind the driver. Now Mr. Hognisko leaned forward very intently; in a small notebook he recorded the RPM and fuel gauge readings. I made a mental note to arrange later for him actually to drive our bus—under supervision—inside the factory yard: a little thing like that for a delegate is very memorable.

As the bus went steadily through the last of the morning fog, I walked the aisle and answered their polite queries: Those salt flats at the edge of Upper Bay, were in production? The Alameda container-shipping facility, was it eighty-percent automated? Concerning Blacks in major California cities: how much Blacks?

The Korean's backpack was in the aisle beside him. Intensely, mostly with his arms, he was speaking to a man across the aisle; the man

267

listened, did not change expression, but finally repeated the question to me in English:

"Gentleman with valuable pack here say he makes fashion-purses— very many. Also: how far is Disneyland?"

I replied that Disneyland was in the Los Angeles area, specifically at Anaheim, which was approximately four hundred miles south, about one hour flying time.

"Gentleman says Disneyland not so far away."

At first the factory appears on the horizon as several hundred aligned ventilators, exhaust stacks, and air-scrub towers; closer, the immense roofs rise slowly from the ground and fill the bus windows. Only then do they really see the factory walls.

I understand the reaction: they have flown a long way to see this absolutely state-of-the-art complex; in their own countries they may wish to build a replica. When at last in a moment of bus-window vision our factory becomes manifest, they fall silent, are a little reverent, a little stunned. I, myself, often view it at mid-morning in the California sunshine and still I have some slight feeling of awe.

Our bus stopped at the entrance gate: There will be a slight delay.

Actually, I believe these foreign-delegation delays have internal function. Not every unit of our Younger factory operates at any given time; therefore all tour routes are selectively programmed.

The question is a good one: as an experienced guide, have I seen the complete layout, all units in production? Or: have I ever been programmed twice on the identical tour-route? Possibly, but my sole interest is professional: the art of tour-satisfaction.

In about twenty minutes, as expected, a young woman in her three-wheeled golf cart rides out across the vast parking lot to our bus. She hands me the route-skip chart. Often we work together.

Inside our bus, the young woman from Public Relations speaks to this delegation in English, German, and then in Turkish. First, an apology for this routine delay. Then her rundown of statistics: number of fenced areas, square-footages under roof, water gallonage daily; the architects and major contractors for the Beginning, Middle, and Final Coordinate modules.

Her speech is always impressive. No questions.

As our delegation enters routinely through the East-Arch plaza, I sense the usual change of mood: casual talk ceases. Here the corridors are vaulted-steel, air conditioned, and are virtually aseptic. The big surprise is the color-coding systems: all Receiving and Primary Incalculation areas are in tones of red; at tour's end, near the West Exit gates, the color coding ranges from indigo through violet.

Therefore, when one delegation looked down from the catwalk into their first full-production module, they saw that the nitrous tubing, conduits, and the work-persons' smocks were an identical shade of green. Because the high-speed machines are virtually silent, my voice was easily heard.

"Below, Gentlemen, our syntax looms. From left to right, inside trans-lucent tubes, the Youngers are admitted, then loomed."

Each delegate at once became fascinated with a single aspect of the process: with the emission tubes or water-recovery sumps; with the sensor areas or the green, intricate thread-lines which glisten in the cool light. As though they were encased, merely passive objects, all Youngers are sorted, then pass at high speed through the looms. Here all syntax patterns were confirmed. No one person can ever register all the coordinated movements; in the end, all visitors merely stare.

"All loom thread is 90% nylon—linen is no longer used." And to Mr. Hognisko, "Syntax is a general term: in addition to speech, it also encompasses larger cultural patterns."

He made a note.

In the loom pits below, the machinery seemed to breathe, and for an instant to glow deeply inside the intricate thread barriers. A workper-son, a woman in a green smock, emerged from the corridor between the extraordinary, winking shuttles, as though ejected or born from the loom itself; she glanced upward, gestured, then placed one hand lightly—testing for heat—on a rotor housing. The breathing looms slowed perceptively. The vault darkened as we moved on.

No further questions.

Our delegation lined up behind the glass barriers of a typical organic unit: here all Youngers receive their viral program injections; these mod-ules are typical of one of the more advanced procedures.

All in a row, faces pressed to the glass barriers, the delegates watched intently. Smiling or asleep in their little sacs, the Youngers passing in the troughs seem almost a blur. When twins with Oriental features went past, the delegates gesticulated, were much pleased.

As we watched, the sensor banks read the fluid codes: abruptly, the twins were shunted off together, disappeared. Farther along we viewed the more refined sorting and incalculation: one strain was for sensitivity to metal objects (cars, gold coin, tempered steel—as in guns). This one is standard, takes very well. The more complex motives of power (money and banking) or indiscriminate knowledge (for teachers) is less predict-able.

From my point of view, however, nothing *seems* to happen in the organic modules; they are low delegate interest. The crux forge and the sports verifier are more melodramatic. For Youngers, however, the entire process is without pain; doubtless it passes in a mild semi-biotic dream. As to overall effectiveness, not all types of irradiated tendencies are final; in California, a complete program-rejection at some later age is not common. Being exotic, our viral incalculation modules elicit few questions.

None? Very well: move along now to a typical production unit, V.T.

In V.T. all action is overt. Here all delegates have floor privilege. They may stand at a machine-of-choice. They move about freely. Only a re-peated call for the lunch-snack disengages most foreign observers. I also like these sections quite a bit.

Of course, the unexpected noise is the first contrast. The hubbub is most life-like: here all the machine operators call out. They curse one another and their balky machines; they chew tobacco where they stand. In V.T. the work rules are posted in several languages, especially Spanish; the operators belong to a loose, ineffectual union. Here Management leaves well enough alone.

At once all delegates scattered. Now they stood beside the machines, avidly speaking with the operators, if only in sign language. At last here was something everyone understood.

Mr. Hognisko was immediately beside a Stealth Elaborator. The Younger is placed (in sac) on a rotating metal plate; the eccentrically-balanced flywheel lowers—delicately or too deeply—and roughs the sac with the wheel's random abrasives. All Youngers appear to be terribly shocked, are in momentary pain; inside the sac we see their little hands row the fluid. Oddly, however, certain Youngers laugh; others withdraw or become merely fetal. The fascination, of course, is with the *variety* for at the Violence Tannery no two Youngers ever react precisely in the same way. The reason for this is not known.

No matter: because of altercations and workmen shouting obscenities, there can be neither questions or answers. Naturally these conditions divert delegates from our more refined techniques: A & A (Animal Affiliation, usually of the horse-prone variety); A & T (Alliance and Trauma-consequence, as in multiple divorce); A & C (Attenuated Cruelty, wide-spectrum). If asked directly, I say those more isolated sheds are reserved for some future visitation.

Because this particular delegation would not leave the machines, time did not permit them a view of the flower-decked, elaborately color-coded Reunion Ramps. Here all Youngers are delivered—emotionally, melo-dramatically—to parents, guardians, etc. With manufacturers, a little reconciliation doubtless goes a long way, for their interest is with distri-bution. In any event, after our luncheon-snack I answered questions:

—Yes: all water is re-cycled. Our California model conforms to Regional and Federal clean-air standards, or is being modified accordingly.

—No: Those Upper-Bay salt flats have no bearing on this choice of site.

In some distant area of the plant, at a place I have never been, I heard a reverberating, deep, explosion. All cafeteria lights went dim— then again became bright.

The delegates looked at each other but did not change expression.

Through a third party who spoke some English, the man from Korea asked about profit margins, and projected return on capital investment.

These figures, I said, are not available at the present time.

Before lunch was over, I noted that Mr. Hognisko has disappeared.

When we went outside to our boarding ramp, I saw Mr. Hognisko driving our bus (under supervision). He steered in large, swerving figure-eights, all over the now totally deserted parking lot.

When the regular bus driver saw me waiting, he directed Mr. Hognisko to park at our ramp.

As they boarded, each delegate said the tour had been most interesting and educational.

Whereupon I returned with the delegation to a downtown San Francisco hotel and checked them in for the night.

## II. The Snow Orchestration

A Bedouin party had toured California sixteen days when I was detailed to their "caravan" at a highway intersection just south of Yosemite.

Majestically, their polished-aluminum motor coaches all in a row floated around a curve, became larger; closer, in the mid-morning sun, the silver coaches seemed still wet. They parked in echelons-of-two beside the highway. Beneath the windshields, I saw sprayed-on, national colors; all license plates were of diplomatic issues. Their coaches carried twenty-eight persons, excluding drivers; the TV, radio, citizen's band antennae, and the rooftop air conditioners implied money was no object. They were much more than one hour late.

When no one got out, I walked from my car back to the first motor coach. Above and from behind his windshield, a driver in white coveralls waved casually. Their door did not open until I knocked again.

The Sheik greeted me cordially. He was in native dress and spoke with a distinct Cambridge accent. We shook hands. Inside it was a series of elaborate, meaningless introductions in Arabic; I presumed the names and titles were also on my roster.

The large forward compartment of this coach was lined with satin pillows; a white canopy of cloth hung overhead. With waterpipes and provocative sex magazines scattered about, the effect was that of a lavish tent, temporarily at ease on a desert oasis. From each dais, however, I noted each Arab could see both the driver's back and the instrument panel of the coach.

Naturally, my concern was to discuss at once our exercise: its engineering, cultural function, project costs, and projected useful life—everything. Unfortunately, either it was now tea time or I was served ritualistically. Inwardly I fretted at this further delay but made conversation and watched them drop many lumps of sugar into their delicate teacups. Time passed. The canopy filled with blue, sweet, Arabic smoke.

Suddenly an older man who had remained withdrawn in shadows leaned forward. He spoke emotionally in Arabic. I understood not a word, but I felt accused—of something.

"This cousin," the Sheik said not calmly, "*believes* one of our drivers is a State Highway Patrolman. In disguise, of course."

I requested details.

"As we go, we hear only this driver: *his* citizen-band radio is *active*. On our monitor in this coach we hear his *every* word."

They nodded: it was a communal judgment.

"This Number-Three driver conveys—Oh, slyly in code—information."

Patiently, I explained: all caravan drivers assigned are Teamster-Union members. By custom these drivers, via CB, convey harmless greetings to other passing Teamster-Union drivers. They alert one another to speed traps, the presence of Highway Patrol cars, and so on.

"But we have diplomatic plates!"

Finally I resolved it by two promises: a possible substitute driver; secondly, immediate warning to Number Three. Meanwhile, with their permission, I would brief all drivers; on this final leg to the valley ahead their caravan would simply follow my official car. This was discussed at some length: agreed.

Therefore I walked back to the other coaches to alert the drivers and to counsel Number Three—who appeared to be Pakistani. The third and fourth coaches carried only women and children. On identical television consoles I saw the identical program, an episode from "Gunsmoke"—with Arabic soundtrack. The women in *perda* and their children watched the screens very intently.

Number-Five coach carried servants, supplies, one accountant-scribe, and a physician; inside it smelled rancid with coffee grounds, smoke, and household pets.

At the head of the convoy, from the middle of the highway, I waved one arm in a circle: start your engines.

Slowly I led the way upward along the treacherous, curved highway for another sixty-two miles. We were now so behind schedule that the two guards at the gateway arch of stone waved us immediately to the promontory. Not far from the guard rails at the cliff's edge, the motor coaches again parked in echelons-of-two. Again I walked back to their first coach and knocked several times to gain admission.

I said the news was good: although well past noon, the atmospheric conditions at the altitude were still satisfactory. Our observation parapets lay immediately ahead.

Most opportunely, the Sheik said, this pause coincides precisely with the customary hours for lunch. Naturally I would be their honored guest?

"Very well," I had to reply, for clearly my status was that of servant. "Possibly this pause is foreordained—for our better fellowship?"

Everyone who understood smiled; my remark was then translated. The older men nodded wisely, then repeated in Arabic what I thought was the word "foreordained."

Our meal was elaborate. The lamb and the goat had been slaughtered, then fast-frozen in their home country, flown to California, and only last night delivered by taxi to this caravan. I admired the planning; the Sheik replied that such was their custom while abroad. Eventually everyone took a waterpipe and began to smoke. More time passed.

Almost inadvertently, much later, I glanced at my wristwatch.

Everyone stood up as though I, myself, had engendered this by-now-ruinous delay. At once two men took citizen-band microphones from beneath their pillows and began to give orders. Then everyone was talking at once in Arabic.

When all members of the party gathered on the promontory, there was a drawn-out uninformed discussion: was the snow exercise suitable for male children (under puberty), women, or servants? Eventually the physician, all young girls, and the eldest women were returned to the caravan; for security, all drivers to remain *in* their vehicles—and no CB transmissions.

So it was very late when finally I led their party to the viewing ramparts. Once seated, the Bedouins wrapped themselves in their robes and stared at the amphitheater headwalls of granite. Already I saw shadows in the east crevasse.

Over an intercom which connects all observation sites, I gave the set-speech: superb feat of modern technology superbly adapted to the unusual California resources and terrain. The exercise exploits three basic elements: light, wind-activation, and snow. Although apparently preserved in its superb natural state, our amphitheater below in fact is artfully lined with recessed ducting, elaborate banks of discharge nozzles, and panels of sequestered lights. From geothermal wells—Nature's bounty—high-density $CO_2$ rises, is compressed, and is then released sequentially. The gas escaping becomes "snow." All energy-transfer systems draw power from distant hydroelectric sites. Hurriedly, I reviewed the volume of released gasses, miles of buried tubing, square-footage estimates, the main designers, primary contractors, and maintenance budgets, *per capita*. Were there questions?

If the Bedouins registered my voice, they gave no sign.

Oddly—I confess it—when an orchestration begins, I forget the parties visiting. No two orchestrations are identical; I am always surprised. In one way I am proud to be part of it, and at those moments I wish everyone in the world could share this experience, especially when the program is complete and in sunlight at noon—which is the proper time.

As always, and especially with the Bedouin party, I had the usual feeling of anticipation—something like terror—when the first flakes of snow floated upward from the walls. Lights suddenly transformed the vast granite amphitheater into alabaster. The first "winds" blew. The panoramic wall began imperceptibly to writhe.

The snow builds, is caught in random drifts as though the wind were a shaping hand: the first portraits emerge. As it is with the vast faces carved in stone against the sky at Mount Rushmore, so now do portraits of snow range across the light-breathing walls for our initial contemplation. Because of the programmed wind, the hair on the snow-sculptured heads seems to rise as though the massive heads had tossed back in pain from the azure light.

On this particular day the faces at once extended into full-length figures: two prehistoric Asiatics in postures of sacrifice, their ritualistic knife piercing again and again the maimed child of snow. Face averted, an Indian woman undulates in postures of sexual invitation below the priest who is riding a burro. Whereupon the amphitheater resolves into concentric rings, each ring smaller and lower until the lowest depths become an eye, an enfolded flower of blazing snow, more fluid, more gold than the sun at noon. From the top rings, driven by winds, the snow overflows then falls like giant slabs of wax dripping into the molten eye. Always I imagine music would contribute to their better understanding of our past, but there is no sound beneath the sky.

The full-length figures dissolve into violet light. Now there is a wall of forests, all trees falling. Oxen and a thousand horses rear or are solidly yoked, pulling first crude sledges across the headwall, and then pulling grotesque mills down, down through a crevasse into that deepest core. All growing things are now gone away, the walls turn incredibly green, are supine beneath the faceless wind. These things I know are prelude only and I wait.

The sun came to rest on the farthest rim of the mountain. That first suggestion of nightfall was like the giant, whistling shadow of a bird's wing scything above our parapets.

The snow orchestration became suddenly frenzied. The lights blinked, shuddered; the wind rose. Everywhere snow erupted, became untrammeled drifts, then rolled down, down, as a thousand small avalanches into the darkness.

The amphitheater became mauve, then red. The wind swirled, lifted the red snow in rising, cyclonic columns. At eye-level those columns tilted, and I saw into the calyx of a monstrous flower. Within, I saw neither face nor figure—only the snows: iridescent, without motion, a roil of fire wherein nothing burned.

The lights turned a violent orange. The snow column died into the fissures of the granite wall; the wind also went away. As though the world itself had ended, there was neither breath nor sound.

In that spectacular, truncated way—abruptly—the orchestration of snows for the Bedouins stopped. If viewed in sunlight at noon, they would have understood everything; they, themselves, had delayed. I made no apology. I did not explain.

Their robes blown by late-evening winds, the Bedouins straggled back in little groups to the darkening promontory and to their aligned coaches. Only the guardrails seemed unchanged.

As it turned, out, however, I never did answer the usual questions. At once their physician and their accountant-scribe requested audience.

Very mysteriously, Number Three driver had disappeared. He had transmitted no CB messages; no property was missing; no known enemies. With the Sheik, I inspected the coach; the driver had simply vanished.

At once the Sheik withdrew with his immediate family and counselors. I waited outside the closed vehicles for what seemed a very long time. Finally, everyone reappeared and I was told a decision:

Most assuredly this thing was unfortunate. On the other hand, could it be entirely astonishing: had not I, myself, agreed previously both to reprimand and also to driver-replacement? Being a Pakistani—very possibly naturalized for convenience—the man was obviously incompetent. For this surely the Teamsters Union bears much blame. Concerning the driver's family: in any way, here or abroad, might they be contacted?

I said probably in some way they could be tracked down.

Excellent. But to the main point: an alternate driver.

I did not reply.

"Being the most qualified," the Sheik said, "by reason of my own extensive limousine holdings, *I* will drive this vehicle for the remainder of this day. I have closely observed all drivers—also the instrument panel. For me this will be educational. Agreed?"

I said the next stop was outside Fresno, where they were expected.

"Well done," the Sheik said very affably, for he was eager to drive.

One-by-one the engines started. Their noise reverberated upward in the chilled, rising wind from the mountains.

Going back down the highway, the Sheik followed my automobile much, much too closely. Continually he honked the airhorns. He drove recklessly—on the inside of all curves.

At that time—and to this day—it was pointless for me to report to anyone higher up that very plainly I saw bloodstains near the driver's seat when I inspected the vehicle. I suspect their physician. But as the Sheik had so rightly said, "We have diplomatic plates."

No matter: at the final intersection their caravan turned south. I honked once, and waved goodbye. In my report I intended to say that—in fact—the delegates noted many parallels between snow orchestrations and their own rich, essentially Persian cultural heritage.

Exactly at the speed limit I drove north to my motel which was at the edge of Stockton.

### III. At the Coma Pavilions

"My hobby geology," the surveyor from Penang told me. "Long time ago this place under water."

I said probably so.

On our drive south to the coast this group of scholars, a recuperating Swiss physician, educators, etc., had become better acquainted and were now a lively, well-motivated interest group. Our station wagons were to park here; older ladies—probably ex-schoolteachers—changed to hiking boots for this last-mile descent to the valley floor.

No recording equipment or cameras beyond this point, please.

Below, melodramatically, the valley divides; each parallel branch ends in white sand at the beach. Beyond, the sea was iridescent, rising, turquoise. For me this tour marked the season's end; already I was thinking of Palm Springs.

Energetically, our ex-schoolteachers started down the path; farther along, one voice, in German, began a marching song. Mainly to permit the Swiss physician a moment's rest beneath the rock overhang of a shelter carved years ago from solid rock by the first inhabitants, I called a halt and then reviewed our inspection guidelines:

Speech with inhabitants permitted *only* if resident-initiated. However: technically qualifed observers—physicians, our pathologist, etc.—may touch or otherwise manipulate comatose subjects. Only gross anatomical evaluations are customary; use of a stethoscope is all right. "Why-type" queries are unsettling, hence counterproductive. In a word, ladies and gentlemen, we are professionally-oriented observers.

"Yes, yes," the group responded, mostly in English. "Is understood." Questions?

—Certainly: All of them enjoy State, Federal, and Constitutional safeguards regardless of race, etc. Percentage of resident, native Californians is not available—estimates vary, yes.

—No: not an "exhibit" or a "theme park" impulse (e.g., Under Six Flags). If motivations appear incomprehensibly complex, consider the complexity of life today.

No others? I thank you.

Around the first, abrupt corner, against the sky and almost bridging the canyon walls, they saw their first Counseling Mobile. The light was very good.

To me, this one is largely amusing. To all educators and to our shockingly emaciated priest, *en route* to the Vatican, it was fascinating. At once, they climbed the ladders and from the high platforms leaned over the railings the better to observe.

I explained the site-logic: here coastal winds converge where the canyon narrows. The boom and cable arrangements suspended also converge—then regress—from the Resource Wheel—the large one, centered horizontally. The dissonant noises are their voices and also wind among their cables. In mid-air, the subjects forever pass; being electrically charged, however, they can never touch. By attraction then repulsion they move continually—what, one hundred fifty feet above these rocks?

Suddenly, exhibitionistically, one in a loincloth, its body dried totally by the winds, swooped down: arms outstretched, wide-eyed, the sun caught as fire on its enormous, steel-rimmed glasses. For a second it was suspended above our astonished heads, then with a tackle screaming, it rose in a great rush of air, was gone.

"Dead," the Swiss physician said. "Long time." Our pathologist from Edinburgh concurred.

Aloft on the highest platforms the educators tried to interpret the sound of the cables and the voices in the sibilant air. Again I called: Rejoin, please, your group immediately?

Because the sun was not yet too high we walked mostly in the shade of the canyon walls. Being of mature years, this group viewed with little interest the Excess Pavilions: a Consumer Cavern, the Cervix-Renewal and Depletion Station where desires of a purely sexual nature are changed monthly by surgical intervention. Surprisingly, the emaciated priest scarcely paused at an elaborate Meditation Pavilion dedicated to programmed Faith-Loss.

Their age-group considered, possibly I kept them overly long at the Matriarch Escarpment. I, myself, am oddly drawn to this ever-expanding sequence which is best viewed from elevated walkways along the opposite canyon wall. I explained:

Opposite: a typical encampment painted ochre and blue. Architecturally, the primitive forms hang on: seen in the platforms, square or shaped to the cliff face; seen in the shelters, rooflines peaked or typically convex; observed in the child-transfer poles (one per sibling) anchored like horizontal flagpoles, extending out from the platforms; also below— bars vertical or horizontal—their individual men-pens. Now: either supine or pacing continually in the prescribed patterns—two examples visible, extreme left—the woman controls all architectural improvements, equipage, monies. Moreover. . . .

"A-hoh!" the priest said, for he was coughing. Deeply absorbed, the Swiss physician said nothing, but his nurse spoke vehemently, "Disgusting, I think." The physician nodded, "Is so."

Along the cliffs, the women had finished eating and had fed the little children—gentle or with cruel dispatch. Actually, I find the children very pleasing to watch, for they frolic about the platforms, at times terrifyingly near the unguarded edge. Now, however, it was time for them to descend.

Note the psychological play. Having been fed, the children understand they are to be lowered, head-down, from the anchored flagpoles to the man-cage level of the structure. While being rigged by the ankles for their over-the-canyon suspension, the children whimper or kick. If a reactive type, the mother screams; if brutal, she often abuses the child.

Observe: at the instant of lowering, a child now smiles, laughs, calls to the man! See the Black babies bounce and whirl themselves and sing out?

At cage-level, the man reaches out. Variously he speaks, touches the girls' genitals, see? Swings them far out over the canyon—their play. Soon the man gives each suspended child its ritualistic mid-day bath. So: now along the escarpment, high and low, the children are raised back to the mother's platform. Now their little faces are very sober, or they simulate tears, or great glee—as the mother requires. There: all done for this day.

Being myself the son of parents long separated, a Pomona College graduate, and as a person who lives in celibacy—save the two winter months at Palm Springs—really, I am drawn to this escarpment. In fact, I forgot to ask for questions.

The surveyor from Penang spoke. "How make more babies?"

"At night," I replied. "Someway at night."

"Surely," the pathologist said, "there is a hole in the platforms. Possibly a trapdoor access is gained—after dark or not."

"Hole somewhere," the surveyor replied. "But why he go up there anymore?"

A discussion ensued and eventually I led this group to the place where first we hear plainly the long, cloth-tearing sound of waves dying on the white sands.

Among thwarted beach pine and oak trees at the valley's mouth, in pits, or aloft on poles exposed to the heavy sledge of the sun, abruptly, we came upon crucifixion platforms.

The stench of kelp and ruined shellfish at first is shocking, but this group did not draw back from this littoral of self-imposed agonies. The pathologist and the surveyor and the German philologist (ret.) ran forward to see more. In a second all the others scattered wildly among the trees.

Abandoned, I watched them go. Officially, I appear interested in a great many things; unofficially, however, my enthusiasms cannot be totally legislated from higher up. In my work-year of ten months, I see no other place of such consummate, natural beauty; yet, inwardly, I find this quarter-mile of sand truly revolting. Farther along I hear even the ex-schoolteachers cry out among the oak trees at some macabre, almost-sought-for recognition. In this place I keep my personal participation to the level of description, and the tight little smile.

In general: our Crucifixion Beach presents three general categories: Situations-Financial (Credit Pits, Tax-Supplicators, and others); Conformist Poles (Stakes, also Bamboo); and finally, the Coma-Pavilions proper. Since no one in the party either wanted or needed to hear more, I went directly ahead to the place where they would re-assemble. As I walked rapidly ahead, certain members of our party called out.

Two school teachers, their walking boots deep in sand, asked about a woman, burned by the sun, her hair blowing, seated—or buried—navel-deep in her pit. Mechanically, steadily, the woman threw sand upward into the wind; the wind blew the sand back into the pit and into her eyes. "Either credit-possessive," I explained, "*Or* a person forever sailing on packaged tours. It is the same. By going deeper she expects—some-time—to find water, from the sea."

The Swiss doctor was separated from his nurse. He was beside a platform about the height of a hospital bed, the platform larger than a circus ring, made up of old hatch covers, planks, and other flotsam from the sea. The bodies—perhaps one hundred—were hopelessly intertwined, comatose, save for the eyes which at random opened, stared for awhile at the sun, then closed. Stethoscope in place, the doctor was tracing the arterial blood supplies in the arms and legs of the men and women. On his right hand the doctor wore a rubber, surgical glove. He glanced up from his very serious examination and said, "Nefer hemorrhoids in a homosexual—I have nefer seen it."

The professional educators and also the German philologist (ret.) called down from the very top of a conformist pole. Aloft those poles sway in the wind, first towards the valley of stone, then towards the sea. Their voices seemed to be calling, "Accounted for . . . allll accounted for. . . ." but I could not be certain.

Even the priest, who was said to be *en route* to the Vatican and who had heard so much during his life, was apparently overwhelmed. Withdrawn in shadows, I passed him beside the pilings of some vast towering platform. In sand, from below, he stared aloft at the underpinnings. The priest was extraordinarily pale beside the black, creosoted poles.

The surveyor from Penang was the first to join me as I waited at the exit path where pines and oak and sand almost touch the tides running.

Without wishing to be so, I was sitting eye-level before the final and certainly the largest single pavilion. Here incredibly old men and women sit on a platform, elaborately put together, iron-reinforced against any storm. In the wind, in the terrible sun, at night and in salt spray these persons beyond speech each hour thrust thorns, or splinters of wood, or even fractured abalone shells—any debris—beneath their own flesh, and into the shoulders and the backs of one another.

In the end, always, their infections are overwhelming and they lie down, more than a thousand, still working, still moving a little, then comatose, unable to register either the sea or clouds, the valley or the sun burning in the sky overhead. Forever, their large and their small wounds fester, suppurate, fester, and grow.

"Okay," the surveyor said after awhile. "They pay for something?"

I said probably so.

Only when the first shadows rose from the sea and fell all at once across the beach did this party leave the Pavilions and gather at the exit path. Going back, no one at all sang. This day and this season were now ending. For the first time since I began this kind of employment, I found it a little depressing: for the past hour I had waited, and had thought vividly of Palm Springs. The station wagons were still parked on the cliff above.

Only after we were on the freeway returning to the hotels and to the city from whence we had come did the surveyor from Penang whisper in my ear:

"German, one who start singing. He stay back there. On a pole."

I did not reply. The pathologist and the priest and the Swiss physician were already asleep, and besides these things happened more often than the surveyor knew: about two per party, on a yearly average.

The station wagon seemed to throw itself even faster through the dark, headed towards the high, lighted escarpment of the San Francisco skyline. I thought only about tomorrow—and of Palm Springs.

This year, again, no doubt I will meet someone interesting.

I always do.

# JOANNE GREENBERG
# THE SUPREMACY OF THE HUNZA

Born in Brooklyn, New York, in 1932, Joanne Greenberg has lived for more than twenty-five years in Golden, Colorado, and has published numerous works of fiction including *I Never Promised You a Rose Garden* (1964), *Founder's Praise* (1976), *The Far Side of Victory* (1983), *Summering* (1966), *Rites of Passage* (1971), and *High Crimes and Misdemeanors* (1979), these last three being collections of stories. "The Supremacy of the Hunza" first appeared in *The Transatlantic Review*, 1971, was selected for *Best American Short Stores 1972*, and was collected in *Rites of Passage*, a work that reveals Greenberg's early interest in anthropology (subject of her degree from American University in Washington, D.C.) and in social commitment. (She has assisted in setting up mental health programs for the deaf in various places throughout the country, she teaches sign language, and she is an active member in answering medical calls for the Highland Rescue Team.)

In the story, an anthropologist, Margolin, has moved to an old house in the Rockies west of a metropolis (such as Denver, Colorado) only to have his pastoral peace disturbed by installation of power-towers. Protest seems useless, and Margolin, who believes that so-called civilization can't be stopped, is bored by his neighbor, Westercamp, who thrives on "organized complaint." But two events arouse Margolin's anger and compassion: Westercamp sickens, and an encounter with mentally-ill Indians at the state hospital creates a feeling of shared hopelessness. At this juncture, Margolin begins to think constructively of the Hunza, a Himalayan people alleged to lead "natural" lives without crime or anguish. Suddenly the Hunza cease to illustrate "primitive man," for their simplified life seems a better one than that imposed upon contemporary Westerners by the forces of progress and technology.

# THE SUPREMACY
# OF THE HUNZA

Margolin's house was four miles down Ridge Road, and part of his keen pleasure in coming home each day was in turning off the highway onto its blacktop. It was a slow road, one of the old wagon trails, lined with trees and made without the raw wounds of blasting. The way wound through hills, past meadows and upland pastures. Turning north, a wide vista opened on blue-dark pine mountains, and then the way turned down and Margolin took the dirt road to the right, to home.

It was an old house, square but leaning in its age as the ground did. Marbles put down by Margolin's youngest boy rolled west in some rooms, east in others, as though the center of the earth was in some question. The rear of the house looked out over the pine hills and back the way Margolin had come. He and Regina had never owned land or a house before this one. Because of its age, its place, and its view, Regina lived with the house's ancient crochets and Margolin became a commuter, submitting to the shocking erosion of his leisure time in travel. It was worth it, they told their incredulous friends. There might not be much time, but there was a sense of time here, and of stillness. Then the power-towers came.

The first was neatly placed, whole, while Margolin was at work. It stood ninety feet tall and gleaming silver at the side of Ridge Road. The next day there were two; then five. Then there was a row of towers across the road and down in hundred-foot strides. They climbed hills, walked valleys; they were hung with great muscles of cable. Two-hundred foot swaths were cut through the woods to accommodate them until they stood in a cable-hung line fifteen miles long, crossing all the forest and hill country between Emmettstown and Hale.

Margolin felt invaded, betrayed. He called the Power Company and was told that the land was a long purchased right-of-way. He called his lawyer, who looked into it and found that the land had been deeded in 1913, when there had been no zoning statutes, and that the owners

285

were held only by what applied at the time of purchase. Margolin hung up, fuming.

"There's nothing we can do," Regina said. "We'll just have to learn not to see them, that's all."

"That's the whole point!" he raged. "We came here so we wouldn't have to un-see everything. They have no right to make us un-see the damn things! They could have buried the cables and they know it!" When a neighbor called and told him about the protest meeting, Margolin was eager to go.

Regina shrugged, "The law is on their side—I think it's useless to fight it."

"But if we *all* protest—"

"Okay," she said. "Okay."

So he sat on the familiar folding chair in the school gym and waited for the meeting to start. Regina was right. What could they hope to do? The Company was within its rights; its eyesore towers were on its own land, owned long before the people who wanted to see these hills and meadows had come and begun to destroy them with houses. A man can spend his lifetime protesting and petitioning but there can never be any real protection for the ephemeral, unnamable joys of life. Across the gym a man stood up and waved to him. He saw it was Larry Westercamp.

Margolin seldom saw Westercamp except at meetings. There had been the school battles over sex education and busing and bomb shelters before this. The Margolins had gone dutifully to be counted, but Westercamp and his wife seemed to come alive in the atmosphere of organized complaint. They had been on numberless peace marches and zoning protests; their anger instantly took form as a petition, and in the meetings Westercamp was always at the core of the group, passionate and indignant and demanding action. Now he was coming over. Margolin sighed and began automatically to formulate an excuse. The meeting wouldn't end before midnight, and now he had Westercamp too.

Watching the lithe man move across the gym, Margolin realized that part of his irritation was envy. Westercamp was over forty and there wasn't an ounce of flab on him. His face had a striking, ascetic angularity; it was a face popularly imagined on poets and saints. Margolin was slightly sagging in the middle; he wore glasses and was getting bald, but Westercamp's hair was a magnificent steel-gray mass which he tossed in moments of restlessness, like a proud horse or a boy.

"Hi!" and he came over, smiling. He always seemed delighted to see Margolin and sat down beside him with a neatness that made Margolin feel older. "Ave's home with the kids," he whispered. "Measles."

"Oh?" Margolin said.

"She wanted to come, but measles can be serious, you know."

"Yes, I know." Margolin nodded.

"The doctors around here are prejudiced by their union. They're against anyone who wants to keep his health by natural means. Drugs, vaccination—it's all they know. We've had the kids on vitamin C to build them up. The school nurse called us fanatics."

"Oh, well," Margolin said, grateful for something on which he had no opinion.

The meeting began. The problem of the towers was described in agonizing detail. Their height and distance, number of lines and voltage was argued for over an hour. Everyone who said "ninety-foot towers" was reminded by someone else that the towers were ninety-three feet eight inches. Westercamp was often on his feet, explaining, urging. A woman said the towers might be a safety hazard and then the question of their falling or the lines falling was argued for another hour.

At the beginning Margolin sat listening in excruciating impatience. Slowly, his restlessness thickened into a kind of leaden boredom which turned down gentling as it released itself toward sleep. His head moved forward, his arms relaxed. Behind him a chair scraped and he shot up, shocked into wakefulness, not sure where he was. Beside him Westercamp was following each anguished point and question with alertness, rising to explain and embroil himself and each side issue.

At last the meeting broke up, having settled nothing but that there would have to be another meeting to decide the main thrust of the protest. It was very late and people left quickly. Margolin was tired and disgusted. He hung back out of boredom, staring at the display of children's art work on the walls above the gym equipment.

When his eye had worked itself twice around the empty room, he knew it was time to go, and he forced himself out through the back door of the gym and into the darkness. The night air brought him awake. He breathed in deeply and found himself smiling. He stretched and felt the air widening in his lungs. Suddenly he was alert and hungry, his senses keen. The autumn wind had sharpened the edges of everything; a wind-apple scent twisted past him from the orchard farms on the other side of town. There was late-cut grass too, and as he turned, a faint, resinous smell—pine trees from the woods miles west of where he stood. He was smiling, relishing the night and his solitude and how ancient a pleasure it was to sort the scents of the wind. He was sorry he had brought the car. It would have been good to walk the three miles home, warming himself from the work of it. He looked out toward the parking lot. Beyond it stood the line of towers, now with red lights on top of them to warn away aircraft. The pyramid, he thought and sighed, the most stable structure there is. They were in for good and a million meetings wouldn't move them.

"Civilization!" He jumped. The voice was Westercamp's, behind him. Damn! Margolin felt caught at something. He turned and there was Westercamp pointing to the towers. "Why do we let ourselves be used by these . . . gadgets . . . America's gone soft."

"I don't like the towers either," Margolin said uneasily. He didn't want to hear about Soft America. Searching for something else, he remembered a half-heard fragment of table conversation. "Hey, the kids say they saw you on TV. How does it feel to be in Show Biz?" He saw he had said the wrong thing.

Westercamp tossed his head nervously and dug his hands into his pockets. "It's just another part of what I've been trying to fight; the mechanization, the reduction of everything. The news media made a big joke of it."

Margolin wished he had remembered more of what his children had said. "Uh—I didn't see it. What happened?"

"Our section in Fish and Game has been working on a new strain of brook trout. We needed a species with a high tolerance for the common pollutants. Last week the Governor invited the four other governors here for those Regional Conservation talks of his. We were supposed to give a demonstration of the trout, but we didn't know it was rigged as a stunt. They announced that the Five Governors were going to do a little fishing, that away from all the pressures and publicity they might be able to work out the issues. Then Fish and Game got the word that the Governors had better catch something, and what better than the new trout? I had to take almost all of our new fish upstream of their 'secluded spot' and release them to be dragged out three hundred feet away."

"That's kind of standard, isn't it?" Margolin said. "Honor of the State and all that?"

"There were newsmen in that 'secluded spot' taking pictures of me throwing the fish *in* and others taking pictures of the Governors pulling them *out*. On the six-o'clock news they mentioned the specially developed trout, and they mentioned conservation talks, but nobody paid attention. It was all a big comedy. They had spliced my section and the Governors' sections together and speeded up the film. They even set it to music. Me throwing and them catching. It looked like a sort of dance, fixed in rhythm, in, out, my face, the Governors' faces, and then the fish, so we were all doing a kind of dance."

Margolin had begun to laugh. He couldn't help it. He imagined the look on the faces of the men and the faces of the fish. The Governors were clad in skins, grunting as they pulled out fish in a steadily quickening rhythm, Westercamp working faster and faster, the wide-eyed fish more and more confused. He tried to stop and tell Westercamp that he wasn't laughing at him or his job. The man just stood there looking wounded until Margolin forced himself to stop and offer a ride home. The answer was stiff, but Margolin hadn't wanted to be cruel and Westercamp knew it.

"I'm sorry, really," Margolin said. "I suppose feeling strongly about a thing puts it out of the joking category." They got into the car.

Westercamp, still earnest, persisted, "It's just that you, of all people, must know how important it is—not only conservation, but human—dignity. The average man doesn't see, but you're an anthropologist; you study uncorrupted people, people who live as nature intended. . . ."

For a minute Margolin didn't understand. "What?"

"I mean you can see how far we've gone from the true pattern, the way people were meant to live."

Margolin turned out on the road and then glanced at Westercamp. "Larry, all men impose a pattern on nature. The lives of the people I study are often more artificially determined than ours. I just study the patterns, I'm not looking for Utopia."

"But there are people whose lives aren't complicated by—by . . ." and he gestured out the window to the few lights in a deserted shopping center.

"I don't know that it's better to have a life complicated by dead ancestors whose clan taboos must be remembered and followed—"

"I'm not saying that others don't go wrong—tribes full of superstition and fear, but there are others, certain groups . . ."

They pulled up at Westercamp's house. Margolin wondered if he should shut off the motor. It was late and he was tired, but he didn't want to seem impatient or draw attention to his waiting. Westercamp was still working. "Doesn't it disturb you that we—the richest nation on earth—are plagued with mental illness, moral decay, pollution of our air, our water, our values—?" He was aware that he had lost a connecting point in his idea. "Well, you *understand*," as though Margolin had only been teasing him. He looked up at the dark house, "Ave's probably gone to bed."

He opened the car door, got out and then turned back to Margolin, "Look, we've got to fight those towers. We can't give up. Come to the meetings—we need you. People get excited at first, but after a while they drop away and without organization, we're lost. You have to be vigilant—so vigilant, all the time."

In the dashboard light, Margolin saw his tight little smile, a condemned Saint, encouraging at the fire. Then Westercamp turned and went to his house.

Margolin could see by his walk that Westercamp was tired. The youthfulness seemed to have fallen from him like a disguise, with only the physical props still there, the hunting boots, the soft old shirt with half-rolled sleeves; young Westercamp forever just returning from the woods strong and uncompromised. Except that suddenly the forty-three-year-old man was in disguise and admitting to his age. Margolin wondered why he should be so comforted by that admission.

He headed home, keeping the window down and trying to relive some of the enjoyment he had had in the beauty of the night. Now it was only cold and late and going to be hard to get up tomorrow. "Primitive man!" he muttered. Then he thought about Westercamp again, beautifully choreographed, feeding fish to the Governors' mountain stream, and by the time he got home, he had orchestrated in order, a minuet, a tango, a wild "primitive" native dance.

In following weeks the Margolins began to get phone calls and mail from some of Westercamp's conservation groups. Regina laughed at Margolin's "new hobby," but he found himself inordinately angry at Westercamp's violation of his privacy. The letters and calls were so importunate, so desperate and convinced: Did he know that Strontium 90 was building up in our bodies? Did he know that the water table was dropping, the world was burning its resources, wastes were poisoning its soil, war eroding its morals? *Act Now!* He put the pamphlets in the bottom of the filing cabinet when Regina wasn't looking.

The second meeting about the towers was held on an evening when Margolin had to be at the University and he was relieved not to have to go. The next day Westercamp called. "Ted, I didn't see you last night. I hope you haven't been sick or something."

"No, I had to stay over at school."

"I hope you can make it next time. We're getting up a petition. Frank Armbruster is going to see if we have good grounds for a lawsuit and he'll let us know."

"Uh—Larry, I've been caulking the windows, and I left things where the kids—"

But Westercamp wasn't listening. "It's going to pick up this time. This time we'll make them see. Oh, and I was talking to someone there and we got into a discussion about the Chontals. That's the way you pronounce it, isn't it, Chontals?"

"Who?"

"Chontals, those Indians on the southern Isthmus of Mexico—"

"Oh?" Margolin tried to sound professional and interested, but he was fighting an annoyance out of all proportion to the cause. Spontaneous Discussion of the Chontal. He sighed.

"I was reading," Westercamp went on, "about this man who went there. He never saw an adult strike a child. Crime and insanity don't exist there. He never saw violence. The people live on their land simply and in peace. He saw women of seventy and eighty carrying water in huge jugs for miles without tiring. I admire people who can live like that—simply. Don't you think that's wonderful?"

Margolin wanted to say, "Yes, wonderful," and go upstairs and caulk windows and curse, but he couldn't conquer his irritation. "I've never visited that group," he said, "but I know the area. I'll lay you odds that the 'women of seventy' were thirty and *looked* seventy. Employment means staying alive till tomorrow; the absence of crime is the absence of an idea of private ownership. The harmony is chronic malnutrition, the tranquility is cocoa-leaf."

"Ulcers and heart trouble are unknown," Westercamp argued doggedly. "Diabetes and mental illness—"

But Margolin couldn't stop either. "They have rickets, pellagra, TB, smallpox. The infant-mortality rate culls out everyone but natural survivors. Mental illness 'exists' only where people accept the possibility of changing human behavior."

"But diseases like rickets are cured by decent diet, medical knowledge that we—"

"Larry, if the Good Life depends on decent diet and medicine, then the Good Life isn't Chontal, is it?"

"Well what about Tristan, then, Tristan de Cunha?" The big proof, the cap.

"What about it?" Margolin said, remembering the magazine stories. "The Islanders were warned and later evacuated to Liverpool because an earthquake had been predicted."

"Yes," shouted Westercamp in triumph, "but they found themselves getting cavities in their teeth; they saw their old people getting respiratory diseases, and their children picking up the values of the gutter; so they packed up and they got out, all of them, back to a decent life, a life away from 'civilization'!"

"After seeing six months in a Liverpool slum as 'civilization,'" Margolin said acidly. The magazines had played it Westercamp's way, he remembered: The Good Life vs. Sin & the City. "The men with the rotten teeth and bad morals were the ones whose machines had predicted the trouble and saved the Islanders in the first place. Too bad about cavities, but the people of Tristan were unskilled and illiterate in a world that demands both skill and literacy. The population in paradise is dwindling anyway, aging and dwindling, because in spite of clean air, good morals, and no cavities, the general health is poor. With a single occupation possible and almost no choice of mates, there is very little dimension to life on Tristan, because Tristan as Utopia just doesn't work. . . . OK?"

The phone-voice sounded wounded. "Well, you know more about them than I do, I guess," and Westercamp said good-bye, leaving the victory of the dead line to Margolin.

"Be as little Chontal," Margolin muttered, and hung up. His mind passed over other words to where his envy was: What right did Westercamp have to make heroes? That ugliness scared him so badly that he had to promise himself to be decent next time, and generous, and leave Westercamp's illusions alone.

In time the mailbox glut slowed a little, and it became peacefully automatic to put the tracts away in the filing cabinet. They had a place. Outside the power-towers showed no sign of departing the landscape, and Margolin tried his best to ignore them, look through them, adjust them to his eye in some automatic way, but none of the tricks worked. He missed the third meeting and the fourth, and after that he wasn't called again.

The autumn moved from abundance to its lean old age. The trees shriveled and darkened, the frosts fell dry. Winds screamed in the towers. Margolin began to have daydreams about those towers blowing over; they were juvenile, self-indulgent dreams and they made him ashamed. Then it snowed and the towers stood out like skeleton sentries overwhelming the hills where they stalked, watching. They had been up for five months. He knew they would never come down; he knew that defacing the land with them was wrong, in Westercamp's word, unnatural, and that there was nothing he could do.

It worried Regina to see him sitting in the chair by the window, looking out dully as an invalid at trees, sky, and the graffiti of birds and small animals in the snow. The sun picked out the towers in a blue-white blaze. He knew she was able to strike their ugliness from her mind. If she had been asked to draw the meadow in front of their house and the hills stretching beyond, her painstaking sketch would have shown no towers. They had spoken about her gift for ignoring ugliness once or twice, and when he thought about it, it frightened him. Now it was one of her sources of strength. He thought she might try to coax him away from the betrayal keeping him busy. His special project was coming in December. He would be home until then.

He was correct. She began to invite people over for dinner, for cards, for nothing. Soon the guests reciprocated until every evening was filled, until he complained that he didn't have enough time for his reading or his work. What was the matter with her? Why was she so restless?

It was at one of these automatically reciprocating forced marches that he saw Westercamp again. Remembering his stubbornness he thought that Westercamp might turn away, but whatever losses Westercamp had suffered, he seemed to have forgotten them and he hurried over smiling to greet Margolin, "Ted, hi!"

"Hi, Larry," he said. "How's it going?"

"Fine, fine," and Westercamp grinned. They went over to get drinks and Margolin dug around for something to talk about. "Say, how is the group coming on the towers?" Westercamp gave the dip of his head that showed he was embarassed.

"Well, it's just about disbanded. . . ." Margolin realized the embarrassment was for him—one of the Righteous who hadn't been there.

"We had too few coming to make a real fight of it," Westercamp added. "We did make some calls; we sent the petition and Armbruster is still looking into the legal angle, but"—and his taut, ascetic's face gave a quick twitch of a smile—"people aren't willing to back up their beliefs."

"Oh, come on, Larry!" Margolin said. "A well-led group could have gotten it done in fifteen minutes, and instead of group therapy we could have had our petition going right away. I went to the meeting to register a protest, not start a career. There was no firm leadership and we got bogged down in side issues. The thing didn't die of apathy, but of incompetence."

Westercamp stared at him with the shock of having heard something obscene. Margolin muttered an excuse and slipped away.

The Margolins left early. It was a thick, ugly night. As they came toward home, he looked around for the towers, but they were hidden in fog; even the mean-eyed red lights. "Damn things! I hurt Larry again, Reg, but he's so naive!"

"Then why are you so hard on him? Why can't you leave him alone?"

"I don't know. He's using me, and . . . I don't know."

He escaped into work gratefully. It was almost time for Christmas vacation and he had been asked by a therapist at the State Hospital to spend some time with three Sioux who were patients there. "They dream," the therapist had said, "and I'm out of my depth with the symbols they're using."

Margolin had been looking forward to going. It would be a relief to
be called from the twilight window where he could see the towers
closing upon his house. Perhaps he might be able to help in some way,
although he was no expert on the Sioux. Some insight here might
freshen his classes, anyway.

When the day came, he packed delightedly and told Regina that he
would come back rested and stimulated and looking forward to writing
*Acculturation* on the blackboard again. He left earlier than he needed
with a feeling of excitement, as though he were going to set off cross-
country to a place unmapped but where all Towers were his to deal
with. He called her from a hotel near the Hospital and a few times after
that to find out if everything was all right, and he called her when he
was getting ready to leave. His voice on the phone hadn't prepared her
for the way he looked when he walked into the house again. He stood
without moving, gray and sick and deeply tired, so changed that she
was stunned and couldn't think of anything to say. For a while they
simply stared at each other. "Ted?"

"Hi."

"Darling, what happened? You look exhausted."

"Tomorrow," he said, "not now."

"Let me take your coat—come on in the kitchen and have some
coffee. It's all ready. . . ."

The whole house had been readied for his homecoming; Regina in
her diaphanous blue thing, the kids in bed, the rooms orderly. He sat
in the quiet room with his coffee and realized that as exhausted as he
was, he wouldn't sleep. He was afraid even to try.

After a while she asked, "Did you have a nice room at the hotel?"

"It was fine." Then he laughed, shaking his head at the lie he was
beginning; he would have to tell her something, and if it wasn't what
had happened, it would have to be some kind of lie. "It wasn't fine,"
he said. "I can't even remember what it was like. What I remember is
a series of gray-smelling interview rooms, two senile old Sioux and
Benton Song." He spoke slowly, seeing himself again in those rooms,
listening as he had, cold and alone, to tapes of Benton breaking asunder
with astonishing dreams. In the nightmare landscape's vastness, the
symbols of The People had become cheapened parodies, like Made in
Japan trinkets Benton sold summers from a plastic wigwam off the
highway.

"Start at the beginning," she said.

"In the first place, Benton isn't Sioux at all. He comes from Arizona;
his mother was Navaho, his father one of the Tewa living in Taos Pueblo.
At the staff-meetings they talked about The Indians, not Navaho or

Tewa. Benton is the product of a marriage like that of a Japanese geisha and Sicilian grape-grower. I tried to help him, Reg, and I couldn't. I didn't patronize him or play the scholar, but I couldn't help either. In the middle of our first meeting he got up and yelled, 'Your mother is full of cowboy pictures!' and left."

"What happened? Did he come back again?"

"No, I went to see him on the ward. We talked there at first. He needed all kinds of proofs of my honesty and competence—you can't give that in two weeks and he knew I had that time limit, that neat vacation, 'two weeks with The Savages,' he said. There've been too many fake-authentic Indian things and too many bad books. Even the simple facts of Benton's life give him pain. Sometimes he was—well, never mind. His mother was a professional Indian, going around the country to march in parades and 'do' conventions while his father waited back in Taos and wondered why his wife couldn't be the way women are supposed to be. Later she took Benton on tour with her."

"But that's no Indian background—it's . . . nothing."

"It was this Indian's background—" and he smiled sourly. "At one time I did try to pin him to a category—'With which people were you most at home?' He only shouted at me: 'With the warriors of the Silver Screen! Apaches in feathers, bathing trunks under their breechclouts, Sioux in sneakers. Tonto, him my brother!'

"I tried to make him see that even his mixed symbols had meanings that Anglos might not know: 'The hawks you see in Dr. Ferrier's tests and the ones you dream about—he's trying to find a way to help you . . .' He answered, 'I don't know about that! They threw me out before the movie ended!'"

"You can't be expected to do psychoanalysis in two weeks," Regina said, defending.

"I was supposed to know the context of those dreams—to show Ferrier where the symbols carried cultural weight." He began to repeat one of the dreams that Benton, tonguetied with tranquilizers had given to the tape recorder to haunt Margolin's evenings:

"The sky is clear—it's someplace near Window Rock. It's noon and the sun is riding the world. Something is going to happen, but I don't know what, and I'm afraid it's a sign I won't see or recognize—that I'll miss it. I'm sitting on a mesa, a small mesa, all piled with rocks, alone. I'm watching everything, and I'm watching me. I'm born from the sun —I look down and see the me that's down there, far, far down. I'm a hawk. I despise that crawling thing so far down there. I begin to dive toward it, to kill it, and I feel a heat and a chill in me, a kind of crying, like crying for air when you can't breathe. I open my big wings and my shadow darkens the man and the rock. What the wanting is—it's to join that shadow—to be all one. I scream, dive head-on toward myself, man and shadow, and hawk, all one, and when I hit, it's dying, the end—a terrible pain, and I wake up."

"It has a beauty to it," Regina said.

He sighed. "I suppose it has." He looked around at the kitchen, shining and clean for his homecoming. "There are tribal realities in it, and universal ones, and a self-wounding satire of the White Man's Red Man, and I can't really tell where one leaves off and another begins. We soon stopped having 'interviews' and just talked; that is, when we could. He would fight on the ward at night sometimes. Then he would come in the next day black and blue and groggy with drugs. I liked him, so it hurt—that business. Before I left this morning, I stopped in to say good-bye and we shook hands. I hadn't thought he would commit himself like that. I wanted something—anything that could make it better for him. He's intelligent and he knows it in spite of all the 'injun-talk.' I told him to help Ferrier and the Group Therapy people by telling them about the differences between Navaho and Tewa, not letting them get away with phony symbols and a phony reality. He shook his head, and said, 'Maybe it's better to be a character in a white man's movie. When the Eagle speaks for my life what language will he use? A language I don't know? A language nobody knows any more?'

"I told him to keep trying to hear the words. He looked at me and shrugged and said that at least I had been a change from sitting around on the ward, and we laughed. Then very quietly he said, 'You tried.' I—uh—gave him our address and told him to come and see us when he got out. . . . Don't worry, he won't. He folded the paper up very carefully and put it away, but we both knew he wouldn't come."

"Oh, Ted, you don't know. Maybe he will. Maybe you did do more than he said, even more than he knows himself, and then too, you helped the doctors—"

"Sure. I took the notes I'd made and brought them to a big hospital staff-conference. Everybody listened politely and when it was all over, they thanked me and complimented me and kidded in a very gentle way about the scholarly monographs to be derived from this source anguish."

"They tried to make you see that you had helped."

"Oh, Reg! They were pitying an amateur who couldn't fight away the awful hopelessness wound up in those damn tape-spools. They'll forget Benton isn't Sioux; they'll forget I told them I hadn't helped. They'll take the notes and make them law and do more studies on *The Mental Patient*, and I'll do 1 or 2 on *Acculturation* when I need something published, and Benton's pain is so awful and so frightening and nobody knows how to help!" Then he stood up and shook his head and went to bed, leaving Regina alone in her sexy blue, staring at his half-finished cup of coffee.

The next day was Saturday and he resolved that if he didn't want to be ministered to, he'd better stop acting like an object of pity. He dressed quickly and with a great show of heartiness, fixed the loose steps on the back porch, and took the kids out for hamburgers and a monster movie. Although there was nothing real in his good spirits, he was comforted by the deception. He was standing in well for the real owner of his life.

The movie struck him as being subtly obscene. Its symbols, which he understood more clearly than Benton Song's, were homosexual and fetishistic. Worried for his children, he questioned them afterwards about what they had seen. They answered from untroubled, open faces and spent the ride home delightedly reliving the crucial scenes with themselves and the monster and the world gone small and helpless.

Regina looked at the greasy-fingered, bleary-eyed spectacle they made and her face relaxed. "Honey, I forgot to tell you last night—I put all the mail in the top drawer of the desk so it wouldn't get misplaced. There were some calls. I took the messages and they're in there too."

"I'll look at it all later," he said, and still working, went upstairs to see Mark's science project.

When he did get to it, he understood why Regina had let it wait. It was mania; Westercamp again, and oh, the air, the water, the food, outer space! the benthos off the continental shelf! . . . And the phone calls. They had heard he was interested; did he wish to become a member? Did he know there was a group to—? a Council for—?

"*Regina!*"

"I had to save them for you. . . . Now, you've seen them you can throw them out."

The phone rang. It was for him. Did he know about the protest against the mass shooting of elk in Wyoming? He hissed his answer into the phone and hung up. Regina was standing in the middle of the room, watching him, her hands raised slightly, defensively, and the gesture infuriated him.

"This is ridiculous!" he said. "I won't have that damn fool involving me in every hysterical cause he's hooked on!" He went for the phone book to get Westercamp.

"Ted. . . . Just a minute. I think you should know—-something's happened to Larry. Avis told me while you were away. He's sick, Ted; he's been home all week and it has to do with his job, somehow."

"What's the matter with him?"

"Avis never talks about their troubles. She must have thought it was important that you know, because she told me to tell you. You're a very special person to Larry."

"I know, I know," he said.

"Maybe you should call, but not about the protests."

"I'll tell her to put him on vitamin C," Margolin said, and felt ugly for having said it and so, had to defend the ugliness, "No wonder he's sick, with all the fuss they make over health and vitamins. Reg, how am *I* supposed to help him? I just got back from *not* helping someone I *liked*, someone I'm 'trained' to help." Her eyebrows rose slightly. "Okay," Margolin went on, "he's naive and I'm jealous of it, but I resent being used as a talent scout for his damn tribes!"

"You don't own primitive man any more than he does." Getting his look, she shrugged. "Well, I've told you about him; you can do what you like," and she left him and went upstairs to oversee the baths.

"Do what I like!" he muttered, and dialed Westercamp's number. He had concocted a vague, neighborly beginning, but when he heard the hope in Avis Westercamp's voice, he knew he wouldn't be able to use it. What did they expect of him? Westercamp got on and Margolin was unprepared for the lowered, pinched quality of the voice; its youthfulness had been conquered, the naive enthusiasm was gone, narrowed to the effort necessary to lift the phone. He was even puffing from the walk. They traded greetings and Margolin found his neck and arms aching with the strain of holding the phone to his ear. He began to throw words into it, needing the sound to listen to. He told Westercamp a wildly doctored story about his visit to three Sioux Indians, and how one had turned out not to be a Sioux at all. He tried to make a little joke about the mailing lists. He pushed away heedlessly and the thoughts fled before him into hiding. When he stopped, he was winded.

Westercamp began to speak slowly. "I suppose your wife told you what happened. . . ."

"Not really," he said.

"Trout . . ." Westercamp whispered. Margolin held his breath. "We were developing—uh—resistant to certain—uh—contaminants in the water. I told you."

"I remember," Margolin said.

"We put some in Ede Lake about two months ago. By last week they had died—all of them. And in Swanscombe creek too. The fish could live in foul water"—his newly old voice cracked—"but not in sewers. The river—is a sewer. The lake—is a sewer."

"I know the trout took time to develop—"

"Not the *time*," Westercamp interrupted querulously. "It's us. We had everything, everything, and we burned it, poisoned it. Why didn't we stop before it was too late? Why can't we stop destroying? Why can't we live *simply*, like the Hunza?"

Margolin caught his breath. The Hunza? New entries in The Noble Savage Sweepstakes.

A student had asked him something before vacation—he should have seen this coming. His old notebook had given:

> The Hunza: small group of Moslem, Subsistence herders, slopes of Himalayas. Close, precarious adaptation to high altitude, short growing season, rugged terrain.
>
> (P.8, C.50, IC.6)

The codes indicated the typical Tibetan pattern, but the Utopia-hunters must have been there and come back with the eternal, impossible tales—no anguish, no crime, no locks, men living in vigor to great age. The old dream was blowing into bloom, like a wild poppy. It would be cut back on the edge of fact and lie dormant for a winter only to come bright again somewhere else. Margolin sighed and thought: Your mother is full of cowboy pictures.

He said gravely into the phone, "Yes, the Hunza."

He could hear Westercamp breathing in his ear, sick now, and wary of more pain. Suddenly Margolin wanted to beg his foregiveness; for polluting his air and fouling his water and for permitting the hideous towers to stand.

Westercamp breathed into the phone again. "People who have seen them say there are no words for greed or envy."

"There probably aren't," Margolin said gently.

"They live simply—pure food, good water."

"They are a small, closely knit people," Margolin added quietly.

". . . and they reverence wisdom. The elders live to a hundred and twenty." Westercamp's voice had lightened.

"Moslems," Margolin said, "tend to venerate age." He was glad when Westercamp missed the point of this.

"Yes, and wisdom. They don't worship fads, material things—they're happy, I think, because their lives are natural. It's good for men to work hard . . . " The voice had some of its suppleness again. Margolin was moved. His own torment could never have found relief in some unknown tribe's good fortune. He knew that if Utopia existed, he would have envied it, and not, with Westercamp's singular goodness, wished it well.

"You see," Westercamp went on, "they're not compromised and humiliated all the time. They live as they should. . . . They don't have to try to convince everybody of the simplest truths . . . the most obvious truths."

"A Hunza can understand another Hunza's work," Margolin said, "and I think that is a beautiful thing."

"I'm glad you agree. If only we were like them!"

". . . and their language is interesting too," Margolin said, "an old and complex tongue."

When he hung up, he found he had a headache. At three in the morning it was still pounding. The red lights on top of the power-towers were winking on and off, on and off, outside the window.

Margolin sometimes used a hand-made spear-thrower to shock his freshman classes on their first day. He would send the spear into the wall at the back of the class and then, in the sibilant wash of amazement, wade dramatically to his beginning: Primitive Man. . . . At six in the morning Regina traced the strange sound to the basement and found him practicing with the spear-thrower, sending the makeshift spear across the laundry room with terrible savagery. When she asked him what on earth he was throwing it for, he said, breathing hard, "Ninety-three feet, eight inches."

# WILLIAM EASTLAKE
# THE DEATH OF SUN

William Eastlake came relatively late to the Southwest's high, dramatic country. Born in Brooklyn, New York, in 1917, he discovered New Mexico in the mid-1950s (after he had served as a soldier in France and Belgium during World War II and had been wounded in the Battle of the Bulge) and settled on a ranch in the Jemez Mountains, eventually moving to Bisbee, Arizona. He has felt the meaning of the Southwest and has translated it into literature in eight novels—notably *Go In Beauty* (1956), *The Bronc People* (1958), and *Portrait of an Artist with Twenty-six Horses* (1963), all recently reprinted by the University of New Mexico Press—and in more than sixty published stories. As Walter Van Tilburg Clark noted, "William Eastlake has brought into sharpest focus all the questions about modern man and his values . . . with the most unimpeachable blend of sardonic realism and far-reaching myth."

"The Death of Sun" originally appeared in *Cosmopolitan*, 1972, and was reprinted in *Best American Short Stories 1973*. Whimsical and high-spirited, though at the same time gravely serious in its implications about the West's future, it is a mock-"Western" which has Navajo Indians, led by a white teacher, Mary-Forge, set out on horseback to pursue and defeat a white rancher named Osmun who uses a helicopter to hunt and kill an eagle named Sun. The posse succeeds in destroying Osmun and his machine but not before Sun has also been destroyed. Just as the heroic Victims are a composite (nature, eagle, solar deity, women, intellectuals with natural instincts, and person with a sense of individuality and purpose in life), so is the Outlaw a composite (technology, racism, capitalism, anti-environmentalists). Authentic civilization, associated with nature and the natural self, is threatened with extinction: Eastlake's fable brings us up sharply against the facts of Western history and makes us see the interrelationship between people and the natural world of which they are a part.

# THE DEATH OF SUN

The bird Sun was named Sun by the Indians because each day their final eagle circled this part of the reservation like the clock of sun. Sun, a grave and golden eagle-stream of light, sailed without movement as though propelled by some eternity, to orbit, to circumnavigate this moon of earth, to alight upon his aerie from which he had risen, and so Sun would sit with the same God dignity and decorous finality with which he had emerged—then once more without seeming volition ride the crest of an updraft above Indian Country on six-foot wings to settle again on his throne aerie in awful splendor, admonitory, serene—regal and doomed. I have risen.

"'Man,' Feodor Dostoevski said," the white teacher Mary-Forge said, "'without a sure idea of himself and the purpose of his life cannot live and would sooner destroy himself than remain on earth.'"

"Who was Dostoevski?" the Navajo Indian Jesus Saves said.

"An Indian."

"What kind?"

"With that comment he could have been a Navajo," Mary-Forge said.

"No way," Jesus Saves said.

"Why, no way could Dostoevski be an Indian?"

"I didn't say Dostoevski couldn't be an Indian; I said he couldn't be a Navajo."

"Why is a Navajo different?"

"We are, that's all," Jesus Saves said. "In the words of Sören Kierkegaard—"

"Who was Sören Kierkegaard?"

"Another Russian," Jesus Saves said.

"Kierkegaard was a Dane."

"No, that was Hamlet," Jesus Saves said. "Remember?"

"You're peeved, Jesus Saves."

"No, I'm bugged," Jesus Saves said, "by people who start sentences with 'man.'"

"Dostoevski was accounting for the high suicide rate among Navajos.

Since the white man invaded Navajo country the Navajo sees no hope or purpose to life."

"Then why didn't Dostoevski say that?"

"Because he never heard of the Navajo."

"Then I never heard of Dostoevski," Bull Who Looks Up said. "Two can play at this game."

"That's right," Jesus Saves said, sure of himself now and with purpose.

"What is the purpose of your life, Jesus Saves?"

"To get out of this school," Jesus Saves said.

Jesus Saves was named after a signboard erected by the Albuquerque First National Savings & Loan.

All of Mary-Forge's students were Navajos. When Mary-Forge was not ranching she was running this free school that taught the Indians about themselves and their country—Indian country.

"What has Dostoevski got to do with Indian country?"

"I'm getting to that," Mary-Forge said.

"Will you hurry up?"

"No," Mary-Forge said.

"Is that any way for a teacher to speak to a poor Indian?"

"Sigmund Freud," the Medicine Man said, "said—more in anguish I believe than in criticism—'What does the Indian want? My God, what does the Indian want?'"

"He said that about women."

"If he had lived longer, he would have said it about Indians."

"True."

"Why?"

"Because it sounds good, it sounds profound, it tends to make you take off and beat the hell out of the Indians."

"After we have finished off the women."

"The women were finished off a long time ago," the Medicine Man said.

"But like the Indians they can make a comeback."

"Who knows," the Medicine Man said, "we both may be a dying race."

"Who knows?"

"We both may have reached the point of no return, who knows?"

"If we don't want to find out, what the hell are we doing in school?"

"Who knows?"

"I know," Mary-Forge said, "I know all about the eagle."

"Tell us, Mary-Forge, all about the eagle."

"The eagle is being killed off."

"We know that; what do we do?"

"We get out of this school and find the people who are killing the eagle."

"Then?"

"Who knows?" Mary-Forge said.

Mary-Forge was a young woman—she was the youngest white woman the Navajos had ever seen. She was not a young girl, there are millions of young girls in America. In America young white girls suddenly become defeated women. A young white woman sure of herself and with a purpose in life such as Mary-Forge was unknown to the American Indian.

Mary-Forge had large, wide-apart, almond-shaped eyes, high full cheekbones, cocky let-us-all-give-thanks tipsy breasts, and good brains. The white American man is frightened by her brain. The Indian found it nice. They loved it. They tried to help Mary-Forge. Mary-Forge tried to help the Indians. They were both cripples. Both surrounded by the white reservation.

High on her right cheekbone Mary-Forge had a jagged two-inch scar caused by a stomping she got from high-heeled cowboy boots belonging to a sheep rancher from the Twin Slash Heart Ranch on the floor of the High Point Bar in Gallup.

Mary-Forge did not abruptly think of eagles in the little red schoolhouse filled with Indians. A helicopter had just flown over. The helicopter came to kill eagles. The only time the Indians ever saw or felt a helicopter on the red reservation was when the white ranchers came to kill eagles. Eagles killed sheep, they said, and several cases have been known, they said, where white babies have been plucked from playpens and dropped in the ocean, they said.

You could hear plainly the *whack-whack-whack* of the huge rotor blades of the copter in the red schoolhouse. The yellow and blue copter was being flown by a flat-faced doctor-serious white rancher named Ira Osmun, who believed in conservation through predator control. Eagles were fine birds, but the sheep must be protected. Babies, too.

"Mr. Osmun," Wilson Drago, the shotgun-bearing sado-child-appearing copilot asked, "have the eagles got any white babies lately?"

"No."

"Then?"

"Because we are exercising predator control."

"When was the last white baby snatched by eagles and dropped into the ocean?"

"Not eagles, Drago, eagle; it only takes one. As long as there is one eagle there is always the possibility of your losing your child."

"I haven't any child."

"If you did."

"But I haven't."

"Someone does."

"No one in the area does."

"If they did, there would be the possibility of their losing them."

"No one can say nay to that," Wilson Drago said. "When was the last time a child was snatched?"

"It must have been a long time ago."

"Before living memory?"

"Yes, even then, Drago, I believe the stories to be apocryphal."

"What's that mean?"

"Lies."

"Then why are we shooting the eagles?"

"Because city people don't care about sheep. City people care about babies. You tell the people in Albuquerque that their babies have an outside chance, any chance that their baby will be snatched up and the possibility that it will be dropped in the ocean, kerplunk, and they will let you kill eagles."

"How far is the ocean?"

"People don't care how far the ocean is; they care about their babies."

"True."

"It's that simple."

"When was the last lamb that was snatched up?"

"Yesterday."

"That's serious."

"You better believe it, Drago."

"Why are we hovering over this red hogan?"

"Because before we kill an eagle we got to make sure what Mary-Forge is up to."

"What was she up to last time you heard?"

"Shooting down helicopters."

"All by herself?"

"It only takes one shot."

"You know, I bet that's right."

"You better believe it, Drago."

"Is this where she lives?"

"No—this is the little red schoolhouse she uses to get the Indians to attack the whites."

"What happened to your other copilots?"

"They got scared and quit."

"The last one?"

"Scared and quit."

"Just because of one woman?"

"Yes. You're not scared of a woman, are you, Drago?"

"No, I mean yes."

"Which is it, yes or no?"

"Yes," Wilson Drago said.

Below in the red hogan that was shaped like a beehive with a hole on top for the smoke to come out, the Indians and Mary-Forge were getting ready to die on the spot.

"I'm not getting ready to die on the spot," Bull Who Looks Up said.

"You want to save the eagles, don't you?" Mary-Forge said.

"Let me think about that," Jesus Saves said.

"Pass me the gun," Mary-Forge said.

Now, from above in the copter the hogan below looked like a gun turret, a small fort defending the perimeter of Indian Country.

"Mary-Forge is an interesting problem," Ira Osmun said—shouted—above the *whack-whack-whack* of the rotors.

"Every woman is."

"But every woman doesn't end up living with the Indians, with the eagles."

"What causes that?"

"We believe the Indians and the eagles become their surrogate children."

"That they become a substitute for life."

"Oh? Why do you hate me?"

"What?"

"Why do you use such big words?"

"I'm sorry, Drago. Do you see any eagles?"

"No, but I see a gun."

"Where?"

"Coming out the top of the hogan."

"Let Mary-Forge fire first."

"Why?"

"To establish a point of law. Then it's not between her eagles and my sheep."

"It becomes your ass or hers."

"Yes."

"But it could be my life."

"I've considered that, Drago."

"Thank you. Thank you very much," Wilson Drago said.

Sun, the golden eagle that was very carefully watching the two white animals that lived in the giant bird that went *whack-whack-whack*, was ready.

Today would be the day of death for Sun. His mate had been killed two days before. Without her the eaglets in the woven of yucca high basket nest would die. Today would be the day of death for Sun because, without a sure idea of himself, without purpose in life, an eagle would sooner destroy himself than remain on earth. The last day of Sun.

"Because," Mary-Forge said, and taking the weapon and jerking in a shell, "because I know, even though the Indians and us and the eagle, even though we have no chance ever, we can go through the motions of courage, compassion, and concern. Because we are Sun and men, too. Hello, Sun."

"Stop talking and aim carefully."

"Did I say something?"

"You made a speech."

"I'm sorry," Mary-Forge said.

"Aim carefully."

Mary-Forge was standing on the wide shoulders of an Indian named When Someone Dies He Is Remembered. All the other Indians who belonged in the little red schoolhouse stood around and below her in the dim and alive dust watching Mary-Forge revolve like a gun turret with her lever-operated Marlin .30-30 pointing out of the smoke hatch high up on the slow-turning and hard shoulders of When Someone Dies He Is Remembered.

"Why don't you shoot?" More Turquoise said. He almost whispered it, as though the great noise of the copter did not exist.

"The thing keeps bobbling," Mary-Forge shouted down to the Indians.

Looking through the gunsights she had to go up and down up and down to try and get a shot. She did not want to hit the cowboys. It would be good enough to hit the engine or the rotor blades. Why not hit the cowboys? Because there are always more cowboys. There are not many eagles left on the planet earth, there are several million cowboys. There are more cowboys than there are Indians. That's for sure. But what is important now is that if we give one eagle for one cowboy soon all the eagles will have disappeared from the earth and the cowboys will be standing in your bed. No, the helicopter is scarce. They will not give one helicopter for one eagle. A helicopter costs too much money. How much? A quarter-million dollars, I bet. Hit them where their heart is. Hit them right in their helicopter.

But it danced. Now Mary-Forge noticed that although it was dancing it was going up and down with a rhythm. The thing to do is to wait until it hits bottom and then follow it up. She did and fired off a shot.

"Good girl," the Medicine Man said.

"That was close," Ira Osmun said to his shotgun, Wilson Drago. "Now that we know where Mary-Forge is we can chase the eagle."

Ira Osmun allowed the chopper to spurt up and away to tilt off at a weird angle so that it clawed its way sideways like a crab that flew, a piece of junk, of tin and chrome and gaudy paint, alien and obscene in the perfect pure blue New Mexican sky, an intruder in the path of sun. Now the chopper clawed its way to the aerie of Sun.

The eagle had watched it all happen. Sun had watched it happen many times now. Two days ago when they killed his mate was the last time. Sun looked down at his golden eagle chicks. The eaglets were absolute white, they would remain white and vulnerable for several months until the new feathers. But there was no more time. Sun watched the huge man junk bird clawing its way down the long valley that led to Mount Taylor. His home, his home and above all the homes of the Indians.

Like the Indians, the ancestors of Sun had one time roamed a virgin continent abloom with the glory of life, alive with fresh flashing streams, a smogless sky, all the world a sweet poem of life where all was beginning. Nothing ever ended. Now it was all ending. The eagle, Sun, did not prepare to defend himself. He would not defend himself. There was nothing now to defend. The last hour of Sun.

"Catch me," Mary-Forge shouted from the top of the hogan, and jumped. When she was caught by More Turquoise, she continued to shout, as the noise of the chopper was still there. "They've taken off for Mount Taylor to kill Sun. We've got to get on our horses and get our ass over there."

"Why?"

"To save Sun," Mary-Forge shouted. "Sun is the last eagle left in the county."

"But this is not a movie," the Medicine Man said. "We don't have to get on horses and gallop across the prairie. We can get in my pickup and drive there—quietly."

"On the road it will take two hours," Mary-Forge said. "And we'll need horses when we get there to follow the chopper."

"What would Dostoevski say about this?" the Medicine Man said.

"To hell with Dostoevski," Mary-Forge said.

Outside they slammed the saddles on the amazed Indian ponies, then threw themselves on and fled down the canyon, a stream of dust and light, a commingling of vivid flash and twirl so when they disappeared into the cottonwoods you held your breath until the phantoms, the abrupt magic of motion, appeared again on the Cabrillo draw.

"Come on now, baby," Mary-Forge whispered to her horse Poco Mas. "What I said about Dostoevski I didn't mean. Poor Dostoevski. I meant seconds count. We didn't have time for a philosophical discussion. Come on now, baby, move good. Be good to me, baby, move good. Move good, baby. Move good. You can take that fence, baby. Take him! Good boy, baby. Good boy, Poco. Good boy. I'm sure the Medicine Man understands that when there are so few left, so few left Poco that there is not time for niceties. You'd think an Indian would understand that, wouldn't you? Still Medicine Man is a strange Indian. A Freudian Medicine Man. But Bull Who Looks Up understands, look at him go. He's pulling ahead of us are you going to let him get away with that Poco?" Poco did not let the horse of Bull Who Looks Up stay ahead but passed him quickly, with Mary-Forge swinging her gun high and Bull Who Looks Up gesturing with his gun at the tin bird that crabbed across the sky.

"You see, Drago," Ira Osmun shouted to Wilson Drago, "we are the villains of the piece."

"What?"

"The bad guys."

"It's pretty hard to think of yourself as the bad guy, Mr. Osmun."

"Well, we are."

"Who are the good guys?"

"Mary-Forge."

"Screw me."

"No, she wouldn't do that because you're a bad guy. Because you kill eagles. People who never saw an eagle, never will see an eagle, never want to see an eagle, want eagles all over the place. Except the poor. The poor want sheep to eat. Did you ever hear of a poor person complaining about the lack of eagles? They have got an outfit of rich gentlemen called the Sierra Club. They egg on Indian-lovers like Mary-Forge to kill ranchers."

"Why?"

"They have nothing else to do."

"You think Mary-Forge actually has sex with the Indians?"

"Why else would she be on the reservation?"

"I never thought about that."

"Think about it."

"I guess you're right."

"Drago, what do you think about?"

"I don't think about eagles."

"What do you think about?"

"Ordinarily?"

"Yes."

"Like when I'm drinking?"

"Yes."

"Religion."

"Good, Drago, I like to hear you say that. Good. What religion?"

"They are all good. I guess Billy Graham is the best."

"Yes, if you're stupid."

"What?"

"Nothing, Drago. Keep your eye peeled for the eagle."

"You said I was stupid."

"I may have said the Sierra Club was stupid."

"Did you?"

"No, how could you be stupid and be that rich?"

"Why are they queer for eagles then?"

"They are for anything that is getting scarce. Indians, eagles, anything. Mary-Forge is against natural evolution, too."

"What's natural evolution mean?"

"When something is finished it's finished, forget it. We got a new evolution, the machine, this copter, a new bird."

"That makes sense."

"Remember we don't want to kill eagles."

"We have to."

"That's right."

The eagle that had to be killed, Sun, perched like an eagle on his aerie throne. A king, a keeper of one hundred square miles of Indian Country, an arbiter, a jury and judge, a shadow clock that had measured time for two thousand years in slow shadow circle and so now the earth, the Indians, the place, would be without reckoning, certainly without the serene majesty of Sun, without, and this is what is our epitaph and harbinger, without the gold of silence the long lonely shadow beneath silent wing replaced now by the *whack-whack-whack* of tin, proceeding with crablike crippled claw—the sweet song of man in awkward crazy metallic and cockeyed pounce, approached Sun.

Sun looked down on the eaglets in the nest. The thing to do would be to glide away from the whack-bird away from the nest. To fight it out somewhere else. If he could tangle himself in the wings of the whack-bird, that would be the end of whack-bird. The end of Sun. Sun jumped off his aerie without movement, not abrupt or even peremptory but as though the reel of film had cut, and then proceeded to a different scene. The bird Sun, the eagle, the great golden glider moving across the wilds of purple mesa in air-fed steady no-beat, in hushed deadly amaze, seemed in funeral stateliness, mounting upward on invisible winds toward the other sun.

"If he climbs, we will climb with him, Drago. He is bound to run out of updrafts."

Wilson Drago slid open the door on his side and shifted the Harrington & Richardson pump gun into the ready position.

"How high will this thing climb, sir?"

"Ten thousand feet."

"The bird can climb higher than that."

"Yet he has to come down, Drago."

"How much fuel we got?"

"Fifty gallons."

"What are we consuming?"

"A gallon a minute."

"Shall I try a shot?"

"Yes."

Sun was spiraling upward in tight circles on a good rising current of air when the pellets of lead hit him. They hit like a gentle rain that gave him a quick lift. Sun was out of range. Both the copter and Sun were spiraling upward. The copter was gaining.

"Shall I try another shot?"

"Yes."

This time the lead pellets slammed into Sun like a hard rain and shoved him upward and crazy tilted him as a great ship will yaw in a sudden gust. Sun was still out of range.

Now the upward current of air ceased, collapsed under Sun abruptly and the copter closed the distance until Ira Osmun and Wilson Drago were alongside and looking into small yellow eyes as the great sailing ship of Sun coasted downward into deep sky.

"Shall I try a shot?"

"Yes."

Wilson Drago raised the Harrington & Richardson shotgun and pumped in a shell with a solid slam. He could almost touch Sun with the muzzle. The swift vessel of Sun sailed on as though expecting to take the broadside from the 12-gauge gun that would send him to the bottom—to the floor of earth.

"Now, Drago."

But the gliding ship of bird had already disappeared—folded its huge wing of sail and shot downward, down down down downward until just before earth it unleashed its enormous sail of wing and glided over the surface of earth—Indian Country. Down came the copter in quick chase.

There stood the Indians all in a row.

"Don't fire, men," Mary-Forge shouted, "until Sun has passed."

As Sun sailed toward the Indians the shadow of Sun came first, shading each Indian separately. Now came the swifting Sun and each mounted Indian raised his gun in salute. Again separately and in the order which Sun arrived and passed, now the Indians leveled their guns to kill the whack-bird.

"Oh, this is great, Drago," Ira Osmun shouted, "the Indians want to fight."

"What's great about that?"

"It's natural to fight Indians."

"It is?"

"Yes."

"Well, I'll be."

"My grandfather would be proud of us now."

"Did he fight Indians?"

"He sure did. It's only a small part of the time the whites have been that they haven't fought Indians."

"Fighting has been hard on the Indians."

"That may well be, Drago, but it's natural."

"Why?"

"Because people naturally have a fear of strangers. It's called xenophobia. When you don't go along with nature you get into trouble. You suppress your natural instincts and that is dangerous. That's what's wrong with this country."

"It is? I wondered about that."

"There's nothing wrong with shooting Indians."

"I wondered about that."

"It's natural."

"No, Mr. Osmun there is something wrong."

"What's that?"

"Look. The Indians are shooting back."

Ira Osmun twisted the copter up and away. "Get out the rifle. We'll take care of the Indians."

"What about the eagle?"

"We've first got to take care of the Indians who are shooting at us and that girl who is shooting at us."

"Is she crazy?"

"Why else would she have intercourse with the Indians?"

"You mean screwing them?"

"Yes."

"She could have all sorts of reasons. We don't even know that she is screwing them. Maybe we are screwing the Indians."

"Drago, we discussed this before and decided that Mary-Forge was."

"What if she is?"

"Drago, you can't make up your mind about anything. You're being neurotic. When you don't understand why you do something you're being neurotic."

"I am?"

"Yes, get out the rifle."

"I still think it's her business if she is queer for Indians and eagles."

"But not if she shoots at us when she's doing it; that's neurotic."

"You're right there, Mr. Osmun."

"Get the rifle."

"O.K."

"You know, Drago, people, particularly people who love the Indians, are suppressing a need to kill them. It's called a love-hate relationship."

"It is? You can stop talking now, Mr. Osmun. I said I'd get the rifle."

Below the helicopter that circled in the brilliant, eye-hurting, New Mexican day, Mary-Forge told the Indians that the copter would be back, that the ranchers would not fight the eagle while being fired on by Indians. "The ranchers will not make the same mistake Custer did."

"What was that?"

"Fight on two fronts. Custer attacked the Sioux before he finished off Sitting Bull. We are the Sioux."

"We are? That's nice," the Navajo Bull Who Looks Up said. "When do we get out of this class?"

"We never do," Jesus Saves said.

"Get your ass behind the rocks!" the teacher Mary-Forge shouted. "Here they come!"

The copter flew over and sprayed the rocks with M-16 automatic rifle fire.

"That should teach the teacher that we outgun them, Drago," Ira Osmun said. "Now we can get the eagle!"

The golden eagle called Sun spiraled upward again, its wings steady, wild, sure, in the glorious and rapt quietude of the blue, blue, blue New Mexico morning, a golden eagle against the blue, a kind of heliograph, and a flashing jewel in the perfect and New Mexico sea of sky. The gold eagle, recapitulent, lost then found as it twirled steady and upward in the shattered light, followed by the tin bird.

Sun knew that he must gain height. All the power of maneuver lay in getting above the tin bird. He knew, too, and from experience that the tin bird could only go a certain height. He knew, too, and from experience that the air current he rode up could collapse at once and without warning. He knew, too, and from the experience of several battles now with the bird of tin that the enemy was quick and could spit things out that could pain then kill. All this he knew from experience. But the tin bird was learning, too.

The tin bird jerked upward after the golden eagle. The golden eagle, Sun, wandered upward as though searching and lost. A last and final tryst in the list of Indian Country because now always until now, until now no one killed everything that moved. You always had a chance. Now there was no chance. Soon there would be no Sun.

"Remember, Drago, I've got to stay away from him or above him—he can take us with him. The last time when we got his mate he almost took us with him; I just barely got away when he attacked the rotors—when the rotor goes we go, Drago—we fall like a rock, smash like glass. They will pick you up with a dustpan."

"Who?"

"Those Indians down there."

"Mr. Osmun, I don't want to play this game."

"You want to save the sheep, don't you?"

"No."

"Why not?"

"I don't have any sheep to save."

"You don't have any sheep, you don't have any children. But you have pride."

"I don't know."

"Then fire when I tell you to and you'll get some."

"I don't know."

"Do you want eagles to take over the country?"

"I don't know."

"Eagles and Indians at one time controlled this whole country, Drago; you couldn't put out a baby or a lamb in my grandfather's time without an Indian or an eagle would grab it. Now we got progress. Civilization. That means a man is free to go about his business."

"It does?"

"Yes, now that we got them on those ropes we can't let them go, Drago."

"We can't?"

"No, that would be letting civilized people down. It would be letting my grandfather down. What would I say to him?"

"Are you going to see your grandfather?"

"No, he's dead. We'll be dead, too, Drago, if you don't shoot. That eagle will put us down there so those Indians will pick us up with a dustpan. You don't want that, do you?"

"I don't know."

"You better find out right smart or I'll throw you out of this whack-bird myself."

"Would you?"

"Someone's got to live, Drago. The eagle doesn't want to live."

"Why do you say that?"

"He knew we were after him. He knew we would get him; he could have left the country. He could have flown north to Canada. He would be protected there."

"Maybe he thinks this is his country."

"No, this is civilized country. Will you shoot the eagle?"

"No."

"I like the eagle and the Indians as well as the next man, Drago, but we have to take sides. It's either my sheep or them. Whose side are you on, Drago?"

"I guess I'm on theirs."

The helicopter was much lighter now without Drago in it. The copter handled much better and was able to gain on the eagle.

Ira Osmun continued to talk to Wilson Drago as though he were still there. Wilson Drago was one of Ira Osmun's sheepherders and should have taken a more active interest in sheep.

"The way I see it, Drago, if you wouldn't defend me, the eagle would have brought us both down. It was only a small push I gave you, almost a touch as you were leaning out. By lightening the plane you made a small contribution to civilization.

"We all do what we can, Drago, and you have contributed your bit. If there is anything I can't stand, it's an enemy among my sheep."

The copter continued to follow the eagle up but now more lightsome and quick with more alacrity and interest in the chase.

The Indians on the ground were amazed to see the white man come down. Another dropout. "Poor old Wilson Drago. We knew him well. Another man who couldn't take progress—civilization. Many times has Drago shot at us while we were stealing his sheep. We thought anyone might be a dropout but not Wilson Drago. It shows you how tough it's getting on the white reservation. They're killing each other. Soon there will be nothing left but Indians."

"Good morning, Indian."

"Good morning, Indian."

"Isn't it a beautiful day. Do you notice there is nothing left but us Indians?"

"And one eagle."

The Indians were making all these strange observations over what remained of the body of the world's leading sheepherder, Wilson Drago.

"He created quite a splash."

"And I never thought he would make it."

"The last time I saw him drunk in Gallup I thought he was coming apart, but this is a surprise."

"I knew he had it in him, but I never expected it to come out all at once."

"I can't find his scalp. What do you suppose he did with it? Did he hide it?"

"The other white man got it."

"I bet he did."

"They don't care about Indians anymore."

"No, when they drop in on you they don't bring their scalp."

"Please, please," Mary-Forge said, "the man is dead."

"Man? Man? I don't see any man, just a lot of blood and shit."

"Well, there is a man, or was a man."

"Well, there's nothing now," Bull Who Looks Up said, "not even a goddamn scalp."

"Well, Drago's in the white man's heaven," More Turquoise said. "On streets of gold tending his flock."

"And shooting eagles."

"Drago's going higher and higher to white man's heaven, much higher than his what-do-you-call-it—"

"Helicopter."

"—can go," Jesus Saves said.

"I don't like all this sacrilege," Mary-Forge said. "Remember I am a Christian."

"What?"

"I was brought up in the Christian tradition."

"Now you're hedging," When Someone Dies He Is Remembered said.

Ah, these Indians, Mary-Forge thought, how did I get involved? And she said aloud, "Once upon a time I was young and innocent."

"Print that!" Bull Who Looks Up said.

"We better get higher on the mountain," Mary-Forge shouted at the Indians, "so when Osmun closes on the eagle we can get a better shot."

"O.K., Teacher."

"There's only one white guy left," she said.

"I find that encouraging if true," More Turquoise said.

"Load your rifles and pull your horses after you," Mary-Forge said.

"My Country 'Tis of Thee," Ira Osmun hummed as he swirled the copter in pursuit of the eagle. You didn't die in vain, Drago. That is, you were not vain, you were a very modest chap. We can climb much higher without you, Drago. I am going to get the last eagle this time, Drago. I think he's reached the top of his climb.

Sun watched the tin whack-bird come up. The tin bird came up *whack-whack-whack*, its wings never flapping just turning in a big circle. What did it eat? How did it mate? Where did it come from? From across the huge water on a strong wind. The evil wind. Sun circled seeing that he must get higher, the tin bird was coming up quicker today. Sun could see the people he always saw below. The people who lived in his country, filing up the mountain. They seemed to be wanting to get closer to him now.

Ira Osmun felt then saw all the Indians in the world firing at him from below. How are you going to knock down an eagle when all the Indians in the world are firing at you from Mount Taylor? It was Mary-Forge who put them up to it, for sure. An Indian would not have the nerve to shoot at a white man. You don't have to drop down and kill all the Indians. They—the people in the East—who have no sheep would call that a massacre. Indians are very popular at the moment. If you simply knock off Mary-Forge, that would do the trick. Women are not very popular at the moment. Why? Because they have a conspiracy against men. You didn't know that? It's true, Drago. The woman used to be happy to be on the bottom. Now she wants to be on the top.

No?

Did you say something, Drago?

I thought I heard someone say something. I must have been hit. My mind must be wandering. What was I saying? It's part of the conspiracy. What's that mean? Something. I must have been hit. What was I doing? Oh yes, I was going to get Mary-Forge—the girl who is queer for Indians and eagles. The eagle can wait.

And Ira Osmun put the copter in full throttle, then cradled the M-16 automatic rifle on his left arm with muzzle pointing out the door. With his right hand he placed the copter in a swift power glide down.

Sun saw the obscene tin bird go into its dive down. Now would be a chance to get it while the tin bird was busy hunting its prey on the ground. Sun took one more final look over the aerie nest to check the birds. The eaglets were doing fine. Drawing the enemy away from the nest had been successful. The eaglets craned their necks at the familiar shape before Sun folded his great span of wings and shot down on top of the tin bird.

Mary-Forge mounted on Poco Mas saw the tin bird coming, the M-16 quicking out nicks of flame. She could not get the Indians to take cover. The Indians had placed their horses behind the protection of the boulders and were all standing out in the open and were blasting away at the zooming-in copter. Mary-Forge was still shouting at the Indians, but they would not take cover. They have seen too many goddamn movies, Mary-Forge thought, they have read too many books. They are stupid, stupid, stupid, dumb, dumb, dumb Indians. How stupid and how dumb can you get? They want to save the eagle. Standing exposed naked to the machine gun. The stupid Indians. Mary-Forge raised her rifle at the zooming-in copter in a follow-me gesture, then took off in a straight line, the horse pounding, and the flame-nicking copter followed, so did Sun. So now there were three.

The tin bird was alive in flame all at once, something had hit the fuel tank and all of everything exploded in fire, the rotors of the tin bird were still turning and fanning the flame so that it was not only a streaking meteor across Indian Country but at once a boil of fire that shot downward from the terrific draft laying a torch of flame across the desert so that the mesquite and sagebrush became a steady line of flame ending where the tin whack-bird hit into the rocks and went silent in a grand tower of fire.

"It was Sun that did it," More Turquoise said.

The death of Sun.

All of the Indians and Mary-Forge were standing around the dying fire of the big whack-bird in the smoke that shrouded the death of Sun.

"When an eagle," the Medicine Man said, "—when a true bird has no hope—"

"Yes?"

"When the eagle is no more," the Medicine Man said.

"Yes?"

"Then we are no more."

"Yes," every person shrouded in smoke said.

Look up there. It was within three months when When Someone Dies He Is Remembered remembered that an eagle named Star by Medicine

Man sailed in one beginning night to reclaim the country of Sun. Now Star's wide shadow passed over the dead tin whack-bird then he, the great eagle Star, settled on his throne aerie in awful and mimic splendor, and again admonitory, serene—regal and doomed?

# DAVID KRANES
# THE WHOREHOUSE PICNIC

Born in Boston in 1937 and a western resident since 1967, David Kranes teaches creative writing at the University of Utah and is artistic director of the Playwrights' Lab at Sundance, a program of Robert Redford's Sundance Institute. *Hunters in the Snow* (1979), a collection of stories, was followed by a novel, *The Hunting Years* (1984); his newest novel, *Keno Runner*, will be published in the winter of 1987 by Peregrine Smith. His play, *The Salmon Run*, was winner of the National Repertory Theatre Playwright's Award, and *Montana* was done in 1986 by the Philadelphia Festival Theatre.

"The Whorehouse Picnic" was published in *Writers' Forum*, No. 11, 1985. Historically the territory for a fresh start, the West depicted in Krane's story is so burdened with a history of nuclear-age violence and dehumanizing commercialism that the American Dream of success would seem to hold no tomorrow for Chase, who nonetheless cannot abide feelings of inferiority, failure, and loss. As solitary builder of an atomic bomb, he believes he will establish respectable credentials in the world and impress Dixie, the whore. When Pomo, his Indian friend, accidentally explodes the bomb, the "chase" for success is over, but not the hope for self-fulfillment. Catching an enormous trout, Chase, like many an American and western hero, tests himself against the forces of nature. He returns to society—Dixie's whorehouse picnic—prepared to accept life on its own not-so-respectable terms. And life in the West is once more transformed to wonder.

# THE WHOREHOUSE PICNIC

C hase watched Dixie cleaning herself over the blueplastic dish-basin, sponging and laughing. The brain Chase liked, his *smart* brain, had thought something funny for Dixie, and Chase had said it, and Dixie had laughed, her stomach muscles tightening and relaxing. She was wonderful, beautiful, and Chase felt so good that he wanted to say his secret out loud, tell her about the bomb, describe his hearing a man on "Good Morning, America" announce that any bright person could learn to build one by going to a public library, and that the man in the green suit and the bow tie had been right. Part of Chase, even at forty-one, in fact *was* bright. He had gone and read and found out and had been building an atomic bomb now for nearly seven years and was almost ready to test it way back in The Shell Creeks. Still, in his reading, once, on a trip to Carson, Chase had learned about The Rosenbergs and about their disclosure and where it had gotten them. But, God, she was beautiful! And he certainly wished she didn't work at Carole's-93 Club Lounge & Brothel, where half the men from the Ruth Copper Pit came, men who, except for his friend, Pomo, Chase would turn down if they answered an ad to be his brother.

"You're adorable!" Dixie said.

"You have beautiful skin," Chase told her. He walked over and turned the Wayne Newton tape down on her Walkman.

"My skin stinks," Dixie said and laughed. "It's too tight on my bones. And it's like wax."

"Get dressed and walk outside with me," Chase suggested.

"Delores will put a hole in my head!"

"I'll pay another half hour."

"She doesn't want us hanging around out front. She says it's cheap. She says it looks like we're soliciting."

"Some time I'm going to ask you for a regular date."

"Promises, promises!"

"So walk out back," he said. "Just put your robe on and walk out back with me. I want to stand outside with you just a minute."

Dixie looked at Chase. She squeezed some gel from a tube onto her hands and ran her hands between her legs, then over her breasts. "I'll

323

say one thing for you," she said. "You're different."

"Good," Chase said. "I hope. I sure don't like most of what passes itself off for Life in this state."

"You don't like Nevada?"

"Nevada killed my mother."

Dixie picked her robe from a brass hook. She knew what Chase meant; she'd heard his story—about how his mother's bones had changed to cream o'wheat before he'd even turned twenty and how it had happened to other people at about the same time, in the 1950's, in Caliente.

"Walk out back."

The dark outside was turquoise, veined and growing into new light. "This is what I like," Chase said, and he pulled Dixie in her orange silk robe to him like a colt or calf. "I hate the mine. I hate the drunks. I hate the Fords and Chevies banked all along Steptoe Creek. And The Mustang Club. And the Hotel. All the dealers who think *they're* beating you. . . . But I *do* like this. I like this air. I like this sky. And I like feeling my nose in your hair like this."

"You're a very different kind of person," Dixie said, her words against Chase's shoulder.

"You keep saying that."

"Well, it's true. I think you're probably very intelligent. Not that I think it's wrong to be intelligent. But things roll over in your head, like stones in a creek. And. . . *I* don't know: I get a chill, sometimes, when I'm listening to you."

"When's your next day off?" Chase asked.

"Monday."

"I'm going with Pomo . . . on a fishing trip, tomorrow, for three days. Up over into the Ruby Marshes. But we'll be back. I'm asking you to go on a regular date with me next Monday. Evening. No money. What would you say?"

"Where are we going?"

"I don't know. I'll have some trout. We could drive over to Ward Charcoal Ovens State Park, and I'll grill them. And I could even bring us along some cold Blue Nun wine. We could start that way at least."

"Would you ever marry me?"

"Where'd that question come from?"

". . . What time?"

"About five o'clock?"

"Okay."

Then Delores's voice sounded *Dixie?!* beyond. Dixie bit Chase playfully on the neck and ran inside.

Driving his Silverado in the near-dawn over to Hotel Nevada, Chase could almost smell the explosives in back under his double tarpaulin. When Chase was a boy, the Atomic Bomb had started killing his mother. Sometimes he saw her ghost in the AG, hosing down sugar beets and cucumbers. And it had made his father into a person who could rarely talk. Chase remembered The National Guard coming to Caliente and requesting vehicle owners to drive down to Earl's Sunoco for a free carwash. Chase had seen *Escape from Alcatraz* six times on his trailer on a VCR. "A person has got to free himself from what's bad," Chase had told Pomo, after the man had come six years ago and talked on "Good Morning, America."

"I agree," Pomo had said.

"Then maybe he'll marry a woman who won't roll herself over in a pickup, drunk on Oly beer."

"Damn rights," Pomo had nodded. "Damn rights. You definitely got yourself a winner there—with that attitude."

Chase almost ran his van into the back of a '76 Camaro. He pumped his brakes. So if you were smart enough, then maybe you could stop hating your life. True: Chase's bomb wasn't *exactly* like the 1945 bomb. Still, according to what he'd been able to read, he had the essentials. So Chase probably wasn't a fool.

Waiting for his *huevos rancheros* in the Hotel Nevada coffeeshop, he drew nuclei and neutrons and gamma rays on his napkin. His eggs came. The Mexican waitress asked: "You make a map?"

"*Sí,*" Chase said. He cocked his head. He laughed. Then he said, "I'm sorry."

The Mexican waitress looked confused.

He called Pomo to set the time that they would leave for their fishing trip to the Ruby Marshes. His mind was still full of Dixie. Pomo said he was waiting. Chase said he needed the morning for other things. "What *other things*?" Pomo wanted to know. Chase said he would pick Pomo up at two.

"You have salmon eggs?" Chase checked.

"Three kinds," Pomo said. "And cheese marshmallows. And garlic cheese."

Everybody at the pit treated Pomo as an Indian. Chase knew he wasn't. Chase knew that, when Pomo was just a little boy, he had lived in a palace in South America somewhere. He and Pomo had talked. Pomo had told Chase that one night many men had climbed up over the palace wall and Pomo's father had told Pomo that he should run and that he should never come back, and Pomo's father had shown Pomo a passageway underground and Pomo had run until the passageway had come up in the woods, in some trees. Then, over time, Pomo had ended up in Ely, Nevada. "I'm not an Indian," he had said to Chase. "I was a boy in a palace." Chase respected Pomo.

Chase hung up the phone and looked out over the lobby and the casino of the Hotel Nevada. Everything was dead light and dust. The carpet looked unraveled and like lint. The furniture was fat; it was tired and scarred. The whole thing was like a waiting room, Chase thought, for people who were so bored they had made appointments to die. One man, with a blue hardhat on, playing alone at a blackjack table, had a cup beside him, the coffee steam seeming to slide *down* and over the ratty felt and never to rise. It was a place you could never repair or renovate. All you could do is blow it up and start over.

Chase had built his bomb in the Duck Creek Range, in an abandoned shaft where a man named Hildebrand had once prospected for gold. Chase had found Hildebrand's claim in a can. Approaching, over the rutted road, always made his pulse beat in his head, afraid that some rock or sudden ditch would upend the van and set everything off. His brain made pictures of enormous craters and of huge funguslike clouds all the unimproved thirty-seven miles.

He parked at the mouth of the shaft and put the tailgate down. The mine went back a hundred and thirty feet and averaged five feet in height. This was his last load and Chase unwrapped it and packed it in and attached it up so that when he was done, his Atomic Bomb, radio-timer-detonator included, was in the side of Monitor Mountain and ready to test.

He'd rigged a pulley, and with it Chase packed a flattened '52 DeSoto against the shaft. Then he piled rocks. Sometimes he felt *outside* his bomb. Other times, he felt *in* it. It was curious. Also he felt very solitary with what he'd done. Was that how the fellow, the scientist, Edward Teller, the man he'd read about, had felt? And the other man? Oppenheimer?

But he also felt proud. He was not the stupid person that some tourist, seeing him leave the Ruth Copper Pit, day shift, black lunchpail in his hand, might think. All Chase needed now was to set his CB radio to the proper frequency at the proper time and the whole mountain should go off.

Chase imagined a conversation with Dixie. "It's an atomic bomb," he said and pointed. "There. In the mountain."

"God: amazing!"

"It took seven years."

"You have to be a genius!"

"I built what I hated," he said. "So I could stop hating it."

He brushed his hands. He looked down. He looked at the dust. He looked at the mountainside and saw a mule deer bound into camouflage. He looked at the chill broken light, now at noon, through the trees. Red-tailed hawks rested here. His muscles felt hard. His brain had a fire. He would fish with Pomo, who'd grown up in a palace! He would land enormous trout! He would find a place somehow, somewhere, with Dixie.

Pomo stood out in front of his shack when Chase arrived, practicing casting with a chicken bone at the end of his line, tied there with a nail knot.

"How're they biting?" Chase asked Pomo.

"I caught a small dog," Pomo said. "But I threw him back."

"Shove your gear in the back," Chase said. "Just unlatch it."

Pomo gathered a bedroll and backpack, tacklebox with his rod and moved out of Chase's vision until he filled most of the rear-view mirror, throwing up the hatch on the back of the vehicle.

"You ready for the big ones?" Chase asked his question to the mirror.

"What're you doing with *this*?" Pomo asked.

Chase could feel an oily jolt snake his spine. He set himself and turned slowly around, knowing that he would see what he saw: Pomo holding a stick of dynamite that had hidden itself in some fold of the tarpaulin. "I smoke that," Chase said.

Pomo looked at the dynamite then at Chase then at the dynamite then at Chase again. "You gonna blow lunkers out of some hole you scouted?" Pomo asked.

"Who knows?"

"You steal this from work?"

"One thing I have to tell you," Chase said. "We can't turn on the radio. It wears the battery down. It's important." Chase had not *planned* exactly when he would set the bomb off. Maybe he would just drive around for a year or so, knowing that he *could*. Or maybe he would set it off Monday night, on his regular date, and impress Dixie. Still, he tried, nevertheless to make it clear, without hurting his friend's feelings, that the CB radio had to be out of bounds for Pomo. "I mean it," Chase emphasized. "Don't turn the radio on. I'm extremely serious."

They drove past the gravel pit through Ruth and over Little Antelope

Summit. At Eureka, they turned north on 46, up along The Diamonds, along Huntington Valley, then, just before Jiggs, east to Franklin Lake and the Ruby Indian Reservation. They talked about the day. "I like the shape of the sky," Pomo said. Then they argued whether sky actually had *shape* or not. They ran down lists of people on the crews they worked with.

"You like McLaren?"

"If McLaren had a brain, he'd be dangerous. You know Luker?"

"Luker has to sleep with snakes. Angelari?"

"Angelari's a loser."

"Definite loser."

"The next time Angelari takes a bath, it'll be the first."

There were random thunderheads when they set up camp, and they could hear a far, offhand rumbling that neither took to be dangerous.

"Think it'll rain?" Pomo asked.

"I don't care if it does."

They walked the Franklin River along some railroad tracks. Neither had fished the area, but a man they'd met once on the Owyhee River had recommended it.

"There are trout in there." Chase pointed down to where a drape of reeds flagged along a section of the bank.

"How do you know?" Pomo asked.

Chase touched his glasses. "Polarized lenses," he said. "Cuts the surface glare. I can see them."

Pomo studied Chase. He nodded. "You've got brains," he said. "You are one guy with brains if I ever met one. You figure things."

Chase enjoyed Pomo's respect. It occurred to him to tell Pomo his secret. Instead, Chase asked whether Pomo had ever thought about marrying.

"Maybe you and I'll talk about it sometime," Pomo said. He picked a handful of gravel up from the rail bed and hurled it.

Chase resented Pomo's gesture. His privacy. Were they friends or weren't they? Did they discuss things or didn't they? Did Pomo think that just because he'd grown up in a palace he was better than Chase? Chase's impulse was to fish a hole off somewhere by himself for what was left of the afternoon.

They fished a wide bend together, just below where a fast churning creek angled in from the north. There were eddies and holding pools and a lovely, smooth *V* just above some swifter ripples. Pomo landed a 16-inch cutthroat. Then Chase hooked an enormous brown. "Holy shit!" Chase said. The drag on his reel made a sound like Dixie sometimes made. The brown broke water. "Jesus Christ!"

"He's a monster!"

"You bet he's a monster!" Chase said. "That's a monster that's been in that pool for a *million years* just waiting for me!"

"Don't let him head over toward those logs!"

"I'm watching him!"

"He's headed over toward those logs!"

"Get out your net!"

"He's going to wrap himself around those logs!"

"Let *me* worry about that! Get your net out!"

"He's *in* there!"

The enormous brown tangled Chase's line around submerged tree roots; Chase lost the fish's resonance against the play of his fingers, the direct tension. He felt blood pumping into his face and scalp and arms and charged, working his reel, into the stream. "What are you doing?!" Pomo shouted, but Chase rushed the logs and his submerged trout. He fell, scrambled up, fell, scrambled up again. "Chase! Jesus! Be careful! Don't be crazy!"

He was not going to lose this! He had lost too many things here where hope just went up and blew back so hot and dry that your breath felt like ashes. He had not made a date with Dixie or spent probably ten percent of his life building an atomic bomb for *nothing*. Chase dove into the pool.

Underwater, he searched for his trout. He grabbed a log, let his pole go but followed its filament into the hatchwork of branches. He felt strange. He felt in danger. He felt a delicious madness. Then Chase's hand touched skin, and he knew that the brown was still possible; and he almost shouted. He could feel his chest beating. He could feel his breath wrestling with itself, making itself still. Then the yellow belly of the brown flashed. Chase's better brain ordered his breathing to relax. He could see the root that the brown had wrapped himself, again and again, around. And with one hand to the right of the snarl, the other hand to the left, Chase positioned himself, feet planted in the rocks of the streambed, and twisted, rotating the root so that, somehow, it snapped just outside both his hands, and he rose to the air and to Pomo's vision of him with the branch high and level over his head and the enormous brown he had chased dangling from it. "*Bring the net!*" he yelled.

That night, Chase made a package for his trout with aluminum foil. He poured dark rum in and closed the package and buried it in the coals of their fire. He and Pomo sat on rocks and passed the rum bottle

between them. "You should use lemon," Chase said. "And butter. But
I didn't bring them." And then he confessed to Pomo: "I may love
Dixie." Pomo nodded. He passed the rum bottle to Chase. They could
hear an owl, in a nearby tree, eating a potgut.

Later, suddenly, Chase was awake, bolt upright in his bedroll and crying
out. The earth lifted. The whole eastern sky trembled and flared. It was
like being in the belly of a world, suddenly enraged. He felt terrifying
failure, awful loss. But he understood, too, in an instant, what the
moment was all about. He knew. Pomo was sitting, door open, in his
Silverado with the CB radio on, looking ashen. "Oh, fuck," Chase said,
"Goddamit-shit-piss-crap-and-doublefuck!"
 "Jesus Christ, man!" Pomo said. "What was *that*?! Chase, man, *look!*"
But Chase was already looking. "I couldn't sleep. I got up," Pomo said.
 *Well, there it was!*
 "I took your car keys from your jacket pocket and . . . "
 *Boom!*
 ". . . figured if I couldn't sleep, then I'd get some company."
 *Seven years!*
 "And so I turned your CB radio on, and I was dialing back and forth,
looking for a band, when. . . !" And all Pomo could do was gesture
toward where the sky was green like phosphorous and making sounds
like a huge, hungry stomach.
 "I told you twice. . ." Chase contained himself. ". . . driving over
here . . ." He gritted his teeth. ". . . I said . . . I *warned* you . . ."
 Pomo swallowed.
 *"Don't use the radio."*
 Pomo wet his lips. "I forgot," he said.

Two mornings later, Chase and Pomo shoved their gear and their Cole-
man cooler full of trout into the back of the Silverado and started home.
Pomo had been a rage of questions. Chase wouldn't talk. Something
had been taken away. Something had been made incomplete. "But what
could it have *been?*" Pomo kept asking. And "Chase—really—shouldn't
we *leave*? Shouldn't we get a paper and *find out*? Maybe it was the *mine*.
Maybe it was the *pit*. Maybe it was the whole of *Ely*. Maybe something
happened."

They stopped for coffee in Eureka on their way home and bought a
paper. The paper had a picture of an immense crater on the front page
and the headline: ENTIRE MOUNTAIN COLLAPSES EAST OF ELY.
The article kept repeating phrases: "confounds scientists" and "baffles

experts." And at several points it said things like: "with the near-force of a thermo-nuclear device." Chase felt some part start to shift position inside himself—though he wasn't sure, really, what it was.

"Aren't you *interested* in this?!" Pomo said.

"What's the deal?" Chase said. He thought of Dixie. He tried to stay remote. He tried to act dispirited and failed. "A mountain blows up. So what. I'm glad no one was injured. That's all. Or killed."

"*Look at this!*" Pomo pointed to a whole inside page of pictures of the crater. "Sure, they *say* no one died. But there are all kinds of people— sheepherders, prospectors—living up in those mountains. Twenty years from now! *Then* they'll start giving a list!"

Chase felt confused. He pushed his coffee mug away and stared into the gallon jar of beef jerky on the counter as if it would answer something.

He sat in his trailer most of Monday and thought of taking his life—it made sense—but he worried he would hurt Dixie's feelings if he didn't appear at five that afternoon for their first regular date. So he washed. And shaved. Put a clean shirt on and a string tie. And he drove to Carole's 93 Club Lounge & Brothel at the time he and Dixie had set.

The door was locked. The lights were out. Dixie came around the far corner of the building. "Hi," she said.

"Hi," Chase said.

She was wearing an orange summer dress with spaghetti straps. "I have some bad news," she said. "I'm sorry."

"What?"

"I should have remembered—but I'd forgotten."

"You don't have the day off?"

"No—it's the picnic."

"What do you mean?"

"It's the whorehouse picnic," Dixie said. "We have it each year. Did you hear about the mountain?"

"I did," Chase said. "I read about it in the paper. So you can't see me?"

"We have the picnic. It's at the natural arch. Up Elderbury Canyon. It's just us. Once a year. No one else is s'posed to be invited."

"You look beautiful," Chase said. And just then, an orange White Pine Co. School District bus pulled up in front of the brothel. "When is it through?" Chase asked. "When's it over?"

"It depends," Dixie said. And she came close and gave Chase a kiss on the side of his head.

"It's *here!*" Chase could hear Delores calling out to the other girls inside. Chase couldn't help himself. He started home, but then drove up to Elderbury Canyon and parked in a turnout before the natural arch. He could hear shrieks and music, and he approached through trees to see all the women from the brothel arranged—plastic drink glasses in their hands, some with paper plates. Carole was grilling steaks on a standing fireplace. There was a large battery tapedeck playing Bette Midler from *The Rose*. Dixie was there, talking with a girl named Satin and another girl Chase had never met. It was curious. It made Chase feel wonderful. It made him feel shy.

He stayed in the trees, circling, and the dusk came on. At one point, someone saw him and pointed and Dixie gave a tiny wave, but no one seemed really affected. When the dark came, Carole and Delores set halogen lamps around the picnic's circle, and the girls all started to dance. Someone put on a Neil Sedaka tape. Someone lit the lamps. A number of the girl couples close-danced; some even kissed each other with their mouths open. They were all high. Chase found himself with his arms wrapped around a lodgepole like a wife. His bomb only came to his mind once, flickering, like the wings of a bat. He watched Dixie. She danced with Annette. But it was friendly dancing. They joked and teased. Once they danced cheek to cheek.

Chase stayed on the edge, in the trees, watching, until midnight, when Delores called that the bus would be leaving in ten minutes. Then he came out and signalled Dixie. She strolled over. "You obliged to drive back with them?" Chase inquired.

"I'm off 'til noon," Dixie said.

He looked at her. It was hard to talk.

"I wouldn't mind driving over to see the Red Lion in Elko," she said. "I haven't seen it—and they say it's nice."

So they did that. Dixie threw up out the van window once, just north of Currie. She'd had too much to drink. She apologized. "They've surely done a good job with this," Dixie said when she saw the new Red Lion Casino and its impressive carpet. Chase bought her a breakfast steak in the coffee shop; then they took a room and undressed in silence. "It's different," Chase finally said. "Yes, it is," Dixie said. She was standing near light from the window: "It is really. . . . So? Well? What would you like?" she asked.

"What would *you* like?" Chase said. "You always ask me. What would *you* like this time?"

She told him. And he tried. And it seemed to work. Just after four they woke up a Justice of the Peace, behind the Commercial Hotel, and married each other and drove back to Ely with Dixie's head on Chase's shoulder talking about different planets that were in the sky sometimes that you could see.

They were tired, and they went to sleep for a couple of hours in Chase's trailer. Chase scrambled eggs for them and made them toast and coffee for breakfast. They smiled at each other, then Dixie said: "Have to get to work." And she stood up and kissed Chase on the cheek, and he kissed her.

"You want to take the car?" he asked.

"Why don't you drive me."

So Chase did. Then he went to the Hotel Nevada for a third morning cup of coffee. And sat. And looked around. And he had to admit—it had the look, somehow, of a different place.